P9-CLE-896

Baldwinsville Public Library
33 East Genesee Street
Baldwinsville, NY 13027-2575

WITHDRAWN

ALSO BY MARY GORDON

Fiction

There Your Heart Lies
The Liar's Wife
The Love of My Youth
The Stories of Mary Gordon
Pearl
Final Payments
The Company of Women
Men and Angels
Temporary Shelter
The Other Side
The Rest of Life
Spending

Nonfiction

Reading Jesus
Circling My Mother
Good Boys and Dead Girls
The Shadow Man
Seeing Through Places
Joan of Arc
On Thomas Merton

Payback

WITHDRAWN

Baldwinsville Public Library
33 East Genesee Street
Baldwinsville, NY 13027-2575

Payback

Mary Gordon

PANTHEON BOOKS

New York

This is a work of fiction. Names, characters, places, and incidents either are the product of the author's imagination or are used fictitiously. Any resemblance to actual persons, living or dead, events, or locales is entirely coincidental.

Copyright © 2020 by Mary Gordon

SEP 1 1 2020

All rights reserved. Published in the United States by Pantheon Books, a division of Penguin Random House LLC, New York, and distributed in Canada by Penguin Random House Canada Limited, Toronto.

Pantheon Books and colophon are registered trademarks of Penguin Random House LLC.

Library of Congress Cataloging-in-Publication Data
Names: Gordon, Mary, [date] author.
Title: Payback / Mary Gordon.
Description: First Edition. New York : Pantheon Books, 2020.
Identifiers: LCCN 2020000079 (print). LCCN 2020000080 (ebook).
ISBN 9781524749224 (hardcover). ISBN 9781524749231 (ebook).
Classification: LCC PS3557.O669 P39 2020 (print) |
LCC PS3557.O669 (ebook) | DDC 813/.54—dc23
LC record available at lccn.loc.gov/2020000079
LC ebook record available at lccn.loc.gov/2020000080

www.pantheonbooks.com

Jacket images: (center) Miroslav Boskov/E+
(bottom) hatman12/iStock, both Getty Images

Jacket design by Jenny Carrow

Printed in the United States of America
First Edition
2   4   6   8   9   7   5   3   1

For Marvin,
who is not afraid of getting lost

PART I

Brimston, Arizona

February 2018

The Arizona sun is strong this February afternoon, but all the women are quite cool and comfortable. You might think that they chose the colors of their shorts and sleeveless tops to match the colors of the fruits they are eating: cantaloupe, watermelon, honeydew. Their fingernails and toenails are painted in various shades of opalescence: silver, rose, robin's-egg blue. This is their weekly ritual: water aerobics, a manicure, a pedicure, then lunch (raw fruits, raw vegetables, whey protein–enriched smoothies) in front of one of their wall-sized TVs. Their children are grown; their husbands are somewhere.

They are waiting for the show that is their favorite, and for which they feel a proprietary pride because it started as a local cable show here in their own Brimston and has now gone national. But they knew it *when*.

"I just love her. I always have."

"I'm crazy about everything about her."

"When she goes after someone, I just feel good about things, like the world's on the right track."

"Blah blah blah and boo hoo hoo," they say, imitating Quin's inflection, toasting each other with their pastel smoothies.

"Good afternoon, lovers of justice. This is Quin Archer. And this is PAYBACK.

"Today's show exposes a greedy dishonest father, Winston La Marr. He cheated his daughter Cindy of a legacy left by her grandmother and fled the country with a new woman. Cindy's loving grandmother, Thelma La Marr, Winston's mother, created a trust to ensure that her granddaughter would always be provided for . . . she particularly wanted Cindy to have a college education. But she was too trusting . . . perhaps not in her right mind . . . and the trust was set up with only herself and Winston as trustees, not Cindy. She felt secure giving Winston the money to invest, and he invested it in what were called 'bearer bonds.' Bearer bonds, my friends, are named as they are precisely because anyone holding them in their hand . . . or bearing them . . . can cash them in. And that is precisely what Winston La Marr did. Cashed in the bonds, fled the country, leaving his daughter impoverished.

"We've connected with him in this leafy upscale suburb of Philadelphia, an idyllic setting, my friends, I'm sure you all agree. Observe the wide, quiet street, the lush old trees. But I'm here to tell you that for Cindy growing up, life was far from idyllic. She went from living a comfortable middle-class life to being an impoverished child of a working mother—her mother went back to work as a secretary when her husband left and barely made ends meet—so Cindy was the victim and her victimizer went scot-free. Time and the world healed her; she is a brave, brave woman—married for thirty-six years with two lovely daughters and five sweet grandkids—until today. Because we're here, all of us, you and I, and finally the victim will no longer be a victim but a payee. When she will get her PAYBACK."

On the screen, dark storm clouds brood. Then from somewhere, from anywhere, a golden arrow pierces the clouds, which part like curtains, revealing shining gold letters: PAYBACK.

The gold letters disappear to reveal the severe face of Quin Archer.

Standing in front of a large white house with out-of-place Colonial pillars, at the crest of a perfect lawn, is a grim-looking woman, possibly in her late fifties. On the right, slumped, stricken, stands a man in at least his eighties. Quin Archer approaches them. The old man bursts into tears. "What I did was terrible; I was the victim of the disease, gambling . . . it's a disease like cancer or diabetes. You throw away everything valuable, for the disease. I wouldn't be surprised if you didn't forgive me. By the time I got myself together, I couldn't find you. I tried, I really tried, but you'd moved, your mother remarried, you took her husband's name. I tried, I really tried. I only wish I could make it up to you somehow."

Winston La Marr begins weeping.

"You well may shed tears, Mr. La Marr. But until Cindy gets her PAYBACK all I can say is blah blah blah and boo hoo hoo. Tears are not PAYBACK, Mr. La Marr, and this is why we're here. Because it is time for you to make it up. To pay it back. I'm looking at your beautiful home here . . . and Cindy has provided us with images of the homes she lived in growing up."

Drab ranch houses on treeless streets appear on the screen, each one more dilapidated, more dispiriting than the last.

"And this is the home Cindy and her husband, Tom, have made a home, through sweat and tears and struggle . . . a home, modest by any standards . . . no pillars for Cindy, no great lawn and majestic trees. So I would say there *is* something you could do to make it up to her, because it is obvious that you are enjoying a lifestyle far superior to that of the daughter you abandoned."

"It's . . . it's not mine . . . it's . . . it's my wife's."

"Let's see what your wife has to say about all this," Quin says, walking up the three brick steps to the front door.

She rings the bell insistently, and the door is opened by a tall woman, her hair a stiff tower of copper red, her arms crossed across her large, heavily corseted chest.

"I want you off my property," the woman says.

"Well, I'm afraid it's too late for that, as your husband has signed a release."

"But it's my property, not his."

"I think, Mrs. La Marr, that this is not the case. The deed, which we have found, is in both your names."

The woman tries to close the door, but Quin has wedged her foot against it, so it is impossible.

"Your husband has said that he wishes he could make up to his daughter for the deprivation he caused her. He says that the money is in your name, but I'm sure you'll see the injustice, Cindy deserves some PAYBACK."

"Over my dead body."

"Are you sure you want the scandal of your husband being taken to court, exposed for the thief and cheat he is, his past laid out for everyone to see . . . not just your neighbors, but all the viewers of this show?"

"Marie," Winston shouts from the bottom of the lawn. "Marie, it's only right."

The woman pushes the door against Quin's foot, and Quin, having no choice, moves her foot away, takes off her high black pump, and rubs her foot with the greatest possible expression of inflicted pain.

"I'll make it right, Cindy, I swear I'll make it right," says Winston La Marr.

Cindy falls into her father's arms, and weeps. "Everything happens for a reason, Dad."

"And remember, Cindy," Quin says. "If your father is unable to make his wife act justly, you have legal recourse. You need not be a victim. You will get PAYBACK, I guarantee it, if you just take your life in your hands, the only life you have, Cindy, the life that your father nearly stole from you—if you use the strength that helped you survive, I guarantee that you will get your PAYBACK."

Quin Archer turns her back on the embracing father and daughter. "Till next week, then. Remember: Justice may be slow in coming, but together we will bring it home."

She walks down the hilly lawn to the sidewalk. She looks into the camera with a fierce intensity.

"My friends, my real true friends, all of you out here, I've never had the courage for this until now. But your love and support have made me feel safe and strong. You see, what I have kept shut inside my heart is the truth that I, too, was a victim. And my victimizer, my betrayer—well, I didn't have the strength then to confront her, and there was no one to support me—she should have been the one—and so I ran, like so many victims, I ran. Ran into a life of self-destruction, which through so much support and love I was able to turn around. But now, my friends, my community of justice seekers. It's my turn. I am proud to say that I have helped many to give up the status of victim, and it's my turn now. You've heard me say it: Don't call yourself the victim, call yourself the OWED. Next week, my friends: you'll hear my story. Next week my victimizer will be the one to PAY BACK. And remember, my friends, FORGIVENESS WITHOUT PAYBACK KEEPS A VICTIM IN HIS CHAINS."

In a trailer parked in front of the brick house, two girls, bright and fleet as birds, dab at Quin Archer's face with a white towel, leaving on it splotches of makeup the color of a pretzel. "Santa Fe Sunset" is the name of the foundation shade Quin favors. She is proud of her even, youth-bestowing tan, and although people warn her of the danger of tanning beds, she doesn't listen. She mistrusts all doomsayers and believes that if there are consequences to something, she will find a way around them.

She snaps her fingers for one of the girls to give her a hand mirror. She examines her face with calm satisfaction. With pleasure, she runs her hands over her skin's firm, wrinkleless texture. She is lean and taut; there is no looseness, no sagging on any part of her body. She wished for years that her eyes were bigger, but now she's made her small eyes a kind of trademark, emphasizing them with lines of thick black kohl. She worries that perhaps her arms are starting to look ropy, but for now she favors sleeveless sheaths and high heels. She pats with pleasure her signature hair: silver spikes, baffling speculations about her real age.

She applies a thick coating of her signature orange lipstick— "Tangerine Sunrise"—and outlines it with a darker pencil: "Blood Orange." She swivels around on her chair and says to her two birdlike assistants, who pretend to understand, "Well, that almost didn't work . . . I hate it when they fall into each other's arms. Thank God for the wife. But wait and see, girls, this next one, the one I was just talking about. I'm going to nail this one. I'm going to nail her to the wall."

PART II

New York
New Canterbury, Rhode Island

April 1972

Halfway down the wide stone staircase she stands still. Just for a moment, then she walks down three steps and is still again. Fifth Avenue. She looks to her right—or south, as she believes. It opened, the avenue, and that was just the right word for it: *avenue,* not *street* or *road,* but *avenue,* with its suggestion of expanse. The tallest buildings show themselves in mist, thin as needles, then rise up, dissolve in silver.

She knows that she must turn around; she has to look behind her for the girls—the meek, abashed ones trailing close behind her, the daring ones who chafed and tried to flee, calculating the possibility of wild escape. But there would be no escape: there was the yellow bus a hundred paces from the bottom step, and there was Mrs. Golding, tapping her clipboard with a light green mechanical pencil, come along, girls, come along. Kind Mrs. Golding had agreed to take the girls back to Rhode Island without Agnes, leaving Agnes in the city, on her own to do whatever she wanted. Take a holiday or half a holiday, for goodness' sake, kind Jane Golding had said.

Agnes waves the bus off till it is entirely out of sight. She hasn't moved; she doesn't know how long it's been, long enough to be noticed if anyone was watching. But no one is watching. She's completely on her own.

Is that the problem? That no one was watching. No one expecting, no one requiring. Was this what immobilized her? Because she just can't decide. Here she is, on the steps of the Metropolitan Museum, and she is an art teacher—*the* art teacher at the Lydia Farnsworth School for Girls, New Canterbury, Rhode Island. A school to be proud of, founded by bluestockings, suffragettes before the First World War; she herself had been a student there, an atmosphere of deliberate but genteel tolerance, an unspoken insistence on decorum, mixed with an insistence on intellectual freedom, laced with a New England asceticism that despised, in equal measure, cheap luxury and received ideas. But now there would be no girls trailing, no masterpieces to explain, no passing by the Carpaccio she would have preferred for the Titian she felt they ought to know about. The whole of the world's great art, and she had only to go back up this staircase, into the building and up the truly grand stairs, and it was all hers.

But just as easily, she could go down the stairs, turn right, and make her way down Fifth Avenue.

She can't stand there any longer. It's making too much of it to stand like this, as if the question were a great one. Even if she put the matter in large terms—art or life, the past or the present— she knew that was ridiculous. The great questions were not for her, to put it in those large terms was nothing but vanity, and vanity was one of the faults she knew she was susceptible to and therefore must fear.

Go on, then—up or down.

Down it was, and to the right.

And after two short blocks all doubt is done. This was the right thing . . . the budding trees make her breath light and easy. Wasn't it possible to say that observing these was as good as looking at the Turner sunsets or the Goya boy? Wasn't it, after all, another kind of learning?

Is it possible that everyone she passes is as interesting as they seem? Even the dogs look clever, ready to discriminate, their wedge-shaped or triangular heads full of information picked up as they sniff the sidewalks or each other's trim behinds. The doormen raise their white-gloved hands and whistle for the yellow cabs. Possibly the people getting in the cabs don't bother thanking the doormen, or perhaps they do. The new babyish leaves are slight but prosperous. The sky is not quite brilliant but in no way overcast.

In front of her, a mother carries a baby on her back: a complex frame, steel tubing, but the cloth that makes the pouch through which the baby's legs poke is a tie-dyed blue-red-green, and in the center, a yellow peace symbol. The baby's head lolls to one side; he drools; his lips make little sucking motions. The mother's hair catches the light: gold, curly wires that rise and fall with each step that she takes in her high red boots. Her skirt is very short, but Agnes thinks she must be comfortable in her purple tights, and the skirt, though short, is sturdy corduroy. Wonderful hair, she thinks, and she would like to tell the mother, Your hair is wonderful; your baby is beautiful; and do you know how lucky you are that it is 1972 and you can let your hair be as it is? Kinky, we might have called it five or seven years ago. Frizzy. It would have been required that you sleep all night in hard, excruciating rollers so that you could appear acceptable in the morning, in the world, with bone-straight hair. Like mine, Agnes thinks, touching with regret her thick hair, shoulder length, the longest she has courage for. Because she is Miss Vaughan, the Art Teacher. At the distinguished Lydia Farnsworth School, which has, it must not be forgotten, standards.

But it's not true, she thinks, we are not fortunate in 1972. You shelter your baby in a cloth that urges peace, but there is no peace. We are at war. This terrible, this absurd, this evil war. Impossible to put out of the mind for more than a few hours the television images: mothers like this one running with babies, both aflame. Napalm. Unfriendly fire. But you and I are on the same side, she wants to tell the mother. We may have been on the same marches. She remembers her first march. The Pentagon, September 1967, in a yellow bus with Jo and Christina: the three of them the youngest teachers, newly hired. Now inseparable. Friends, they know, for life.

The headmistress, Letitia Barnes, had hired three young teachers to replace three retirements: Agnes Vaughan, Christina Datchett, and Jo Walsh to replace Miss Hastings and Miss Lloyd and Miss Fuller, all of whom had been there since the last days of the Depression. Agnes taught Art History and Studio Art, Jo taught History and Civics, Christina Biology and Chemistry. An alum had funded a new Chemistry lab. When Agnes was a student there, they made do with out-of-date equipment, it being understood that science was not their strong point. This was something Letitia Barnes was dedicated, now, to changing. And hiring Jo had been a radical decision; her husband was in prison in Danbury for having burned his draft card.

None of the three new teachers was attached to a man. Jo's husband was in jail. Christina, the only real voluptuary, had plenty of offers for dates, but she never allowed a second one, saying, "They bore me to crumbs, I just can't take it."

Agnes is engaged, but Roger Jenkins, her fiancé, is on an archaeological dig in Iraq. He has been away for six months; he will be away for another twelve. She is ashamed to admit, even to herself, that what she misses most is the sex. Sometimes she isn't sure exactly how she became engaged. She loves Roger, she knows she does: his steadiness, his ease in the physical world, his belief that all problems were solvable using a mixture of reason and determination. She loves the hair on his chest and his long narrow feet. But she doesn't think about him constantly; his image doesn't swim up to her consciousness whenever nothing else has taken up habitation. She knows they will, together, make a good, perhaps even a rich, life. But sometimes, in the first moments of waking, she must tamp down the suspicion that she agreed to marry him because the estate of daughter, her strongest connection being to her parents, has grown obsolete to the point of being disreputable. Sometimes she is afraid that what she likes best is how they appear, the way they are seen as they walk together. She likes the look of their hands clasped on a table.

She sees her parents' happiness, but knows somehow that her father's passion for her mother has never been returned. So she tells herself it is all right: a love, warm but not incandescent, the prospect of a large and fertile meadow rather than towering mountains or raging seas. And she wants sex, sex on a regular basis without the fraught dramas that finding a comfortable horizontal surface seem increasingly to entail.

But if she is honest, she enjoys herself more with Christina and Jo than with Roger.

Roger's humor is dry and ironical; he is very fond of puns; it has nothing in it of Jo's zaniness, Christina's delight in the absurd, her gift for mimicry. The three young, pretty teachers, spending their weekends together, watching the mixed couples at the adjoining tables when they are in restaurants, or down the bar from them at the happy hour they've discovered two towns away. With Roger, she never feels this freedom, this full-throated sense of being in the world.

Being unattached allows the three of them to give extraordinary attention to their students, as the older spinster teachers did, but without the over-genteel (or lesbian) cast that turned off some prospective parents. The three of them spent their weekends together, Agnes the glue that held the three together because Christina could be impatient with Jo's political earnestness and Jo could be quick to take offense at what she saw as Christina's "Noël Coward to hell with it all" approach.

Agnes adored them both and found them more admirable, more exciting than she believed herself to be. On the marches they went on together, they were able (as she is sure the mother with the baby on her back would be) to shout the slogans at the top of their lungs. *Hey, hey, LBJ, how many people did you kill today?* The most Agnes could do was make the *V* sign with her fingers. *V* for *Victory*. But what would victory entail? She wishes she were more like her friends, more like what she is sure this mother is like. Do you understand, she wants to ask the mother, walking ahead of her, how awful it is to know yourself to be a timid person? *Timid*. What an awful word. She hates the word. She would like to spit it onto the sidewalk. But that too is something she could never do.

The mother and the baby turn, head off the avenue, west, Agnes thinks, and disappear into the park. She wonders if she should follow them. No. Suppose the mother turned and showed a menacing or angry face. A sneer, a grimace. Suppose she was scarred or deformed. What then would be required? No, it was best to let them go.

Fifty-Ninth Street. The Plaza. Memories of afternoon sweetness. Her mother and her mother's best friend, Frances Fletcher. Always college girls with each other, roommates, although they hadn't lived together for thirty years, but in their minds, perhaps, they always had. Christened Henrietta and Frances, they called each other "Hank" and "Frank."

Frances had not married. Frances was what was called then a "career girl." One of those glamorous jobs teenagers could dream over: an editor at *House and Garden* magazine, although she had neither house nor garden but was urban, a New Yorker to her fingertips (always the same blood red). And her mother always said, incomprehensibly for Agnes at the time, but later sensible, "A shame really, she was a first-rate poet." Frances, her cigaretty voice, her red-painted nails, her high heels (a reference point for Agnes, whose mother would risk nothing more than a medium heel, "It's no accident they're called spikes"). Frances, who had not married but specialized, Agnes's mother confided later, in affairs with unsuitable married men. Frances, large boned, presenting an image of health that was only just not aggressive, in contrast to Agnes's mother, who had suffered asthma since she was a child.

Her trips to New York with her mother, culminating in drinks with Frances, were always about seeing art. The Metropolitan, where she is today. The secret jewel: the Frick with its polished, pricey quiet; the courtyard, the quietly plashing fountains, her mother's favorite Bellini, Agnes's secret favorite, the Ingres in the blue satin dress. Her mother had wanted to be a painter. "But if you aren't great, you may as well be useful." She became a medical illustrator. She took a pride in her own hardheaded common sense, painting only with Agnes: watercolors of flowers, this is how to put in shadows, how to blur a line.

Agnes started college believing that she would be a painter because she was the artist of her class at the Lydia Farnsworth School. Lauded among her friends for her ability to capture their faces. Rewarded by neighbors who want her to render the view of the sea from their back porch. Her self-portrait hung in her parents' bedroom, "Look, Paul, how she got the arch of the eyebrows." Then at Brown she is told she is hopelessly conventional; realism is dead, even abstraction. One teacher praises her "delicate eye, and delicate hand," but then, leaning over to correct a line, he rests his not-delicate hand on her breast, and she understands that it is time to give up painting.

She had her own lunches with Fran at the Palm Court, without her mother, uneasy at the exclusion but unwilling to give up the pleasure. A gimlet. You must know how to drink and not get drunk.

Sometimes she spent the night with Frances. Her apartment: a source of crucial information. A shelf of cosmetics and small deliberate brushes, mascara, eyebrow pencil, eye shadow, eyelash curler, lipstick, lip brush, liquid rouge, solid blusher. "I have to put my face on," Frances says in the morning, as if after closing the bathroom door she will be shedding her unadorned face for a new one.

But Agnes was drawn to Frances as the cavemen had been drawn to the one among them who realized that meat was better salted, cooked.

Frances was romantic, not about her own romantic life, which she described with a brittle cynicism, but about Agnes's parents' marriage. They had all met in college; Frances and Agnes's mother at Mount Holyoke, her father at Amherst. "I've never seen anyone as taken by anyone as your father was by your mother. For a long time, she didn't accept his attentions, his obvious devotion. I think she knows that he loves her more than she loves him. Oh, she loves him, they are one of the few genuinely good matches I know. But he's not the love of her life. You are. I've heard her make a joke of him . . . his earnestness, what she calls his 'moral finickiness.' But she's never made a joke of you. Not for a minute. I think perhaps you have been perfectly loved."

On one of their visits, Frances said, "Has your mother talked to you about contraception? It's no good blushing, not knowing could have hideous consequences. I remember a girl in our class at Mount Holyoke, a few of them, really, over the four years, they'd leave for a weekend and never come back, and you didn't know if they'd died or just had a baby. Barbaric. But should you ever need anything like that I have a very good doctor friend who could help you."

Agnes approaches Fifty-Seventh Street. Fifty-Seventh Street was only one thing: Carnegie Hall. And only one person: her father.

It had been another kind of adventure when her father took her to New York. It was always to Carnegie Hall, and their route was always the same. They got off the train at Penn Station and

walked east to Fifth Avenue so her father could make his pil-
grimage to the New York Public Library. His cathedral, his Vati-
can, his Taj Mahal. Not surprising: he was a professional, Paul
Vaughan, head librarian of the Providence Public Library.

Agnes and her father would walk up Fifth Avenue from Thirty-
Fourth to Forty-Second, a stop in at the library, "just to see how
the old girl's doing," and then lunch at Schrafft's. And then, the
arrival at Carnegie Hall, the trip up the red-carpeted staircase,
the buzz and then the hush, the high, lustrous whiteness of the
auditorium, the beams of light, as if they'd been trained to it,
falling on the brass of the balcony railings, but they didn't sit in
the balcony, they had box seats, always the same, and the thrill of
the maestro entering the stage. Leonard Bernstein: a god to her
father, the sacred personage as the Forty-Second Street Library
was the sacred space. She could never recall what she had heard,
only the sharp, anxious thrill of anticipation, the first shocking
notes, and being carried up to a level where she and her father
could, momentarily, soar together. But even in that magic space
there were rules: Do not tap your foot, do not clap at the end of
a movement. The worst sin possible: to fall asleep.

And then, their trips to New York were over, like some trace-
able moment in a chronicle: the beginning of a war, the end
of the plague. The destruction of Penn Station. Her father had
taken it as a personal affront. He made one trip to the new facility and came home in a tearing rage. "I will never set foot in that
city again. I am grievously disappointed."

She crosses to the west side of Fifth at Fifty-Seventh. She looks
in the window of I. Miller, the shoe store that takes up nearly the

whole block. And, there, right in the window, there they are: the wonderful red boots that the mother of the baby wore.

There's nothing in her that resists the impulse to try those boots on, and she knows it's unlike her, she was never very interested in clothes; she didn't want to stand out . . . although she didn't want to be one of those words that ended in *y: dumpy, frumpy, dowdy, homely.* But something about these boots made her heart race in the way that certain songs did—songs that her father would call *vulgar* but that she loved to dance to. (It was a secret she kept from her parents, that she loved to dance; loved, particularly, girl groups—the Supremes, of course, but even the ones whose names she had to admit were embarrassing: the Dixie Cups, the Shirelles.)

A tall blond young man with a red carnation in his buttonhole approaches her. Even before he opens his mouth, she knows he's gay; *gay,* the word she'd learned to be comfortable with halfway through college because so many of her friends were. Pete, her closest friend in college, had said, "Watch it, lovie, you're well on the way to being everybody's favorite fag hag." Her father, who was quick to say he had no problem with homosexuality, refused to use the word *gay,* saying he loved it too much to see its meaning diluted. Maybe, she thought, that meant he really did have a problem.

The salesman shows her to a seat, but before she sits down she tells him she wants to try on the red boots in the window.

Looking around the store, she is convinced that she is the youngest of the customers, and the poorest. She feels herself begin to sweat with her own sense of unfitness; it was fortunate that her salesman was quick, because she was on the verge of sneaking out.

He kneels before her and helps her with the boots.

Never before has any article of clothing given her such a sense of rightness. She's embarrassed at her response: she giggled, giggled in a way that would have been mortifying for one of her students.

"Stunning, absolutely stunning," he says. "Take a look."

She stands in front of the full-length mirror, afraid to meet her own reflection.

They look as wonderful as they feel. She's almost hypnotized by the rightness of everything about them.

The salesman stands behind her. "I think they're very fine, though they'd probably be better with a shorter skirt."

"I'm a teacher," she says, feeling foolish at the response.

"You're not a teacher all the time."

"In the town I live in, I'm afraid I am."

"Then, sweetie, you need to get out of town more."

She isn't sure whether he's kidding her or insulting her, but she decides to make a rueful face, one she had learned while dealing with challenging students. It threw up a barrier, but low enough so that it could be climbed over, if the inclination arose.

"I'll take them," she says.

"Do you want to wear them? I think you love them *that* much, if I'm not presuming."

"Yes," she says. "I would like that very much."

"Listen, they're great on you. Wear them in good health. I see by your ring that you're engaged. I'm sure your fiancé will be pleased."

"My fiancé is in Iraq. On an archaeological dig."

She sees that his opinion of her has risen. She wasn't just a provincial schoolteacher, engaged to an accountant or the town lawyer who drew up everybody's wills.

"All the more reason to live a little, no?"

She turns west onto Sixth Avenue. On the corner of Fifty-Fifth and Sixth was the character everyone seemed to know about: a mountain of a man dressed in a red cloak, his legs bare in lace-up sandals, on his head a Viking helmet, complete with horns. He was blind, one eye bleached of color, almost turned in on itself. Moondog was his name. Two of her students had come back from a weekend in the city full of excitement after their encounter with him; had invited him to join them at Shakespeare in the Park—*As You Like It*—and he had nodded, silently, and followed them. "He's kind of like a god, kind of like Homer, Homer was blind, right, and kind of like Jesus, but kind of like a Viking hero." Nearly unable to contain themselves, they presented her with copies of his poetry. He sold the poetry for pennies. She remembered two of the poems; they were easy to remember, rhymed couplets, but she had made the mistake of showing them to Jo and Christina, who were less prone to sympathize with student silliness.

> *An armored knight fell off a ship and sank into the blue.*
> *He looked a lobster in the eye and said, "You're armored, too?*
> *We have to buy new cars each year or we'll be classified*
> *By all the Joneses in our town, who must be pacified."*

Agnes wanted to use her father's word, *ridiculous*, because that's how the poems seemed to her, and when they said they thought he was like Homer, they thought he was like Jesus, she had to work doubly hard to silence her father's voice . . . those sweet, silly girls. Margaret Kiley and Joan LeBeau. They said they didn't know whether they wanted to be painters or poets; they said they wanted to live together after college on a sheep farm in New Zealand.

She was relieved that she wasn't their English teacher, because she thought their poetry was trite and sentimental. She was grateful that she was their art teacher; she could teach them some skills: perspective, shading . . . which didn't require her to voice judgments on their subject matter, which was as trite and sentimental as their poetry—although their triteness and sentimentality moved her as it expressed itself in their lives.

Often, she asked herself: What can you really teach anybody? She could let them know that Fra Angelico came before Goya; she could explain the techniques of each, and place them in the context of their culture. But if the student thought the paintings weren't worth her interest, Agnes couldn't do anything at all. Too often she realized that they said they loved the paintings because they loved *her,* because they wanted to please *her.* Once they were out of her sight, and she of theirs, would they ever go to a museum or a gallery, or put a mark on paper to record something they found engaging or arresting?

She knew they loved her, or that they believed they did. She enjoyed the love, but she didn't deceive herself that it was real in the way other loves in her life had been, and she had learned quite quickly that it was not long lasting. Sometimes she thought it was like the frosting on a cheap birthday cake: sugary, succulent, but of no nutritive value whatever; the colors false, the decorations hard and tasteless. So she could teach skills but she could not teach vision; she could not impart the seeing eye. And, looking at the decay of New York, of the horror of the war, of the cities on fire with race hatred, she wondered whether what she was doing was of the slightest value. She knew she was good at it, she was better at it than she'd been at anything else, and her life had not been devoid of successes, of achievements. But she wondered whether doing it was of any use at all.

This is what she felt on the bad days when all at once doubts, like fast-growing weeds, sprang up from nowhere, when the room was staticky with minor malice, overheated with the girls' pent-up animality or unmoored with the distraction of their dreams.

But mostly, she believed that she was doing something fine. She could use without self-consciousness the plain word *beauty*, on its own, and not linked to some other word: *parlor, pageant, queen,* a connection that implied it was a currency. She could suggest that beauty was of no clear use at all, but something luminous, some added luster that could neither be explained nor explained away. She could give them this, and if they took it, it might be thought to last. Sometimes her heart broke at their naïveté—she was only seven or eight years older than they, but she couldn't remember having been so naïve. They believed that they could simply approach life like a temperate ocean whose waves would carry them but would never, ever overwhelm them, never be the cause of their destruction. Sometimes their beauty pierced her, when the light fell on their shining hair, or the bones of their wrists, or the napes of their necks as they bent, absorbed, unconscious, to a task she had given them that they desired, above all, to finish well. When one of them took an interest in an artist she believed they never would have known

if it had not been for her—Vuillard, Morandi, Caspar David
Friedrich—it was as if they shared a family treasure, secret and
quite rare. She feared that in her love for them, there was a generous measure of self-love. But she knew that she loved them,
although she worried that they were, perhaps, too easy to love.

One of them was not easy to love, and it made Agnes believe
that her love was worthwhile, precisely because of its difficulty.
Heidi Stolz. Of all of them, the least obviously lovable, certainly
the least generous, the cruelest, the most begrudging. Of all of
them, the true original.

She thought of Heidi's final project, which was a direct slam
at Margaret and Joan, who had papered the school with copies of
a poster: a daisy with childish lettering that spelled out "War Is
Not Healthy for Children and Other Living Things."

Whereas most of the girls were anchored firmly in the impres-
sionists, arguing among themselves whether Monet or van Gogh
was the greatest painter ever, Heidi was devoted to pop art. She
had made a presentation that would have shocked the other girls
if they hadn't long ago written her off as "a weirdo," "just too
conceited," "a big drag."

Pop artists, Heidi said, were the only people who were really
honest about what most people liked looking at. They were
the only non-snobs, and they didn't pretend not to care about
money. Everybody wants money, she said, they just pretend they
don't. She said that their refusal to draw a line between high art
and low art, between the commercial and the purely beautiful,
was one of the most important ideas in the history of thinking.

Her final project was so openly antagonistic to Margaret and
Joan that Agnes didn't display it. It was a comic strip. In the first
frame were two girls, direct and nearly perfect likenesses of Joan
and Margaret. They were holding posters that said "War Is Not

Healthy for Children and Other Living Things." The second
frame included the character Steve Canyon from the comic strip
that appeared in the Sunday paper. The square-jawed, impossibly muscled pilot was saying, "You're right, girls. War is not
healthy." The third frame showed Steve walking among hid-
eously mutilated corpses, their guts spreading out, their unattached limbs randomly spread around the field where they lay.
The fourth frame was a Vietcong soldier throwing a grenade.
The fifth frame revealed who he was throwing the grenade at. It
was Margaret and Joan, being blown to smithereens, along with
their posters.

Heidi Stolz. Even her name was ugly. It was a terrible word, *ugly*.
Laide, the French, was kinder . . . sometimes her mother referred
to someone as *jolie laide*, a woman whose looks were not conventional but still somehow appealing. Was Heidi Stolz appealing? It would be kind to call her a *jolie laide*, probably because
of her eyes, which were unusually small, the color of olive pits.
Their smallness and colorlessness was exaggerated by her dark,
thick brows, which she took pride in not plucking, and her thin
lashes, which even on the way out of school when makeup was
allowed she would not enrich with mascara. She had a fine,
high forehead, and distinguished cheekbones; her chin ended
the reversed triangle of her face in a graceful end-stop. Her lips
were full and well formed; they might have suggested generos-
ity, but their perpetual position was a smirk, or, when she was
distracted, an almost stupid slackness. She had a slight overbite,
which Agnes imagined a certain kind of man, perhaps older, dis-
criminating, might find sexy.

She was, Agnes often thought, the one real rebel in the Lydia

Farnsworth School. The ones who thought themselves rebels were really conforming to the spirit of the times, in which to be rebellious was to be fashionable, in the swim. A true original was never in the swim. A true original would be struggling against the tide, as Heidi was, and often the sight would not be pleasing, the strokes awkward, the swimmer choking and sputtering and rising up covered with flotsam and jetsam that might not always be easily lovely to behold. Jo and Christina loathed her, Jo because she had no time for anyone whose politics were not far to the left of Hubert Humphrey, and Christina because she distrusted anyone whose approach to the world suggested anything of hiddenness, anything not straightforward, anything indirect. "She reminds me of a coyote. She slinks around the corner—even if there isn't a corner she makes one to slink around, she fixes those mean little eyes on you, and she's ready to pounce if you make the slightest error. And the mother, oh my God, hasn't she heard the Anita Ekberg look is out of style?"

Christina was right about Heidi's mother. She swanned into her parent-teacher conference in a black mink coat, her husband and Heidi trailing behind her like tugs behind an ocean liner. Her husband stood listlessly, waiting to take her coat. She didn't sit at one of the student desks, as the other parents did, but, after looking around for a second, took Agnes's chair, requiring that Agnes place herself alongside Heidi and her father, as if Liesel Stolz were, in fact, in charge. Which of course she was. She reached into her red leather clutch, took out a pack of cigarettes and a small gold box the size of two postage stamps. She put a cigarette to her lips and snapped her fingers. Heidi's father jumped to his feet and lit the cigarette. Liesel Stolz opened the small gold box, and Agnes saw that its purpose was to collect the ashes from the cigarette. Liesel was wearing a heavy perfume, and the scent, mixed with the cigarette smoke in the small classroom (was smoking even allowed in the Lydia Farnsworth School . . . it was possible, Agnes thought, that no one had ever even attempted it), made Agnes feel dizzy and nauseated. She coughed, and brought her handkerchief to her lips.

"Your daughter is very, very gifted. A pleasure to teach. I might even say a privilege. She has a real eye, a real sense of form and color, and a fine critical sense."

Liesel snorts. "Yeah, well, that and a dollar will buy her coffee and a donut."

Agnes is anguished for Heidi, but Heidi seems to be taking all this in stride, and this adds to Agnes's sadness: She's used to it, Agnes thinks, it's all she knows of a mother.

The following Monday, Heidi arrived early in class and said, "I'm sorry about my mother. I mean, the cigarettes, the perfume. Joy, she calls it. Her perfume. Supposed to be very expensive. But it literally makes me sick. I'm very sensitive to smells . . . I'm wondering if you are too."

Agnes was touched at Heidi's observation.

"Well, yes, I am, Heidi, and as my mother says . . . she's sensitive to smells too . . . it's not a blessing, it's a curse, because bad smells are more disturbing than good smells are delightful. Not, oh, no, not that I mean to say that your mother smelled bad . . . I mean . . ."

"Relax, Miss Vaughan, I know what you mean. It's just another thing we have in common. Like on the ski trip when we realized we wore the same size shoes."

Agnes talked about Heidi and her mother to Letitia Barnes, the headmistress. "Yes," Miss Barnes said. "Yes, I agree with you entirely. When I saw her with her parents, I could see that their eye never fell on her with . . . well, not only with love, but with pleasure in what they saw. I've seen a lot of parents looking at their children, and I know the difference between the look that feeds and the look that starves. There's something pathetic in Heidi's trumped-up vanity. Like the time she came in to tell me that she'd been admitted to Mensa, and I was actually embarrassed for her. I wanted to say, Mensa is just a moneymaking operation, no one who is really intelligent needs to join an organization that certifies their intelligence. But I didn't want to take anything away from her; she seems to have so little. The very prototype of the poor little rich girl."

So Heidi Stolz was no one's favorite. Was it vanity that inspired Agnes to take Heidi under her wing, to make the girl hers? It wasn't supposed to happen, that teachers had favorites, but of course they did, it was part of the job, one of its dangers and its strengths—you saw the gifts of your students, saw which matched your own, and moved to cultivate them: watering here, pruning there, feeding, propping. It had not been easy to convince Heidi Stolz that Miss Vaughan was on her side, was singling her out for special recognition. Agnes asked Heidi to come speak to her after class after she had made her presentation on pop art.

Agnes said, "It was a very fine job. You worked very hard on it; you did a great deal of real research."

"Is that your way of saying it's not quite your thing?" Heidi said, with that look that made Agnes remember what Christina had said about Heidi and coyotes.

"To be honest, it's probably *not* 'my thing,' but I'm always interested in trying to find out about something not immediately congenial to me, and I always respect a well-considered opinion, even if it's not my own. I'm impressed that you had the sophistication to be interested in a movement that's not . . . well, usually accessible to people your age."

Agnes dislikes her own tone; she hears its falseness, its condescension. She hopes that Heidi takes of her words what can be of use . . . she is too aware of Heidi's perceptiveness to imagine that she doesn't pick up the unnaturalness of the tone . . . but perhaps she expects unnaturalness from her teachers. And so takes it as the norm.

"I had a friend . . . she lived next door for a year . . . she was house-sitting for the people who really lived there . . . she was a RISD student, and we really got along. She was really into the pop art movement and she took me to some exhibits at RISD. She said all the best people in her class were working in this way, and . . . well, it just made sense."

"That was very lucky for you, making such a friend."

"I don't really see her anymore. She moved to London."

Agnes saw the sorrow that Heidi was trying to conceal behind a look of nonchalance.

"Well, perhaps you'll go and visit her someday."

"No," Heidi said, pulling on a ripped cuticle. "When people are gone, they're gone."

"I don't think that's necessarily true, Heidi. It hasn't been my experience."

"But that's just your experience."

Agnes felt chastened, but it was as if a child had slapped her, just to show she could.

"You have to admit, Miss Vaughan. You have to admit, you have to admit the pop artists are onto something," Heidi said, her eyes gimlets now, intent and, for the first time in Agnes's experience, alive. "About the way we look at the world."

"That's exactly what you helped me to see, and I'm grateful," Agnes said.

～～～

AGNES TURNS SOUTH. She wouldn't stop at the Forty-Second Street Library; last time she'd been there, she'd been disheartened by what had happened to her father's sacred place. The surrounding park was full of drug dealers and derelicts; when she went into the building and looked around, at first it seemed itself, only a bit shabbier, but when she approached the great staircase she saw a person asleep in the phone booth—man or woman, she couldn't tell—muffled in newspapers and giving off a stench of filth and misfortune. Had there been so many beggars when she came with her father? Only one had caused her to stop and drop coins into his hat. He was a young man, filthy but not unhealthy looking, sitting on a filthy blanket beside an equally filthy but equally healthy-looking dog. His sign said simply, "The dog comes first."

She would make one gesture in memory of the pleasant times with her father: she would stop for a bite to eat at Schrafft's. The truth was, she didn't know places to eat in New York, except for Schrafft's and the Plaza, and Schrafft's was, above all, a place of comfort and safety where nothing unexpected, including the menu, would even think of approaching.

She orders what she had always ordered: a BLT and a Coke, for dessert a butterscotch sundae. The waitress is a version of all the waitresses at Schrafft's, Irish, encouraging but not intrusive in her black uniform, with a white lace collar, which suggested that she was serving as one's personal maid. Agnes takes out her copy of *The New Yorker* and turns to "The Talk of the Town," which always makes her feel like a foreigner, or an orphan with her nose pressed up against the window of the candy store that was New York, a candy store full of confections whose names were unfamiliar to her but which, she was sure, if she got up the courage to taste them, would be delicious.

Her sandwich is perfect and so is her butterscotch sundae. But the place itself seemed to have lost some sheen. Was it always peopled only by old ladies, brooding over creamed chicken and a too-early cocktail? She remembers thrillingly fashionable young women lunching here with stable but successful-looking dates; there isn't a man in the place now, and she is the youngest woman in the room by thirty years. One of the black-and-white tiles on the floor is chipped.

She has just enough time to make her way to ugly Penn Station. Her father was right; it was a monstrosity, no one would want to spend one extra moment there. She would use the Schrafft's bathroom. She knew it was always clean; a dirty bathroom could plunge her into a hopeless state.

After she washes her hands, combs her hair, and applies fresh lipstick, she looks around the ladies' room; no one else is there. She stands in front of the full-length mirror and does something she would have been mortified for anyone to see. Something the moderately rebellious girls did on their way out of school: she rolls down the waistband of her skirt to make it shorter. She had taken seriously the salesman's opinion that her boots would take on their full value with a greater proportion of visible leg. She walks up and down the small space; she turns looking over her shoulder at her reflection. And is pleased.

The heavy door opens. A woman in a peach-colored suit with a fur collar, a hat of a darker peach, maybe it was apricot, in the shape of a crescent moon. The woman looks her up and down; Agnes is sure she notices the rolled-up waistband. She looks contemptuously at Agnes's raincoat, flung carelessly on the counter near the sink. Her back as she approaches the toilet is full of reproach, and Agnes knows that she deserves it. But it's her father's voice she hears.

Ridiculous, she hears him say. You've made yourself ridiculous.

She runs up the stairs to her table—she's left a bit of her Coke and would like to finish it; shame has turned her whole body hot, she's sure that her face is flushed. It's another thing she dislikes about herself, how prone she is to blushing.

She pays her check and walks outside. All the well-being that had been hers before she entered Schrafft's is gone now. She is only one thing: ridiculous. What made her think that buying those boots was the right thing, that they had anything to do with who she was, with how she lived? They weren't for her; they were for the young mother with her baby in the peace-symbol pouch, for someone freer, more at ease with the attention boots like that would inevitably bring. She thinks of all the beggars on the street; perhaps she would take the boots off on the sidewalk and give them to some poor wreck of a woman, who would be delighted with a gift from the usually begrudging gods.

And then it comes to her: there is something she could do that would make sense of the whole enterprise, that would make it not ridiculous but an opportunity for real good.

She would give them to Heidi Stolz. She remembers that they wear the same size shoe, because Heidi had remarked on that, with a childish simplicity that touched Agnes because it was so unlike her usual cutting slashes.

What Heidi needed was to know that she was regarded with favor, was thought about, considered, singled out.

There is no one sitting beside Agnes on the train. She takes off the boots and places them in their box. She puts on her sensible black low-heeled pumps.

Her father is waiting for her at the station. He had said to be sure she called him as she was leaving New York; he didn't like her driving herself in the dark. It would make her mother a nervous wreck.

They both knew that wasn't true; he was the worrier, the fearful one. Her chief inheritance from him. The legacy that worked and worked to muffle her from all the world's harsh lines, to keep, as he would say, her two feet on the ground. Her feet that would not wear those boots, now. In order that she would not be ridiculous.

∿

IT WAS always tricky when you were singling one student out—for favor or for censure—but Heidi Stolz's personality made it even trickier. Agnes would have liked to ask Miss Barnes for advice—or Christina or Jo, for that matter—but she knew that none of them liked Heidi or approved of Agnes's taking her under her wing.

The more they warned and spoke against Heidi, the more determined Agnes was to prove them wrong, to trust her instincts (You're a new teacher, Miss Barnes had said. Remember that you're not that much older than they are and they can be very clever at manipulation), to do something unusual for her: not to listen to her elders and betters, but to go her own way.

Giving Heidi the boots was an extravagant gesture, with an exciting tincture of excess. How would she manage to present Heidi with the large box without anyone noticing it? Although Heidi's proud nature and her isolation from the other students made it possible that the others would be afraid to ask her what she was carrying. She only hoped that Heidi's desire to one-up the others wouldn't make a braggart of her, displaying the boots, "They're from Miss Vaughan," for all to see. She believed, though, in Heidi's appetite for secrecy, her belief that her greatest power over those who despised her was to keep them in the dark.

She asked if Heidi could come to her classroom when the girls on the field hockey team were practicing . . . which was the same time the glee club met, and the newspaper. These were the activities of the popular girls. Heidi belonged to the debate club, which met—Agnes double-checked—at a different time.

Heidi knocked on the door and, at Agnes's "Come in," entered the room, with that slinking motion that Agnes found regrettable, that she hoped someday to counsel her against. "You wanted to see me, Miss Vaughan."

Always, when called to see a teacher, students expected the worst. But what could Heidi Stolz have to fear from her? Agnes had given her nothing but praise, encouragement that might even be named extravagant. The thing that she most disliked about her job was the idea that she might instill fear.

"Come in, Heidi. I have something for you."

Still the wary look, the raised shoulder, the torso that corkscrewed around itself as if it were trying to make itself invisible.

Agnes reaches under the desk where she had kept the shiny white bag with the words in script "I. Miller."

"This is a little strange, I know, and I'm going to have to ask you to keep it between us."

She could hear Miss Barnes's words, "Don't create any divisions among students, there are enough already, God knows. And don't ever make any of them feel you're on their side against the others."

Heidi would always be the exception, the one who called for exceptional responses. And if teaching were just a matter of a one-size-fits-all set of responses . . . well, she was sure that wasn't what it was meant to be, what she wanted it to be.

Agnes tries to make herself look like someone in a 1930s screwball comedy: daffy Miss Vaughan, you never know what will come out of her mouth. Which was, she knew, never the way anyone would have thought of her, not for one moment since her birth. And since her birth, she had had very little practice in lying. It had so rarely seemed to be something that was needed, something that might be of use.

"Well, it is strange. A friend of my parents gave me these . . . they thought I'd like them, and I do . . . but, what is it that you said about me and pop art . . . it's just not my thing. But I thought they might be your thing . . . I thought of you when I saw them, and I hope you like them, I hope they'll be fun for you."

Suspicious, Heidi looks into the bag as if she were afraid it might explode on her: a joke or a sickening surprise. She opens the box, giving Agnes a suspicious look that narrows her narrowed eyes even further.

"You're giving these to me," she says, an accusation.

"Only if you'd like them."

For a moment, Heidi almost looks her age, a girl, capable of a girl's responses. She's beaming, Agnes says to herself. But then another look replaces it and, unable to read it, Agnes feels herself stepping back, as if a jet of something unnamable were being sprayed at her, unnamable and not for her good. The glimpse of innocence that she had seen on Heidi's face is gone. What is there now . . . something not innocent, something quick and cunning, as if a prisoner had found a chink in the wall and were enlisting the help of a hapless guard.

"May I try them on?"

"Of course," Agnes says But she felt, in the seconds that Heidi's expression had changed, that giving her the boots had been a mistake.

Heidi turns her back to Agnes, takes off her loafers, puts on first the left boot, then the right, and zips them slowly. She turns and takes three, four, five steps toward Agnes.

Heidi has lovely long legs. But the boots, a joke against the blue serge of her uniform, give her the look of a child dressing up in its mother's clothes . . . or a refugee taking what was offered from the bin of discards. It would be better when she was wearing something else, the kind of short skirt the man in I. Miller's had suggested. No, Agnes should not, but on Heidi . . . well, it would be interesting to see.

"I think this is the best thing I've ever had from anyone," Heidi says, her eyes softening, her slight, not unappealing overbite (had braces been tried, and only partially succeeded?) giving her smile a vulnerable look. So maybe it would be possible to think of her as a rabbit rather than a coyote. Rabbits had small eyes, but that made them look hyperalert rather than predatory. Little rabbit. In French: *petit lapin*. Although it wouldn't be possible to think of her as hopping. But that made her even more vulnerable: that she could not ever be imagined to have hopped.

"Off with you, then," Agnes says, deliberately choosing the archaic diction. "And it's between us."

Heidi pretends to lock her lips with an invisible key, and Agnes is pleased to see the childish gesture.

Heidi stops in the bathroom down the hall from Miss Vaughan's classroom. She hates that bathroom, the smell of shit that should have been completely nonexistent but was not; she always imagined filthy sanitary napkins susurrating in the garbage cans, as she imagined mold growing invisibly in the grout between the snot-green tiles. There is a window made of crushed glass (insuring insulation from prying eyes, which, she imagined, the founders had thought of as potentially everywhere), but it was never opened.

She feels sick to her stomach. She wishes she could vomit . . . the smell as she kneels makes her retch, but the relief of vomiting would not come.

Miss Vaughan's gift had made her sick. Agnes Vaughan. What had she meant by it? What did she want in return?

For it was one thing Heidi Stolz knew as surely as she knew anything: if someone gave you something they wanted something back. And if the gift was extraordinary, they would want something extraordinary in return. Her job would be to discover what that was, and then refuse to give it.

She thinks of the last gift she had given her mother and how she had gotten what she wanted: she had exposed her mother, let her know that what she thought was hidden was out there for everyone to see.

Did they really believe, her mother and her father (who was her mother's accomplice in it), that nobody knew where they went every spring, to her mother's home in Switzerland, they always said, family business. But Heidi knew it wasn't family business; her mother had cut herself off completely from her family—it was why they went to Aspen to ski every winter instead of to Switzerland. "They told me never to darken their door again, and I've taken them at their word," her mother said. More information had not been given; her mother's sin, or transgression, because none of them was in the slightest bit religious, remained in darkness.

When everyone remarked, again and again, how young and lovely her mother always looked, didn't they know (they must) that every spring she disappeared for two or three months (leaving Heidi with Hans and Elsie) so that she could have her face torn up and put back together again? Heidi had been fourteen— two years ago, it was—when she'd figured it out, when she saw the prescriptions in French from the Swiss pharmacy, lined up like squat soldiers on the bathroom counter. But it was only last year that she noticed her mother's hands.

It was one of those moments that could have seemed supernatural—classes in comparative religion were required at the Lydia Farnsworth School, and she had felt like the blind man cured by Jesus, the sudden removal of scales from her eyes—when she looked at her mother's hands, lying slack beside her white plate on the white tablecloth.

Her mother's hands were old. They were mottled with brownish spots, some larger, some smaller, some nearly black, some—was it the newer ones—only a shade or two darker than the color of her ordinary skin. They had nothing to do with her mother's face.

Her mother saw Heidi staring at her hands—how she wished she had been quicker so her mother wouldn't have seen that she knew, or she wished it at the time, but later she was glad of it—and she quickly hid her hands in her lap. But they both knew: there was nothing that could be done with Liesel Stolz's hands; she could disappear for six months or six years and she would still come home with the hands of an old woman.

And her mother looked at her, and it was clear, so they both knew it, so clear, that Heidi heard her own voice, clear as clear, saying in her mind, "My mother hates me."

And she didn't mind. Because it was something to hold on to, a sharp stone that would never lose itself, never dissolve. Precious. Valuable. As valuable, more valuable, than the ordinary talisman most children held: "My mother loves me." Both were a sure way of knowing who you were. But Heidi's was more valuable because it was more rare.

And hatred implied a relationship of equals, whereas—what was its opposite—contempt, revulsion . . . suggested power on only one side. She had known, as long as she was capable of knowing anything, that her mother found her revolting. That was why she liked looking up the roots of words: *revolting,* to turn away from. Her mother turned from her daughter every time her eye fell on her. Unless the impulse to look was too strong, the impulse to look away not strong enough.

Once Heidi had been sitting at her mother's feet. Her mother was on the yellow satin couch where Heidi was not allowed, reading a magazine. Heidi took her mother's hand, and her mother dropped it, and her face showed disgust. "Why are your hands always so clammy?" And then the time—she should have known to stay away from her mother, because her mother was in one of her rages, and it wasn't like Heidi not to be careful of her mother in that state—but perhaps there was something she needed in the room where her mother was, or perhaps she was just attracted to a natural disaster, like watching a storm or an accident on the highway. Her mother was in one of her silky negligees, a word whose roots she liked because they were connected to neglect. Her mother walked, not stormed, over to her, and said, "Why is your hair always greasy . . . it always looks filthy . . . it's disgusting . . . ," and she picked up scissors that were on her husband's desk, pulled Heidi by the hair, and chopped her hair off in clumps until it fell on the cream-colored carpet, and Heidi could see that it was not lovely, the way her hair lay on the carpet like thick dead snakes. Silently, afraid of her mother's wrath, she felt the tears course down her cheeks, fall onto her shirt . . . she tried to dry them with her hands, but she couldn't keep up with the tears that would not stop. "My hair, my hair" was all she could say.

"Oh, Liesel, oh Liesel," her father said, wringing his hands. Her mother looked over his head, both their heads, and lit a cigarette. "Blah blah blah and boo hoo hoo," she said—her only response to Heidi's tears. "She's better off."

Liesel rang the bell for Elsie to come and take Heidi away.

Then she sat on the couch, placed the scissors on the table, reached into the ceramic box for a cigarette, and snapped her fingers for her husband to light her up. Elsie did nothing to comfort Heidi, only took another pair of scissors and tried to repair the butchered hack job.

No one said a word to suggest that what her mother had done was in the slightest way a cruelty. Everyone around Heidi was afraid of her mother. Everyone around her was weak, particularly her father, who cowered before her mother's blazing rage or simmering unhappiness. But it was more than that: her mother was physically the strongest. An athlete. A competitive skier: all around the house, her medals, her trophies, pictures of her holding something aloft, her blond hair gleaming against a clear winter sky, her shapely body, alluringly female even in the bulky ski outfits, her hand being shaken by some grand gentleman with a moustache or a crown of snow-white hair. Heidi couldn't imagine how it had happened, that her father—her father, who could make nothing happen (except with money, where he was called a wizard, a magician)—could have, as her mother said, "forced me to give it all up to come to this godforsaken part of the world." And so they traveled, looking for enough snow so she could do what she was "born to do" (not born to be anyone's wife or mother, this was the clear implication). Originally, they had lived in Vermont, but, now (was it her father's business?) they were in Rhode Island, where there were only minor hills. They had to travel: to Aspen in the winter, to the Southern Hemisphere in summer (a house in Chile, opened for only two months). "A great athlete," her father always said, abashed, apologetic, and Heidi had no reason not to believe him.

She tried to discern if she hated her mother as her mother

hated her. She liked to think that her hate was different from her mother's; her mother's hate was hot; hot hate could cause you to make errors, and she liked to think of herself as cold, cold and dry as a polished steel figure standing above everything, impermeable, invulnerable to natural shocks or the careless or malignant assaults of anyone or everyone. Certainly, she did not love her mother. How could anyone? Oh, but her father did. Her father did because she was beautiful. Heidi had not been very old before she learned that everything followed from that. If you were beautiful, you were beloved, and if you were not . . . and she was young, very young, when she knew that she was not . . . well, everything followed from that. She heard her mother saying it . . . saying, not only that she was not beautiful, it was much worse than that.

Who was she talking to? It was probably Simon Randolph—he was always around then. Even now, Heidi can't figure out if he was her mother's lover or if he was homosexual. It didn't matter; he was taking her father's place, he was the one her mother wanted to be with, not her husband, certainly not her daughter.

They were drinking . . . those wonderful-looking drinks— they would first shake them up in the special shining metal vessel, then pour them out, rich, amber colored, into special glasses, and then put in a cherry—how Heidi wanted those cherries, once she ate a whole bottle of them and was sick and Elsie said, "It serves you right, they were not for you, they are special for your mother." Even Elsie worshipped her mother, because she was beautiful, and "a real blonde, a perfect blonde," she had heard Elsie say.

Simon and her mother would lean back on the sofa, covered in yellow satin, that Heidi was told she must never sit on—Why do you always seem so dirty, her mother would say, lifting Heidi's hands, which she had scrubbed and scrubbed but never seemed to her mother clean enough—they would sip their beautiful drinks in their beautiful glasses and they would talk quietly, but Heidi always managed to place herself somewhere where they couldn't see her but she could hear them.

"Will you tell me what perverse god placed himself at my cradle so that I got exactly the opposite of what I wanted. What I wanted was a girl child, a beautiful idiot—because believe me there is no sense being born female, there's nothing in it but heartache, unless you're a beautiful idiot—and then a fine, strong, brilliant son who would care for me in my old age. And what have I got? A son who is a beautiful idiot and a daughter who's just a hideous little smarty-pants. I can't bear to lay my eyes on her. It's wrong . . . don't you think, darling . . . wrong and monstrously unfair."

So Heidi knew. She was a smarty-pants. As if her intelligence, which she valued in herself, and her teachers valued, was just a kind of joke garment, something to be mocked and despised. And then there was her brother. The beautiful idiot. Jimmy. James.

She wouldn't have known what to say if anyone had asked her, "Do you love your brother? Did you ever?" She refused to allow the question to inhabit her mind, and no one else would ask the question because no one she knew had any idea that he existed. The hidden brother. Given away. Bought off.

How could she have loved him? She had only met him once. She was never sure whether she was glad that she had met him or wished she hadn't. For years, she hadn't known she had a brother. And then in one of her mother's rages, an insistence: It shouldn't be hidden from her. She has to know it's in her blood . . . should anyone ever choose to have a child by her she has to know. She's getting of an age.

Blood. It was all about blood. Her mother had insisted on her meeting her brother when she found out Heidi had gotten her period. Late, later than other girls in her class; she was nearly fourteen. Strange to think it was only two years ago, strange to think that one of the ordinary facts of life . . . my period, my friend, the curse, my time of the month . . . why didn't anyone just say menstruation . . . I'm menstruating . . . she couldn't stand the coyness around it. Her mother had, of course, been away. Her mother had, of course, told her nothing of what to expect, and, as she had no friends, the information had not come to her. So one day she thought she was dying and—she was proud of this—calmly she went to Elsie and spoke about blood on her underpants. And Elsie said, "Did you soil your clothes or only your underwear?" The word *soil* . . . as if she had done something filthy.

And Elsie, sighing, turning her back to Heidi and returning with a mysterious box, with a word she'd never known printed on it, Kotex, and beside it a ballerina, and sighing again, said, "I've been expecting this for a long time. Well, you're in for it now."

How soon after that did her father come to her room and say, "I must tell you something that may be hard for you to understand." Elsie had given her a book called *The Facts of Life* that had been mildly shocking, but interesting. But that wasn't it at all. She was told nothing about "the facts of life" from either parent.

"We didn't tell you before, sweetheart"—had he ever called

her sweetheart before?—"because we felt you weren't old enough to handle it. But now you're a woman, and it's time for you to know."

A brother. The shock, as shocking as the blood on her underpants, and a new word she hadn't heard, although words were what she was good at, better than almost anyone she knew. Certainly better than her parents or Hans or Elsie, who spoke with accents—her mother, too, but hers was less—and her father seemed almost never to speak.

Autistic. No one knows why. Retarded. He can't really speak. Sometimes he gets out of control. But we think it's time you met him.

Why, she asked herself a million times. Why tell me. Why introduce me. It meant nothing to Jimmy: nothing did. That was what *autistic* meant. Nothing meant anything to him, except what did: the numbers of bricks in the building, the schedule of trains from Providence to New York.

They drive to Cape Cod . . . it's the only time she's been alone in a car with her father, and the minute they get in the car, he turns the radio on. "I need to listen to the news." But he keeps the radio on and listens to some kind of music that people his age listen to.

At a gate, which is guarded by a man in a uniform in a booth, there is a sign: SHADY GROVE. They drive through an impressive grove of trees.

"It really is a shady grove," she says to her father, hoping he'll be pleased at her observation.

"Well, at least there's no false advertising," he says. "I guess you get what you pay for."

Heidi laughs, not thinking what he said was funny, but sensing that a laugh was called for. But perhaps it was not; her father looks at her strangely.

At the end of the long drive, really a road, there are a series of small white cabins that look like the houses in the children's books she was given before she was able to read. Only the colors of the shutters are different: green-blue-red, and then the pattern begins again, green-blue-red, green-blue-red, until Heidi stops counting.

She has pushed from her mind all images, all expectations of what she might have been driven to see. A brother. Fourteen years older. So he is twenty-eight. A man.

But nothing she could have imagined could have prepared her for the sight of the creatures . . . she didn't want to call them people . . . walking up and down in front of the storybook cabins.

Until then, her idea of what the form of a human being might be like had been, she saw instantly, limited. Walking, shuffling, were grown people walking like seals perched on their hind flippers, people walking with their hands held up in the air in front of them, a tall thin man with a head much too small for his body, a woman whose torso was normal but below the waist of elephantine size, barely able to put one foot in front of another, a man standing still except for incessant rocking, someone turning in circles around and around until a nurse led him by the shoulder, made him walk forward.

Heidi is desperate to run back to the car, why won't her father see that this is too much, that she is still a child and no one who is his child should be forced to see these things. She puts her hand in his, but he takes it away and rubs the palm of his hand on his trousers. Her mother is right: her hands are always clammy. It's not my fault, she wants to say, but I'm better than these people. Normal. A normal girl with clammy hands.

A hideous little smarty-pants.

But better than these.

They are shown into a room that is almost as bare as a room can be. Four hard-backed chairs, linoleum floor, beige with a faint swirl of darker brown. And nothing else. Absolutely nothing.

She and her father sit in the two chairs that are next to each other. They say nothing; she knows, and she imagines he does too, that there is nothing possible to say.

The door opens then. Two people walk in. "A beautiful idiot," her mother had said, and Heidi is struck by his extraordinary beauty: their mother's blondness, their father's high, pale forehead, and the eyes, she has never seen eyes like those, she imagines there have never been eyes like these. Blue-green, the color of the sea, turquoise, but glistening, focused like searchlights on the empty wall ahead of her. His nurse half drags him to one of the empty chairs, and he shuffles to it, feeling for the leg with the back of his heel, sitting uncertainly, with no faith that the chair will hold him.

"Jimmy, your father and your sister Heidi are here to see you," the nurse says.

"Jimmy's father and Jimmy's sister Heidi are here to see him. Did Jimmy's father bring Jimmy Nestlé Crunch?"

Her father reaches into his briefcase and takes out a bag of miniature Nestlé Crunch bars. He hands them to his son. From this Heidi understands that he has been here before.

Jimmy rips open the bag and unwraps one of the candy bars, then another, then another.

"Jimmy likes Crunch bars," he says, liquid chocolate spilling out of his mouth. But nothing can mar the beautiful high forehead, the brilliant sea-green eyes.

"Say thank you, Jimmy," the nurse says. "Say thank you to your father."

"Thank you to my father," he says.

Jimmy wipes his chocolatey hands on his khaki pants. The nurse hands him a paper towel, a stack of which she has in her pocket.

"Jimmy, this is your sister Heidi," her father says.

Jimmy looks at the wall across from him.

"Jimmy Stolz has a sister Heidi," he says, not looking at her.

Then he stands up and pulls away from his nurse. He begins rocking. Then he walks in circles. The circles become increasingly smaller, his pace more frantic.

"Jimmy doesn't like this place, Jimmy doesn't like this place," he says. He picks up a chair; he is about to throw it across the room.

"It's your home, Jimmy, you're at Shady Grove, where you live, just in another room, where your father and sister have come to see you," the nurse says.

Jimmy lifts the chair over his head and Heidi and her father jump out of their chairs and back toward the wall.

The nurse, who is much larger than Jimmy, wrestles the chair from him.

"It's not a good day for him," she says. "It's one of his bad days."

"You'd better take him back," Heidi's father says. "We'll come another time." But Heidi knows they won't and they drive home in silence, except for the radio, which her father plays too loud.

A few weeks later, her father says, over breakfast (her mother is still in bed), "You have another brother. He has estranged himself from the family. You will never know him. Lawrence is his name. Lawrence Stolz. But he has cut himself off from us. Entirely cut himself off. We have no idea, even, where he is, or even if he is alive. We think he's in the Marines. Somewhere, we think, in Asia."

And Heidi knows not to ask anything, to nod, to raise her teacup to her lips and drink slowly, as normally as she can.

Two brothers: one a whirling, a whirring; one blank.

She does not allow herself to think of them. It is easier with the one called Lawrence, no images come to her mind and she refuses to create them. And when the whirling boy, the beautiful idiot, enters the space behind her eyes, she banishes him. Ensures that he is, as the other brother is, entirely cut off.

Why is she thinking about all this now? Kneeling in front of the toilet, trying, failing to vomit. Because she has been given a gift. And she doesn't know how to understand it. Miss Vaughan. Agnes Vaughan. Who pretends to understand her. Because she doesn't know. Finds her interesting. Original. But knows nothing of who she is.

And if she did?

I would have to give the boots back, Heidi thinks, and then, clutching the bag to her, as if someone had actually threatened to take it away, she stands up, her full height, and in the closed bathroom stall enacts a posture of heroic resistance. *These are mine. No one can take them from me. They were a gift.*

That's why she was thinking of her family. That's why all

these things came back. Because she was thinking of her mother, the gift she gave her mother last Christmas, and the knowledge: a gift was powerful, a gift could be a weapon, it made a link between giver and gifted and the link could be used.

Her mother had looked at her with hatred when she realized that Heidi understood about her hands. That there was nothing she could do about them. There was no fixing them. They were old. And they would mark her as old, however smooth her face, however perfect the proportions of her youthful body. Her hands would make a mockery of it all.

Saks Fifth Avenue. The store a voluptuous display of Christmas luxury: smells, music, lights, ribbons, the famous windows with families dressed up to suggest an innocent time of unadulterated joy: the nineteenth century, Dickens, the stalwart father cutting down the perfect fir in the pristine, benevolent, and never-threatening snow, the cool perfumed air, the cool reassuring yet enticing Christmas music.

She went to the glove department. "My mother is just mad for gloves. She says a lady is known by her gloves. I guess it's old-fashioned, but it's the way she is," Heidi says to the saleslady, hoping to conjure a fragile, genteel mother, horrified by the turn the world has taken, lovely in her ivory tower. "So I want the loveliest gloves you have, one pair for every season."

The saleswoman, sleek, coiffed, brushed, bound, buffed, bends down, becomes invisible, then rises, her hands full. She presents the gloves in seasonal order: navy kid, sheepskin-lined tan suede, lemon cotton, a sinister-looking smoky half-transparent lace. Heidi knows she's meant to show enthusiasm, filial delight in the anticipated pleasure of a loving mother, and so she lifts each of them, strokes them, remarks on the different textures, asks that they all be wrapped together, because she'll have to carry them in her suitcase. This is true; Christmas will be, as always, at the Aspen "chalet." She wants them to be in one box because she wants to absorb the fullness of her punishment; if they are in separate boxes her mother might open only one and leave the others unwitnessed.

If only she had had the red boots then. They would be perfect for walking down Fifth Avenue, zealous, triumphant, ready to render justice. A soldier. A saint.

Christmas. The most hideous day, Heidi believed, of all days in the year. The day she got her own back. She liked thinking of it that way. She inflicted nothing, she simply claimed her due.

Her mother had awakened early for a sunrise ski, and had come back glorious: enlivened and nearly benevolent, the cold freshening the perfume on her skin and hair so that for once Heidi wasn't sickened by what it suggested to her of rot and rut.

Elsie had baked stollen, their traditional Christmas breakfast. Her father had risen late and came down so freshly shaved, his hair so slicked back wet from the shower, that he looked to Heidi like a rabbit ready to be pulled up by the ears and stuck in a steaming pot.

She had considered coming down in the dressing gown her parents had given her the last Christmas, a light blue satin quilted affair with a neck-to-ankle zipper that was difficult to navigate and chafed her chin. But she decided against it: she wanted nothing that suggested vulnerability. And it was possible that her mother would throw her out, would banish her not only from the house, but from the family, as the blank brother, Lawrence, had banished himself.

"I took a long time selecting these, Mother," she said, and for a moment her mother's almost natural look gave her a hesitation she hadn't counted on.

But soon that was over. Having seen what was in the box, Heidi's mother's whole being was covered in a hard, brittle shell, as if someone had dipped her in glycerin and then locked her in a freezer.

Never had Heidi seen a look so cold, so killing. And she returned the same cold killing look.

She knew herself to be a killer. With a killer's pride. She had driven a stake into the heart of any possible goodness there could ever be between them. She had done it gladly, purposefully, and with pride she looked over her handiwork like a general looking over the city he had conquered, after the bodies had been dispatched, and the plaza with its heroic statue hosed of all remaining blood, and the new flag, immovable, aloft, demanding plain acknowledgment, and rendering impossible the prospect that it should ever be ignored.

But very soon she told herself the terms were too grand. What she had done was pierce the smooth skin of a rotten fruit, releasing into the air the poison juices, sticky, stinking, spent.

Did her father understand what had happened? She didn't know. He opened the box she had passed to him. He lifted it out of the box, turned it over, looked at the label, thanked her mildly. She had bought him a dark blue tie.

Heidi hears the bathroom door open; she is no longer alone.

She stands up, flushes the empty toilet, and walks into the main room.

Of the people at the Lydia Farnsworth School, the only one

she admires, the only one whose regard she genuinely cares for, is Jeanne Larkin. Because Jeanne Larkin needs no one at the Lydia Farnsworth School; perhaps Jeanne Larkin needs no one in the world. She's the scientific one, Miss Datchett's prize, she and Miss Walsh . . . MIZZ Walsh and Miss Vaughan are fast friends; it's all too predictable and cute: the three pretty young teachers, art, history, science. Heidi has no use for Miss Walsh and her band of earnest peaceniks and weepers over endangered species. But Miss Datchett . . .

Heidi would respect her if she had any interest in science because Miss Datchett likes facts, and so she likes Jeanne Larkin. Jeanne Larkin with her short blond curls when everyone else has long hair parted in the middle (except for Heidi, who keeps her hair in a single plait—people think it's because she wants to be eccentric but it's because her mother is right, her hair always looks greasy, and the plait disguises that best). It was Edwina who advised her to adopt the plait. She doesn't want to think of Edwina now.

But Jeanne Larkin needs to disguise nothing; she keeps her hair short because she's a dressage rider and so has a helmet that would be a problem with longer hair. Jeanne Larkin does things because they are convenient, and then everyone wants to do them but they can't; when people try to copy her they look ridiculous.

She makes no effort to please, and Heidi has tried to understand why, sharing the same desire, she is spurned and Jeanne sought after. And then she realized that other girls hungered after Jeanne's attention because she was genuinely not interested in them. There was no need for her to be contemptuous of them; she simply didn't take them in. She told Mrs. Gould, the sappy

English teacher (whose eyes tear up when she talks about Keats's early death), that the only poetry she really likes are limericks. And she produced a series of limericks about animals.

> *Upend the kind orangutan*
> *You may be pleased to find*
> *Instead of his bland brother's lot*
> *A cherry-red behind*

> *The sloth has forfeited respect*
> *In favor of a luscious rest*
> *Despise him, but can you be sure*
> *His choice is not the best?*

And after that, limericks became the rage at the Lydia Farnsworth School. Everyone was writing or trying to write limericks. Not to be outdone—because despite herself she wanted to be like Jeanne—Heidi wrote one about her parents:

> *My father's a financial whizz*
> *My mother is voluptuous*
> *You might think this would make a rhyme*
> *But no dear readers not this time.*

She handed it in to Mrs. Gould for her extra-credit "creative assignment," and Mrs. Gould called her in and asked if she wanted to see the school counselor, and said that it was very clever but she couldn't possibly share it with the other students.

Which, of course, Heidi must already have known, but she had held a secret hope that she might become admired because of her shocking honesty. It was 1972, after all, and shocking honesty was in vogue.

But not at the Lydia Farnsworth School.

No one calls Jeanne Larkin "Jeanie." If they ever do she says, "I don't have light brown hair, so it's Jeanne."

There is no nickname for Heidi. Except Hide. And no one ever wanted to be close enough to her to try to seduce her with a nickname. No, that wasn't true. Edwina's friends called her Scotty . . . their little mascot. But Edwina is gone, and hasn't answered her letters.

She wants to leave the room before Jeanne Larkin . . . she doesn't want to have to try to figure out a stance in relation to Jeanne that won't leave her abashed.

She looks at herself in the mirror as Jeanne Larkin enters one of the stalls. And for the first time, she feels no need to be abashed, no need to feel inferior. She picks up her white shopping bag. A gift from Miss Vaughan. Miss Agnes Vaughan, who allowed Jeanne Larkin to do botanical drawings because she said, "I don't have a creative bone in my body. But I like to get the look of things right."

But Miss Vaughan had singled Heidi out, not Jeanne Larkin. She had singled her out with the gift, in the shiny white bag. She had singled her out, and trusted her with a secret. It would be a problem for Miss Vaughan if Heidi told anyone. She never would, and Miss Vaughan knew that: it was the truest sign of her regard.

Heidi has something that no other girl in the Lydia Farnsworth School has. A secret. Which she would not reveal, but could, causing embarrassment, perhaps even censure from the totally uptight headmistress. And if the other students knew, it would be bad for Miss Vaughan in another way. Because they would think there was no good reason for anyone to favor Heidi Stolz. And it would make them wonder, and their wondering would make Miss Agnes Vaughan, whom most of them adored, much smaller in their eyes.

Standing behind her desk in the empty classroom, with its over-laying smell of chalk and overripe apples, the light striking the polished desks from the large schoolroom windows, Agnes knows that she has made a mistake. She tries to go back to the moment in New York when she was convinced that making a present of the boots to Heidi Stolz was a perfect idea. She had thought that until she caught that split-second look in Heidi's eyes, what she thought of as a mix of unease and calculation, not the frank delight she had imagined from a girl thrilled to be so singled out.

But wasn't that why she was so fascinated by Heidi Stolz, because her reactions were nearly always unexpected? Because she was never taken in by the popular enthusiasms, by conventional responses or tastes. Even the way she presented herself went against the grain of every other girl: her hair in a single plait, her black winter coat, a throwback to the '40s, which, when Agnes admired it, Heidi confessed to having bought in a thrift shop. Agnes remembered what Letitia Barnes had said to her about Heidi: that she was a starved creature, that her mother had looked on her with the look that starved rather than nurtured.

She wishes that Heidi could see that she was in her own way, if not lovely, then striking: the high forehead, the prominent but distinguished nose, the slight overbite. Her eyes were not large, and that might have made the difference. And it was unfortunate that her name suggested a rosy-cheeked blond, an Alpine Shirley Temple. Her legs were enviably long, and she was surprisingly voluptuous; her stooped walk was, Agnes was certain, a tactic to try to hide her large breasts. Obviously, she had inherited her breasts from her mother, Agnes thought, remembering with unease the unsettling limerick Heidi had shown her.

It was a terrible thing to have such contempt for your parents at her age, a pitiable thing, and Agnes's heart went out to the poor starved creature, because she knew she herself had been extraordinarily loved and loved her parents easily, especially her mother, and if she had some difficulties with her father, there was nothing like contempt that touched her daughterly imagination. Such hateful words, the words in that limerick about her parents . . . and yet they had stuck in her brain.

She had asked Letitia Barnes about Heidi's family.

Miss Barnes had let her preternatural discretion lapse; she looked down at her blotter. "Well, the mother is foreign, Swiss, I believe an athlete in her youth. A skier. When she talked about her past, she mentioned the war only to say that it prevented the 1940 and '44 Olympics, in which she might have successfully competed. I must say, I find her a thoroughly unpleasant woman, mutton dressed as lamb, you'll forgive my saying. The father is the head of a large pharmaceutical company, although he seems rather beaten down for the tycoon I know him to be."

"I worry for her," Agnes had said.

"You're not wrong. But be careful. New teachers often get entangled in ways that have unfortunate consequences."

Is that what she had done? Had she done it precisely to go against Miss Barnes's warning? And was she entangled now?

She thinks of the old proverb that never seemed to have any application to her life: Oh, what a tangled web we weave when first we practice to deceive. She tells herself she hadn't deceived, not really, but she knew that giving Heidi the boots was something that had to be kept secret. But why? Because it was not a thing teachers were supposed to do. Give students expensive gifts.

She had told her mother about it, because she knew that what she was doing was questionable and she also knew that her mother didn't immediately write off questionable behavior. She had shown her mother the boots. "They're wonderful . . . Agnes, keep them for yourself."

"Mother, they were a stupid impulse. I have nothing to go with them."

"Then maybe you ought to get some new things," her mother said. Her mother, having no appetite for large extravagances—furs, jewels—indulged in a series of smaller ones. Antique combs that decorated her chignon or French twist, a collection of hats that her father regularly, properly teased her for; she traveled to Providence to get her hair colored by the most expensive salon in the city; she prided herself on her blouses of real silk and her thin gold watch.

"Nobody else likes this girl, Mother, not even her own parents, not even Florence Gould . . . and she likes almost every student. Jo and Christina just roll their eyes when I mention her name. Jo because Heidi smirks whenever one of the ardent antiwar girls carries on, and Christina because she thinks Heidi slinks like a coyote, that she's always plotting. I understand, maybe they're right, but she has a genuine imagination, she's not afraid to go against the grain. And then she's so lonely, so shocked that anyone would show her the slightest kind attention. She just seems like such a wounded creature to me . . . so undernourished."

"And you want to nourish her?"

"Yes, Mother, I do."

"Well, I love you for that. I always loved you for bringing in wounded birds. For trying to domesticate feral cats. You remember the one who gave you such a bad scratch we had to take you for a tetanus shot? I suppose I'm guilty of the same temptation myself. With my prisoners."

"People said you were mad to volunteer in the prisons giving art classes."

"Well, they were wrong. But I have made mistakes. Do you remember Ronald Simonson? So gifted . . . well, untutored, and rather vulgar in his taste, but with a remarkable ability to do a likeness in a few strokes. I wrote letters in his support for the parole board, and then he got out and beat his ex-wife almost to death a week after his release."

Agnes was silent, remembering her mother's remorse, her mother's visits to the ex-wife, her financial support of the woman . . . who had also, Agnes and her father believed, taken advantage much longer than she had a right to.

"But then there was Leo Johnson, who I thought had the makings of a great draftsman, and he did, he actually got himself to college and is working for a big architect in Boston. So if I hadn't had it in me to believe in possibilities, on the one hand, I wouldn't have supported Ronald Simonson. But then I wouldn't have supported Leo Johnson either."

"Heidi Stolz has no one, Mother. Which is why my heart goes out to her."

"I've come to believe that about sixty percent of things we do from the heart turn out badly. But it would be dreadful not to do them."

Agnes laughed, and ruffled her mother's hair. "Where did you come up with that statistic, sixty percent?"

"Well, I knew it had to be more than half, but I didn't want to make it seem impossibly discouraging."

Heidi's aloneness was Agnes's greatest concern. She seemed to have no friends, and no interest in making them. The only non-contemptuous thing she ever said was about her admiration for Jeanne Larkin. Jeanne Larkin, who rather frightened Agnes; she had never met a girl so self-contained. Jeanne had told Agnes she wanted to be a vet or an astronaut, and Agnes could imagine her, helmeted and suited, hanging, attached by a cord to her rocket ship, dangling happily alone in space, or helping some large animal caught in a trap or a difficult birth. Jeanne was not one of the girls who Agnes knew adored her, but Agnes had at least won her respect by giving her some pointers in the botanical drawings she wanted to do for her project.

She would talk to Jeanne Larkin about perhaps taking Heidi under her wing.

Jeanne was Christina's protégée: the only student at the Lydia Farnsworth School whom Christina considered genuinely scientifically gifted, for whom she mourned the inadequate laboratories, the clear preference for the humanities.

They were driving back from Danbury, the one visit per month on which they accompanied Jo on her visits to her husband. The drive down was always tense: Jo was always afraid that Jack had been beaten, raped, given poisonous food. This had never happened, and on the way home, Jo was always a little

annoyed at Jack's good spirits, his success at tutoring fellow prisoners, the fact that he had a lot of time to write—he was working
on a biography of Thomas Paine—and his delight that he was
in the same institution as Daniel Berrigan, his hero. "It's like he
got locked up with a movie star and gets to have lunch with him
every day," Jo said. "It never rains on Planet Jack. It drives me
nuts," Jo said, but her friends knew she was secretly proud.

"Chrissy, tell me your thoughts about Jeanne Larkin," Agnes
said.

"Jeanne Larkin. Well, she's the best student I've ever had. A
real mind. She's kind of inhuman, but in the best sense of the
word," Christina said.

Agnes and Jo laughed: Christina's malapropisms were a
source of great joy to them. Fortunately, Christina didn't mind
being teased. "I do numbers and formulas, not words," she said.

"Why do you want to know about Jeanne Larkin?" Christina
said. "I didn't think she was one of your arty types."

"She's not . . . she makes a point of telling me that she sees no
point to painting or sculpture. So I let her do botanical drawings,
which she's of course very good at, and I even got some points
for showing her how she could improve things, and by telling
her my mother was a medical illustrator."

"So why the interest?"

"Well, it's Heidi Stolz, I know you can't stand her but she's *my*
most gifted student, and she's so terribly isolated . . . really, her
family is just a nightmare."

"I've checked out the mother. I don't think she has one inch of
skin on her body where it was originally meant to be."

"Well, I really feel sorry for Heidi. You know, Jo, you keep talking about looking out for the poor. She's really one of the poor."

"Her poverty is of her own making. She's a nasty, sneaky little thing. That's why Chris was so right to call her the coyote."

"That's like blaming the poor for being poor, which you claim to be against."

"What does it have to do with Jeanne Larkin?"

"Jeanne Larkin is the only person I've ever heard Heidi speak of without contempt, with anything like admiration. So I was hoping maybe there was some way we could cook something up so they were doing some kind of project together, or something."

"What, you're matchmaking now?" Christina said.

"Well, in a sense. What I was thinking was this. I know that Jeanne goes down to Columbia every Saturday for the special class for scientifically gifted students that you found for her. I was thinking I could find something for Heidi to do so they could go down on the train together. I was thinking maybe we could arrange for a joint project—something about, oh, I don't know, relativity and cubism . . . something like that."

Christina tapped on the armrest of the back seat. "That's actually not the craziest idea I ever heard of."

"I'm out of it," Jo said. "I'm the history teacher, remember, and history would suggest this is a bad idea."

"What history?" Christina and Agnes asked at the same time.

"There's always something," Jo said. "I'll think of it."

Christina agreed to meet with Heidi and Jeanne in Agnes's classroom. Heidi arrived first, slinking into the room, as she always did, looking around her as if she expected someone to spring out and do her harm.

"How are you, Heidi?" Agnes asks.

Heidi shrugs. "Just putting in my time in this genteel prison until graduation."

"Have you thought about what I said about a liberal arts college instead of art school?"

"Well, my parents think you're right."

"We can talk about it next year. Have you been doing any more painting or printing?"

"I'm looking forward to showing it to you when I'm done. You're the only one I trust to look at my work."

"I'm pleased," Agnes says. She was, and her pleasure, she knew, was somehow wrong. "But I'm sure there are some other people, other students here, who would be a good sounding board for you."

Heidi snorted. "You, Miss Vaughan, are the only person here whom I don't consider a visual ignoramus."

Christina and Jeanne walked into the room together. Agnes noticed that Jeanne's shoulders were disproportionately wide; without them she would have been merely the perfect gamine, but instead she suggested something regrettable, slightly alarmingly powerful . . . and Agnes was sorry, as someone who had drawn from live models, that the wide shoulders spoiled the line.

"Are we in trouble?" Jeanne said, with a half smirk, knowing full well that she was not.

"On the contrary," Christina said. "It's that we had an idea for a senior project for the both of you. We're aware that you're quite far ahead of most of the other students—you, Jeanne, in chemistry and physics . . . you, Heidi, in visual arts. So we thought perhaps you had something unique to offer each other, something that would add a kind of dimension to your experience here. We were thinking that perhaps you could write a joint paper, as your senior project, on the link between relativity and cubism."

"I'll be spending a lot of time on dressage next year," Jeanne said. "And I'm competing with my horse."

Heidi seemed to shrink into her torso, but she shot Agnes a look of angry accusation. Agnes knew what she was thinking: This would never work, why did you think it would work.

Agnes drew herself up in the way that she had seen her father do when he encountered opposition. She didn't know where the muscle memory came from; she had no thought of ever having called on the posture before.

"All the more reason, Jeanne," she said. "We could speak to the headmistress about being more flexible with your schedule so you could be freer of class time to pursue your outside activities."

"You mean, like time out of school," Jeanne said. For the first time, there was a change in the absolute level of her gaze. For the first time, she looked surprised and young.

"Yes, that's precisely what I mean," Agnes said. She saw Christina's panicked look. There was no guarantee that Letitia Barnes would agree to it. But Agnes knew that she was Letitia Barnes's pet. She had asked for no favors since she got here; she would call her markers in.

"That might be kind of cool," Jeanne said.

Agnes tried to read the look in Heidi's eyes. It was fear, she decided, the same fear with an undercoating of anger she had seen when she gave Heidi the boots.

"If you want to," Heidi said. "Anything to spend some time away from this place and the idiots I have to spend my days with."

"Let's shake on that," Jeanne said, and Agnes let her shoulders relax. This, she knew was a wholly good thing. This, she knew was a triumph.

Agnes was eager to lay the groundwork, so perhaps over the summer the girls could spend time together. An Oxford art historian was giving a lecture on *Guernica* at the Museum of Modern Art. The lecture was on a Saturday, and Agnes knew that Jeanne traveled to Columbia on Saturday mornings. That was why she had pressed Christina to propose the plan to the girls that very day, so they could work on the idea on the train that weekend. She didn't know when there'd be another opportunity for her to suggest—or did she mean *insist*—that Heidi travel to New York.

"Jesus, Agnes, why don't you just put leashes on them and take them down there yourself?"

"Am I being that, well . . . bossy?"

"You know, what I love about you is everyone thinks you're a delicate little flower but when you want something, you're as stubborn as a mule. I'm quite sure this is a terrible idea, but I'm exhausted from arguing with you."

"Do you really think it's terrible?"

"I do, but I want it to be great because I need to believe that good intentions from a good person can be of some good in the world."

"I don't think I'm such a good person. You don't know some of the thoughts I have."

"If you're not a good person, I would have to relinquish everything I think about the possibility of a good person. And I'm not willing to do that. So you'd better be right about this."

~~~

HEIDI KNOWS she is ridiculously early for the train, but she didn't want Jeanne to be watching her approach, and she wanted to make sure she could make her way without the ignominy of rushing. She watches Jeanne make her way up the stairs and across the platform.

Jeanne is wearing jeans and a poncho: a light brown background with alternating black and white animals. The wool looks so soft, so comforting, that Heidi longs to touch it; despising herself for the impulse, she steps back as Jeanne approaches. Her boots are square toed and low heeled, and they make a heavy determined sound on the cement of the train platform.

Heidi feels that what she's wearing is ridiculous. She had bought the shortest possible skirt to show off the red boots Miss Vaughan had given her. And the jacket she had bought with Edwina on one of their thrift shop expeditions, a vintage World War II army jacket, with ribbons, insignias, brass buttons—Elsie had tailored it so that it fit her perfectly; the lieutenant colonel must have been very tall; the jacket reached just below her knees and she could cinch it tight with the fabric belt—which she had thought so original, so distinctive, now seemed merely showoffy. But she wishes she had thought to dress as Jeanne did: protected, contained, yet with the suggestion of warmth and an almost sleep-inducing comfort.

Jeanne nods, and Heidi nods back. Neither of them speaks.

As soon as they're seated in the train, Jeanne takes a book from the canvas rucksack she carried. It was called *Relativity: A Primer.*

"I thought you could get started on this."

"Thanks, I'll take good care of it."

"It's not mine. It's Miss Datchett's. Give it to her when you're done."

"I'll ask Miss Vaughan to give you something on cubism."

"Fine. I know nothing about it, as I imagine you know nothing about relativity."

"You're right there."

"I guess you have some good reason for doing this. I'm doing it so I can have more time to work on dressage before the big meet."

"I'm just doing it because any minute away from that hellhole is good for me."

"It could be worse. You should hear what some of my friends in this Columbia class I'm going to say about their schools."

"Well, school is a prison they consign us to because they're afraid of what we'd be up to if they let us out."

Jeanne looks at Heidi as if she were speaking a foreign language. She takes off her poncho. Underneath it is a black cotton turtleneck. Once again, Heidi feels she has misjudged; she's wearing a V-neck sweater, light blue mohair; she hadn't thought that the heat of the compartment would render the wool irritating to her bare skin.

"Is your cape alpaca?"

"Yes, my parents know these people in Vermont who raise alpacas."

"I always get alpacas mixed up with llamas," Heidi says, feeling that for the first time she had said something acceptable.

"They're actually very different. Llamas are more than twice the size of alpacas."

"Oh," Heidi says, feeling rebuked.

Jeanne takes a large textbook out of her bag.

"I have to look over these equations before my class."

"Sure," Heidi says.

She takes out the book on Picasso that Miss Vaughan had lent her.

"I'm going to a lecture on *Guernica* at the Museum of Modern Art."

"Nice," says Jeanne, not looking up from her equations.

They pass the rest of the trip in silence. Heidi is pretending to read, but, in her misery, none of the words make sense. The Blue Period, the Rose Period, the impact of *Les Demoiselles d'Avignon* . . . none of it seemed to make any difference. She had hoped that she and Jeanne would become friends out of a sense of shared superiority. But Jeanne Larkin knew perfectly well that she was superior to everyone, including Heidi Stolz, and it was clear that she felt no need of friends. Heidi feels herself begin to sweat, and she's terrified that before the end of the trip she will be stinking. She goes into the filthy tiny bathroom and smells her armpits, but the stench of the shit of strangers and the disinfectant intended to cover it means she has no idea how to judge the presence or absence of her own offensive smells.

Jeanne says a perfunctory goodbye as they arrive at Penn Station and heads for the subway. Heidi envies the sureness of her step; not for a second did she have to look around for where she was going, but then, she'd been doing this for months, since the beginning of junior year, when Miss Science Datchett had found this course for her, because obviously Jeanne was too brilliant for the rest of them.

Heidi tries to look like she knows where she is going; Miss Vaughan had advised that she walk to the museum, it wasn't far; she had only to walk two blocks east to Fifth Avenue and then the walk was less than a mile, and Miss Vaughan thought Heidi would enjoy "taking in the sights. I know you have a wonderful eye; it will be a good exercise for your powers of observation."

An educational experience, Heidi nastily repeats Agnes Vaughan's words, her soft voice in her mind. She was full of rage. How pathetic Agnes Vaughan must have thought she was, giving her the gift of the boots, setting up this stupid project so that she and Jeanne Larkin would have a connection. She isn't sure whether she resents Miss Vaughan or Jeanne Larkin more.

She decides it's Agnes Vaughan, because she pitied Heidi, whereas Jeanne Larkin thought her simply beneath notice. Of all things, pity was the worst, the most impossible to bear, and in her refusal to bear it, she once more recognized herself.

She saw almost nothing in the walk up Fifth Avenue; vaguely she takes in the lions of the Forty-Second Street Library, the Atlas statue in front of Rockefeller Center, the big church across the street. But mostly, she concentrates on her rage, and her desire to be free of them, free of them all, after another year of imprisonment in the oh-so-cozy Lydia Farnsworth School. Then she would surprise everyone; maybe she wouldn't even go to college . . . she could hear Miss Vaughan's gentle insistence on the importance of a liberal arts education, that she had a wonderful mind that needed to be cultivated, but she would refuse cultivation; she would look for something savage, something to mark the contempt she woke up with every morning and fell asleep cradling against the too-large breasts, her mother's breasts, that she despised as she despised everything about her mother.

Miss Vaughan had given Heidi her pass to the museum, so she

didn't have to pay or stand in line with the rest of the people, so proud of themselves for being where they were. She's grateful for that; she hated standing in line; she hated hearing the ridiculous conversations, weather, food, love affairs, all of them, she believed, not worth the breath spent on them.

She had never seen *Guernica*. She had never been to the Museum of Modern Art. But Miss Vaughan didn't know that. The only times she'd been to New York, she came with her parents, and they came so that her mother could shop. She'd passed Saks Fifth Avenue, where she had bought the gloves for her mother, and she knew that a few blocks up there was Bergdorf Goodman, which her mother approached, awestruck, like a pilgrim approaching a shrine.

She's early, and she takes a seat toward the back of the auditorium. She doesn't want to take out her book on Picasso, so she opens a small notebook that she carried for sketching, and begins to write random sentences, in order to appear engaged.

Jeanne Larkin is a stuck-up bitch.
Jeanne Larkin can go to hell.
I hope she doesn't get into Harvard or Yale or wherever
    she wants to go.
I will not go to college. That will upset them all.

The room begins to fill, and two men appear on the stage. The younger one introduces the speaker, a professor from Oxford,

Trevor Havisham. He is going to talk about *Guernica* in relation to the Spanish Pavilion at the exhibition of 1937. There would be special access to the painting itself, the young man said; it would be cordoned off for this audience, the ordinary museumgoers would be kept back.

She allows herself to indulge in her favorite fantasies. She is successful, she is famous. In this fantasy she is not the lecturer but the subject of the lecture: her groundbreaking work as a brave, daring artist. Enviable, envied. Heidi believes that being envied is the most desirable thing in the world.

The lecturer is William F. Buckley, whom she admires and finds enormously attractive. Her father watched his show, *Firing Line,* every Sunday and Heidi sat next to him, both of them cheering Buckley's demolition of the hapless opponent who had put himself at Buckley's mercy. It is one of the few times she feels close to her father. He says he is a conservative: "Liberals believe in the future, they think it's a great blank wall and they can write any nonsense they like on it. As if there were no past . . . nothing to press on the wall. A conservative is someone who deals with the reality of the darkness of the past." In seventh grade, she had expressed herself as a conservative, and everyone fell on her as if she were carrying a germ that could infect them all. None of their arguments moved her; she was bored by their optimism, and from then on, she refused to engage in political arguments. She hopes one day to be as articulate as William F. Buckley. She loves his voice, always contemptuous but never aroused, adding extra syllables, there was some liberal historian he loathed named Schlesinger, and he said the name *Slezinger,* drawing it out to make him seem somehow loathsome, reptilian.

She imagines William F. Buckley saying her name, *Heidi*

Stolz, with reverence. He had never known how to look properly at art before he discovered her work. He says he doesn't know how she managed to achieve all that she did at such a young age. She is always twenty-five in her fantasies, but older looking, like the picture of Marlene Dietrich in her mother's dressing room.

The real-life lecturer is not interesting. He is speaking about a war Heidi has never heard of. The Spanish Civil War. Nationalists, Republicans . . . the words tumble around her brain and confuse her, and she resents the confusion: she blames the speaker. He mentions names she doesn't know, Durruti, Prieto, and some she does, Dalí, Joan Miró. She has to think of something to tell Miss Vaughan, so she has to pay attention. If she tells Miss Vaughan the lecture was boring, she will get that sad look, that disappointed look, and Heidi will despise her and yet regret that she was the cause of that look.

She writes a few things in her book. Hitler's bombs, she writes, Hieronymus Bosch. Hieronymus Bosch is a painter she likes. One of the girls who was known for taking a lot of drugs, Linda Frank, made Miss Vaughan laugh when she said, "I think he was tripping," when Miss Vaughan showed a slide of Bosch's *Last Judgment.* Heidi hated it that everybody laughed, especially Miss Vaughan. She knew that she could never think of anything to make a whole class laugh. Even the teacher.

The lecture is over. They are being shown to the painting.

Heidi has seen it a million times, in reproductions, in slides in Miss Vaughan's class. But never has the horror of it, the terror, the pain of the animals, particularly, the sheer panic of the horse, struck her as real. She would like not to be moved by it, as she has wedded herself to Andy Warhol's cutting remarks about "great art." But she can't make herself move away She is still looking when the guard moves the velvet rope to allow the ordinary museum-goers access.

"Too bad he was on the losing side."

She hears a voice behind her, an English accent, even more alluring than William F. Buckley's, which she knows to be some version of American. She forces herself to turn slowly, as if someone behind her, speaking in an English accent, were of no importance to her.

He looks nothing like William F. Buckley; he looks something like the actor who plays Marcus Welby, MD. Robert Young. Silver haired; he wears gray trousers and a blue blazer, light blue shirt, and (this *does* excite her) an ascot instead of a tie. He is not quite smiling; he radiates calm, a large composure, and he must want to talk to her, or he wouldn't have come up behind her and said what he said.

Who will she be for him? Nothing like this has ever happened to her. He is, after all, a stranger, the category she has been warned about since early childhood. But he is nothing like the kidnappers in her imagination, wild eyed, grizzled, their clothes grimy and redolent of their desire to do her harm. This man gives off a slight, not quite masculine fragrance, yet it isn't feminine . . . is it lavender, something like that, something sweet and spicy, something she has never experienced before, certainly never in a man. A man who wants to talk to her.

She knows that this is a rare opportunity; she can become whoever she wants to be for him. He knows nothing about her, nothing about her history, he has never heard of Jeanne Larkin or Joan LeBeau or the giggly girls with their stupid athletic boyfriends. He knows nothing about her mother; and she understands that she must make herself the most different from her mother that she can imagine. She must convey an extraordinary original mind, unmoistened by sentimentality or ordinary received ideas.

"What does it matter? He couldn't have stopped anything happening. No artist could. By the time he painted this, all the people, all the animals, were smashed to smithereens. I wonder how much money he made off it. Now he gets a million dollars for drawing an apple on a napkin."

"So cynical for one so young."

"How do you know how old I am?"

"I'm trying not to think about it."

"Well, let's not," she says. This, she knows, is called flirtation. How did it come to her? Perhaps it was always there, just waiting for a worthy recipient, like a tennis player who has never played because she knew no available opponent who would be worthy of her skills.

"Might I invite you downstairs for a coffee? Or in my case, forgive the cliché of my birthplace, a cup of tea?"

Her heart races. This is the first time anyone male has ever asked her for anything. She tries to look undecided, consults her watch.

"Briefly," she says, proud of her word choice. Accepting, but with an undercurrent of reluctance, the delicious spice of holding back.

She asks him to bring her a coffee, black, which she doesn't enjoy but seems sophisticated.

He is drinking tea, with milk and sugar.

"What brought you to the lecture," he said, "since you are obviously not a worshipper at the shrine of Santo Pablo?"

She would rather die than say, "My teacher wanted me to

come." She shrugs. "A friend gave me a ticket and I thought, why not?"

"And what did you make of our Oxford don?"

It is her turn now to present everything she's learned from Edwina, from reading *ARTNews, Artforum,* which she subscribed to after Edwina left, everything she can get her hands on about Warhol and the Factory.

"Well, I don't think art should be political . . . I don't think it should be anything. It's just there to amuse. Warhol says the most important thing is to not be boring. And let's be honest, how many of us aren't just bored to death in museums, after about half an hour people are screaming inside, dying to get out. Because they are, simply, not amused. Warhol is always amusing. He makes you laugh at yourself when you're being your most serious. He makes you stop pretending. That's what a great artist should do: make you see when you were pretending, make you see what it is you really value."

"And what does he value?"

"Money and fame, just like everyone."

"Is that what you value, Miss Red Riding Boots, whose name I don't even know?"

"Just like everyone," she says. "Heidi," she says. "Heidi is my name."

He laughs.

"What a wonderfully ironic name for someone who is the opposite of that good little girl. I'll bet you've always been a bad little girl, haven't you?"

"That's what I've been told," she says. It isn't true; she was never called bad, only hideous, annoying, stuck-up.

"And what about beauty? Because you know, of course, that

you are a beauty. Not candy-box pretty, but a real beauty, a rare, challenging beauty, that the eye can never rest on but it hungers for more, for what is behind those piercing eyes, for the next words to come out of that fascinating little mouth. It's a kind of beauty a boy would not be able to appreciate. Or even a young man. I pride myself on my connoisseurship."

She is grateful that her skin is olive toned and doesn't show a blush, because inwardly she is blushing furiously. The sentence she has always waited for. And she didn't even have to ask; she didn't have to do anything. It was given to her, a pure gift. He is the one she was always waiting for. He has called her beautiful. But she mustn't allow him to think that it matters to her, must make him think it's something she's always had and doesn't need to prize.

"Beauty is something people want to believe in because they want something to believe in, because they're afraid of not having anything to believe in. Beauty is what people will pay to be near."

"Oh, my dear . . . I think we have many things to say to each other . . . we can be the missing parts of each other's education. I'll tell you what, you take me to your favorite Warhol, and I'll take you to my favorite. You'll have to wait to find out who it is. That will be part of your education."

Education. Somewhere she had learned that the root of the word *education* was the Latin "to lead out." He was leading her out of the trap, the prison of her life. The man who would tell her who she really was so she could at last truly know herself.

"Why not?" she says. She believes that something very important, something that will change her life forever, is taking its first steps.

"You first—ladies first, as they say. Only we can't say *ladies* anymore, can we? It has to be *women*. And I guess you have no ambition to be a lady."

"You never know what my ambitions might be. I like to keep my options open."

"Ah, the luxuries of the young. I'm afraid my options are quite limited. And so when I see something quite wonderful, I don't want to let it go."

He brushes his fingers along her cheek, and she feels an excitement unlike any other she has ever known. Is this sex? Sex—that has always seemed to her brutal and sweaty and overbearing. This is nothing like that.

She leads him to the Warhol Marilyns. "You see," she says, "he's making the point that she is the object of our worship, that she's no different from the Madonnas of the Middle Ages or the Renaissance. And it's not just random . . . you see the way the color of her lipstick, her lips—the lips that everyone wants to kiss—blend into the background. It's the kind of harmony that the old masters were all about, only it's true to our times."

"What a fascinating little thing you are," he says. "Lovely and brilliant. A dangerous combination. May I take your arm? It's my turn now, a different floor of the museum, a different era . . . quite a different way of looking at the world. Do you know Ensor?"

She knows that he'll be able to tell if she's lying. "He's not someone I've really paid attention to," she says.

"Ah, that's the tragedy. Most people don't pay attention to him at all. But I think he's got the same fearlessness that you like in Warhol, the same insistence that we see the world as it really is."

He leads her to a canvas that Heidi has to force herself not to turn away from. *Horrible* is the word she wants to use. Two skulls against a candy-pink and blue sky. One wears a fur hat. Each has in his teeth one end of what looks like a leaf or a stick. But the title is *Skeletons Fighting Over a Pickled Herring*.

She understands that this is some sort of test, and she knows just what she needs to do to pass it. She laughs. "That's hilarious," she says. "I love it."

"Yes, that's exactly right. The hilarity of nightmare. Your friend Warhol thinks life is a joke, and my friend thinks it's a nightmare . . . a nightmare that can only be survived by its absurdity."

She will use those very words to Miss Vaughan . . . she's not sure what she'll tell Miss Vaughn about . . . about this man, whose name she doesn't know.

"It certainly is enough to kill your appetite, but I wonder if I could invite you to my apartment for some lunch. I'm quite a passable cook and I'll make you some real food, not the overpriced bibelots they serve in the café here. I promise not to offer you a herring."

Everything she's been told should, she knows, make her refuse him. But he isn't like anyone she's ever known. She doesn't want her time with him to end.

"Sure," she says. "I just need to be on a five o'clock train."

"To where, if I may be so bold to ask."

"Providence," she says. "Providence, Rhode Island."

"And what do you do there?"

Alarm spreads beneath her ribs, the pure hottest blue inside the flame. She must think of something, so he doesn't realize she's just a high school girl.

"I'm waiting to think of something to do with my life that

doesn't bore me. Meanwhile, I live in my father's house. He's what's known as a tycoon."

"One of the great houses of Newport?" he asks.

She will steal the history of the people in town whose ancestors are in the graveyard by the Congregational church. That, she knows, always arouses interest, even from people who like to pretend it doesn't. She will steal a sentence from Miss Letitia Barnes, speaking of ancestors in what she imagined was self-mockery but Heidi knew was camouflaged pride.

"Oh, no, those overblown mansions were for the nouveaux riches. We think of the people who came over on the *Mayflower* as *arrivistes*. My family arrived on the *Arabella*, which landed months before the *Mayflower*. And then they founded my town."

"The true American aristocracy," he says.

She doesn't know what will happen when he finds out her last name. Because she knows he will be part of her life, and eventually she'll tell him that what she said was all a tease, and he will laugh and chuck her under the chin. Perhaps call her a minx. A vixen. One of those words from the novels she read when she was combing the library for books that would tell her about the life she knew she wanted, but did not know how to name.

It's raining hard, with a cold wind, as if it weren't late April at all, but some wrathful November day; the rain is making it hard to see the buildings across the street, and she only has her jacket.

"Luckily, like all true Englishmen, I have an umbrella. If I may ask you to take my arm."

The umbrella is large and his arm is thin but reassuring; she can't see where they're going, but she knows they'll be all right. She is walking, under an umbrella, holding the arm of a man who finds her fascinating. She remembers the scene in *Little*

Women when Jo takes Professor Bhaer's hand. He was much older than she, and better educated. She had loved *Little Women*, she and Lorena Wilcox, the one true friend she had, who had lived next door until her parents moved from Vermont, she and Lorena Wilcox acted it out every day, taking turns playing Jo, obviously the only person in the book to be. They were friends; they were really friends; they enjoyed each other; they wanted to be with each other all the time. Heidi had cried when she drove down the street with her parents, waving at Lorena until she was out of sight. "I'll miss her so much," she told her parents.

"Blah blah blah and boo hoo hoo," her mother said. "You'll write each other for a couple of months and never get in touch again."

Her mother had been exactly right.

Lorena was her only friend for years until Edwina. Whose house sat next door. Whom she had adored. Edwina encouraged her to wear her hair in a single braid, as she did. Edwina took her to Providence to see art exhibits; included her when she and her friends went to coffee shops and drank their coffee black and smoked unfiltered cigarettes. But when Edwina moved to London, she never sent Heidi her address.

The man, her new friend (she doesn't know his name), is English. Possibly he is from London. Is it possible he knows Edwina? No, that's ridiculous. But thinking of Edwina makes her frightened, and she takes hold of his arm, as if to ensure that he will break the pattern, that he will be fond of her as she is of him and will stay in her life. He begins singing a song she knows is quite old, "Isn't it a lovely day to be caught in the rain."

"Do you know that song?" he asks.

She won't lie. People lied about knowing things and got

caught out. It was one of the things she liked doing: catching people out when they were pretending to know something.

"No, I don't."

"Fred Astaire," he says. "It will be the first step in my education of you. Fred Astaire."

"I've seen a movie of his on TV. I really like old movies."

"Of course you do, you little marvel," he says, taking her arm and pinching a bit of the fabric of her sleeve between his thumb and third finger. "Look at your sense of style, choosing this old jacket, which might look absurd on some people but on you is exactly right. You like old movies, then?"

"Yes. I like black-and-white films best," she says. It's almost the truth; she loves the dark anxiety-filled movies with 1930s criminals and detectives, although her favorite movie is *My Fair Lady*, but she admits that to no one.

"Cinema is my life," he says, and she imagines him having had a career cut short by the vulgarity of Hollywood; she thinks he must be gallant, enduring the corruption of something he loved.

He kisses her hand.

"Fortunately, I live quite near," he says, but the umbrella is so big and she has been so absorbed in the pleasure of being with him that she has no idea where they are when he walks up the stairs and turns the key to the door of his building, keeping the umbrella open until she is safely inside.

The corridor is dark, the light coming only from a tarnished fixture on the ceiling; the elevator is papered with a pattern of ferns; it groans and wheezes like an old dog. Their heels make a satisfying sound on the black and white tiles of the corridor they walk down after they have left the elevator. He has indicated the way with a gallant sweep of his arm.

Just inside, there is a tall ceramic cylinder with Chinese figures against a black background climbing up a steep green hill. He deposits his umbrella in it.

"You must take off your lovely boots," he says. "I'll stuff them with newspaper, so they won't lose their shape from the rain."

Under her elegant boots, she is wearing a schoolgirl's navy knee socks, and she doesn't want him to see them . . . but it's impossible for her to walk around in her wet boots, so she flings the knee socks off and rolls them into a ball, placing them inside her jacket pocket.

Now she is barefoot, and this seems wrong, but there is nothing for it. She must just pretend that it is the kind of thing that always happens to her in this careless life she has suggested that she lives.

"Luckily, I have a lentil soup, which is just the thing for this weather, then perhaps an *omelette aux fines herbes,* and a little cheese. The *pièce de résistance* will be dessert: it is the thing the English are best at; the rest of our cuisine is rubbish. I remember a French friend saying, *'Tout est bien avec custard.'* I feel fortunate that there's one store in this benighted city where I can buy Bird's Custard."

"You don't like New York?"

"Alas, my work has brought me here."

Eventually, she knows, she will be told the story of his career. But sensing that it is painful to him, she asks nothing.

He pours her a glass of red wine. "Something to take the chill off," he says, and she is worried; she has drunk almost nothing in her life—champagne at New Year's, a sip of beer on a hot summer's day. But to refuse a glass of wine would be to reveal her youth, her inexperience. He has taken her for a sophisticate, and she wishes to be nothing else in his eyes.

The apartment is small; the kitchen is a little slit of a corridor off the living room, whose walls are covered with books, as she knew they would be; on one wall are a couple of paintings of cows drinking from streams—this disappoints her at first, but she decides it fits his gentle English character. The largest pictures are posters from old movies: *Laura*, the red letters matching the slash of the brunette's lipstick, the yellow background insisting on danger, doom. Across from it, *Notorious*, which she is thankful she saw recently on *The Late Show*, Cary Grant carrying the semiconscious Ingrid Bergman to safety from the weak but lethal spy and his terrifying mother.

At one end of the living room is a small table with forest-green place mats, one with a napkin in a light tan wooden ring. The man goes to a drawer in the small kitchen and brings out another napkin for her. The soup smells rich and nourishing; she is very hungry, as she was too nervous for breakfast. How ridiculous it seems now, that she was nervous about Jeanne Larkin. Her friend (she still doesn't know his name, and it seems too late to ask now) would have no interest in Jeanne Larkin, and Jeanne Larkin would be as out of place in this situation as a fish in a cocktail bar.

"To the beginning of things," he says, raising his glass, and she knows enough to raise and sip from hers.

She tells him that her mother is Swiss, and her father is in the pharmaceutical business. That she is an only child. That she'll be making her way to New York, she knows, but not before she's ready.

He tells her he was in France during World War II, that it was terrible, terrible, and yet one had a "fantastic sense of being alive, and that life was meaningful."

He cuts a slice of bread and hands it to her on the point of the knife.

He is talking about the liberation of Paris. She hadn't realized that she had emptied her glass, and he pours more from the bottle in the middle of the table.

"I'll just see to the omelet," he says.

She drinks more from her glass. Everything is very, very pleasant, everything seems quite simple, as delightful as perfect weather. The omelet is wonderfully buttery, the bread is warm and crisp, the butter, a small rectangle in a crystal covered dish, seems cheerful, wholesome, eager to please.

She seems to be talking a lot, she is talking about the conformity of everyone she knows in their opposition to the war in Vietnam . . . and she repeats her father's words: "If you're going to have a war, then do it properly and get on with it and get out."

"I couldn't agree more, having been in war myself. But that's rather an unfashionable position for people your age, who are intent on burning everything up in the name of . . . God knows . . . freedom, I guess they call it."

"I'm a conservative," she says. She quotes verbatim from her father. "The trouble with liberals," she says, "is that to them the future is a blank wall, they think they can write anything they want on it, as if all the writing on the wall of the past didn't exist."

"Oh, let's not be too serious," he says. "I'm about to present you with the famous dessert. Pudding, we call it. For you Americans, pudding is only some poor imitation of our custard. You're going to begin thinking I'm obsessed with custard. Perhaps I am. Well, a man needs to have a hobby."

She laughs too loudly, she knows, and she covers her mouth as if to make a joke of the idea of laughing too loudly.

He goes to the record player and puts on a record that was at the top of the pile. "I knew there was a reason that Fred Astaire song came into my mind," he says, and she hears the rhythmic lighthearted song "Pick Yourself Up."

Her friend is whistling the melody in the tiny kitchen. He comes in with two dishes: some sort of fruit covered with something yellowish, thicker than cream but more liquid than what she would have thought of as custard.

Underneath the fruit is a layer of damp cake, soaked through in liquor. The differences in consistency—the wet cake, the firm berries, the warm liquidy custard—seem absolutely fascinating to her; it seems like the best dessert she's ever had.

Now Fred Astaire is singing, "Must you dance every dance with the same fortunate man," and her friend stands beside her chair, half bows, and says, "May I have this dance?"

She is frightened; she's never danced with a man, or a boy, before. In all the dances with the corresponding boys' private schools, she has never once been asked to dance. But she had been given dancing lessons, and she knows that if the man is a good dancer, you just follow. And she knows her friend will be good.

He is singing in her ear, so sweetly she's afraid she'll fall asleep dancing. He must sense this, and he leads her over to the couch and sits her down. Then it happens, what she has been waiting for. He is kissing her. "I am being kissed," she thinks. But then it isn't like what she wanted at all; his tongue is inside her mouth; she feels like she can't breathe, and he is trying to make her lie on the couch, but she doesn't want to lie down, she doesn't want his body on top of her like this, and she says, "I don't want to, I don't want to."

And then he is someone else; the man she has been with, the

man who made everything happen that she'd wanted so much she was even afraid to wish for it, has turned into a panting, grasping animal, and he says, "Of course you want to, of course you want to. What did you think you were doing, coming here in that skirt that's barely decent in those boots that are just shouting fuck me fuck me . . . you can't do things like that, you can't do things like that to me, I'm not some pimply faced boy you can tease until his balls turn blue. You did want this, this is what you were asking for, everything you did was asking for it."

It is easy for him to reach up her tiny skirt and pull off her underpants, and then . . . it is happening, the thing every girl has been told is worse than death, and it hurts, it hurts terribly, and she feels blood, but then he is making a horrible half-screaming noise and then he is gasping on her, and she will not cry, she will not, but she will make him get off her. She pushes him away, and he falls onto the floor.

"Wash yourself off," he says. "And don't go around telling everyone how terrible men are."

He pulls on his pants and half sits, half reclines on the couch, covering his eyes with his arm, as if he can't bear to see what has just happened. She knows he wants her to leave as soon as she can. But she will wash herself first. She feels the blood between her legs; worse than the beginning of a period.

In the bathroom, she wets the sour-smelling washcloth, rubs it over the sliver of green soap until it makes a lather. She washes herself, rinsing again and again. She makes a kind of sanitary napkin for herself out of layers of toilet paper. She places it in the crotch of her underpants, and then looks in the mirror, to see if she looks different, if she can recognize herself. On the shelf under the mirror she sees a plastic name badge. She recognizes the logo "Lowe's Cinema." Underneath the logo, in smaller print, "Henry Smith, projectionist."

She sees her face in the mirror. It is no longer tragic, it is no longer the face of a victim. Henry Smith, projectionist. "My life is the cinema . . . I came to New York for my work." He runs a movie projector . . . that's his work. He's not a director, or a screenwriter, or an actor, or even a cameraman. He threads the tape, he switches the light; he makes sure the tape doesn't snag or snap or burn up. Nothing he has done to her can really hurt her now. She walks out, no longer the crushed wet bird who made her shameful way into the bathroom.

He is still leaning back on the couch, his face covered with his arm.

She puts on her coat, takes her socks out of her pocket, removes the paper from her boots, puts them on, as slowly as she possibly can, and zips the zippers with a loud vindictive tug.

"Henry Smith, projectionist, my life is the cinema," she says, imitating his accent.

He takes his arm away from his face, and the two of them exchange looks of what is too shallow for hatred.

"Go to hell," he says, "and get someone to teach you about douching. You stink like three-day-old fish."

Her short-lived triumph over him has completely disintegrated. He has let her know that there is nothing more loathsome than her body, that she is the kind of female who will engender nothing but disgust. There is nothing she can say that could reduce him to the level she is now; she is surprised that she can stand upright; and she knows that she is oozing a noxious substance, he's perfectly right, that her femaleness is open and putrid and impossible to fully cleanse. She runs down the corridor, she won't wait for the elevator, frightened that, in an elevator, close to another person, her offense will become public, a public nuisance, a danger to the larger health.

She has to wait in the rain for a taxi, because she has no idea how to get to Penn Station, because she doesn't know exactly where she is. There is one mercy: she will be able to get a train soon; her ticket is good, and she will be home before dark.

She chooses a seat far from any other person, because she is still terrified that her stink will cause anyone who comes near her visibly to shun her. The army jacket now smells of age . . . mildew, perhaps, or mothballs, or the stink of whoever owned it. It is soaked through; her mohair sweater clings to her body like a sick wet animal. She curls up against the window and tries to sleep, but sleep will not come.

How can this have happened? How can this man whom she thought of as the figure of her dreams, so elegant, so romantic, have turned into a monster? Was he right—had she been asking for it? She thought she was asking for a few ardent kisses . . . hadn't he understood that . . . or was it she who had not understood?

She needs someone to tell her how to understand this. But who was there for her to go to? If Edwina were still around, she would have been able to tell her. But when Heidi wrote to her she never wrote back. So maybe she'd changed addresses . . . there was no way of knowing where she was, and Heidi understood that Edwina was finished with her; she had no need of her mascot, her Scotty . . . she was on to other things. Heidi had decided she would never write Edwina again, and she was angry that she had even allowed the thought of her into her mind.

It's unthinkable that she would go to her parents, and anyway they were in Switzerland, on one of their secret trips, from which her mother would come home with a new, young face.

Elsie and Hans—they were her enemies, as she had allowed them to understand that she knew they were stealing from her parents; they would probably be pleased at her misfortune. The people she had met at the Mensa meetings . . . she didn't even know how to get in touch with them from meeting to meeting. And there was not one person at the Lydia Farnsworth School whom she did not despise.

But that isn't true. There is one. Miss Vaughan. Miss Agnes Vaughan.

Heidi knows where she lives; she has driven around her house . . . had it been curiosity or a hope that she would appear and Heidi could pretend to just be in the neighborhood and they would chat outside of school, two equals, on a street like any other?

For the first time since Henry Smith told her she stank, there is a chink in the black wall of her misery. She would go to Miss Vaughan. Miss Vaughan would tell her how to understand what had happened.

She parks the car in front of Miss Vaughan's house. She walks up the brick path. She is shivering; she is still wet, although it wasn't raining now in New Canterbury. The moon, a thin crescent, allows a sliver of light on the dark approach to the front door. There is a knocker in the shape of a dolphin. Also a doorbell. She chooses the bell.

For a while, there is no response, and Heidi is afraid no one is home, although she can see a light through the closed curtains. Finally someone opens the door. A woman; probably Miss Vaughan's mother, of course she is, they look almost alike, although Mrs. Vaughan's posture is stooped and she looks weak, unhealthy.

"I need to see Miss Vaughan," Heidi says.

"Yes, come in. You look cold."

"I'm all right. I just need to see her."

"I'll be a moment. She's upstairs. It takes me a moment."

Heidi nods but says nothing.

"Please, come in and sit down?"

So this is Mrs. Vaughan's mother. She seems to have a bad cough; her shoulders are stooped and she leans heavily on the banister, but Heidi doesn't want to start feeling sorry for her.

This is Miss Vaughan's house. There is nothing special, nothing memorable about it. Comfortable, comfortable places to read books, to talk quietly. The couch and the chairs are a rose-colored chintz; she can't see what pictures are on the walls; there is a fireplace; one beam from a standing lamp falls on the knob of one of the brass andirons.

She watches Mrs. Vaughan make her way, with difficulty, up the stairs. She would like to say, "I'll go, I'll go and get her," but she knows that's impossible.

She hears soft voices, a few words, and then Mrs. Vaughan makes her way slowly back down.

"She'll be right with you," Mrs. Vaughan says. "Can I get you a cup of tea?"

How odd, Heidi thinks, she has no idea who I am, and she lets me into her house, offers me tea. She feels she has entered a foreign country, a country of kind children who have no idea that danger might be in the world in the person of a stranger. She feels older than Mrs. Vaughan, and a bit contemptuous with her new knowledge, hours old. She had trusted a stranger . . . and what had happened, had happened, this thing, which she didn't yet know what to name, since she didn't yet understand it. This is why she was here. Because Miss Vaughan would help her understand.

Miss Vaughan is coming down the stairs. This is not what Heidi had been expecting; Miss Vaughan had been sleeping; she rubs her eyes, she ties the sash of her pink chenille robe. Ugly, Heidi thought. Why does she have such an ugly robe?

"Heidi, are you okay?"

"I was raped. I went to the lecture in New York and I met this man and he invited me to his apartment for lunch and then he raped me."

Agnes Vaughan puts her hand to her mouth, as if, Heidi thought, she were holding back vomit.

"You went to a strange man's apartment? How could you have done that? How could you have let that happen? You knew better than that."

The words rise up and crash against them, an ice-cold wave that covers them, then disappears, and leave them frozen where they stand. Where did those words come from? The minute they are out of her mouth, Agnes wants to take them back . . . they aren't what she meant, they aren't her words, they have nothing to do with her. But she doesn't have even a moment to take them back. Heidi looks at her, and the look changes in an instant, from crushed disappointment to the clear bolt of pure hate.

And then Heidi turns and runs, runs, down the brick path, runs down the three stone steps and into her car. Agnes runs after her, but she's wearing bedroom slippers and the path is slippery from the morning's rain. She falls forward on her face, and she feels her teeth cut through her lip, tastes blood, and as she stands up, she hears Heidi's car engine start and the sound of the car racing down the road.

Agnes's mother is standing at the door.

"You're bleeding. Come in, come under the light."

"I can't. I need to go after her."

"You're bleeding, you can't drive like that."

"I have to."

Agnes puts her coat on, grabs her keys from her purse, and runs to the garage where her car is parked. She backs down the driveway, drives as fast as she can down the street. And then she realizes: she doesn't know where she's going.

She doesn't know where Heidi lives. It was part of school life: in school, you were not a part of a family; you were on your own, and teachers made a point of separating school from home life.

She drives in the direction that Heidi went, as fast as she can. Her mouth is bleeding and she cups her hand under her chin to catch the blood.

She will not find Heidi, not tonight. Tomorrow. She would call Letitia Barnes, get Heidi's address, drive to her house, and express her sorrow, her shame, offer to do anything to make it up to the poor wounded girl, whom she had just wounded further.

Heidi drives dangerously fast down the small decorous streets of New Canterbury. The dull misery that had been the climate of her mind lifts, and her mind is cleansed, as if she had withstood a violent storm, with lightning that struck down the obscuring trees, leaving behind a bare and flattened plain. She had thought that she could rely on Miss Vaughan, that Miss Vaughan could understand, that Miss Vaughan cared about her. She had even thought it possible that Miss Vaughan loved her.

But now she knows, and her new understanding makes her feel valorous to herself. You could not count on anyone to understand. This need for understanding was a weakness. She would not indulge in it again.

Before she gets home, her plan is settled in her mind. Elsie and Hans would not be home yet. She would go directly to her bedroom, take off her wet clothes, and bathe . . . she would scrub herself hard, hard, as if she were shedding an old, diseased skin. And then she would go into her parents' room.

She knows where everything is kept. In all the time she has been alone in her house, she has explored, carefully, her parents' bedroom. She knew where her father kept a thousand dollars in cash. She knew which of her mother's jewels were real and which were cheap paste copies. She would take the money and the jewelry. Then she would disappear.

They wouldn't be able to find her. And they would blame themselves. Her parents. Miss Vaughan. Miss Vaughan would never be able to forgive herself. Miss Vaughan would never forget her.

PART III

Rome

April 2015

S he said no to everyone who offered her a ride to the airport. She wanted to leave as she'd arrived, to end as she'd begun, but she knew that was foolish, it wasn't an end really. She would be back.

But she didn't know how and when.

It would never be her home again. She would always be a guest . . . staying at the house of someone who would empty a drawer or two for her, make a place in their wardrobe. She'd have to start buying things like a ribbed plastic coffin for her toothbrush, small plastic pots for moisturizer and eye cream. In one of the cavernous American drugstores that would soon be familiar to her, she'd head for shelves marked TRAVEL SIZES, and stock up on mouthwash, shampoo, conditioner. She would never again have the familiar bed, the familiar pillow, the mirror that gave back her reflection with all its changes, containing them somehow behind its transparent front. Now when she looks in the mirror she sees a woman past middle age, say it, she tells herself each morning, an old woman. She came to Rome a young woman, unmarried, and leaves a grandmother. Not quite a crone but closer to that than any other noun. There is no word for men, she thinks, that corresponds to *crone*.

She waits at the Piazza Belli for the H bus, paradise of pick-pockets. She will take it to the Stazione Termini and then take the new fast train to the airport. The Leonardo Express, she found it funny to link the two words . . . Leonardo and express. But maybe, she thinks, that's right, the past and present should be linked, even in ways that seem incongruous, or else what is left . . . an emptiness, a rootlessness. It is important not to lose the thread. She has to believe that her life has a line . . . thin, nearly invisible, sometimes, sometimes hidden by a pattern: fruit, flowers, stains, but always there if you look closely enough. A life like a bolt of cloth, rolled up on itself like those bolts of cloth that fascinated her when she went with her mother to the fabric shop. The saleswoman she and her mother made fun of, Mrs. Wilberforce, her endless supplies of smocks, each one with a ridiculous print: somersaulting babies, monkeys, gingerbread men, Martians. "What a serious name for such a silly woman," Agnes's mother would say.

Mrs. Wilberforce would throw the bolt of cloth onto the counter, unrolling it, turn after turn, measuring it out with a device Agnes thought magical: it was clamped to the table; the top half a dial, the bottom half invisible. The fabric was fed between the top half and the table and the dial registered the length of fabric. At the right moment, her mother would say "Stop" and Mrs. Wilberforce would cut the fabric with pinking shears, and then fold it in tissue.

.   .   .

She has only one small bag; everything else has been shipped ahead. Her nephew Paolo arranged for the sale of the furniture; she told him he could keep whatever money it produced.

The bus lumbers over the Garibaldi Bridge. St. Peter's is to her left, but she has never liked the sight of it, and preferred looking to the right, at the glass-roofed synagogue, the Byzantine cupola of Santa Maria in Cosmedin. Lurching like a clumsy rhino, the bus heads down the busy Arenula, past the Largo Argentina (Mussolini's Disneyland, Pietro had always said). Her eye rests with loving sorrow on the buildings' walls, the tender colors of Roman stucco, blue-gray, pink. The more expected ochre and burnt sienna. When she first arrived, she was amused that colors she had known only from her childhood Crayola box were real, a commonplace here. She knows these walls well; she has known them in different lights, in different seasons. She feels she has a right to call them hers. Will she feel the same right when she no longer lives here? This is what she will miss most: the light on a wall, the sound of her heels on the cobblestones, the refreshment of the fountains with their endlessly replenished outpouring.

She's glad she has a seat to herself because she knows she is whispering nonsensical words, words she wouldn't want over-heard. "Goodbye, my life." Absurd, not even true because she had a life before she came here. A happy one, intact before it was shattered . . . but she will not allow herself to use the passive verb, because she knows she was the one who shattered it.

And she has more life to live, but she can't believe that it will consist of anything but diminishments.

Impossible to say that leaving Rome is not a loss, Rome that had nursed her, healed her, brought her back to life. She arrived forty-three years before, broken, or more correctly scalded, like the victim of a fire, disfigured, the slightest touch a torment. So covered in self-loathing that she once picked up half a pastry from the gutter and ate it, as though some voice had told her: This is your due. This is what you deserve.

It was a long time before she was able to take in the famous beauties. They were too strong at first . . . she was ready only for the colors of the walls, the markets, the fountains. And Jasper, who took her in as if she were a heroine from a nineteenth-century novel, fleeing scandal. Fleeing to Jasper. Who saved her. He and Rome.

But there had always been someone to save her from the ultimate crash; her falls have always been of the nonfatal sort, the kind from which you are able to raise yourself, shocked, looking around, surprised that you are on hard ground, that you are not alone. If you looked around to find no one, that would be desolation. And she has never been entirely desolate. She has never been abandoned.

She was the one doing the abandoning.

She was marked, but not destroyed.

The only prayer she has ever really prayed: Please let Heidi not be destroyed. Please let me not have destroyed her.

She doesn't even know if Heidi is alive.

Heidi.

She'd hardly slept for weeks after Heidi ran down the path in front of her house, running in the red boots Agnes had given her . . . she had tried hard to follow her, to find her, but failed. The summer nights were long and bright; this was a curse and not a blessing. The picture would not leave the stretched canvas of her eyelids. The words would not stop repeating themselves on the stretched skin of her eardrums. "I met this man in the museum. He was English. He invited me to his apartment for lunch. He raped me."

And her response: "How could you have let that happen?"

Words impossible to take back . . . and the running girl, impossible to catch or stop.

It upset her parents that she wasn't eating. And the dramatic flare-up of her eczema, which she'd been prone to as a child, mostly in winter, always in times of stress. But now every inch of her body was covered with angry red skin that flared and flecked. She let her nails grow long because long nails were better for scratching. She raked her forearms raw; it was the only thing she allowed herself—the momentary or less than momentary assuagement of the constant itch, leaving behind it a burning, satisfying, preferable to the itching.

One night her mother lifted Agnes's shirt sleeve and said, "My God, Agnes, this has to stop," and insisted on taking her to the doctor, kind Dr. Boyle, who had treated her all her life and was familiar with her eczema. But this, he said, this was something quite different.

"Are you eating properly? You're very thin. And sleeping? Not boyfriend trouble, I hope . . . I thought you were all set up with that nice archaeologist. I was so taken with him at your engagement party."

It was only when the doctor said those words that she realized she hadn't thought of Roger at all. Even the word *archaeolo-gist* was a shock, as if someone had reminded her of a country she once visited but of which she had completely lost track. She could hardly believe that Dr. Boyle didn't know about Heidi . . . she could hardly believe that there was anyone in the world who didn't know. But, in fact, the interest was much more limited than she could have imagined . . . extending only to the Lydia Farnsworth School and Heidi's parents . . . although the meager-ness of their concern was shocking to Agnes. Their decision not to postpone their trip to Chile for summer skiing.

The Stolzes had hired a private detective, someone recom-mended by their lawyer, to find Heidi. Rupert Longman. Agnes was convinced that Rupert Longman wasn't his name at all.

The Stolzes had hired the cheapest detective their lawyer could find. He was an absolute cliché of the seedy private detec-tive: a dirty raincoat, a greasy comb-over, loafers with a chain across the instep, the office in Providence on the third floor of a building with other dubious-looking enterprises: check-cashing services, medical supplies, a bail bondsman. For a month, she went back and back to that office, and in all that time, she never saw anyone go in and out of any of the other offices, nor did she ever see anyone entering or leaving Rupert Longman's office. She would hesitate at the door, his name painted onto a glass obscurity, the misleadingly elegant lettering: RUPERT LONGMAN. She had never seen such an ugly room: dusty manila folders in piles that looked always about to topple, the smell of stale ciga-rette smoke and a lingering miasma of anxiety and shame left by the clients she never encountered.

Longman always seemed surprised to see her, although she always called first to make an appointment. He knew Agnes was checking up on him; he knew she believed he wasn't doing his job. His response to her was made up of equal parts of defensiveness, contempt, and condescension.

"What I've learned, Miss Vaughan, and you may come to learn it too, is that someone who doesn't want to be found . . . well, you'll probably never find them. It's harder with someone that age. She doesn't have a credit card, even a Social Security number. Usually you'd start with friends, but she doesn't seem to have had any. And you people at the school don't seem to have a clue."

"I think she's probably in New York," Agnes had said, and he snorted, "Well, that narrows it down," enjoying his own wit so much that his laughter ended in a sickly coughing spasm. "New York, New York. Needle. Haystackville. Drug dens . . . abandoned apartments this kind of kid might find her way to . . . where would you even begin."

"And where *did* you begin?" Agnes had asked him, taking a bitter pleasure in her unaccustomed rudeness.

"I made some calls . . . I went to that neighborhood where they all are. You know, near the Chelsea Hotel, and I showed her picture around . . . I asked about her . . . I went to cafés and bars and luncheonettes . . . no one had heard of her. I have to say no one really cared that much. I left some of my cards around. I did a lot of things you wouldn't understand. I walked the leather off a good pair of new shoes."

She didn't believe him; she knew she had to look for herself. She didn't take the sleeping pills Dr. Boyle had prescribed because she wanted to be as wakeful as possible for as many hours of the day as she could. She stayed at her mother's friend Frances's apartment. Frances was impatient with her, but she didn't care. She walked around Chelsea, the Village, the Lower East Side;

she printed photos of Heidi from the yearbook. She walked and walked and when she took her stockings off at night they stuck to the blisters on her feet, there was blood inside her shoes, her hands and arms were bloody from scratching. And always inside her head was a buzzing, the whining of a mosquito or a gnat, the words . . . *Your fault . . . all your fault.* No peace, no respite, only the sense that she had to be doing something because no one was really doing anything.

Three weeks after Heidi disappeared, Agnes wrote Roger, calling off the engagement, but he was in so remote a part of Iraq that the letter didn't reach him for two months, and when he finally called, it was too late. She was another person, a person he hadn't known, and she had to force herself to be polite to him, not to be impatient with what seemed to her an egregious lack of comprehension.

Just after she spoke to Roger, she turned in her resignation to Letitia Barnes.

"I consider this unwise," Miss Barnes had said, her diction the oral equivalent of copperplate.

"I'm not fit to be teaching young people," Agnes had said.

"I believe you are quite wrong. You are a very gifted teacher."

"If Heidi Stolz is dead, it's my fault."

Agnes knew she sounded brutal, but she wanted to shock Letitia Barnes into admitting the enormity of what had happened.

Miss Barnes put her hand to the lace at her throat. "You have no reason to think she's dead. You don't even know that what the girl said really happened. She's quite a fabulator. She claimed she was an only child, whereas in fact she's one of three. She is absolutely starved for attention. That kind of appetite can never ever be satisfied."

Hearing those words, Agnes hated Letitia Barnes, and they never spoke again. For years, she had loved Miss Barnes, looked up to her, and with one sentence, it was wiped away. She must be dead now, Agnes thinks, and the whole way of life she represented is dead too. She regrets not having gone to see her again, regrets not having said some sort of goodbye; now she can mourn Letitia Barnes, although it is too late; her mourning does no good.

She's often wondered what would have happened to her if Frances hadn't come up with the idea of sending her to Jasper . . . Jasper, who had always hung in the air above Frances and her mother's heads whenever they met, for they never met without speaking of him, incandescent, fantastical: Jasper, the third of the glittering triangle—two Mount Holyoke girls, an Amherst boy, inseparable, delighted in each other's company . . . a throwback to some girl's novel of college life. He disappeared romantically from their American lives, relocating to Rome, where he worked as a restorer of paintings . . . they didn't know what kind of paintings, only that his clients were rich and he didn't admire most of what he saved. Jasper—the more alluring for being faceless, for Frances and Agnes's mother often regretted that they had no picture of him. Agnes had never met him; he had only come to America when Agnes was an infant and he served as godfather. She knew him only as the provider of magic gifts for birthdays and Christmases—a doll dressed as a Neapolitan peasant, a music box with a view of a volcano that played "Santa Lucia," a toy gondola with oars the color of red lipstick, and a gondolier with a striped shirt and an elaborate hat. For her eighteenth birthday: a cameo that had belonged to his mother. For her college graduation, a Pontormo drawing.

She had never believed that it was only a happy accident that Frances reported that Jasper was desperate—she showed Agnes the letter—"I am in desperate need of a cultivated young person who can organize the chaos that is my life."

But Agnes didn't question; she was desperate to get away, away from anyone and anything who could remind her of Heidi—and she was so entirely deflated that she couldn't begin to make a plan for herself.

"When you see him, you won't entirely believe him," Frances had said. It would have been easy to write him off as absurd, his unruly hair, sticking straight up, as if he'd been permanently startled or electrocuted, his muttonchops, his watch on a watch fob, his three-piece English tweed suit. All his clothes, even the most casual, looked as if they had originally belonged to a much larger man who'd lost a great deal of weight, although Frances and Agnes's mother assured her that he'd always been "Falstaffian in girth." His teeth were large and square and a bit yellowish—he smoked a pipe—and his lips were surprisingly youthful, full and red, surprisingly healthy looking, because he gave the impression of a lifetime of unwise eating, an entirely indoors existence. When he was alone, walking from room to room, he often seemed to be conducting an invisible orchestra. He enjoyed saying that there was no place for him in the twentieth century, and his entertainments seemed to come from another age: sherry parties, afternoon teas, musical evenings. Often when you were with him you felt like you'd walked into some costume drama, perhaps a local production of *The Barretts of Wimpole Street*.

That first day, when he answered the door, he stood for a

moment and then said, "So here you are, then," which she would learn was his customary greeting. But she felt it had been perfectly designed for her, and his words gave her such a sense of safety, of repose, that she had to hold herself back from falling into his arms.

"You must put yourself entirely in my hands . . . no one knows Rome as I do, not even Romans," he said. Later, knowing him better, she thought that she must have been a trial for him in those first weeks, when she was nearly mute and covered with unsightly red blotches. He did all the talking at meals; what he said was always interesting but required no response.

"There is only one rule for guests of my establishment," he had said. "You must see one beautiful thing every day and tell me about it at dinner.

"I've arranged some things so that your days won't be quite empty," he had said. Every morning they bought the day's fruit from the market. He arranged for daily Italian lessons with the impoverished countess, who, he had said, fled an unhappy marriage by night with only the clothes on her back and her little dog. Agnes never knew whether or not his descriptions of people were true, but she always chose to believe them. The *contessa* was a demanding teacher, and it was a relief to swim in the temperate lagoon of verb tenses and noun-adjective agreements in her company. She insisted that Agnes also read newspapers and fashion magazines so she would have an up-to-date vocabulary.

Jasper would leave for his studio, which was a few streets down the Viale Trastevere on the Lungaretta, they would lunch, Jasper would nap, and then they would walk, avoiding the famous great sights in favor of cloisters and chapels and private parks that tourists rarely visited.

And then she would accompany him to his studio, where he

and two assistants restored paintings . . . it was rich with the smell of turpentine; the windows were high and let in enough light to make the paintings' imperfections all too visible. Sometimes Jasper seemed charmed by something he was working on, but often he would say—and she didn't know whether his regret was real or put on for her benefit—that once, just once, he would like to feel he had restored something great. "But there's not nearly so much money in greatness as there is in flattering the vanity of the aristocracy, or, more important, the newly rich."

He was right about the details of his records being in chaos. She began to realize that it was the result of his reluctance actually to charge people for his work. In one corner of the studio was an old roll-top desk; it was overflowing with bills and invoices. The task of creating order for Jasper—whose kindness made her feel the only brightness she had known since the night Heidi had run off—was the perfect occupation for her. Because she knew it troubled him—the disorder of that desk. Everything in the apartment was perfectly chosen and properly placed. Hanging from the ceiling in the middle of the living room was a polychrome wooden angel from the fourteenth century; one wall of the room was a display of antique keys, another a series of Piranesi etchings. The rugs had come from his family in Delaware. He was an only child, and his parents had died young. He was vague about their deaths. "Let us just say that they conform to my favorite writer—E. M. Forster's—idea of plot. The king died and the queen died of grief." He was indulgent to Maria Rosa, who cooked and cleaned for him, but he could fly into a rage if she put the toilet paper on in the wrong direction. "It must be pulled down, not over." Sometimes when he was bored, he would straighten the towels in the bathroom so that they were exactly level.

It was such an orderly abode that the jarring note (his disorderly desk was kept in exile in the studio) was even more jarring to Agnes than it might have been in a home that had anything in it of the ramshackle. Regularly, he brought home boys. Agnes was mortified trying to decide how to place herself when she heard them at the dining room table. She would hide in her room, afraid even to walk into the bathroom. She dreaded embarrassing him. But he was not embarrassed. One day he said simply, "There is no need for you to tunnel into your wardrobe, like some abashed mole. There is no need for you to hide. I have nothing to hide. It is all quite simple. They want money and I want sex. Often, there is fondness between us. Sometimes misunderstandings that more money usually smooths out. You needn't join us for chitchat if it makes you uncomfortable, but you can if you like. Sometimes they are quite amusing, and they are always lovely."

She never joined them, and she never quite understood. Paying for sex. Prostitution, that ugly word, suggesting nothing of pleasure and everything of tinctured commerce. And Jasper, at fifty, seemed to her too old for that sort of thing; she was twenty-four and most of the boys were younger than she.

She disappointed her parents by saying she didn't want to go home for Christmas; she wanted time away from anything that might remind her of Heidi; there were whole days in Rome when Agnes didn't think of her.

"Oh, dearie me," her mother had said with a sharp intake of breath when she told them she wasn't coming, but her father quickly insisted, "Then we shall come to you."

It was an uncomfortable visit. Agnes's father was at his worst, his most stiff backed, his most puritanical. He found Jasper's way of life appalling—and he didn't even know about the boys.

When he discovered that Jasper didn't take a newspaper, his face got very red and he clenched his hands into fists. It didn't help when Jasper said, "I deliberately don't take any newspaper and when I happen to lay hands on one, in a café, for instance, I put it down instantly, as if I'd stopped myself biting into a particularly nasty confection, artificially colored. I keep myself from politics because I want to be able to invite all sorts of people to my home: it is often the case that people who are fascists at heart have marvelous things in their homes to look at, dress well, and are wonderfully witty. And the same thing is true of the most militant communists. It's better not to know."

She saw that her father was enraged. It was a relief to everyone when he left the apartment in search of a newspaper. She saw her mother brushing her father's bad mood away, like buzzing flies that you resented because they made you go inside on an otherwise beautiful day, spoiling the perfect picnic.

Guiltily, she and Jasper admitted that it was a relief when they were gone: "We've become quite the settled couple, I suppose." When Christina and Jo came in the spring, it wasn't a success either. Jasper liked young women to be quiet and decorous; it wasn't difficult for Agnes to fit the bill. But in different ways, Christina and Jo did not. Christina seemed to have brought with her only overalls and what looked like the tops of men's long underwear. And Jasper's adamant refusal of political consciousness bothered Jo, in a different way from Agnes's father. She insisted on trying to engage him in conversations about the Red Brigades, kept asking if he knew anyone who was involved, or knew where there were bookstores that could give her access to the kind of literature about the Italian situation that she couldn't get in America. "Oh, my dear, I'm sure I don't know . . . it's not

the sort of thing people in my circle would have a purchase on."
Agnes wished he hadn't used the words "have a purchase on,"
she saw the look on Jo's face—the kind of look, she thought, that
Savonarola must have had when a bejeweled lady crossed his
path—but Jo had good manners. And she could see that Agnes
had been in terrible shape and was better and that was because
of Jasper. Jasper was a tough sell for anyone whose only terms
were ethical. He and Jo would never be at ease with each other.

"I understand exactly," Agnes said to her friend. "And yet I
have never known anyone to do more good."

"I see that, I do," Jo had said. "But it's a tough one."

Christina said of him, "I feel like I'm an animal who's wandered onto entirely alien terrain, but the food is succulent and
we just inhabit our separate lairs. And besides, the strange creature that he is, he's healing you . . . I can see you're healing. Take
it from me; I'm in med school now."

When Christina said that, Agnes began to understand that
something was happening to her, something was changing, and
healing was as good a name for it as any. It was impossible for
her to point to a time when the healing had begun. She knew it
had to have been a gradual thing, but when Christina said those
words, she realized that she was better, but she had no idea how
it had happened or what the turning point had been. It was, she
thought, like one of those experiments she'd been fascinated
with as a child: someone lifts a calf who gains a few ounces every
day until one day the calf is simply too heavy to be lifted. Healing, she thought, was something like that, only in the opposite
direction.

The second year she was in Rome, Jasper invited "a few hundred of my closest friends, well, my dear, thirty," for an "Ameri-

can Thanksgiving." He cooked a turkey and sweet potatoes and
creamed onions, to the horror of Maria Rosa, who called him a
savage and held her nose when she wrapped the leftovers, saying
that only savages would eat such food.

He decorated the table with pumpkins and Indian corn—he
was vague about where he'd gotten them and Agnes didn't want
to press—and there seemed to be no unifying principle behind
the people at the table: at-large ex-pats, distinguished ladies in
reduced circumstances, wealthy clients.

It was only when Jasper toasted America and said we must
all think of something we were thankful for but by no means
say it aloud that Agnes realized how much better she was. That
Christina had been right; she had been healed by something as
the calendula ointment that Maria Rosa had brought back from
her village in Umbria had cured her eczema. That she no longer
woke every morning thinking of Heidi; no longer went to sleep
with Heidi's face behind her eyes; she dreamed of her much less
frequently, and the dreams were sometimes merely neutral.

∿

IT WASN'T until the following June when Jo and Christina were
visiting that Agnes first paid attention to Pietro di Martini.

Looking out the bus window, she twists her wedding ring
around her finger. It is hardly possible to believe that there was a
time when the words *my husband* did not apply to him.

He was there for one of Jasper's musical evenings; he was part
of Jasper's string quartet. Jasper's quartet was made up of his
dentist and an ex-priest, who played violin; Jasper on viola—the
instrument, he liked to say, of the dim-witted; Pietro, the cel-

list, sold Jasper his tobacco from an elegant shop on the Via dei Coronari.

Pietro was at all the musical evenings, but he and Agnes had barely spoken. On one of their visits, Jo and Christina were helping to clear the plates from the evening's refreshments and Pietro was putting the furniture back to its original position. Jo and Christina were complaining about the heat and asking where they might go to swim, and Pietro said, "Nowhere near Rome . . . the beaches here are horrors. *Brutta, brutta.* You must come with me to my family's house on Lago di Fiastra in the Marche."

It made Agnes feel strange that suddenly they were all invited by someone whom she ought to have known, but somehow did not.

The weekend was full of people attached to the di Martini family. Everyone slept anywhere—beds were apportioned, but every morning there were people on the living room floor in sleeping bags, or on one of the rickety couches. With what was clearly mock exasperation, the mother of the family trailed after her children, saying, "Do you never pick anything up . . . do you never understand that windows must be kept open, doors shut . . . do you have to use so many towels." And Pietro or one of his brothers, all a foot taller than their mother, and fifty pounds heavier, would pick her up and twirl her around and call her *strega,* strega mamma, witch mamma, and everyone would bustle around as she sat on the couch and somehow, a temporary order was restored.

"You must forgive my family's disorder, they are, every man jack of them, quite harum-scarum," she said to her American guests in English, explaining that she had studied in London for a year and enjoyed speaking the language.

Agnes hadn't realized how much she'd missed swimming. New Canterbury abutted the Atlantic, and a quarter mile from her house there was what New Englanders called a pond, what others would call a lake, and every year she prided herself on being the first in the ocean, the first in the pond on Memorial Day, the last to swim in both of them in the chill of October. She was never happier than when she was swimming, relishing the release from gravity, the water making lightness real, the detachment from the earth like an astronaut, only not so lonely.

But this was not like any swimming she'd ever done. The water had no tinge of grayness in it, as all North American water did: What should I call it, she asked herself as she was swimming out farther than the others, is it turquoise or aquamarine? She imagined that when she got out, her skin would be iridescent, covered with something like sequins, and when she shook the water from her hair the drops would shine like jewels. She swam out, far from the others, and for the first time since Heidi had run off, she felt lightness; she felt delight.

And then she noticed that she wasn't alone. Pietro had swum out. "My mother was afraid you'd decided to swim to Greece," he said. "My mother worries about everyone. It's what she does."

Agnes resented his intrusion, but it had happened to her many times: she would swim far out and someone would come after her, breaking the membrane of her perfect world.

"Please tell everyone not to worry. Ask Jo and Christina. I'm famous for swimming long distances."

"There is no need for you to come back, then, if you're happy. I hope that you are happy."

It had been so long since she had thought it possible to use the word in relation to herself that she laughed, then saw he was offended.

"I'm sorry," she said. "It's just . . . oh, I don't know, I think people expect Americans to be happy one hundred percent of the time."

"But you see, I know that you are not."

"Not what?" she said, feeling a playfulness that surprised her. "Not American or not happy?"

"Oh, I know you are American. I can tell by your mania for ice in your water. And the way you relished all that white food at Thanksgiving."

She was grateful for his tact in not pursuing the question of her happiness. And for not insisting that she return to shore.

She enjoyed watching him swim away, unrushed but moving steadily through the water, with a kind of lightness she'd begun to notice in all of his movements. She watched him get out and dry himself with a small pink towel; it had been so long since she had taken any interest in any man's body that she had to remind herself that her interest was not the interest she was taking in the water, or the trees of Rome or the fountains. She remembered what she had lost—a sense of herself as a body drawn to other bodies—and was not sure she was willing to have this new sensation. She wished that she could just stay in the water, cool, detached, alone.

But when they returned to Rome, she began to look forward to Jasper's musical evenings in a way she hadn't before, and she was glad when Pietro stayed behind to help with the furniture. She found herself looking at him almost furtively, when he was playing in the quartet and there was an excuse for her eyes to rest on him. She saw that all his gestures were curved; most men, when they spoke, used chopping gestures, slicing gestures, but he seemed to shape the air with a deliberate non-coerciveness. She found herself wondering about the way his body seemed to combine unlikes but still present a harmonious whole. The question of how he gave the impression of slightness and broad-shoulderedness at the same time. She determined that it was because his arms were quite long, the biceps muscular but the forearms slight, leading to hands that could almost be called feminine, his calves thin but his thighs well muscled.

He missed one musical evening, and she felt deprived, let down and disappointed, like a teenager whose favorite rock star had canceled a performance. She knew she was acting like a teenager, a teenager with a crush—what a word for it, she thought, implying simultaneously unseriousness and annihilation. She told Jasper that she had decided to buy a bracelet she'd been looking at for months in a shop on the Via dei Coronari, and she said while she was there—did he suspect the exaggerated sense of the accidental in her tone—she'd be glad to pick up some tobacco from di Martini's. She deliberately didn't say Pietro's name, as if that would provide a clue that Jasper would take between his teeth and run with. Like a puppy making off with the family lunch.

Di Martini's Tobacco. Gone now, she thinks. In its place, another antiques store, specializing in Asian art—she didn't like to think of what might be its provenance. Di Martini's Tobacco . . . source of her comfortable income . . . Pietro's family's comfortable income since the early twentieth century. DI MARTINI—the letters of what would be her name, gold script against a background of black marble. 65 Via dei Coronari, just off the Piazza Navona. One of those streets tourists find by accident and then consider their private treasure. A street of beautiful ochre walls covered by vines.

She remembers that day, the day she pretended to just happen to be in the neighborhood, oh, and while I'm here I'll just pick up Jasper's tobacco . . . Pietro is behind a counter, holding in his feminine hands a pipe with a carved ivory bowl.

Seeing her at the door, he excuses himself to his new customer, rushes from behind the counter, taking her hand, half pulling her into the store, kissing her on both cheeks. "Welcome, welcome," he says. "To my commercial establishment, let me take your coat, what a lovely scarf . . . it's a bit warm in here, I hope you won't be uncomfortable." And the customer, a German, resentful at the loss of Pietro's attention, walks out of the store, closing the door with a loud, accusatory bang.

"Oh dear, I think I've made you lose a sale," she says.

For the first time, she sees his characteristic response to any misfortune, the raised shoulders, the upturned palms, the nearly uninflected syllable, "Beh."

He cups her elbow and leads her up the wide staircase to the second floor. She feels for the first time what she will always feel in the shop, that she has been spirited through, or allowed behind a door into a dream world: another time, a fantasy of a deliberately male, deliberately polished civilization, the transgressive, slightly shameful thrill of being the one girl—you would always be a girl there, never a woman—allowed into the men's club, fascinating artifacts whose use sometimes she can only guess at. The delicious smell of pipe tobacco—confectionary but carnivorous.

It is a shop, everything is for sale, but everything about it suggests that any transactions resulting in the transfer of hard cash are rather beside the point. There are leather couches, carved coffee tables covered with magazines devoted to the love of pipes, leather-covered books—English mostly—memoirs, accounts of exotic travels or the creation of formal gardens. Pietro knows everyone who sits in the deep sofas or fingers the pipes on display on the open shelves.

One area of the store is especially devoted to cigars, and she feels swoony because of the insistent but deliberate seduction of the expensive smoke.

"This," he says. "And you will forgive me if I seem to be attacking your country . . . is my blow against American imperialism . . . a counterblow to the one America has dealt to Cuba because of its phobic anticommunism." (Everyone in his family, she will learn later, calls themselves some kind of communist, although they seem not to feel the conflict created by the source of their wealth: commercial, capitalist.)

"Here we are able to provide for the Italian connoisseur—and, it must be said, for Americans, who have felt the loss created by their country's foolish obstinacy—the finest Cuban cigars. At the same time, I am proud to say, contributing to the health of Fidel's economy."

Entering the shop, she purposely put behind or buried any puritanical scruples . . . even in the first days of her romance with Pietro, it was known that tobacco killed. But it was impossible to believe that anything connected with this artful welcoming and above all civilized place could be in any way destructive.

Gone now, all gone . . . and what reasonable person could say it was not for the good.

But she has lived in Italy too long to believe in the ultimate power of reason.

The day of her first visit, he invites her to lunch and then wonders if she might be free for dinner that Saturday. She was embarrassed at her own excitement at the invitation, as if it were her first date. But it *was* her first date after the collapse, the shattering of her old life. Her life after Heidi.

When she was with him, the lightness that had been hers when she swam in Lago di Fiastra returned. She was drawn to his lightness as a freezing person would be drawn to a fire, a fire that did not blaze and crackle . . . only a constant comforting warmth . . . that gave no sign of possible diminishment or possible harm.

He said he was exhausted by the high volume and supersaturated palate of both his country and his family; he had made an early and surprisingly successful decision to find life amusing whenever possible, interesting always, as a scientist finds whatever evidence he comes upon of interest. He was passionately non-introspective. When he had no choice to respond to an event that was sad, unfortunate, tragic, disastrous, he resorted to his all-purpose monosyllable, "Beh." One of his most frequent comments was: "We will hope for the best."

She had no impulse to share with him what had happened with Heidi; rather, her impulse was in direct opposition; she would keep it from him and him from it, as you would keep a healthy person from the site of infectious disease.

When she looked into his eyes, she saw that there would be no place in his understanding of the world for her sense of having been marked permanently by an act that nearly everyone else called an accident . . . not your fault not your fault, everyone would say . . . but she knew the truth that pounded in her skull— not constantly, as it had been, but she was never free from it . . . your fault your fault. She imagined how he would respond: he would be dismissive; he would be impatient; an initial sympathy would give way to a frustrated incomprehension. So when thoughts of Heidi intruded, she willed them away, challenging herself to come up with the right words to describe his eyes . . . the two she came up with were both unsatisfactory: root beer, ox blood. She rejected both because she associated him with her father, who loved an old-fashioned hard candy called root beer barrels and whose favorite shoes were a color called oxblood. And it was clear that Pietro and her father could not have been more unalike.

Did all women, on the verge of love, she wondered, compare the potential beloved with their father? When she thought of her father, she thought of the word *grave*. A grave man. Possessing gravitas. He was denser than Pietro and shorter; his legs (for years, he'd bicycled everywhere, long before it was fashionable), both calves and thighs, heavily muscled, his biceps unremarkable, his shoulders tending toward the narrow, his palms wide, his fingers rectangular or squarish. He brooded; he ruminated; his laugh came from the middle of his chest, reluctant, like a car starting reluctantly in winter. What was the opposite of gravitas, she wondered, that quality Pietro had that drew her to him? Lightness seemed too light . . . because what he had contained its own force, its own power, a power to lift her from the nullity that had been hers since Heidi had disappeared. She could not imagine Pietro disappointed.

Nine months of dinners, hand holding, and increasingly unchaste kisses passed before he invited her to Arezzo for a few days. It was January and the famous antiques market was on and he told her she could buy lovely things for a fraction of their worth and after a day when the city was crowded with shoppers it would be empty and they would have the Piero della Francescas to themselves. He talked about it as if it were an outing to buy antiques and look at art; nothing was mentioned about hotel accommodations, and certainly nothing about sex.

They were both twenty-eight; neither was a virgin, she'd slept with two boyfriends before Roger and Pietro was Italian; she didn't ask but hoped that his experience was not scandalously wide. But with the same surprise that had struck her when he first asked her to dinner, they surprised each other at the delight their first encounter brought, as if they had been hungry for a particular food that they had heard of but not discovered.

"Lovely," she said, running her hands up and down his body, wanting the English word, the word of home.

"Lovely," he repeated to her, and she realized that the boys she had slept with before had been boys only.

The following September he asked her to marry him, and she refused him.

"But why," he said. "We love each other. We are young and healthy. There is no reason for this."

"We're happy as we are," she said. "So many marriages are unhappy. I don't want things to change."

"I will persist," he said, and did not press her then. "Because I do want things to change. I am tired of what Jasper calls our 'naughty weekends,' and yes, I agree it would be unseemly for us to come together in the home of my parents or in Jasper's home . . . although I am not quite sure why."

She couldn't explain to him that somehow, despite his appetite for rough trade, the image of her room as a shrine to some idea of her as a girl was important to Jasper.

She couldn't tell him that the reason she couldn't marry him was that it was not possible for her to choose a normal, safe life for herself, a secure position in the world, when Heidi could be anywhere, unsafe, unlodged, unplaced. She allowed him to believe that it was because she was reluctant to leave Jasper on his own.

But then, she became pregnant. A fierce animal joy, an animal pride rose up in her and she wanted this baby . . . and yes, she told Pietro, now they must be married.

Only Pietro's family and Jasper and her parents came to the wedding. The reason for the hasty marriage was not kept secret; no one was shocked; everyone was pleased.

One day a couple of months later, walking home from the market, she felt a cramping, and then, to her horror, a gush of water, right there on Via Fornaia. She rushed home, went to bed, phoned Pietro and the doctor. But there was nothing to be done.

Miscarriage. Suggesting a failure of attention or a train not caught. Was this preferable to the clinical Italian phrase *aborto spontaneo* . . . spontaneous . . . suggesting a desire on the part of . . . could that be the right word, *fetus* . . . suggesting something cooked up in a laboratory rather than in what should have been the safe haven of a womb. Five months. A child but not a child. Nevertheless, hers.

Even in the darkest days after Heidi's disappearance, she had never felt more alone, never more a failure: this was rooted in her flesh and her flesh only. There was no one who could share what she felt because no one had known this—what, this creature, this being—its growing life had been a secret only the two of them had shared. Pietro was kind, but temperamentally was made uncomfortable by sadness, and she had no impulse to express to him what he could never understand. When people said, "You're young, you'll have healthy children and all this will seem like a distant memory," she wanted to strike them to the ground, or at least walk out of the room. Her mother came, and sat, and held her hand . . . but her mother had not experienced what she had, and her mother couldn't know that part of her grief was her sense that she had brought it on herself, that it was her just punishment for what she'd done to Heidi. *In loco parentis,* "in the place of the parents," that was what they were told was their role as teachers, and so she was taking the place of Heidi's highly inadequate mother. She had failed her, the primal female test: she had deserted the child at her moment of greatest need. So perhaps it was right that she should not have her own child, nature understanding that she was, in her very essence, unfit.

And yet a kind of desperation took her over . . . she must have a child . . . stronger even than her sense that she did not deserve one: the necessity to have a child, the nullity of a life without one.

It changed things between her and Pietro. Their bond, which had grown gradually rather than following the lightning path of a *coup de foudre,* had nothing in it of the tragic, and so had no place for a sense of failure and loss as deep as this. Lovemaking had something of a job about it, a task with a product in mind, and both of them grew almost to dread it; the failure seemed to fall on them both. There was no reason, no reason at all, the doctor said, that she should not have a healthy baby. But it did not happen. Month after month, her period came on time, each month a disappointment tinged with what she knew was foolish hope, each spot of blood a cause for tears. How primitive it was, how melodramatic: the sign of blood. A messenger without language or with two words only, yes/no. And then the information traveling in a hot wire from the female base up through the stomach and the spine to the brain: Bad News, Bad News Again.

And then, sixteen months after the miscarriage, her period was late. Then later. Without saying it to each other, she and Pietro had both given up hope. The doctor confirmed that she was pregnant, a healthy pregnancy. After five months, one day spotting, she rushed to the doctor, who ordered her to stay in bed. "You have what is called an 'incompetent cervix,'" she said. "We could do an operation to stitch it up, but that too has risks. So we will keep you in bed and hope for the best."

Agnes resented the use of the word *incompetent,* with its suggestion of carelessness or stupidity.

It was summer, and everyone flocked to keep her distracted. They didn't know that what she needed distraction from was not only the fear of losing the baby, but the sense that somehow, from a distance, Heidi was making this happen, or some just god acting on Heidi's part. Her parents came and stayed for a week; Jo came alone, and was tactful enough not to bring the children, and Christina arrived with a friend in tow; to Agnes's astonishment it was Jeanne Larkin. Christina was in medical school; Jeanne Larkin, now a graduate student in physiology, was her teaching assistant. It became obvious that they were lovers. She was surprised that Christina was a lesbian; Agnes wondered whether she had always known and hadn't told her friends, or if it had come on her by surprise. And she worried that if she appeared overeager or overpleased Christina would read it as uneasiness, so she didn't speak about the subject until Christina said, "Oh, for God's sake, don't you want to know the gory details, which are not gory at all? We're very happy, of course."

Jasper was not surprised. "Darling, I could have told you years ago . . . but mum's the word, I always say."

Pietro's family brought food and sweets and books and puzzles; his nephew hooked up the television so that she could see it comfortably from her bed; his sister washed her hair and provided an endless supply of frivolous nightgowns. Pietro read to her in Italian, in English . . . they read Proust together in French. He and Jasper played duets for her, but she was restless; terrified that because of one false move she made, her body would fail her again.

Then it was December, the magic date: she could deliver any time now and the baby would not be considered premature. Her due date arrived and passed. Her doctor urged her to deliver before Christmas so she would not be away. And the hospital staff not be denuded.

And so, on December 16, when the pains began, Pietro paced like a caricature of an expectant father and his brother came in the car that all the brothers shared. Then, after only three hours and what seemed like an endless series of pushes, the words, *bambina, bella bambina.* And her child was in her arms.

A tide crashed over her, wave after wave, of marvel, gratitude, past thought, past language, tears poured out, and she lay in a pool of tears and sweat, almost terrified to hold the little one, because her desire was to enfold her child completely, perhaps to take her back into her own body . . . did she really have to share her with the world? Pietro came into the darkened room. They hadn't settled on a name, fearing to tempt fortune and not knowing the child's sex . . . agreed that the child not be named for anyone in either of their families, for fear of giving offense to anyone not chosen . . . and although she assured Pietro that offense could not be taken by her parents, this was a category of behavior in which he could not believe. The name could be neither Italian nor English; they had no appetite for the Germanic, the French and Spanish were too near Italian; they settled on an Irish name, since they both liked the Irish and neither had a drop of Irish blood. Maeve. Maeve di Martini. An alliteration prevented by two innocent letters, always lower case. Many Italians simply could not pronounce the name; incomprehensible to them that a word would end with a consonant sound. For many of them, she was *Mahvee*.

~~~

THE BUS STOPS at the Via delle Botteghe Oscure. The street of the dark shops. Jasper had bound volumes of a literary journal called *Botteghe Oscure,* one of the jewels of '50s Rome . . . there were so many things like those bound volumes whose fate it seemed excruciating to preside on. The past. The relics of the past.

It's almost impossible, she thinks, at moments such as this, a major leave-taking, a transition to a new life, not to look back on your life and look for analogies, or similes: my life was like this, my life was like that. The happy years when her life seemed a string of brightly colored beads, the precious, the ordinary, all together, each taking their place. Or to think of your life as one of those pie charts that, when you were in grade school, explained the percentage of manufactured goods or the growth of population. One wedge: the life before the incident with Heidi, then the dark time separating it from the fogged-out period, then the time of her Roman healing, the beginnings of life with Pietro. And after that—is it true, she wonders, of all parents who adore their children—wedges marked to correspond to the stage of the child's life. The wedge marked Maeve's birth to age six would be, if she had to color in the chart, and those charts were always colored, a sunny yellow. The time when she rarely thought of Heidi—except in nightmares, where Heidi would demand Maeve, and Agnes would, feeling she had no choice, relinquish her, or those moments when some accident of the body brought Heidi to mind: meeting a friend of Pietro's whose palms were damp as Heidi Stolz's palms were always damp. When she thought of Heidi, she prayed for her, although she thought it was likely that there was no God. But she believed in the Madonna, somehow protective, somehow looking out for everyone, and when she was in a church—not to pray, but to look at something beautiful, which made her feel like an intruder when she walked past old women fingering their beads and mumbling incomprehensibly—and saw an image of a tender-seeming Madonna, she would light a candle in front of it and pray . . . *Let her be safe.*

She'd loved being the mother of a young child. It wasn't isolating, as it would have been had she been in America, she wasn't just the mother of a young child; she was the mother of a young child *in Rome,* where a baby's father could kiss and croon at her with no self-consciousness, where everyone on the street could join in their adoration, like the shepherds at the Christmas manger, where an endless series of arms and laps would be not only available but longing to be of use.

Maeve was an easy baby, then an easy child. Mother and child—they were each other's favorite person; no other company measured up. It was the purest pleasure for Agnes to walk the beautiful city pushing her beautiful baby in her stroller. She always felt a fool saying anything about Rome because so much has been said, but silently, she allowed herself to share with Maeve the most extravagant similes as she walked the streets: a baby in a stroller would never criticize you for saying, "Today the sky is the color of blue grapes, today the sky is the color of a peacock's head."

The fountains never ceased to lift her heart, the plash (no one ever uses the word *plash* for anything but fountains, she often thought, and it was a perfect word for that sound); every corner you turned brought the eye some joy: the light on a building, the white of the marble, the vines climbing the cracked walls, the moss untidy on the ancient heads or limbs.

She was lucky that Maeve didn't mind being in a stroller till she was three, so for those years she could walk and walk with her, long, extravagant walks, some would say ridiculous, walking across the river from Trastevere, heading to Pietro's shop on the Via dei Coronari, her daughter's playroom, her private gallery, the place where Maeve was petted, treasured . . . there was a separate corner of the back office where a child-sized table had been set up for her . . . the finest paper, French crayons, pastel chalks . . . coloring books from around the world, and Maeve knew no other child would ever touch them. Lunch with her father in the trattoria where he lunched every day, carried like a princess, told to ask for whatever food she wants and it will be prepared for her. *Che desidera, Mahvee,* what do you desire, Maeve: that promise that any desire can and will be immediately fulfilled.

Then down the Corso, averting her eyes so she didn't have to see the sturdy or elegant shops turned into outposts for the cheapest American consumer junk. A quick peek into some church with its singular masterpiece . . . the steep climb up the

Pincio (a challenge with a stroller) to the Villa Borghese, park of princes, the pocked busts flanking the paths, the identity of the heads she never learned though she always told herself she would, pleasant conversations with other mothers whom she wouldn't see from one day to the next for months on end, so they could speak lightly and without fear of offense. The kind of conversation, the kind of relationship, that made her glad to be living in a large city.

She still worked for Jasper three afternoons a week: there were times she could use her brain without leaving Maeve, who played on the floor beside her mother's desk, Jasper providing scraps of fabric, spools, paper, scissors . . . and the young assistants who were happy to take a break and play with the lovely child.

And then Maeve started school at five. Jasper, who always looked at Agnes closely, said, "You're always complaining of being tired, darling, and you never were when you had too much to do. Now you have too little, and it's bad for the complexion."

She knew he was right: she knew she was living her days stupidly, that it was taking much too long to do the ordinary things; she spent far too much time making the bed; she started experimenting with makeup and moving the furniture around.

"It's time for you to engage your mind, your very good eye, more actively. I want to train you as I've been trained; time for you to learn the nitty-gritty of restoration. I can imagine what the gritty is . . . but the nitty—does one have to conjure little baby lice?"

And so he began to teach her what he called "the exacting and in some way housewifely art of restoration."

"Always remember," he said, "that ours is a dangerous profession. Capable of doing irreparable damage. The most important quality for a restorer is humility. And never forget that the picture you are restoring is not yours, it has, really, nothing to do with you, with your tastes, your standards. You have to make yourself disappear; you are the servant of an object."

She and Jasper could share the satisfactions—impossible to convey to anyone who hadn't had the experience of getting exactly the right tonality of a belt buckle, a leaf, a fingernail, the moustache of a nineteenth-century nobleman. She learned that his deprecation of the work he did was just a kind of placating of the gods; he did have to do his share of fifth-rate portraits of ancestors and their dogs, but more often what he restored had the appeal of all well-made things, and many had a sense of a place. But she had to silence in herself the idea that there was an inherent unseriousness, perhaps even frivolity, in their work.

~~~

THE BUS MAKES a special stop for a boy in a wheelchair, accompanied by a man Agnes imagines is his grandfather. The driver gets out to help the boy; he arranges the mechanism that will clamp the wheelchair safely, the passengers move aside with a graciousness that she can't imagine in America. The boy's body is twisted, folding in on itself; his face is contorted in what Agnes imagines is a perpetual grimace.

I have been lucky, I have been spared terrible physical afflictions, she thinks, as she always does seeing someone disabled. She wishes she could do what Donatella, her cleaner for thirty years, does when she sees a tragic case like this one: she crosses herself, she prays for the afflicted one. But those are not gestures

Agnes could take on as her own. She cannot even address her gratitude to any being she can imagine possessing a listening ear.

She is most particularly grateful for what she thinks of as her ten shockproof years. The years spanning Maeve's birth to her tenth birthday. Maeve grew and prospered; Agnes was happy in her work with Jasper, although sometimes she felt a certain laxity to her days, and her work with Jasper, though absorbing, seemed sometimes distressingly frivolous. She was happy in her marriage . . . not the greatness of a great passion but the pleasure of a shared life . . . grateful for being part of the di Martini family, spared the cliché of conflict with her mother-in-law; she and Signora di Martini—she could never call her by her first name or—unthinkable—Mama—shared a love of quiet that seemed to escape everyone else in the family. One summer afternoon in the house on the lake when Agnes had stayed home from the beach to help her mother-in-law restore the house from the morning's chaos, Signora di Martini said to her, "You are like our lake, smooth, cool on the surface, but not chilling, no, the springs are warm, and underneath many variations, many surprises perhaps, none of them dangerous, if you would look for them, but my son would not be one who would do that sort of looking. None of my children would."

Then the shockproof years were over; time took its toll. When Maeve was ten, Agnes's father had a slight heart attack, and he informed everyone that he would never cross the ocean again. She could no longer refuse to travel; there was no way any longer to avoid her fear of running into Heidi—even of someone mentioning Heidi, or her family . . . or her fate. Occasionally she would realize that, in Rome, anywhere in Italy, she thought of

Heidi much less frequently than she would ever have believed possible. But in Rhode Island, she would always be looking over her shoulder, listening for the sound of the voice she could hardly remember but knew she would instantly recognize.

Pietro had never been able to understand why she was reluctant to visit her parents in the place where she was born. Their visits to Rome were clearly unsatisfactory; her mother abandoned her father for Jasper and her father wandered, abashed as a cuckold, gripping his guidebook and binoculars with a heroic resolve and a martyred look.

She had never told Pietro about Heidi and none of the Italians she met asked her about her past. She was grateful to be in Italy, where privacy was treasured. She learned that in Italian, there is no word for privacy. She came to understand that although so much of Italian life was lived in the open there was a deep impulse to secrecy, to *secretiveness,* that all Italians shared.

The American summers: she believed that America had stolen her daughter from her. She could see Maeve taking on a new liveliness, a liveliness she disliked herself for being unable to enjoy. Agnes felt her daughter move away from her, a necessary separation, she kept telling herself, a proper one: nevertheless, a loss. Before the American summers, she had taken unadulterated pleasure in being Maeve's mother, she and Pietro were proud, happy parents, delighted with their child: her acute social conscience, her hours looking at and classifying rocks, her taking samples of her parents' blood and saliva to examine under the microscope they bought her for her eleventh birthday. Pietro, being Italian, had no impulse to curb what Agnes feared might be thought of as bragging, fearing punishment from some northern god who looked askance on a parent's pride and pleasure. Neither Agnes nor Pietro had any aptitude for math, and they found it remarkable to watch their child snapping up the math prizes, making her way to the stage when her name was called, skittish and shy like a colt jumping its first fences. It was strange for Agnes to see her daughter doing something she could never have done, excelling at something she would never even attempt. She couldn't imagine what was going on in her daughter's mind as she sat in front of papers filled with numbers that made her mother's head swim. She had never liked thinking about things that she couldn't touch or that were—the stars, the planets—so far away and so numerous that they made ordinary human life seem like nothing.

∿

THE BUS STOPS at Teatro di Marcello and a mother and daughter make their way to the seat across from Agnes. The daughter, nine or ten, Agnes guesses, is dressed for school in black running pants, a white stripe up the side, a fleece jacket, aquamarine. The mother is dressed for work in a navy pinstripe suit, black stockings, patent leather pumps. The daughter's hair is French-braided—Oh, I know how long that takes, Agnes wants to tell the mother, and the pleasure of it. The daughter unhooks her backpack and without even asking plops it in her mother's lap. She yawns, stretches, lays her head on her mother's shoulder, and closes her eyes to sleep.

Enjoy it now, she wants to tell the mother, it will be over before you know it.

She remembers the years when she believed her daughter hated her.

When Maeve decided that her mother was someone whose

presence was an irritation, an annoyance, someone to be avoided whenever possible, endured at best, when Maeve's catalog of gestures consisted entirely of eye rolls and exasperated cluckings . . . which Agnes was not sure were preferable to overt insults. The sweet water of Maeve's need for her mother evaporated, replaced by some astringent gel, ice-cold and biting.

She remembers—with a pang that reminds her that it will be a long time till she sees Giulietta again—her sister-in-law, who had had three daughters, saying to her, "With these girls it is death by a thousand cuts. But you must believe me. It will be over in a decade or so."

A decade or so! Agnes had heard that with a sinking heart. But Giulietta had been right. It is difficult to remember that the present Maeve, competent, compassionate, solicitous of her mother, was the brash girl who could devastate her mother with a quick curl of her lip. At one point, Agnes understood that Maeve found her mother's physical existence revolting; she insisted on doing her laundry separately from her parents', but then Agnes understood that it wasn't Pietro's dirty clothes that were the problem, because occasionally Maeve would say, "I'm doing a load of laundry, Papa, can I put in anything of yours?" Once Agnes saw Maeve moving her mother's toothbrush far from hers, as if even that proximity was a contamination; she held the toothbrush between her thumb and index finger as if it were a filthy specimen.

One day, Maeve asked if she could go to boarding school in America and Agnes said no. Maeve shouted, "I hate you. I just hate you." Pietro took her by the shoulders and, looking straight in her eyes, said, "You may not speak to my wife that way." Maeve, in her turn, was so shocked that her father would refer to Agnes, not as her mother, but as his wife, that she burst into tears, threw herself into her mother's arms, and said, "Please, let me sit in your lap."

Over and over Maeve said that she hated living in Italy, she wanted to be in America. "I live for my summers," she said, and she burst into tears when Pietro made fun of her dramatic diction, throwing his arms over his head and singing, "I live for my summers."

Agnes had to understand that not only did Maeve prefer America to Italy, but that when they were in Rhode Island, she preferred Agnes's father to Agnes's mother. To everyone's surprise he had fully embraced the role of invalid, or, as Agnes's mother said, "valudetarianism." The vigorous, demanding juggernaut assumed an identity that seemed both willed and archaic: wandering around the house in slippers, a scarf around his neck in all seasons.

It was only Maeve's urging him to accompany her into the woods that released him from the constancy of his role. He dusted off the binoculars he'd bought for himself in college and hadn't used since Agnes had failed him as a birding partner. She'd tried pathetically hard, but she could never see what her father had just finished seeing and he grew impatient with her . . . look, for God's sake . . . where . . . just there . . . just there.

Christina and Jeanne Larkin were living together and Maeve discovered that Jeanne too was a birder, and so she, Jeanne, and Agnes's father became inseparable. They made no effort to mask their disinterest in non-naturalists. Once when Agnes was carrying four bags of groceries into the house, not one of them lifted their heads from the specimens they were pasting into the expensive notebooks her father had bought Maeve to help Agnes.

It was shaming what she felt that summer, and, thirty years

later, leaving her Roman life, the shame is still fresh. Shaming to admit that you felt abandoned by a twelve-year-old, jealous of your father and your former student. But she was gripped by jealousy, an emotion she'd never known. There was almost no ease between her and Maeve that summer, and, like the wife whose fidelity is scorned in favor of the mistress's novelties, she hung, abject in the background, waiting for a kind word, an approving glance.

Only when they were swimming did their old ease return.

Despite her devotion to birding and collecting specimens of leaves and lichen and moss, Maeve looked forward to her daily swim. There, Agnes was in the ascendant. Her father had grown fearful of swimming and Jeanne Larkin couldn't swim. She said she'd never been able to learn although she'd been given countless lessons. Christina said, with a pride that to Agnes's unease smacked of the maternal, "It's because she doesn't have an ounce of body fat," and Jeanne, who had a tendency to be literal minded, said, "No one can have not an ounce of body fat. It's that my ratio is quite small."

For a change, Maeve seemed happy in her mother's company, scrambling over the rocks to get to the pond, diving in, the first slow paddles, the first dreamy strokes . . . which never lasted long. Soon she called out, "Race you, Mom."

She had always let Maeve win. Until the day she decided she would not, that she wanted Maeve to know that she, the child, could not always have the whip hand, the child's whip hand that always had the luxury of withholding love, attention, favor.

Agnes swam ahead of Maeve, as fast as she could, and kept swimming, feeling herself propelled by some unkind fuel. She didn't stop to see how far from her daughter she'd gone. And then, she looked back.

She saw Maeve sitting on the rocks, alone, shivering in her towel. She swam back, much faster even than she had swum away; she clambered up the rocks so quickly that she skinned her knees. She chafed Maeve's cold body with her dry towel and wrapped herself in Maeve's wet one and asked herself if she was capable at all of love. Maeve was the person in the world she most loved and yet she had wanted to make her feel bad. She had wanted to assert her own power at her daughter's expense.

She believed that her life was taking on a tinge of the perverse.

WITH THAT PRICKING of the ears that accompanies, always, for her, the sound of English words folded into Italian, like sharp rocks sticking up in a silver stream, she hears the woman in the seat behind her saying, *"C'è un* perfect storm."

She is trying to remember when the phrase "the perfect storm" came into common usage. It was sometime in the '90s, she thinks, a book and then a movie about a shipwreck. Did Italians use it? She hasn't heard it . . . perhaps it's a vision most Italians would prefer not to incorporate into daily life.

There's no phrase, she thinks, for what would be the opposite of the perfect storm, a fortunate coming-together of events that enables, not disaster, but great good fortune.

Chance, or you might call it accident or fate, she didn't know which . . . *chance* seemed too frivolous, *fate* too portentous, *accident* suggested carelessness or a lapse of attention. If you were religious you might call it grace, but that was wrong too, because of what it might imply about a being who cared anything about a particular human life.

So the accident, the fate, the luck, the grace of her finding life's work restoring polychrome wooden sculptures. She'd given up, trying to find the right word for it. Only not given up the gratitude that made her wish that there was, in her life, a prayable being to whom she could render thanks.

A whole way of life, a way of living, a métier, a *mestiere,* floods her now, bobbing up in fragments. *In restauro.* Restoration. She wonders why a work life should come back to her in fragments only, not in stories with a clear beginning, a hard-to-trace middle, a definable end.

Because there was no form for it, there were no romances honoring a life of work, no chronicles, no ancient epics. And there were not enough words for all the different loves. The common loves, the love of man and woman, of parent and child, of God, of country, had exhausted the word *love* so that too often it didn't fit, like a wineskin that had stretched or shrunk, and had no real relation to what it was meant to hold. The love of work: the wind at your back each morning propelling you from your bed, reassuring you that it made a difference whether you lived or died, whether you were well or sick, your presence was required, and invested with a meaning. It must be common, she often thought, this kind of love, you could see it when people were one with their work; her butcher had it, and Roberto, who sold her cheese; welders had it, and seamstresses, and sailors, and the women who polished the brasses on church altars and the men who fixed their shoes.

One night Benedetto Fedele, a guest at one of Jasper's musical evenings, wrung his hands (she would learn that he would literally wring his hands at the first sign of difficulty): his assistant was leaving because she'd gotten pregnant and didn't want to be exposed to what might be dangerous chemicals. More hand

wringing, more desperate, quicker claspings and unclaspings . . .
projects were unfinished . . . projects were unstarted . . . and did
he pick up from the air the flicker that emanated from Agnes's
skin . . . the idea that perhaps she could work with him . . . or did
Jasper pick it up, and was that what moved him to offer Agnes as
a temporary help?

Benedetto's studio, dark and serious, with none of the sense of
play that had been part of Jasper's. The objects to be repaired
nearly always sacred . . . nearly always once the object of
prayer . . . the sense that they contained in them the urgencies
and needs of people year after year, asking for help.

Her first *tratteggio*. "*Tratteggio*, my dear," Benedetto said. "A
kind of sleight of hand . . . a way of pretending that what is missing is not missing." *Tratteggio*, a word that was in her mind, on
her lips every day. A technique of filling in what were called
lacunae, paint that had been lost, using tiny brushes, first you lay
down neutral background and then a series of thin lines, layer
over layer, until from a distance the lacunae seemed to have disappeared, visible only up close and only to the discerning eye.
Skill: the sound of the word not conveying what it contained;
skill, a joke sound, like a kind of game, whereas a skill was
acquired slowly, it was about repetition and boredom and enduring the boredom and the shame of failure, looking squarely at
what was wrong and forcing yourself to go on, go on when you
had no real idea of where you might be going. And the pleasure
when the skill was realized and you understood: this is mine, no
one can take it from me. A deep rich pleasure unlike any other,
unlike sex, or the love of friends or children, unlike the joy of the

natural world or the elation of great art. Simply: the satisfaction of a firm ground, earned, and, she had thought . . . unable to be lost.

The way it had come about: another instance of Jasper's kindness. Jasper, deliberately unheroic in his presentation, in his understanding of himself, but heroic in his instinct to open the closed hand . . . letting her go, *Of course, dear girl, of course, what a relief, I've been waiting with bated breath for you to release me to a life of leisure.* Suggesting that her breaking the news that she wanted to stop working for him and start working for Benedetto was something he'd wanted. A heroism of good manners. Good manners—the words making impossible a linkage with heroic, but perhaps they did more good than the obvious brands of heroism. So there were no medals given for good manners, but, she thought, there should be, because what were good manners but a leveling of the insurmountable cliffs, a filling-in of the brutal cracks? For how could she say, without being brutal: I prefer Benedetto's studio to yours because I love what he works on as I do not love what you work on, I find it more beautiful, more precious, more worthy of being preserved. How could she say, without being brutal: I am more comfortable with the moral implications of working in Benedetto's studio, repairing works that were made from the most natural, least costly of materials: wood, works that were prayed to, kissed and caressed and believed to cure plague or infertility or heartache. That no painting could replicate what these works achieved: the etched grief on the mourning mother, the lift of the hip of the young Madonna carrying her child, the child's playful grasping of the mother's chin . . . these sculptures she felt were unparalleled in what they said about life's fragility, and in the face of it an unquenchable vitality. Forgiving in their half-ruined state as paintings could never be: if there was a hole in a canvas, it could only be destroyed; marble sculptures, even in their ruined state, could not allow for peeling back and replacing, could not present the evidence of human touch or retouch. But missing hands or gaps or abrasions . . . her sculptures could absorb them and still present to the viewer the possibility of elation that came from great works of art humbly conceived. And how she revered the artists who did not feel the need to leave their names, who worked with assiduousness on the unseen backs of pieces that would be attached to a wall or placed so high that no eye could see the perfection of detail.

But after two years of Agnes working for him, it was clear that there was less and less work in Benedetto's studio, as he was aging and refusing more and more commissions. And she felt the limitation of repairing works that only a few people would see, whose value was connected to a marketplace, to money, and more and more she wanted to be part of something larger, something available to everyone, rich or poor . . . that could be visited by anyone in a museum or perhaps even a church and so, slowly, she determined that she wanted to train as a conservator who could be hired by the Italian government to work on public projects . . . which meant applying to the Istituto di Restauro, admission to which was known to be impossibly difficult.

And would they take someone her age?

"Yes," Benedetto told her. "But you must study very hard. Because the entrance examination is brutal, brutal." It had three parts: a practicum in which you would have to show your skills; a test to see your sensitivity to color; and (least daunting to her) a written exam in art history.

Once again, her good fortune at having at her side, at her back, people whose love was effective and constant. Benedetto, instructing and then judging her *tratteggio*, Jasper testing her on colors . . . Pietro and Maeve drilling her on chemical formulas and the history of solvents and glues.

She is accepted. A sense of triumph she had never felt before, because never before had she competed for a prize she desperately desired, competed against almost impossible odds. She must silence the nagging suspicion: Was she accepted because the head of the Istituto had for years gotten his cigars from Pietro, that Pietro's sister's husband's cousin had been for years the bursar of the Istituto? She knew that she would not have been able to do this in America, but living in Italy had given her the skill of pretending that human connections were a deciding factor in nothing.

~

SHE TIES the scarf around her neck a bit more tightly. Maristella. Maristella gave me this scarf . . . when was it, Christmas, my birthday, or did we see it in a shop window and Maristella insisted on buying it, "You must have this. It suits you. You must."

Must . . . it was a word Maristella had no trouble using, and no hesitation.

The first sight of Maristella. Professoressa Ford. How, Agnes wondered for the thousandth time, did European women do it? The straight skirt, gray or black, the jacket or cardigan, gray or black, the discreet scarf, olive or dove colored. Perfectly tied as the hair is perfectly colored . . . pulled back or cut to just the right length.

Maristella Sabbatini Ford . . . colleague. What an unsatisfactory word, she'd always thought, too dry and narrow to contain the idea of a kind of love. She loved Maristella Ford.

The ideas she'd first encountered in Maristella's lectures, the honor of working on objects of heart-stopping beauty: once trees. The wood specially chosen . . . dual in its meaning, connecting the practical and the symbolic or transcendent . . . poplar or pearwood or walnut for crucifixion . . . tradition naming them more spiritual than other wood; willow for the Magdalene, known to weep and bend. The properties of each wood she could have recited in her sleep, or in the moments coming out of sleep: limewood, easiest for carving; willow, the most flexible.

Sometimes she tried to imagine the living trees that had to be cut down. The sacrifice of living beauty for what was meant to transcend time.

Telling no one, sometimes she laid her hand on the wood and thanked the trees that had given up their lives. The ancients believed that trees had bodies like human beings; she always remembered the words of one of them . . . though she forgot the writer . . . wood was like the human body in that it could suffer, rot, or be blessed, and it could be infested with worms.

Trees had always been to her the proof that whatever else nature provided, it provided safety and benevolence, grandeur and delicacy. Shelter. Shade. Her eye falls on the plane trees, common to Rome, unknown in America: their plate-sized leaves, their formal bearing. She will miss the trees of Rome, urbane and cultivated as the trees of Rhode Island are not. She remembers her walks with her father learning the names of trees, then coming home, with samples of bark and leaves and needles and acorns. She hadn't walked in the woods with her mother . . . pollen and mold triggered her mother's asthma . . . but it was with her mother that she made the tree book, the early tree drawings and watercolors. Nature and culture. It was as if this work combined the best of what her parents had given her. Pietro and his family are proud that Agnes is making a contribution to the *patria*. And even Maeve admires her mastery of the science involved. A work that pleased everyone, that excluded no one, that opened conversational doors with everyone she knew.

At first, her relationship with Maristella had the formal circumscription of not only teacher and student but also professor and apprentice . . . and remembering her own error with Heidi, her failure to create a proper distance, she was admiring of Maristella's tone of a formality not unsympathetic yet with no suggestion of the intimate.

The first project she worked on with Maristella: a six-foot Madonna della Misericordia, sculpted in the Marche in the fifteenth century, holding her cape open to shelter a random collection of men, women, and children. The Madonna was mostly intact, the sheltered ones not sheltered enough: their features chipped or abraded, their clothes worn down to nearly bare wood. Thirty years later, her body recalls the sensations that accompanied the first days of her first restoration under Maristella's eye. She remembers the cold hard stone . . . she had to be kneeling to get to the little pilgrim who was her charge: only one, others might say, of a collection of random figures under the Madonna's cloak, but he was hers; he was not one of many to her, he was himself, irreplaceable. His hair was blond, he had only half a nose, his cloak was an olive green, his peasant shoes gray-gold. It will be her job to replicate as nearly as possible the tone of the original paint. How fresh it still is, the memory of the terror that thrummed and throbbed as she held the surgical scalpel—first used by ophthalmologists in surgery on the eye—that she would use to scrape off the paint, with the same sense of the fragility of what the knife touched as she was sure a surgeon had. She remembered the beads of sweat like a band of seed pearls collecting at the roots of her hair where it touched her forehead, the dry throat that made her afraid of the coughs that might escape, the dry lips she licked and licked like an animal sizing up its prey. It was all the more difficult because she was so moved by the idea of it—the Mother of Mercy, the Merciful Mother, the possibility of a generous protective enfolding . . . a safety from the buffeting of a cruel world. Later she and Maristella talked about how hard it was to remember exactly what you did after you had finished the project; what she remembers is Maristella saying, "Look inside the ear; when they repainted, they usually didn't take the trouble to go there, you have the best chance there of finding the original paint."

Months of quiet labor, months without praise or even recognition. And then, the thrill of being selected . . . Professoressa Ford would like Signora di Martini to assist her on the next project . . . and the gradual earning of regard.

So theory became conversation, became the laying-on of hands, the scraping-off of paint, the insertion of tiny or large pieces of treated wood.

They talked about all the different ways things could be destroyed, diminished, degraded . . . all the different words meaning what was lost . . . because of . . . well, Maristella said, because of life. There was nature: damp, mold, dryness; and there was the human touch and its harm: the impulse to redo, to improve, to make something one's own that was not one's own;

and then there was war . . . and Maristella had come of age as a restorer repairing the enormous damage of the war . . . stupid Italians, she said, waiting too long to keep their art safe.

They asked large questions . . . was it ever possible to reproduce the original . . . was the touch of history part of the work of art or should it be removed . . . however beautiful . . . in favor of some dream of an original that could only be guessed at . . . and perhaps never really restored, because that was another thing nature did, some of the elements that made the old colors, the old oils or glues were impossible to reproduce because the plants that were their sources had become extinct. Was the brush of time benevolent or hostile . . . was there any such thing as a recoverable past, was the purpose of restoration to replicate what the artist had intended or was there a responsibility to the aesthetic sensibility of the present: to create, for the viewers, some simulacrum of what the original viewers might have experienced . . . replacing the original with what would be in keeping with what people wanted to see? She had read about but never seen an exhibit of classical statues, replicas of white marble figures but garishly painted, as its creators had intended. So disturbing was it to the viewers, whose sense of the classical depended on pure whiteness, that the re-creation of the original created, in most viewers, a response of anger, betrayal, and loss, and only experts were interested, and their interest was an interest only of the mind. So they could talk and talk about ideas, Agnes quiet in the background as Maristella and colleagues shouted and cursed or blessed the name Brandi, the father of conservation theory, his supremacy unquestioned from the '40s through the '70s.

But then they got down to the work of it, and that was what satisfied Agnes most deeply: that what seemed like abstract questions, merely theoretical, became a task—fill in that crack, scrape off those drops of glue, too much red . . . no, no, let's leave that. Maristella, like Jasper, loved the word *nitty-gritty* . . . you are a good animal like me . . . and when it comes down to it, spit, touch, smell . . . it is an animal's work. Agnes had mastered the techniques of microscopy and ultraviolet photography, the chemical tests for age and decay . . . but in the end, Maristella said, it was the look of the thing, the smell of the thing, that really often determined the right action.

Maristella whom I loved. Whom I will always love. Whom I will—except for an accident or miracle—never see again.

Decades of partnership. "We are a team," Maristella likes the English word. "Like me, you are a good animal," admiring Agnes's sense of smell, her willingness to spit clean with actual spit. "Nothing better," Maristella says. "But the young ones are too fancy for it."

Shared work, and like raisins folded into a batter, the details of a woman's life.

Words no men would utter.

My miscarriage.

My abortion.

Maternal pride, important that it not be brought into the light of the workplaces, where it would inevitably be seen as a sign of unseriousness in a world in which it is far too easy for a woman to be called unserious.

Whispered . . . in cafés or over drinks.

My brilliant daughter.

My beautiful son.

How we love them.

How we love them.

How easy, so easy as to not even merit being spoken of—the thought of dying for them.

The falsely ironic complaints, really a kind of bragging, on the part of prideful wives.

"My husband does not know the meaning of the word *regret*."

"My husband does not know the meaning of the word *vacation*."

Once, after her second glass of wine, she said to Maristella, "Sometimes I feel about our sculptures the way I feel about my daughter. That I have to pretend that I don't believe they're superior . . . as I have to pretend not to believe that my daughter is smarter than her classmates or her friends or the children of my friends . . . I have to pretend not to believe that these images in painted wood are not the most wonderful thing humans have come up with." And Maristella had said, "Oh yes, oh yes, I know exactly what you mean."

The time they giggled when they had to restore a small sculpture of the infant Jesus. Learning that there were many of them around because when highborn Renaissance girls, devout or just unmarriageable, were sent off for convent life, they were given these sculptures, as a substitute for the children they would never have . . . and they wondered, did these holy or imprisoned women take them to bed, pretend to nurse them?

"Be careful with the little hard-on . . . it could easily snap off. You didn't notice it, did you, that the little penis is erect. Well, you wouldn't have . . . you didn't have a boy child."

But never shared with Maristella: the shame of her betrayal of Heidi, the hope that her work was not only a reparation but a sign that what had seemed to be destroyed could be restored, intact, as good as ever, even, perhaps, venerated, loved.

The younger workers would come to Agnes and beg her to prevail on Maristella not to be so publicly critical. She had to comfort one young woman in the bathroom after Maristella had shouted at her because the lines of her *tratteggio* were too thick, "It is a likeness of Saint Sebastian, not a pair of Englishman's pajamas."

Agnes had urged Maristella not to constantly be shouting out *"Cretina!"* when someone had scraped off too much paint, reminding her that when she, Agnes, had once taken off a splinter of wood and had come to her distraught, she had gone to the back of the statue, shaved off a splinter the size of a third of a toothpick, and told Agnes to attach it and paint over, "It never happened," she had said. And Agnes had felt the mercy of that. "You have it in you to be kind, Maristella, you have been kind to me. Try to be kinder to the others." "But you see, you are not an idiot and they are idiots." Always Agnes kept a generous supply of tissues, because it was part of her partnership with Maristella to smooth over the broken pride of the young people Maristella had insulted, restoring it, as she restored the broken areas of the statues they both loved.

Years when her work life was more important than her family life. Maeve had decided on university in America, choosing Brown, which had a seven-year program in pre-medicine— chosen in part because she could be near her grandfather, who was ailing. And then his death, coinciding with the millennium. That Christmas Eve her father died, the heart attack he had feared and tried to fob off for years, a good death, quick, rising from the dinner table, saying he needed a bit of a rest, and when Agnes went to wake him, he was, simply, gone. His death was not entirely unexpected—it had been years from his first heart attack—but she was surprised at how unmoored it made her feel. Even after his heart attack, she had always thought of her mother as the fragile one, the one whose breath she feared and invigilated, his solid body, thickly muscled, rooted to the earth, his legs that she'd thought of as tree trunks. And now this man, this great solidity, was simply absent, simply ash, an unlovely chalky substance scattered in the Atlantic. She felt as if the crust of the surface of the earth had suddenly thinned; she was newly aware of the possibility of its giving way and her falling through it into a darkness.

And then 9/11, unbelievable from the distance of Italy . . . causing her mother to decide that she would move to Rome. She and Jasper decided they would live together in what he called "my scandalously overlarge digs." So Agnes was in charge of two octogenarians, vigorous, but liable any moment to become not so . . . and always, it seemed, in need of medicine to be picked up from the *farmacia* at the drop of a hat.

❧

THE BUS LURCHES to a sudden stop in front of the Campidoglio. She remembers a day . . . not in the first years of her marriage . . . Maeve had already left home . . . when she and Pietro had come to the Capitoline Museums to see an exhibit of the statues of Canova, and, a bit tipsy from two proseccos they had drunk in the museum bar, had understood that they were both aroused, hungry for each other, and, without a word, took each other's hands, ran down the stairs, and hailed an extravagant cab to rush back home for an afternoon of surprisingly ardent lovemaking under the familiar coverlet.

How is it possible, she wonders now, that it was not long after-ward that she could say, knowing it was the only possible truth: "I no longer love my husband."

She knew it wasn't fair; most people considered that what he did was admirable.

The sudden decision, plucked, it seemed from nowhere, from the sky, or like a remnant of cloth snatched, hanging from the branch of a tree. He was going to sell the business.

For years he pooh-poohed the scientific evidence of the harm of tobacco.

When Maeve would accuse her father of enabling the deaths of his customers, he would repeat that he had smoked since he was fourteen, everyone in his family had, none of them had lung cancer, no one he knew well had.

He pointed to his customers in their nineties who flourished, responding with something that was just not glee to joggers and vegetarians who died early and even painfully.

Until his cousin Lucca, who was five years younger than he and an avid pipe smoker, died of cancer of the lip. Suddenly he remembered the fallout of his customers, victims of lung cancer, the *professoressa* of linguistics, the barber who still knew how to give a perfect shave with a straight razor and who used Jockey Club cologne on his clients, the columnist for *La Repubblica*, the dentist he said he would never go to because his fingers were too thick. Agnes firmly believed, although she would never say it aloud, that for an Italian nothing is real until it touches someone in the family. When Lucca died, in the blink of an eye, it seemed to Agnes, Pietro made the decision, consulting no one, presenting it to everyone whose livelihood was concerned: he was going to sell the store.

He disappeared to the house in the Marche for six weeks. He would speak to no one. He called himself a sinner, a criminal. And then, self-shriven, he came home with his new set of plans: he would give half the proceeds of the store to research for lung cancer. He trained as a hospice worker. He read architectural history and practiced the bowing of his cello, which he played for the dying, accompanying them on their way to death with his music, now believing that it, too, had purpose, had a value that it had not had before.

Six weeks of sorrow, of grief, of penitence. And then, a clear sense of purpose. Action. Reparation. A new life. And everyone admired him, and something was done, was over, a new page had been turned, or the book closed; he had confessed, and was forgiven; he was willing to do his penance, make his atonement, and the atonement was clearly and finally made.

He believed he was atoning, and that the atonement counted for something—but Agnes could not imagine how or where. He believed that he had done harm and doing good somehow wiped out the harm as if you had refurbished a house in the town next to the one that had been destroyed in an earthquake, as if there were some kind of currency, liquid and transferrable, that could undo harm.

But Agnes could not believe in that currency. If she had, she might have done something like what Pietro did—volunteered at a home for runaway children to make up for her betrayal of a child who had trusted her—but she believed the exchange was an illusion, a cheat. She wanted to tell Pietro that the people who died because he had sold them tobacco had died terrible deaths, and were permanently dead and that nothing he did for some other dying person had been or could be of any use to them: the harm was the harm and could not be undone. The harm she had done to Heidi could not be undone. She wanted to force him to understand that harm was not like coins that could be passed from hand to hand, exchanged. Harm left a scar, or should: the harmed one had been wounded, and a scar was left behind on the wounded flesh, and so, in justice, the one who had done the harming should be similarly and permanently marked.

The whole time she was back in Rhode Island, she longed for news that Heidi was still alive. Everything in her wanted Heidi in the world, but she had an equally strong desire: never to see her again, because she dreaded seeing once again the look in Heidi's eyes before she turned and ran down the path. And she feared that any reparation Heidi would ask would have to continue until both of them died.

No thoughts like that occurred to Pietro, and because of this she could no longer love him. She knew that it would be possible to believe that the knowledge that atonement was required of both of them might forge a new, a stronger, a more precious bond. But she also knew that it could not. She couldn't forgive him for not having been marked, darkened, hardened, as she had been. For not understanding that some damage could not be undone and so atonement was a delusion. She had never told him about Heidi; it was too late now. And so, in her silence, in her isolation, she envied him to the point of something like hatred, because he believed in the possibility of atonement. She didn't know if he felt the distance between them . . . he behaved no differently. She had no impulse to leave him, though; she had loved him, and she could never explain to anyone why she no longer loved him; they were the adoring parents of an adored child.

He didn't question her taking a job in Urbino . . . quite near where the family's summer house was. She stayed away for weeks at a time, only returning to Rome for the occasional weekend.

It was easy and almost too predictable for her to begin an affair with her colleague, the project supervisor, an Englishman named Michael Forbes. It was unlike any sex she had ever had in that it was just sex, with no pretense of love or future involvement. And he was unlike any man she had known well. Vain (he ran three miles a day, despite the weather; he ate sparingly but as a connoisseur, and she was bored by the amount of time he spoke about food, the purchase of it, the preparation, the analysis of restaurants as if they were theatrical events or items on the stock exchange). But she knew it was precisely his vanity, his incessant connoisseurship, that made him an accomplished and exciting lover.

She learned that there was a part of her that was a very good actress, that even though she was her own audience was an adept at playing the part of the great, the sophisticated, the worldly, even worldly-wise, lover. Which she certainly was not.

But then it was the very aspect of performance, of artifice (sex as art, therefore artifice, therefore artificial), that suddenly almost sickened her. Her mouth and tongue seemed irritated and abraded as if she'd been living on a diet of crystallized ginger and Campari, and all she wanted now was the good plain local red wine and a thick soup made of local vegetables.

She and Michael Forbes worked together for six months, but her desire for him was over a month before the project ended and he went back to England. She rarely thought of him, her time with him took its place in the world of the useless, irrelevant past, tie-dyed shirts, cassette players, transistor radios. It was, she thought, like a summer storm that cleared the thick, fetid air of her resentment of Pietro. She would never again love him as she had, but she began once again to relish his presence. She was grateful that he never suspected, that she had done nothing to mar his happiness: he was a happy man, and she believed she was a good or good enough wife. She knew that Pietro was born to be a happy man and almost anyone would have been a good wife to him. But she understood, in a new way, why she had required him, that, unlike him, she could have been married to no one else. To be whole, to have some sense of health, of not having been irreparably disfigured by what she had done to Heidi, she required Pietro di Martini, with his lightness, his sweetness, his intelligent good humor, his aversion to self-analysis, his hopeful-ness, his faith in the goodness of life that had brought her back to life. He was wonderful with Jasper and Agnes's mother, doing more than his share in helping to care for them.

They went to concerts, to exhibitions; they spent much more time in the country house; they cooked elaborate meals. There were four years that were like a level plain, a tended meadow, when nothing terrible happened and nothing wonderful. There were difficulties: she was the caretaker for two old people, and it required a lot of attention to get them to the places they wanted to go and arrange their increasingly frequent trips to the doctor, the pickup of prescriptions from the pharmacy.

And then the meadow suddenly flowered; the peaceful green monochrome bloomed with joyful color: Maeve told them she was going to have a child.

Agnes remembers the call: the day outstanding, not inter-changeable, as so many days are, with any other day. "Mama, Papa, we're going to have a baby."

It came as a surprise, because Maeve wasn't married. Of course, none of their friends' children seemed to be married; they lived with each other, had multiple children without, as people used to say, benefit of clergy. Maeve had been living with Marcus for six years.

Even now when Agnes thinks of them, it is their physical beauty she thinks of first, her daughter, the tall, fair, lithe beauty, and Marcus, taller, larger than she, and darker. Calmer, kinder too. A landscape architect with whom Agnes was able to share what she could not with Maeve or Pietro: a hunger for what the eye found beautiful. Walking with him through Rome she learned not only architectural details she'd missed for nearly half a century, but also, walking with a black man, how little she had thought of race in her years away from America.

She hadn't thought he and Maeve would have a child; Maeve was so absorbed in her work as Christina's partner in her family practice, and as the doctor in charge of a facility for abused children in Providence, that neither Agnes nor Pietro had given thought to her having a child.

The joyous ringing of the telephone: "He is here, Agnes, Pietro, he is here. Leo. Ten fingers. Ten toes. Perfect," Marcus says.

They fly—and it feels like they are literally flying—across the ocean to greet the new life. They take turns holding the baby, marveling together at the new strand of the new connection, jointly amused at the difference between American and Italian hospitals. When she had given birth to Maeve, hordes of Pietro's relatives had arrived with whole meals, served on china and cutlery they had brought from home, new sheets they had bought, changing the bed themselves so Agnes would be comfortable. In the Providence hospital, only two visitors were allowed at a time; if you had told a nurse or someone in charge that you were bringing special sheets, you would have been thought at best eccentric, at worst someone with an entirely culpable, even dangerous ignorance, of the ways of hospitals, and you would no doubt be refused.

How is it possible, she thinks, her heart lifting at the knowledge that she will see Leo in a matter of hours, that he is seven years old now.

Leo: she says the name to herself, knowing without the slightest doubt that he is now the greatest love of her life. She doesn't know how to find the words for a passion whose very name—grandmaternal—worked against the idea of passion, a word coupled inevitably with the scrapbook, the rocking chair, the ball of knitting wool. But she knew it as a passion, with its accompanying fears, different from a parent's. Now she had to worry that if he needed her she would be unable to help him, because she was too old. Worry without the same inexorable responsibility of a parent's, and she was relieved to be free of the parent's narcissism, and so felt that the passion for this child was the purest of any of her life. She had no ambitions for him, only that he be good and happy. No more than that. But those, she knew, were no small things, and perhaps no more likely than accomplishment, riches, fame.

She was very glad that the distance she had felt from Pietro had vanished, and, holding their grandchild, they could stand together, in joy, in wonder, in gratitude . . . for what seemed a certain sign of the goodness of life.

Because it was less than a year after it had happened, what everyone used the same word for: the accident. The definite article, as if there were only one, had always only been one.

They were staying in their country house. Pietro had gone

back to Rome for a niece's graduation. Agnes had expected him
home around ten, and when he didn't arrive by eleven, she went
to bed, putting his lateness down to traffic or his family's inabil-
ity to make a timely exit.

At two, she was awakened by the doorbell. Two policemen
shyly made their way into the foyer. Pietro had been in an accident; a drunk driver had pushed him off the road and he crashed
into a stone wall.

She didn't know how to ask the question in a way that wasn't
horribly crude. But there was no other way of asking it.

"Is he dead?"

And no other way of answering it.

"*Sì.*"

Yes.

They took her to his body, in the hospital in Urbino. His body
was still warm. It gave her a false hope and she held his hand and
whispered, "Don't be dead, *caro,* please, don't be dead." And for
a moment she believed that if she concentrated hard enough he
would sit up, and tease everyone for being foolish.

She began howling . . . she couldn't recognize her voice, and
she couldn't stop herself. The doctors pulled her away from the
body and held her, trying to comfort her as if they were not
strangers.

When she said, "I must call the family," she felt that the doctor was surprised that she said *the* family rather than *my* family, and that he was prepared for whatever strange behavior an
American would exhibit. And she felt her foreignness. *Straniera.*
Strange.

But she had always found Italian grieving strange. She realized there was no Italian word for "grief," only words for the

observable act of mourning, *lutto, in lutto, in lutto stretto,* or the visible expression of it, *piangere,* but for the inner emptiness, the ongoing invisible state that cannot be assuaged by any human connection—she looked in vain in the language that she felt she knew quite well, noticing that when an Italian wants to express sympathy for a death, often he says, *Ti sono vicino nel suo dolore.* I am near you in your sadness. As if the worst possible thing in grief is to be unaccompanied.

And perhaps, she thought, they were right, because as quickly as she could she acted so that she was no longer unaccompanied. She phoned her daughter from the hospital, and Maeve got on the next plane. Pietro's sister drove from Rome—it was terrifying to think how fast she must have driven . . . Agnes had hardly had time to bathe and dress when she was walking through the door. They held each other's hands . . . as they wept, they picked up and put down the things Pietro had only just been holding: his pen, his reading glasses . . . and Giulietta kissed them, like the little sister she would always be. They drove back to Rome at breakneck speed and she played Beethoven in the car: the crashes, the heroics, were what they both knew they needed. And then the crowds descended, and although Agnes wished for more solitude, it was the one gift she would not be granted.

There was a funeral mass, even though Pietro hadn't entered a church since Maeve was baptized. It had nothing much to do with God or with religion, it was simply what people, his people, had always done: in a way, it was impersonal, and that seemed right.

A moment of particular and unrepeatable tenderness, unique to Agnes and Maeve, wife and daughter, when they discussed what to do with his ashes. They agreed that they should be scattered in places that he had loved and been happy, and they laughed almost uncontrollably when they agreed that there were so many places he had loved and been happy that they might not have enough ashes to go around. They settled on four: the Tiber at the Ponte Sisto; the house in the Marche; the sidewalk in front of the Fountain of the Tortoises in the Piazza Mattei; the courtyard of Sant'Ivo alla Sapienza, the Borrominio church that was his favorite place in Rome to hear music. It was that this was his favorite place, though so unlike him: austere, and geometrical, a monotone white refusing, with a Northern deliberation (Borromini, after all, was Swiss), the slightest hint of color.

She had never thought of Pietro dying before her, as he was clearly the livelier one. And his death was not only his death but a sign of everyone's mortality: if Pietro could die, then anyone could die. Agnes was glad that she'd howled when she realized Pietro was dead; it was a clear memory, a vivid memory, and after a while nothing seemed clear. For months after Pietro's death, she felt nothing but the slackness of everything, its nullity, as if she were participating in the un-aliveness of the dead. She found it hard to make her hands work. She grew clumsy—and she had always prided herself on being adroit with her hands. She dropped things. She seemed always to be sweeping up bits of broken glass or crockery. The food she cooked was either raw or burned. The house became a kind of negative space: everything surrounding an emptiness that was the only real, the only important shape. She missed the conventional signs of Pietro's masculinity: his wood-backed hairbrushes; his change on the top of the bureau; his shoes in the closet, serious with the wooden trees that kept their shape but clownishly large next to hers, which became, beside them, Cinderella's slippers.

Pietro's death had a particular effect on Jasper and Agnes's mother. The wrongness, that he, young, should be dead and they, old, should be alive, weakened them physically. They aged dramatically in the weeks after he died. And it was less than a year after "the accident" that Jasper was diagnosed with pancreatic cancer. It was a painful death, but he did not linger as an invalid, which he would have loathed. "I want to die before I'm either terribly boring or terribly unattractive." He didn't get his wish: he was not lovely in his last days; the indignities of age and illness—shit and spit and stink—he, who was so fastidious, could not be spared them. He was not sorry to die. He said he believed that heaven was a fabulous party where he would see everyone he'd ever loved, eat all his favorite foods, and be treated to endless performances of Bellini's operas.

Agnes and her mother held his hand when he died; he was in a coma. "Do you think he knew we were there?" her mother asked, and Agnes said yes, though she wasn't sure; she wanted to believe that he knew he was not alone.

And quite soon afterward her mother said, "I want to go home now. I need to be back in America. I need to be around familiar trees. And I need to find a church to be buried from. I am, after all, Protestant; in a Catholic church I am always a tourist and to be a Protestant in Rome is to place yourself among genteel spinsters collecting for abandoned cats."

But Agnes put her mother off because she was unwilling to give up her work, which had been the *basso continuo,* the dependable constant that had kept her steady through the losses, shocks, and upheavals she had had to live through.

· · ·

Maristella Ford and Agnes di Martini. A team, which she had never thought of not existing, or only in the vague way that you imagined your own potential nonexistence after death.

And then, one day, as if it were nothing, "I have put in my papers for retirement. We are moving back to my husband's home in Australia." Laurence Ford. A banker from Australia . . . and so, when it is time for him to retire, she cannot possibly refuse him: the return to the home of his childhood. They longed for vistas. The tended hills of Italy, the skies so interrupted by habitation, the small European expanse always a poor substitute.

Their son is in America, in Silicon Valley. But Maristella loathes Silicon Valley; insists that Lauro, the son, travel to Australia to see them. So it was likely they would not see each other again, and Agnes worried that she wouldn't—not being kin, and never having met Maristella's husband—be informed of her death.

Were women always making decisions based on ties of blood? How much more likely that women would make decisions touching work based on ties of blood.

And yet it had not been only blood. They had both seen that their way of doing restoration was being seen as passé, "boys and their toys," expensive holograms as a substitute for standing and looking. Maristella's anger at the mania for laser technology as a way of removing layers of paint. "Do they care nothing for the damage these lasers could do . . . and if we said to them, the best solvent for cleaning off centuries of dirt is spit, they would probably run outside and vomit and suggest to the authorities that we should be sent to a nice facility for the elderly deranged."

And there seemed to be less and less money from the state for restoration, more pressure to do things quickly, with a lack of thoroughness that Maristella found difficult to endure.

With what seemed to Agnes unseemly speed, their work life was over and Agnes had to understand that she was no longer a person with work . . . and would never be again. Her mother's joy at the prospect of returning home made her feel that she had been unkind in postponing her wishes. Often she thought of a philosophy professor who posed the question, "What have you done today to justify your existence?" Was it enough to be the daughter of your mother, the mother of your daughter, the grandmother of your grandson, with the attendant needs of each that you could meet? Why not say that was enough? But she knew that always, there would be an emptiness that had been filled with work . . . something requiring expertise, something, above all, that was done and could be pointed to. You could not point to meals cooked, beds made, clothes washed, even tears dried. Because always there would be more, and always they would be washed away, a message in the sand, which you would be a fool to think could ever be remembered.

〜〜〜

BUT DISENGAGING FROM a life was not so easy. No one had ever told her that; she had guessed at the difficulty, but had not imagined its depth. Jasper had left his apartment to her, as had Pietro. She was suddenly burdened by property, by things. It would take, she calculated, three or four months for her to get rid of everything. But her mother was impatient. "At my age, I think in terms of months, not years," she said. She and Maeve worked out between the two of them that Maeve would take her grandmother home, that her grandmother would live with her until Agnes had sorted out the real estate.

She gave the furniture to Pietro's nephew, newly married,

and to his sisters her beloved dishes and vases, her embroidered counterpane, her perfume bottles. To the community who cared for the homeless she gave two-thirds of her clothes . . . she would not, she understood, be dressing up much in New Canterbury, Rhode Island.

Can it have only been this morning that she made what would be the last of her daily rounds?

She went to the market early as she always had. She said good-bye to Giuseppe, from whom she had bought fruit for twenty years, and before that from his father (she had, she realized, never known their last name). He always asked for Maeve, and for Leo . . . and since she left, for Agnes's mother.

"I'm leaving, Giuseppe, I've moved out. I'm off to America for good on the next plane . . . for good." What did that mean, and was it for good? He embraced and kissed her. Some days he gave her a kiss as they exchanged fruit for lire and then euros and some days he did not—and she could never determine why some days she got *un bacio* and some she did not.

She stopped into the store where she bought cheese, prosciutto and salami, olive oil. Roberto . . . the owner whom she could truthfully and easily say she loved.

He said he did not believe that she would be leaving Rome forever. He said he knew she would be back.

"Oh, I'll be back," she told him, "but I won't be living here again."

"*Chissà!*" Who knows? The Italian hope, she thought, for a kind fate.

He made up a package of cheese and salami for her to eat on

the plane because he said it was a sin . . . *un peccato* . . . to eat airplane food. *Si brutta*. And his embrace was heartfelt, singular, in a way that Giuseppe's was not.

"You must promise me to send postcards and pictures . . . particularly of the little boy . . . I want to see his progress."

She came back to the empty apartment, put the packages on the counter as she always had, but there was no chair or even stool for her to sit on. She leaned against the wall and sank down onto the floor with her back against the wall and her legs straight out, a position or posture taken by no one but a distraught child. She wept like a child, tearing loud sobs, she didn't try to dry her tears; they wet the front of her shirt straight through; she knew she'd have to change it; she was glad she'd packed a change of clothes in her carry-on in case of a delay. She wiped her nose with the back of her hand.

"What are you crying for what are you crying for," she berated herself, as she would berate a child whose tears seemed to connect to no visible, no comprehensible source. But then, she thought, that's always a ridiculous question: What are you crying for . . . as if tears could be explained, articulated . . . weren't they more like sweat than thought?

But she knew what she was crying for. She was crying for the passing of dearness. Of those moments in a life that show its goodness, that have nothing to do with, have not the slightest tincture of, greatness. What might pejoratively be called habit. She was crying because never again would she swim in that gentle sea of small pleasures whose repetition is so nourishing. She knew there were many people who hated repetition and routine, but she wasn't one of them. It was, she knew, because of living in a beloved city, you did the same things every day, shopped at the same stores, had a coffee in the same café, passed the florist on the street and thought while you're doing your shopping, which flowers you'd select. There was always movement, were always new faces, strangers more than likely, construction, changes in window displays, notices of sales. Distractions, and for Agnes distractions had always been the antidote to grief. It was what made her different from her father and Maeve: nature could not console her in the way the streets of Rome could. Because for her, nature was never distracting; in nature, she felt whatever she was feeling more intensely. Sadness was sheer darkness. Elation felt like flying.

So often, when thoughts of Heidi took her over, she could be distracted by walking the streets. Distraction, she thought, has a bad name, but she had often found it a blessing.

She knew she would not have it now. She will drive to a supermarket, the size of a small village, hand money over to someone who will more than likely not be there the next time, carry heavy bundles to the car and drive home . . . unpacking will be another chore because who wants to go to the supermarket more often than they have to: one stocks up.

And she was crying because she could not stop time. Time . . . when people say time what they really mean, she thought, is aging, what they really mean is death. And what is the right response to it? She thought if she could name what she was feeling she could get some control over it. But the words wouldn't come. It wasn't fear; fear was alive, electric, and what she was feeling was dull and grave. Dread was too strong a word for it. Disappointment too weak.

She wiped her eyes; she bent her head as if to accept a pail of freezing water dumped from a high window, or a sudden hailstorm pelting her with cold hard pellets.

Is it only sadness, she wondered, is that the word for it? Sadness, what is lost is lost and there is nothing to be done. Sadness is such a difficult thing, she thought. How pathetic to think of oneself as a sad person . . . no one wants to be the one of whom it is said . . . *She's a sad woman, what a sad woman she is.*

All her past happiness was now only making things more painful, as if she were far out to sea in a boat that leaked and listed and those happy times were highly colored stakes set down in the sand at the shore, of no use except to make clearer how very far out she'd gone.

More than anything that had happened, more than Pietro's death, or Jasper's, or her father's, this leave-taking made her understand that she was going to die. So long, see you tomorrow . . . and what was that but a belief in immortality. Leaving for good. So long.

She sat on the floor of the kitchen, where she had prepared so many thousands of meals, and let herself say out loud, "It's over." She thought of the moment when, as a child, she turned the television off. She pressed a button; the picture would disappear; a black screen would replace it, but in the center a small white dot that grew steadily smaller until at last there was nothing but blackness. And it was simply gone.

As she would be.

She closed the door on an empty apartment. Donatella would come by and sweep the empty rooms, dust the windowsills, the countertops, polish the kitchen faucet till it gleamed, wash the sheets she slept on . . . her last night in what had been her marriage bed, where Maeve very well might have been conceived, five years now a widow's bed, the husband's place taken up by books.

Agnes stripped the bed with a purposeful and unnecessary roughness, stuffed the sheets into a pillowcase, and dumped them in the corner of the room.

She left the keys in an envelope on the marble countertop. Wrote the new owners' names on the envelopes, a Dutch couple, retired, perfectly nice people, but she didn't understand why they needed so many rooms. Pietro and her bedroom, Maeve's, the study where Pietro had played his cello and paid bills and where Agnes wrote letters, lately more and more letters of condolence.

She pulled the heavy wooden door shut, refusing to look at the mailbox with the new owners' names on it, angry that their name was gone, her name, Pietro's, Maeve's, as if they'd never been there.

∼∼∼

THE BUS MAKES its final stop at the Stazione Termini. She will not miss the Stazione Termini, always chaotic, now the home of high-end shops, pushing out the Asians and Africans selling plastic Romulus and Remus, snow globes of St. Peter's and the Coliseum, postcards of the last three popes. She buys her ticket for the Leonardo Express.

From the train window, she sees the ugly new housing and the old walls covered with graffiti. Graffiti tests the limits of her understanding and her tolerance. She hates it, and it is difficult not to think of hating the boys—they are always boys—who defile plain beauty with an impulse to record their names. The sight of laundry hanging outside a window reassures her. A few sheep graze only feet from the train . . . a quarter mile from the airport. What changes for good, she wonders, and what remains?

She sits next to a young American woman, on her way home after a year abroad.

And she thinks: When I came here I was a young woman. In despair, incapable of imagining anything like the life that I've been given. But by whom? The life, that is to say, that I have lived. And whatever life is left to me, I will live it as, whatever else I am, someone no longer young.

She won't say to the young woman, "You have your whole life ahead of you, and you have no idea what it will bring."

Because she doesn't wish, at her age, to be considered strange.

She has lived here more than half her life and will be going home a stranger.

Going home.

But to what?

PART IV

Brimston, Arizona

April 2018

The bitch acted like she was doing some huge fucking favor. She was my assistant, for Christ's sake. I was the one who encouraged her. I sent her to Steven to have her boobs done . . . I mean they were halfway to her knees . . . disgusting . . . and she had to go into hock for the tummy tuck. I was the one to give her the idea to get a black woman and an ex-hippie and do her version of the *View* thing, I mean yes, the black was a no-brainer, you might say that, but I thought: Get some kind of conservative black chick, straightened hair, pull yourself up by the bootstraps like I did, but the ex-hippie, that was me knowing my audience . . . Willow Moonstone . . . but everybody just eats it up, all her old friends and their rehab stories and their suicide kids . . . it makes me want to throw up. It's everything I'm against, this sanctification of victimization . . . it's practically all people want unless they want a kind of mud wrestling and I won't do that either . . . it's almost as bad as the saint-victim thing. You have to give them what they want and what they seem to want now isn't what I wanted . . . not that I ever thought I was doing some kind of fucking service to humanity . . . I did it because it worked . . . I'm slipping a little and I need to do something to get back on track . . . which is the whole reason I'm doing this whole goddamn Disney World, because everything is getting more and more over the top . . . she's got better ratings than me this month. The stupid bitch. It's that ex-hippie, I have to get my market share back . . . now there's going to be a lot of boomers just retired with too much time on their hands . . . they worked for years and never watched daytime TV and I know just what I want, which is why I know this thing with Agnes Vaughan will be just the thing to get me back on top."

"Oh, sweetie pie, not to worry," Rich says. "You're the champ, you'll knock—what's her real name, Veronica Semolina or something—out of the park, they'll see who the real power-house is . . . and then . . . what's important is, you've got the buzz out about your bombshell. Your buzz bomb—I do think this new avocado toast thing is genius, by the way. But it's not the easiest thing in the world to make a really good poached egg." He presses the buttons on the elaborate Italian espresso machine with attachments for cappuccino or latte.

"Oh, darling, the challenges of your life. Hurry up with it, it doesn't have to be for the cover of *Gourmet* . . . oh, didn't that go bust . . . but I have to have some good clean protein . . . no low blood sugar for this."

They eat in silence, and, saying nothing to him, she goes upstairs to her part of the house, her bedroom, bath, and study. A luxury they both insisted was not a luxury but a necessity . . . separate quarters, separate wings.

A good investment, Rich MacParland. She'd hired him first as a trainer; he was certainly good looking, exquisitely fit, and not afraid to be demanding of the pathetic ones who all desired him and so would do anything he asked. How much he wanted what money could buy; his covetousness for fine clothes, good wine, good cars was palpable, slightly dangerous, like a jungle cat circling prey. And his vanity. He had, of course, wanted to be an actor, tried Hollywood, failed. His covetousness made him ambitious and quick to learn. Soon she had made him assistant manager. And then, when her TV show took off, she broached it to him: marriage, she needed it for her image; he needed her money to live the way he wanted. He could have any kind of sex with any boy he wanted—just make sure they were of age, only he had to be ferociously discreet: one slip-up and he was out. He agreed to everything. He was excellent in the kitchen. She contributed lavishly to his amateur dramatic group. As a couple, they cut an exciting, almost threatening dash. A good trade; a good investment. And how much cleaner, how much simpler marriage was without the mess of sex.

She showers quickly . . . she takes no pleasure in her showers . . . scrubs her skin with rough loofahs and pumices and hard, stiff brushes. She dries herself thoroughly with towels that her guests find surprisingly rough, surprisingly unwelcoming to the skin, and, slipping into her black terry robe, sits in front of her makeup table. The makeup girl—she's good, what's her name . . . Estrella, surprising that a Hispanic would have such a good sense of white skin tones . . . she must have to depilate like mad, they're all very hairy, it must be disgusting to have to deal with all that body hair. But she admires Estrella's matte surface, and when she pays a compliment, Quin can allow herself to believe she means it, although probably it's as false as anything that comes from the mouth of someone who's paid to make you look good.

She regards her face in the mirror as she has always regarded it: a problem to be solved. "There will be time to prepare a face to meet the faces that you meet." Where did that come from . . . oh, she remembers now. That stupid poem that Mrs. Gould taught them . . . she thought it was so profound. T. S. Eliot. "The Love Song of J. Alfred Prufrock." Some old guy trying to figure out whether he should live or die. Die, then, she'd wanted to say, and wants to say it now. Get it over with. She's annoyed that something from that part of her past, the Lydia Farnsworth School . . . the Lydia Fuckworth School, she calls it, whenever it enters her mind . . . is presenting itself now. Well, it's because she's going to be confronting Agnes Vaughan.

Mrs. Gould told her that her satiric poetry was very accomplished but not appropriate for class presentation. Ridiculous Mrs. Gould with her glasses on a string that sometimes got caught up with the cross she wore . . . the girls knew she would grab onto it—thinking no one saw—when she felt she was losing control of them, which of course made them wilder, more determined to rebel. Miss Vaughan had praised her poetry and sympathized with her disappointment. One of her lies, that cheap, easy sympathy that Heidi had mistaken for real understanding. That she had fallen for. That she'd been weakened by. Her problem was that she hadn't had contempt for Agnes Vaughan's false promises. Well, Agnes Vaughan will be getting her payback now.

Admiration could be turned into contempt; sometimes it was easier than others. The change with Agnes Vaughan had been painful, like a tooth pulled out without anesthetic: bloody and disfiguring. But sometimes the transition had no pain attached to it at all, as with her brother. With her brother, the change from admiration to contempt had been like a child's tooth falling out because she'd bitten on something hard, and painlessly, the gap appeared, followed soon by the sharp point of the new tooth pushing itself up with a pain you could induce or stop by biting down or not: it was up to you.

Lawrence Russell Stolz. The Marine. The oh-so-successful businessman. Thirteen years older than she, and she'd hardly known him. If she believed in luck, which she resolutely did not, she would have said she'd connected with him again because of good luck. But she didn't believe in luck; it suggested the kind of mystical gobbledygook that Ayn Rand so despised. There was chance, random, unconcerned, neither malevolent nor benevolent. And you either took the chance and made something of it because of the strength of your will or you let it go and called yourself a victim of fate. She had taken her chance, and it had, almost literally, paid off.

Face up to it. She'd admired it because that was, her brother said, the motto he lived by. As if everyone had a motto, needle-pointed, framed, hung over the oh-so-comforting hearth. Well, in the end he hadn't lived by it. Died pathetic, whimpering, asking her to hold his hand. Which she did not. And he had cheated her; she'd learned this only after he'd died and the lawyers had let her know.

She won't think about him now. She'll tell Valerie she was an only child. Which, to all intents and purposes, she was.

She'd never had contempt for Edwina . . . when Edwina comes into her consciousness she banishes her as quickly as she can, because, impervious to contempt, Edwina has the power to wound her. Edwina had never written back. Was it that Heidi—Scotty—wasn't interesting enough, wasn't important enough? But no, that wasn't it, she was sure that wasn't it. Edwina had never promised to keep in touch. Edwina with her perfect ivory skin, her long honey-colored braid that Heidi tried to imitate, the high forehead, the eyes that blinked and blinked when someone said something she didn't like. Edwina had promised nothing, suggested nothing, suggested, even, that she wouldn't write back. "I'm lousy at that, Scotty," didn't suggest goodness or kindness, the goodbye—cool and final—always on the table like an invitation or a thank-you note. There was no false offering, and the meagerness of the terms was attractive. Because true. Edwina, offering little, hurt little. The memory could still pierce, but Quin understood. It was not betrayal. To be hurt by something whose terms had been set out clearly was only a weakness in which she would not allow herself to indulge. The one person she fears seeing again is Edwina; if she saw her, longing would follow, impossible longing, the diminishment and the sense of failure, of inadequacy, of not coming up to the mark.

What she has to be sure of, what she has to be careful not to be surprised by, is what she's going to conceal about her past. The face that she prepares to meet the faces that she meets. It has to be the face she wants seen; she can't be tricked, caught out. By some memory that will trip her up. Her mastery has always been complete; always she has been cool, hard, dry. Now coolness, hardness, dryness is called for. So she has to relive it all, remember it all, which she has refused for many, many years—a temptation to weakness.

Another thing she learned at Lydia Fuckworth . . . that Michelangelo, all the great sculptors, saw what they needed in the block of stone, and their art was getting rid of what they didn't need, turning it to dust and rubble at their feet, and presenting to the world the figure that had to be discovered within the mass of what wasn't needed. This is what she would do now. Get rid of everything that wasn't part of the figure—it was more than a face, really, it had a body—she was going to present to the world.

Who was she going to be today for the TV audience? The audience who had made her place in the world, her fortune— not a great one, but not nothing. The audience for whom she had such contempt, a contempt so layered, so shellacked with a concealing varnish, that no one could see it for what it was. They mistook it for tough-mindedness, clear-sightedness, real-ism. Reality TV. There was nothing real about it. It was an invention, a shape-making, as fictional as any fiction, more so because it denied its fictiveness, made a fiction of truth, a truth of fiction.

What no one understood about her was that she thought of each show as a work of art she was constructing. You have to con-struct the victim; she has to be sympathetic but not pathetic . . . she didn't always get it right, some of them just didn't make it and she had to pay them anyway and now she'd have to do it to herself: present herself as a victim, which she loathed, but it was all a construction anyway, so what did it matter, because in the end she would not be forgiving, although she might appear to. For the camera.

One of the hardest things about her construction of each show was that she had to control, to calibrate, her contempt. Contempt—no one was honest about it, people were afraid or ashamed to say that contempt was delicious, how exciting it was on the tongue, the palate, against the dome-like roof of the mouth. Contempt had been her dearest friend, her most dependable ally. No, it was more: her glamorous, accomplished, dangerous inamorato. Contempt had sheathed her, allowed the soft pulp of attachment to harden into a dagger, or a sword. It had been the cold impermeable steel that covered the swamp of helplessness, of loneliness, of paralyzed abandonment. What people never understood, or never admitted if they understood it, because it made you sound inhuman—but human, what did that mean, usually something weak, "I'm only human," meaning, "I didn't hit the mark." What people never understood was that contempt was a pleasure, a deep pleasure, perhaps the deepest.

Was it such a bad thing to be fueled by contempt? Didn't it show, really, a sense of rightness, a refusal to cover up what stank and rotted when you covered it up? Contempt was a shield, but it also made things possible that otherwise would not be. She was the knight, crusading for justice, ARMED in the impermeable metal of contempt. She liked thinking of her foot shod in a pointy metal, cutting into the ground, making a mark that was perfectly shaped, a perfect point.

She did have contempt for her audience . . . but that didn't matter. She often had contempt for the people on the show, particularly the ones who seemed oh so ready to forgive, those are the ones she couldn't help but she tells herself she's helping them, she's pulling them up from that slough of victimization . . . she's being hard on herself when she says it's just contempt, she's really doing them good. What good does it do to say, "Oh, boo hoo, let's sit down together and weep" . . . and then what? That was the point of her show. That was why people loved it. It was about justice, not mercy. The quality of mercy is not strained. The quality of mercy is strained, like baby food. She was offering people a clean, hard diet of nourishment—clean protein: see that someone who has hurt you is also hurt and then you are free of them, you can move on, stop worrying about them. They didn't worry about you, did they? That was the point. The interviews she couldn't use were the ones where the victimizer made himself a victim: "I've thought of you all my life, a day never passed when I didn't think of you." Bullshit. What did you do about it? You thought about me: blah blah blah and boo hoo hoo. Now you're going to pay.

She had been a contemptuous child, a contemptuous girl. And then Agnes Vaughan had tempted her away from the place of contempt, the high dry place where she was safe, where she had a clear view of everything. It was Agnes Vaughan's time to be paid back.

What was unbearable, what was truly hateful, was what contempt had replaced. Yearning, longing, pleading, the little match girl, so disgusting. Blah blah blah and boo hoo hoo. Her trademark. A knight with a foot shod in iron, pointy, cutting into the earth, leaving a mark.

So who would she be for the audience today? She had made her name by urging people to give up the stance of victim, to replace it with vengeance seeker, justice seeker. But there had to be a moment in which the audience felt sorry for the contestant—the moment when they inhabited the place, that she, Quin Archer, would lead them out of. So would she have to allow that . . . allow that transitional moment in which her audience saw her as a victim? If not, there would be no pleasure for them in seeing Agnes Vaughan brought to her knees.

So she would paint herself a victim, but a glamorous one. A victim of the 1960s, which her audience saw as the bad time and yet were not impervious to its glamour.

There was nothing glamorous about those years. So many of them. Eight. April of 1972 to December of 1980. Wasted years. Sordid. Squalid, but in a limp, mousy way.

She had the thousand dollars, which she kept in a roll in the tip of her boot, all too aware of thieves that were everywhere in New York. Every night she fingered the dollars, damp from the sweat of her feet, spread them overnight till they were dry in the morning. And every week, she paid her hotel bill, the cheapest she had been able to find near Penn Station, a weekly rate of $200. She had only a thousand. After three weeks, she would have to do something.

What had she done those three weeks, walked and walked, aimlessly looking for something, anything, fighting the urge to call Miss Vaughan and say, Come and get me, I need you, it's not too late. Her parents were in Chile, she didn't even know how to get hold of them, and she would rather die than ask Elsie and Hans for help. This was when she remembered the saving power of contempt. She remembered something her father put on his face when he cut himself shaving. Styptic, it was called. Its function was to dry the blood. A styptic pencil. He touched it to the bleeding cut, and it was immediately dried. She had found it magic—sometimes her father could be kind, letting her sit with him while he shaved some mornings—and contempt was her styptic pencil drying the wound made by longing, by belief that someone would be there to help, and the disappointment when there was not.

And so, walking up and down, buying a few outfits—replacing the boots with sandals as the summer approached, a pair of jeans, an Indian print skirt, a leotard, a peasant blouse . . . her pride and her contempt were the styptic that dried out her desire to cry out for help. And with the dryness: pride. I have done this. I am entirely on my own. I need no one.

Someone had left a copy of *The Village Voice* in the hotel lobby. She picked it up and took it to her room, intuiting somehow that this was the place to go for things that would help her make a new life.

She bypassed stories about demonstrations, about experimental films, tried to read someone named Jill Johnston and then Jonas Mekas and then with a start of excitement realized that what she really needed was the Classified section: she needed to find a place to live; soon she'd be running out of money.

She asked the desk clerk for change for five dollars; grudgingly he gave her a fistful of coins but said he couldn't keep doing that, she'd have to go to the bank sometime. She made her way to the phone booth in the lobby, which stank vaguely of sweat and what she hoped wasn't urine.

She called the number on the first ad she saw: "Female seeking female. Share spacious apartment. Washington Heights. River view."

Washington Heights. She had no idea where that was. But if she had a river view, that would be something to brag about when it was time to brag . . . and she knew that someday that time would come.

She had refused to admit to herself that she was lonely, that she wanted company, but the girl on the other phone, Debbie Marshall she said her name was, sounded so enthusiastic, "Hey, if you're not busy, come right up. I think you'll really like it."

She told herself afterward that she should have called more

than one person, answered more than one ad, but it seemed the right thing at the time to seize the opportunity. She took the subway uptown to 157th Street, and walked toward the river.

Debbie Marshall. The thought of her makes Quin sick. The smell of patchouli. The smell of cat piss. Kitty litter under your feet. The loose scarves, skirts, blouses, the hanging necklaces. To hide the fat, the disgusting fat. Calling herself the earth mother when she was nothing but a pig. Her middle-of-the-night gorges on ice cream, on cookie dough that came in tubes that she ate raw, on butter that she mixed with sugar when there was nothing else. Giggling when she was found like a naughty child . . . but she was just a disgusting pig. And Heidi had been taken in for a while. "I'm just an earth mother . . . a mother hen, and I think . . . well, you're like my little sister, my little chick."

There's a view of the river.

I can help you with furniture.

Can you move right in?

Oh, this will be fun. You can sleep on the couch tonight and tomorrow we'll go to Goodwill.

The next day, a mattress on the floor, a table, a lamp, blankets that smelled of mothballs . . . sheets they bought in the Spanish-speaking stores on Broadway . . . cheap, but new.

Debbie buys flowers for Heidi's new room. Contributes a vase from some cabinet. Perhaps her grandparents'.

Treats her to meals: till you get on your feet.

I'm a film student.

But she never goes to classes, or only if there's absolutely no reason not to go. The commute to NYU is long; so if the weather isn't good or if she has a headache or she's just not into it . . . she never seems to go.

An endless stream of "incompletes."

Years, thousands of dollars.

People let her get away with so much. Why? Because she made herself so weak, presented herself as almost boneless . . . had no malice . . . wouldn't hurt a fly.

Disgusting.

The disgusting cat.

The filthy kitty litter.

Would you mind just dealing with that . . . it's just . . . it's hard for me. I have asthma.

So Heidi becomes the cleaner of cat shit, and when the cat sprays (*I can't stand to have him neutered . . . it just seems so unnatural*), she is the one who sprays and sprays ammonia, and then Debbie takes her in her arms, the floppy breasts, *Oh, you're the best . . . my little sister . . . I'll take you out for a really good meal.*

Chinese food. Not expensive. But better than what Heidi can provide herself. There is a view of the river. She tells herself that's why she was taken in, because she did have that to look at: the river, gray in all seasons, but occasionally shining like a strip of metal.

Do you smoke?

Not really.

Debbie had an endless supply of marijuana, so there were days spent in a haze of reclining, eating, watching television test patterns, giggling . . . she had money. Her parents paid the rent; it had been her grandparents' apartment, and the family had held on to the lease. Rent controlled. Which is why she could charge Heidi only sixty dollars a month.

Heidi needs a job and takes the first one she sees, in the dry cleaner on 158th Street.

Two old people, stunted like midgets, the Levensons. Benjamin and Hortense. The husband repairs things . . . he is meticulous and short tempered; he will spend what seems to Heidi an absurd amount of time getting spots out of a tie, a suit jacket, with what is called "white spirit" but smells like poison. But the minute there is no work, he reads books on international socialism. The wife constantly complains about being overheated. She pins the slips with the customers' information onto the garments, places them in a bin, and waits for the person from the central dry cleaner, who arrives every day: the high point of her day, she complains to them; some listen, some refuse to listen and simply bundle the clothes up, turning their backs on her without a pretense even of politeness. Every night it is one of Heidi's jobs to go over the floor with a powerful magnet that picks up the pins. She rather enjoys this, it seems magical. Mrs. Levenson praises her, "Your penmanship is very neat. That's very important. If names are illegible . . . we're lost."

Heidi makes no attempt to ingratiate herself with the Levensons or with the customers. She exchanges only the necessary words, and refuses pleasantries. "You could be a little warmer with the customers," Mrs. Levenson says, and Heidi says okay, she'll try.

Every week they pay her on time.

On Friday nights and Saturday mornings they pay her to turn the lights on and off. To press the button on the electric kettle.

They have no children.

They say nothing about their past, but they were not born in America.

She has no contempt for Mr. Levenson, but they are mute to each other, nodding, allowing each other's existence with complete neutrality.

She works there for two years. Saving her money . . . she doesn't know for what.

She cuts her hair short and dyes it blond so no one will be able to find her.

But no one seems to be looking.

Occasionally, Debbie lures her downtown to where "it's happening." Music, young people . . . parties in dark rooms with plentiful drugs. She goes because there is no reason not to and she doesn't want to pay for pot, which she increasingly needs to get through her days.

Sometimes Debbie brings a man home, and always the next morning she wants to talk endlessly about how wonderful it was, how she thinks it's really going to lead to something, but it never does. She gets fatter and fatter.

Heidi allows no one to touch her.

Only once, she loses her temper with Debbie. She must have been really stoned, because she was trying to put more kitty litter in the box (instead of cleaning it, she just piled litter on top of the shit until Heidi gave in and cleaned it), she was probably trying to make coffee for one of the guys . . . and when Heidi woke up for work . . . walking over to the light switch that was above the kitchen sink . . . she stepped in a mixture of coffee grounds and kitty litter.

She screamed.

Debbie came out.

"You can't do this, you can't do this, I can't live like this," Heidi said.

"It's my apartment . . . you can leave whenever you like. No one's keeping you."

She closed the door. The cat meowed in front of the door; she let him in and shut the door.

The cat. Named Cat. How she hated him; all his effluvia, his hair on every surface and always in the air, as fat as Debbie, who loved overfeeding him as she loved overfeeding herself . . .

Heidi often fantasized about poisoning the cat.

But Debbie would know it was her.

And she had nowhere else to go.

And then, suddenly Debbie decides she's "into women," and Roxanne enters their lives.

Roxanne was a waitress at the Italian restaurant that Debbie occasionally treated Heidi to. Small, compact, quick moving . . . a slash of red on her lips—no one is wearing red lipstick in those days and so it seems original, and daring. She is expert at whisking plates away and making full plates appear: she seems like a magician. "You move like a cat," Debbie says to her, and Heidi can see it: Roxanne has understood Debbie as a mark; Heidi sees that she notices that Debbie always pays. "Come late on a Wednesday or a Thursday, we can hang out afterward, I'll bring you free drinks from the bar."

It happens three times; Heidi is bored by the talk, which is all a kind of sexual bragging; Roxanne has been in porn films . . . goes to visit her parents in New Jersey every weekend because they always put twenty dollars in her jeans pocket. "They haven't got a fucking clue." A brother in Vietnam. A brother cop. It's why she likes both parts of being in porn films, she says, the pay easy money for the movies and her family thinking she's a good girl working in a nice "family" restaurant. "We're all Italian, so it's like they think someone's looking out for me instead of my giving blow jobs for a better station."

Heidi can see that Debbie is excited . . . but she doesn't actually believe half of what Roxanne says.

"What's it like, being in a porn film?"

"Actually, it's kind of boring . . . everybody's like pretending they're just not there."

Roxanne invites Debbie to a "really cool place, a bar downtown." She does not invite Heidi.

And then Roxanne is there, living in Debbie's room, cooking for the two of them, Heidi understands that they want her there, to watch. Roxanne usually walks around in her underwear; sometimes only her panties; she has perfect small breasts and Heidi is aroused, although she forbids the feeling when it comes.

"How much do you make at that dry cleaner?" Roxanne asks when Heidi comes home from work, clearly exhausted and dispirited.

Three bucks an hour.

"Chicken feed, don't be a patsy. I'll get you a job at the restaurant. You'll make more in tips in one night than you make a week working for those old misers."

"I'll try it out."

"Have you ever given a blow job?"

"I don't think so."

"Believe me, you'd know. Come on, we'll practice."

Roxanne takes a banana from a bowl on the sticky Formica counter. Every surface in the apartment is always sticky even though Heidi tries to keep the surfaces clean . . . somehow Debbie's touch undoes all her work almost before it's done.

Roxanne sticks the banana in her mouth. "It's important to

keep your jaw slack, and to keep the dick forward so that you don't gag. And remember: you don't have to swallow. Just tell him you don't swallow."

Heidi is sickened, yet fascinated. This is sex. This is sex with no moral tincture, no sense of attachment. Sex as a skill. Sex as a commodity: a job like any other, preferable because it's quicker.

Heidi quits her job at the dry cleaner. She had thought that the Levensons would have some sort of response, but they just seemed resigned.

For a month, she works in Paisan, the Italian restaurant. Roxanne makes a joke of everything: introducing her to Joe the manager—"She knows the score"—to the other waitresses, much older than she, with thick pained-looking legs and tight dyed curls, probably not candidates for the preferential blow job. But no one ever asks her for one.

But she's not very good at any of it, and she hates doing something she's not good at. She can't make small talk with the customers, and Joe tells her if she wants good tips that's what she needs to do. He tells her she's going to have to stay later to help with cleanup in the beginning, which really disgusts her: the leftover food, fresh from someone's mouth, the greasy pots, the stinking garbage. She regrets giving up her job with the Levensons, the tasks she was good at, writing people's names in her careful script, picking up pins with the big magnet.

She has never spent much money, so she decides she'll find someplace else to live: the years of subservience to that fat pig are over.

She looks in *The Village Voice* for someone wanting a single woman to share an apartment. 200 West Ninety-Third Street. Talia Clark. Frizzy hair desperately clenched to her head with clips and bobby pins; stocky legs, a skirt below her knees, loafers, no makeup. She works for a lawyer, though she tells Heidi she taught high school Spanish until she realized she hated every single kid. When Heidi laughs and says, "I hear you," Talia offers her the room. She wants a month's security. Heidi can give it to her with ease.

Talia Clark is almost completely silent. Each morning she makes herself a cup of Taster's Choice instant coffee with nondairy creamer, Shredded Wheat with a banana and skim milk. She washes her dishes instantly (Heidi is pleased with her tidiness), disappears to shower, and then leaves for work. She asks Heidi about her employment prospects.

"I was waitressing, but I hated it."

"Yeah, of course. Can you type? You need to know how to type."

"I never learned."

"That's too bad."

A week later Talia says, "One thing, and the money's good, these publishers that do law books, they need proofreaders . . . are you good at spelling?"

"Really good."

And so Heidi enters the world of nighttime legal proofreaders; she leaves the house at eight p.m. and goes to a windowless basement in the Fifties where a tribe of moles sit under bad lights and make marks with a blue pencil on long rolls of newsprint that are slapped down in front of them by the foreman who decides who will get what to work on and how much. No one talks very much. She is discovered to be excellent at it, and is offered more and more work.

The foreman invites her into his office. He puts his hand on her behind. He asks her if she is a virgin. She says no. He asks her if she's interested in more hours, more work. She says yes. He says, "Don't worry, I'll be sure you won't get pregnant."

"Taking it up the ass" was what it was called. Parts of it she finds appealing, her body's tight resistance, the possibility of degradation if he pulled out his prick and it was covered with her shit. And above all she didn't want to see anybody's face . . . not at any time, not in the swoon of pleasure or the idiotic release.

The arrangement pleases her. It pleases both of them.

She collects her money, more than enough to live on, and makes her way home at six in the morning. Every day she passes the homeless black man who walks up and down the street, whacking the garbage cans with a big stick, saying over and over, "Everyone think he the big shit. Everyone think he the big shit." It's the closest she comes to regular human contact; Talia leaves while Heidi is still sleeping; sometimes they overlap for an hour or two, but neither of them makes the slightest pretense at wanting to spend time together, which seems to suit them both.

The boss has given her extra hours, so she leaves, exhausted, but glad of the cash, at ten in the morning, much later than usual. She walks up Madison Avenue, heading north to Fifty-Ninth Street, where she will catch the subway on Broadway. In the window of a small, clearly expensive store, she sees a pair of old-fashioned wooden skis; she's curious; she knows enough of the world of skiers to know that they now vie with each other for the newest, lightest equipment; she wonders why anyone would want such a relic, such a guarantee of slowness when speed was the most desirable, the only desirable, quality.

At first, she thinks she's just overtired; it's a hallucination; it must be. But she stands, fixed in front of the window of Climb Ev'ry Mountain.

Her mother. Liesel Haubrecht, not yet Stolz. Smiling triumphantly on her skis on a perfect ski slope: blond, trim, perfectly coiffed, her perfect outfit. My mother. My mother young and beautiful. Has she found me? My mother who never loved me. Whom I did not love.

She tears herself away; she won't look at it, she won't go back. She walks away, and then cannot resist the return. Wooden skis. Wool pants and jackets; a sign: VINTAGE SKI WEAR . . . STAND OUT ON THE SLOPES.

Climb Ev'ry Mountain. The spelling stolen from the musical her mother loves that she loathes. *The Sound of Music.* How her mother swooned. Austria, she would say, her eyes closed, her body swaying, how wonderful . . . the mountains, the blue skies.

Her mother. In a window.

Walk away. Keep walking. Don't come back.

She knows she must. But she'll come back tomorrow.

First, she'll sleep to make sure it isn't only an effect of the fatigue she lives with habitually. She wants to run away, never come back, but she'll make herself come back when the store is open. She will talk to someone.

Where did you get that picture? I need to talk to someone.

Lawrence Stolz. Her brother. Who changed her life undoubtedly for the better. By hiring her to work in his store after they acknowledge each other as brother and sister. But did her the favor at the end of allowing her not to be grateful because he had cheated her, and had not had the courage to face the reality of his own death. She is grateful to him for sparing her the obligation of gratitude because gratitude is another one of those tricks that make a space for weakness. And at first, she had been grateful when he signed over to her the $50,000, which is what he tells her was left to her in their parents' will . . . they had died in an avalanche—she wants to laugh, it's so perfect. Only after his death will she learn that, in fact, he was the trustee and in the trust there is much more coming to her.

But for some time, she was impressed. Oh, yes, Lawrence Stolz could be impressive. Lean, tan, not as tall as he seemed; the military posture added inches, the silver crew cut, the manicured nails. The harsh judgments barked out like the military commander he was—two years a Marine—"The way you live is ridiculous. Your neighborhood is a drug den. It's a miracle you weren't raped on the street." (Oh, I was, my brother, but not on the street.) Not asking her why she ran away, why she cut herself off. "None of my business and I don't want to know. Buy some new clothes. You look like an ex-nun or someone trying to pretend she's not a dyke." Sends her to Saks Fifth Avenue but offers her no money for a new wardrobe, as a brother in a romance might have done. "How much money do you have . . . people are afraid to be honest about money. I'll be your guarantor for an apartment on the Upper East Side but don't ever default on your rent or I'll let you live in the street."

Which she feels she has to be grateful for . . . but she tells herself she would have come to it anyway: the one present he ever gave her, *Atlas Shrugged*. She reads it, and it is a revelation. *The Virtue of Selfishness*. To both of them a sacred text.

But she doesn't have to be grateful to Lawrence, he gave her the books but she went much, much farther than he did, and she never flinched from the demands of the philosophy; not once, not once to this day. Grateful to Leonard Peikoff, for their ideas, for their clarity in expressing them. That was a kind of gratitude that wasn't weakening, that didn't demand or even suggest abjection or abasement, that forbade abjection or abasement, that insisted that one praise, congratulate oneself for having had the sense, the courage, to look truth straight in the face, or to jump on the back of the galloping horse truth. What people called luck was just keeping your eyes open, hearing the horse's hooves as it galloped by and having the guts to jump on its back and hold on. The weak either didn't hear the hoofbeats or were afraid to jump on. So one didn't, really, need to be grateful or concerned about the weak, just to appreciate one's own strengths and demand the same of others. Why did people find that unacceptable? There was only one reason for it: they were weak. There's no weakening involved, though, to be grateful to Ayn Rand, to Leonard Peikoff, whose lectures she attended with the devotion of an acolyte whose loyalty was a pledge for life.

Every week at the Objectivist Center; she was not quite comfortable there, but she felt something she rarely felt: that this was a place worthy of her time, worthy of her attention. What a relief it was to see well-tailored, well-coiffed men and women, not eternal boys and girls, with hair down their backs and clothes that had no pretense even of being made to fit, draping, hanging, too concealing, or too revealing, shabby fabric, imprecise line covered up by a mania for everything excessive, not of use, but only to shout out its presence: fur, feathers, sequins, velvet. What the people at the Objectivist Center wore was a witness for their reverence to work well done, standards respected, adhered to, an awareness that novelty was mostly a cover-up for shoddiness. BESPOKE TAILORING. Sometimes she passed a store on Madison Avenue with that sign in the window, and she was sure that some of the people she sat among had suits that were *bespoke:* the word pleased her, suggesting, as it did, that the wearer had only to say the word and someone would be on their knees, measuring, asking for approval . . . begging, almost, to be allowed to do his work.

She tried to dress more like the women . . . but she'd cut her hair boyishly short, and, to a woman, they seemed to favor long hair pinned up or back and lacquered. She didn't want that; she didn't like the heavy feeling of long hair; when she'd cut her braid off, she felt she was freeing herself from some old promise, some old vow. But she followed their lead religiously in the cut of their straight-skirted suits . . . worn just to the knee—or their sheath dresses . . . simple, classic . . . the colors they favored: claret red, kelly green, occasionally black, occasionally navy blue. When she bought her first pair of flesh-colored panty hose and patent leather pumps, she felt proud of her membership in an admirable cohort, not afraid to look out of sync with the times . . . knowing that their standards were the right ones: the ones that would not change, but would be always desirable, always correctly seen by the right eyes, through the right lens.

And it was exhilarating to hear Leonard Peikoff cut through the nonsense that passed for standards about art and literature.

Abstract, nonrepresentational painting . . . done away with in a thrust: "the dabblings of mediocrities who haven't the talent or discipline to learn the artist's craft"—Jackson Pollock, throwing paint . . . what is that put against the nobility of a Rembrandt, recording the best that an individual could be . . . and Beatnik poets and novelists . . . drug-addled minds chanting nonsense . . . mystical gobbledygook—worshipping the dregs, valorizing the worst, the least that man could be . . . not even a gesture toward the heroic, like a Byron, a Victor Hugo.

She read every word that Ayn Rand wrote, every book, every article in *The Objectivist Newsletter.* There was only one road down which she couldn't follow her: her insistence on the importance of passionate sexual love. Heidi thought that was a slip on the part of the master; were her own appetites so overwhelming that she couldn't see the weakening power of sexual desire? Sex was only two things, she believed: an itch or the species' instinct to reproduce itself. If the basic impulse of civilization was the impulse of trade—why engage in a trade that was so often muddled, unequal, unsatisfying? One day, she hoped, she would meet Ayn Rand, and they would discuss this . . . perhaps Miss Rand would thank her . . . or perhaps explain. For herself, she was proud of the trade that her taking it up the ass represented: clear, measurable . . . cold as coins dropped into a glass dish, clearly interpretable as the shutting of a safe door. She promises herself that when she has enough money there will be no more need for sex.

What had she read before she read that wonderful book? Cheap mysteries. And, picked up on the streets: a complete Shakespeare, which she read almost to spite Mrs. Gould: See, I don't need you; I can do it on my own.

But she reads with a new avidity everything by Ayn Rand, and finds on her own—she didn't need her brother for this, he didn't even know about it, a series of lectures by Leonard Peikoff, philosopher, her mentor. She is excited by the largeness of his terms. She understands everything now; why she had been, all along, on the right track in thinking she needed no one, and that the dead years were dead because she had no system, no philosophy to organize herself, to propel herself to action. Now she knows: she has choice, she has will. That what she would make of herself had nothing to do with her family, her mother who cared nothing for her, her father who enslaved himself, her brother who was nothing better than an animal. She and Lawrence had got themselves out, not by luck, but by intelligence and will.

She works for her brother; her salary is meager, she is making less than she did with legal proofreading, but she doesn't have to be an asshole whore, and she likes commerce; trade, as Ayn Rand taught her, the basic human drive.

She is good at spotting trends because she understands the herd instinct, and she reads high fashion magazines to sniff the air of what will be desired next. Lawrence is grudging in his praise. When it comes, she relishes it, but forces herself not to be too pleased.

These are good years. For the first time she has friends, met at the Peikoff lectures and the Objectivist meetings. She has small drinks parties in her new apartment, for the first time buying furniture of which she is proud: sleek, modern objects without much cushioning; primary colors, a kitchen whose metals gleam like weapons.

But it's her own idea to move to Arizona, she doesn't have to thank Lawrence for that. One of the friends from the lectures tells her it's the new place, the Sunbelt, people don't want to live in cold places anymore; he suggests she make a trip and check it out.

There are no mountains in Arizona but there are people who still want to hike and trek and she scouts the minor cities: she is good at finding markets. She has invested her inheritance well, lived modestly, so doesn't need Lawrence to bankroll her first venture in Sundale: Desertrek: outdoor gear and clothes—she studies and transfers her knowledge of the northeastern ski-based market to something hotter, drier . . . a clientele who like to pretend they love nature when what they really love is an image of themselves.

Nineteen eighty-two. Ten years since her betrayal by Agnes Vaughan, five years of paralysis, of victimization, two at her brother's side, but more important, at the feet of the master, Ayn Rand. *The Virtue of Selfishness.*

Lawrence is angry that she's leaving him. She uses his own arguments against him: nobody owes anybody anything, what is important is the self's own happiness. He can't object; but he is cold and does nothing to make her exit easier.

His life has become very grand. The Reagan years: the glamorous '80s. He has, behind the counter, a picture of Nancy Reagan, who came to the store to look at the vintage ski wear. Brought there by Lawrence's new friend, Pat Buckley, wife of William F. Buckley Jr., whom everyone considers a genius, even she had worshipped him as a teenager . . . but it's Pat, the great society hostess whom Lawrence adores; she enlists him as an escort for some of her friends whose husbands are too busy and too bored to take them to galas and charity functions, because, "darling Lawrence, unlike so many of my dearest friends you have that butch thing. Ex-Marine . . . divine."

Only once was Heidi introduced to Mrs. Buckley, who said to Lawrence in passing, "Pity she didn't get your looks. It would be so much easier if she were decorative."

. . .

Heidi reminds her brother that she doesn't really fit in with his new life, so he doesn't fight very hard to keep her in the store; gives her her "inheritance," which he said he was keeping and investing for her so she wouldn't "throw it away." Only later, when he is dead, does she realize that he has been siphoning off money from her trust fund, one he never told her about, of which he is the executor.

Face up to it. He faced up to nothing. He died nothing but a sniveling coward, tended by other snivelers. Asking for her forgiveness. Which she was glad not to give. But to pretend to give: preferring her contempt for his being duped by the sentimental reproaches of his bedside weepers. And after all, she does owe him something: for the release from the need for any kind of gratitude for him. Contempt rather than gratitude. An infinitely better choice.

None of this will she allow to be known. She has an alternate plan; she has created an alternate life. From that book that got all the attention. Patti Smith. *Just Kids*. Patti Smith and the degenerate Robert Mapplethorpe. The glamour of degradation. That is what she'll provide: the exciting sniff of the degradation of glamour. Nothing about her life working as a dry cleaner, as a nighttime proofreader, as someone cheated by her deluded and ultimately pathetic brother. No: she'll give them what they want.

Reality TV.

The doorbell rings; it's the tech people. Rich can deal with it. It's what he's good at. It's what he's for.

It's crucial that she hit exactly the right tone with Valerie

Singleton. She's not going to be able to use the tone that she's best known for: exigent, probing, sympathetic while refusing sympathy.

It's all about mothers.

What people don't get is that to be a success on TV it's not sex anymore, not in the old way; it's about mothers. People watch the kind of mother they want, what they never got or miss because it's not there anymore. So Oprah's people want the pillow mom, and Laura Ingraham's want the mom so miserly with her praise you'd do anything for it, and it will be the only praise worth having.

Sex. It was something that had never been a problem. After the first time, she knew she was done with it, it wasn't for her. There were only two reasons for it: to scratch an itch or to procreate. Well, if the itch arose she could take care of that herself . . . and as for a child . . . the idea had sickened her from the time she was a child herself. What she had figured out even before she'd read Ayn Rand was that sex was something that was part of a trade. But once she'd made her own money, she had nothing to do with sex. What had it been . . . thirty-five years, maybe. She'd still been young. And so the rejection, willed and powerful, was a more enduring, more satisfying pleasure. The pleasure of distance.

Like setting up camp on the top of a mountain. Cool, high, dry . . . the mountaintop, the company of swooping birds— eagles, hawks, ugly up close but thrilling from a distance, and what people didn't understand was that distance made everything beautiful, distance was the secret to a satisfying life. Birds swooping and landing on the dry high perch.

She'd kept an eye on New Canterbury, on the Lydia Farnsworth School, subscribed to the local paper, checked the school website. So she was ready. Now.

She loves words like *contempt* and *betrayal;* words that are weapons that shock and wound.

Contempt because in order to be on the air she has to pretend to believe in forgiveness, to hope for forgiveness . . . whereas she sees forgiveness as only weakness and weakening. It's justice that makes you strong, but you have to be strong enough for justice. Almost no one is strong enough for justice, and if you are marked forever by what someone does to you it is only justice that they should be marked forever. Forgiveness erases the mark.

She went back, always, to what Ayn Rand had said about trade, that trade was the operative word, in human exchange. But how did you trade, how did you determine a just compensation? The years were unequal, when the mark had been branded on young flesh it was always deeper, the scar more prominent, and the older person had fewer years to live out his punishment. She mustn't use that word *punishment,* she meant *payback.*

Forgiveness was erasure, and why should the mark, the brand, be erased? "Just let it go"—that was one of those new age bullshit clichés . . . just let it go. But where? To what?

Why should the mark be erased? Was it ever erased when the victim had been hobbled, disfigured, dwarfed by what had been done? There were always scars.

What was simple justice people called revenge.

She looks at the framed article on the wall, the image of herself she likes best. She is all in leather, in the pose of a karate attack—she had come up with the idea, Diana Rigg's pose in the old British TV show *The Avengers*. The posture of protection: warning. The article in the *Brimstone Gazette* that was meant to be damning but in fact boosted her ratings to a higher level than they'd ever been. The headline, bold above her fierce, strong image: "The Revenger: Blah Blah Blah and Boo Hoo Hoo."

How it pleased her to think that she had come up with that mantra for herself, "Blah blah blah and boo hoo hoo," called up, taken out when the victimizer tried to explain him or herself, tried to suggest that he too had suffered.

She walks to the wall so she can have the pleasure of reading the article again. It was always a pleasure, more so because the reporter hadn't liked her but she had got the best of him.

"Vengeance is mine, saith the lord," the Bible tells us. But Quin Archer isn't having it. Her reality-TV show, *PAYBACK*, does what it says: it looks for payback. Participants contact Archer when they've found someone from their past who has done them some harm (Quin refuses the term *victim*, prefers the term *the owed*) and has gotten away with it. Followed by Quin and her crew, the harmed confronts the harmer and insists on "payback." Often it's actual money, but sometimes . . . well, let's just say, sometimes the harmed (with Archer's help?) can get quite creative.

Quin Archer originally came to Brimston from the East Coast—New England, she says (pressed, she doesn't reveal details—happy for her participants to spill their guts, she's quite reserved about her own past), by way of New York. She came in 1982 and opened a fitness center called Tough Love, which her husband still runs. Some of you may remember the program that first made her a public figure: Selfishness Boot

Camp. Aimed particularly, but not exclusively, at women, she insisted that putting other people's needs in front of your own was a formula for unhappiness and bad health.

Certainly, Quin Archer is a good advertisement for her fitness regimen. Well into her fifties, she has the lean body of a twenty-year-old athlete. And she insists that anyone can be where she is, with discipline and determination. And a right sense of priorities.

"I became very distressed when I realized that people's—particularly women's—fitness goals for themselves were frustrated because they were putting other people's needs in front of their own. So before I even started on a fitness program, I had to have some assurance from people that they loved themselves enough to put themselves first. It was called 'selfishness'—but that's an invention of people who want to use other people instead of drawing on themselves. I learned about it from the philosophy of Ayn Rand, a great and misunderstood thinker. If we're not looking out for ourselves, we're only involved in a meaningless system of self-sacrifice that, in the end, swallows everybody, leads everybody into a hopeless bog of weakness and self-pity."

"I guess your positions have always been controversial. The people who stayed with your Selfishness Boot Camp program credit you with saving their lives. Others who decided to leave call you a monster, a sadist who gets off on humiliation."

Archer laughs. "And I guess they're criticizing me all the way into the doctor's office for their high blood pressure and type II diabetes."

"You seem to thrive on controversy. Your many fans say you're a lifesaver for victims."

"I refuse the word *victim* . . ."

"Why is that?"

"It's a hopeless word. It calls up pity, or self-pity, which is only a weakener. If you say I've been harmed, then you are looking for justice, not sympathy."

"You seem to really dislike pity and sympathy."

"I dislike it because it doesn't work. It leads to weakness and paralysis. Whereas a desire for justice is strengthening, and energizing."

"The voice-over that starts all your shows says, 'Forgiveness without payback keeps victims in their chains.' But your critics say that you never seem interested in forgiveness; that you push the 'ower' and the 'owed' away from each other every time there seems to be a reconciliation in the air. Your signature phrase—'Blah blah blah and boo hoo hoo'—some people object that you're too quick to interject it when the 'ower' is trying to explain themselves and ask for forgiveness."

"Well, Jada, what I've come to see is that premature forgiveness never lasts. And it backfires. My job is to see that the owed isn't harmed further by being pushed by guilt or misplaced kindness into a too-early forgiveness that in the end serves no one well."

"Do you see a difference between revenge and justice? Isn't it an awfully easy line to cross?"

"It's a line, but just because it's a difficult line—well, that doesn't mean it shouldn't be approached. I believe that things looked at clearly and rationally have the best chance of success."

"So you deny that revenge is what turns you on."

"What turns me on is changing people's lives. It's the best turn-on there is. And if you say I'm addicted to that, I plead guilty." (*PAYBACK* can be seen at 11 p.m. on Thursdays on channel 65.)

. . .

She dresses in front of the full-length mirror, running her hands along the hard contours of her body. Her fortieth-birthday present to herself: a breast reduction . . . she had loathed those fat flopping appendages that threatened to sag and hang. Now there were no vulnerable abutments. She is as lean and taut as a young boy. No need for a bra, but she wears one anyway, because she enjoys the feeling of boundedness. Boyish cotton underpants. Her signature sleeveless sheath, bright orange; the crystal necklace that looks like it was made of ice cubes; her signature black pointed stilettos.

She's completely ready. She has prepared, not only a face to meet the faces that she meets but a perfectly dressed body . . . and, more important, a character for reality TV, which has no more reality than the false eyelashes the makeup girl, Estrella, will be attaching to her any minute.

She's glad to see that Valerie looks uneasy; she won't do anything to lessen the unease.

"Someone offered you something to drink?" she asks, instead of saying hello . . . then air kisses, then, Valerie's gush:

"I'm so excited, Quin. I can't thank you enough for letting me be part of all this."

"Who else," she says, hoping that this will trouble Valerie later—she won't know whether it's a compliment—"Of course I value you more than anyone," or a put-down, "No one else was available."

"Estrella's all ready for you."

She walks over to the makeshift booth that has been set up for her makeup. She suggested they make her up in her own bedroom but Estrella said since they were shooting outdoors she had to calibrate for that.

More air kisses for Estrella.

Estrella runs a comb through the stiff silver spikes.

"It's such a great look, Quin . . . totally you. People try to copy it but it's hard to carry off . . . I don't know anyone else who does it as well as you."

Cheap praise from an underpaid lackey. But it's important to keep in her good graces. Waiters who don't like you can piss in your dinner; makeup artists can add ten years with a stroke.

"I always say, Estrella, if I only had you to make me up every day, I'd be a hundred times happier."

"Oh, sweetie," Estrella says. "You know I'm always here for you. The silver eye shadow . . . the usual."

"You know it."

She gave her credit; she always gave credit where it was deserved. An important part of trade. Estrella improved on the face she made to meet the faces that she meets. Cold, fierce, dangerous, but entirely in control. She pats her spiky hair and kisses Estrella on her smooth matte cheek.

Rich makes his way into the garden.

"Fabulous as always . . . and Estrella, what about a little touch for me?"

"Why not . . . I don't reserve myself for the ladies," she says, and Quin wants to say, Oh, don't waste your breath, he's not for you . . . but if you have a younger brother. She watches him look at himself in the mirror. How he loves himself, she thinks, how he loves the way he looks. If he could have licked his own reflection in the mirror, he'd have done it.

He'd brought frosted glasses of iced tea with a sprig of mint for her and Valerie, and she takes her seat at the side of the small glass table across from Valerie. What a cliché, she thinks, the dyed-blond bob . . . like every anchorwoman from Fox to CNN . . . what a way to make yourself forgettable. Which Valerie deserved to be.

Willow Moonstone and Alicia Spence make their way to the table.

"Rich," Quin calls over her shoulder. "We need two more glasses."

The two women greet her perfunctorily; there is no presence of good feeling, just the merest acknowledgment of a common goal. She would have liked to have some sort of connection with Alicia; she was interested in her; she wanted to tell her that really, they had a lot in common . . . Alicia was ferociously against affirmative action, insisting that people take responsibility and not be given special favor for things that happened before they were born, she railed against rap and hip hop and boys wearing their jeans so you could see their underwear . . . railed against pregnant teens. She wanted people to take their lives in their own hands, just as Quin did.

But she could tell Alicia actively disliked her. She knew when it had happened; when they first met, Quin, fascinated by the stiff helmet of straightened hair, put a hand out and patted Alicia's head and said, "I love your hair." Well, that was something women did . . . what was so terrible? But Alicia had pulled away as if Quin's touch had been a burn. She wonders how much time it takes for Alicia to straighten her hair; if it's uncomfortable; how you get a comb through it. She admires her upper arms, which, as Alicia is in her thirties, are in no danger of looking stringy. Willow Moonstone, as always, looks overdressed; the loose long-sleeved Indian print top, the endless rows of beads, her hair gray and frizzled, shoulder length.

"So, Quin, can you give us a preview . . . I mean, you've told us you have a surprise, something special . . . so. Can you let me in?" Valerie says.

"No spoilers, the effect of your surprise will make everything stronger."

The cameramen position themselves. The sound techs clip mikes and move speakers. The director tells Rich to join the women and makes a dispirited signal to begin.

"Hi there, this is *Morning Circle*. I'm Valerie Singleton with Alicia Spence and Willow Moonstone, and today . . . as I've promised . . . is a very special day.

"We're here in the beautiful cactus garden of our very own Quin Archer, who's graciously invited us into her home today. But first, Quin, maybe you'd take us around your garden . . . you've won a number of prizes for it, in addition to all your other accomplishments. I guess you get tired of people asking, 'How do you do it?'"

"Well, the garden is more a pleasure than a chore, because I just love my cactuses. I love them and I admire them. They're the most self-sufficient of plants . . . the prickles make people keep their distance, but they have a function, they nourish the plant itself . . . and then no promises, just as you least expect it . . . a beautiful flower."

"Would you say you identify with your cactuses, then? Self-sufficient, maybe a little prickly, but full of lovely surprises."

"Why Valerie, what a very nice thing to say. I can't tell you when I've had a compliment that pleased me more."

I wonder where she came up with that, Quin thinks. I wouldn't have thought there was room for it in that tiny brain.

"And here comes her gorgeous hunk of a husband, Rich MacParland. Rich is one of the stars of our local theater group Two Thousand Miles Off Broadway. Who can forget his hilarious performance as Felix in *The Odd Couple* and then, the next year he just tugged at our heartstrings as the sheriff in *A Trip to Bountiful*. And that's another admirable thing about this power couple: they share things . . . originally Rich worked for Quin at Tough Love . . . that was what the gym was called, and now, as her career in broadcasting has taken off, he's taken major responsibility . . . a new look, a new name change. What do you call it now, Rich?"

"Love Your Sweat," Rich says, flashing his expensive smile.

"I like that a lot better than Tough Love," says Willow Moonstone. "It's much more inviting."

"Great, great," Valerie says. "So one memorable example of their partnership was Quin's participation in a talk back when Two Thousand Miles Off Broadway, under the direction of the very talented Julie Gregg, presented their version of *King Lear*. You had one of the leads, as I recall, Rich . . . am I right?"

"Oswald," he says.

"They were considering letting him play the Fool but they were afraid that would be typecasting," Quin says.

Rich's eyes harden, but he laughs and lands a fake punch on Quin's bare arm.

Two Thousand Miles Off Broadway. How she loathed them. A bunch of self-deceived no-talents thinking they're bringing culture to the hinterlands. Bad enough when they were just amateurs, but then they roped in that idiot Julie Gregg, who taught drama at the community college . . . urging them to push themselves, to challenge themselves . . . so, of course, they do *King*

Lear. How they slaughtered the language, how they adored their wigs and makeup . . . Julie had the bright idea of Quin doing a talk back after the last performance, and Rich said, "Honey, just do this for me . . . ," and she went along with it . . . he was owed it, it was justice, and she prided herself on being just. And so the stupid girl thought she'd trip Quin Archer up: "King Lear is a play about forgiveness . . . and you have a very special take on forgiveness."

She'd wiped the floor up with them. "The whole thing is a bunch of hooey," she'd said. "The father's an egomaniac; the two daughters see that, only Cordelia . . . purer-than-thou, can't see that there's no point trying to make moral capital with someone like that.

It was quite a sensation, that talk back." Valerie holds up an article from the *Brimstone Gazette.* "Reality TV Host calls *Lear* Baloney Stew."

"Well, what I said was the whole thing was just baloney. From the beginning. Obviously, the guy is out of his gourd, so just play along with him, the one that really cheesed me off was Cordelia . . . just a vain little girl, oh so honest . . . I won't be like my sisters, just giving him what he wants so they could get what they want. Refusing the fair trade: he wants praise, they want land. What's the problem? No, she has to go all heroic, and everything starts from there. And so he cuts her off . . . and at the end, she dies trying to rescue him, and they forgive each other, 'No cause, no cause.' Blah blah blah and boo hoo hoo. All unnecessary."

"I would have thought you'd like the character of Edmund," Alicia says.

"Oh, Alicia, I didn't know you were a Shakespearean scholar."

Alicia gets that cold look that can actually, momentarily,

throw Quin off balance. "What about me, exactly, makes you think I wouldn't know my Shakespeare?"

How annoying . . . you would think that she'd never play the race card, but occasionally she does. But Quin won't fall for it . . . the "Gotcha, see you're really a racist." "It's just that I don't know you very well, and I mainly think of you as a successful business-woman . . . it's one more sign of your versatility. One more sign that you went after what you wanted and got it."

Gotcha. There is nothing for Alicia to say. But she wants some kind of fight.

"You haven't answered my question."

"I prefer Edmund to Cordelia, if you like, but they all end up badly . . . that's tragedy, which is not the Shakespeare I most like, some flaw that gets in the way of happiness. It's a bad lesson for people. With sense and rational choices, the whole tragedy could have been avoided. It wasn't in the stars, as Shakespeare knew when he knew better."

"Fascinating, but let's not get stuck there. Quin, what is there that you want to tell us about the revelation you're going to make on your show?"

"Don't try to trick me, Val, we're too old friends for that. No spoilers. What I want to talk to you about, what's the most important lesson from my life, is not the harm that was done to me . . . which you'll find out about on *PAYBACK* . . . but that I pulled myself up out of it. And didn't get caught in the coun-terculture swamp, which I wandered into because of the times, because I hadn't yet found the philosophy that changed, that organized, my life."

"You mean the philosophy of Ayn Rand."

"Yes. Briefly: that Man . . . and I say *Man,* not the politically correct alternative . . . through will and reason can achieve happiness . . . and that there's nothing else. And to get rid of the destructive romance about the '60s, which we're still stuck in."

"Tell us more."

She's ready for this. She plotted it all: the false history she'll sell as reality. She knew just where to go. It had irritated her enormously that the National Book Award had been given to Patti Smith, a rock star, not a writer. *Just Kids.* A love song to immaturity and depravity. She had read it like a training manual. She'd created a whole file on her computer: *Just Kids.* Copied out images, details, the most unsavory, the most ridiculous. The National Book Award. A best seller. There seemed to be an endless appetite for the most degraded parts of the '60s and '70s. Well, she could use that. Her greatest talent was knowing what would sell. So she would sell Patti Smith's life as her own.

"Well, I ran away from home at sixteen . . . you'll find out why on the show . . . and made my way to New York. To the Chelsea Hotel, which somehow I'd heard about, it was in the air . . . a kind of magnet for sick depraved weak people who wanted to wallow in each other's filth."

"Are you willing to talk more about it?" says Willow, always, Quin thinks, disgusted, the comforting consoler.

"I'm more than willing, Willow, I'm eager, because as you know one of my major crusades is to expose the lie that drug use is benign, or even productive. So I'll take you through it, briefly, if we have the time."

"The show is yours, Quin."

You bet it is, thinks Quin. I've seen to that.

"Let's see . . . I arrived in New York, sixteen, desperate, and I made my way to Washington Square Park because somehow

I knew that was where hippies gathered, I had this idea that I'd find some musician who'd let me work for him, some kind of roadie . . . remember, I was very young. Well, I did meet someone, I just walked around . . . that's how green I was . . . telling people I had nowhere to stay and asking if they had a spare room.

"I guess I looked pretty prosperous compared to the rest of them . . . they were a ragged and filthy lot, and I still had my middle-class clothes . . . I remember I had this pair of red boots that impressed everyone . . . I guess they thought they could steal them while I slept.

"Anyway, I go home with this guy and this girl . . . I'm thrilled, as you can imagine, like I have my own gang, some kind of made-for-TV movie . . . they take me to this loft . . . the first thing they do is roll a joint, I'd never smoked marijuana before and I get sort of scared, but really hungry. I had only eaten candy bars . . . and I think, oh, this is my new family. And they ask me if I have 'bread,' and I think they want to make sandwiches, but they laugh and pinch my cheek and say, money honey and they start singing, money honey, and I'm so stupid I tell them yes and I can pay rent. And they say cool, we're all artists, we'll share . . . they convince me that I'm a poet and I participate in the endless readings they give. One of them makes films . . . he has some kind of camera he stole from his father, another one takes pictures with a Polaroid . . . he panhandles to get money for film, and the girl draws . . . wispy figures of nudes, until she moves into actual pornographic renderings. Artists. Phooey. Rembrandt was an artist. Victor Hugo was an artist. These were just a bunch of lazy self-indulgent spoiled brats, 'just kids,' and they refused to grow up.

"And that period of my life begins. I console myself that basically they drugged me, because the first thing we did in the morning was smoke pot and the last thing we did at night was smoke pot. And the squalor we lived in. There was no plumbing in the loft. We had to pee in cups. We took showers maybe once a week at the Y. I remember there was a stove, not connected, and a refrigerator, not connected, and when you opened the doors they were just infested with roaches so we just closed the doors and sprayed roach spray . . . God, I can still smell it. The thing is, when you're dirty, you attract animals . . . mice, and then . . . I have to admit everyone seemed to be having sex with everyone . . . there were always strangers sleeping on the floor . . . but there was nothing exciting about it, it was just something you had to do to prove you weren't square . . . and then one day I woke up and my private parts were covered with what looked like little shellfish . . . crabs, they were called. And then we all came down with lice. I had very long hair at the time . . . I wore it in a braid down my back . . . and when we all got lice, in one of my stoned hazes, I decided to just cut my braid off, and one of the artists said, 'Can I have it? I can use it.' And he made an 'art piece' of my braid, with lice, he polyurethaned it and put it in Plexiglas. He called it *Lousy Braid* . . . that was art. So one of the lies people tell about marijuana is that it leads to creativity. That was the kind of creativity it leads to. Fake self-indulgence; no great art ever came from marijuana."

"What about Dylan," says Willow.

"Dylan Thomas was an alcoholic, not a drug addict," says Quin, playing the "I'm so refined I don't take any notice of popular culture."

"No," Willow says, as if she were correcting a slow child. "Bob Dylan. He won the Nobel Prize."

Quin knows she is an excellent mimic. So she growls out, in her Dylan Voice, "She aches just like a woman, but she breaks just like a little girl." That's poetry? That's 'Shall I compare thee to a summer's day' . . . 'Bright star, would I were as steadfast as thou art.'"

"Well, everyone has their own idea of what makes art," Willow says.

"Yes," says Quin, "that's the problem."

"So, Quin, how did you get from here to there?"

"Well, you could say it was a lucky accident, but you know what I say, you make your own luck. Luck is a horse and it comes galloping by your house and either you jump on its back or you let it run off. It was winter . . . I'd been living with these people or some version of them, we kept moving from squat to squat, and I was always the one that tried to make some order, and one day I'd just spent the morning trying to get rid of the roaches and the mouse droppings, and I came back and someone had just left plates of food on the floor and I saw mice heading toward them, and I just got furious, but no one was supposed to care about these things, so I walked out, I thought, Just walk it off, we're all friends, we're all family . . . but I couldn't get over my anger, my sense that I was sacrificing myself for . . . for what? I asked myself. It was very cold and I kept walking. And I passed this store that sold ski equipment and clothes and all of a sudden I realized I'd been a really good skier and I missed it terribly at that moment, and there was a sign in the door HELP WANTED . . . and because I knew a lot about skiing I got the job. And my boss was the one who encouraged me to read Ayn Rand . . . he gave each of his employees a copy of *Atlas Shrugged* when they were hired. And that, you can say, was the beginning of everything."

"Amazing, truly amazing," Valerie says.

"Quite a journey," Willow says. "I guess you arrived where you were always supposed to be."

"You've come a long way," says Alicia, grudgingly.

"Quin Archer . . . our very own Quin Archer, I know you're all eager to find out about the secret she's kept all these years. Keep your eye out for her special program . . . airing when?"

"Not sure . . . there are still a lot of loose ends."

"But knowing you, Quin, they'll be nicely tied up."

"You can count on it," Quin says. She mimes tying a bow and pulls the ends of it tight.

Tight.

PART V

New Canterbury, Rhode Island

April 2018

S he lets the dog out.

The sun is white in a veiled sky. It is seven o'clock; the twenty-third of April 2018, as Jasper would have said, "the year of, if not *our* Lord, then someone's." She has awakened on her own; no need for an alarm; there is no need for her to be anywhere until three thirty, when she will pick her grandson up from school, take him to karate, prepare dinner for him; tonight, he will sleep at her house, and tomorrow she will take him to school. His parents, after a long day's work, will have a night out. Date night, they call it. She is of use, most importantly to Maeve and Marcus and Leo. She is of use as a volunteer, a word she dislikes and is uncomfortable using to describe herself; when she was young, it was a synonym for a woman who valued herself so little she refused to ask for payment. But she tells herself, she had her work, she earned her money, it is all right to volunteer. At the library, she mostly mends books, a shocking number about to be thrown away because of rough treatment. Sometimes, if one of the real librarians hasn't shown up, she works at the desk.

The library is in the same building as it was when she was growing up, a Federalist architect's dream of chaste abundance, large, high rooms, insisting on seriousness. But in other ways it is radically different. As a child, it never would have occurred to her that a library meant anything else but books. Some of her happiest childhood memories were made in this library; walking through the high arched door, at first holding her father's hand, "Good morning, Miss Hilbury." Miss Hilbury, the librarian with her blue-gray or taupe cardigans in all seasons, her distressingly bitten nails, her cat's-eye glasses, Miss Hilbury abashed by Agnes's father, the professional librarian, trained as she is not, the head of the Providence Public Library, in love with him, perhaps. The smell of books, a bit unfresh, but precious in its unfreshness, the colors of the bindings, the first turn of the first page.

At first, her father helped her choose books, but soon he was careful to let her roam, to make no suggestions, and by the time she was ten, he would leave her alone and make his way to the local history section. It was a different kind of pleasure to hear Miss Hilbury say, "Agnes, I was thinking this book might interest you." Knowing that she was thought of by an adult not tied to her by blood. Most often, the books Miss Hilbury chose were biographies of nineteenth-century reformers. Elizabeth Cady Stanton. Dorothea Dix, Jane Addams. Her parents made fun of Miss Hilbury, who always answered your questions in the quintuple affirmative, "Yesyesyesyesyes." She had perhaps never been known to say no; they were sure she dreamed of Agnes's father "in her lonely narrow bed." They giggled every time Agnes pre-

sented a new biography of a new reformer, but Agnes loved those
books: they made her believe that she one day would do something courageous, DEFIANT, SURPRISING ALL THOSE WHO
HAD THOUGHT SHE WAS ONLY WELL BEHAVED. By the
time Agnes was twelve, she was going to the library alone, and
her secret with Miss Hilbury was her appetite for a series called
"Career Romances for Young Moderns." The careers were different; the romances always the same. *Nina Grant, Pediatric Nurse,
Ardeth Livingstone, Cub Reporter.* Always the young, feisty, terrify-
ingly competent young woman has to work "under" a sarcastic
demanding man who gives her a hard time . . . but she gives as
good as she gets, until some act of nature . . . a slip in the hospital
corridor, a storm forcing a car to the side of the road, forces the
supervising male to come to the rescue, admitting, under the
pressure of the blow nature has dealt the career girl, that he has
always loved her . . . and she admits that she loves him. There
was no sense that after marriage, the career gal would be only a
wife. But it was hinted at.

Now more people come to use the computer, or to take out
DVDs, than to look for or read books. And she has had to learn
that even in the genteel and pristine town of New Canterbury,
the library is the much-needed sanctuary for a group of homeless men and women who squat in an abandoned motel made
up of separate cottages. Many attempts have been made to
get the owner to sell the property, but the owner—he or she
is never given a name when spoken about, known only as "the
owner"—is waiting for the right time, for the right price . . . and
refuses to allow the authorities to turn the homeless out, which
must not be the real reason, because the price of land in New
Canterbury is unbelievable, shockingly high. There is no heat

in the motel cottages, and no water, but twenty-five or so people live in them year-round, and, particularly in the winter, four or five of them make their way every day to the library. The head librarian, Laurel Janssen, a young woman Agnes very much likes, says she makes it a point to have a lot of paperback Westerns, because that's what the homeless men like most. They all seem to be veterans of one of the endless wars—Vietnam, Desert Storm, Iraq, Afghanistan.

Two homeless women visit the library regularly, and Agnes finds them more disturbing than the men. One habitually takes to her place three or four Edith Wharton novels, but she never seems to read more than a page or two. She is a large, shambling woman; winter or summer, she wears a black wool dress that covers her from neck to mid-calf. Her shoes are black cloth with a strap; in warm weather, her white waxy legs are disturbingly visible; in winter, they are hidden by several layers of wool socks. Her face and neck are covered with a foundation much too dark for her; she wears bright blue eye shadow and navy-blue mascara, and it is obvious that she leaves her makeup on for days. Once Agnes came upon her in the bathroom, wiping her armpits with wet paper towels.

Of course, Agnes understood that it was difficult for these people to bathe . . . although the YMCA allowed them in to shower . . . this is something arranged for by Maeve and Christina . . . with Jo's help on the town board. All the people she loves can be of help to these people, but she cannot. For one reason: their smell was a torment to her, and once, the woman in the black dress saw Agnes cough and put a handkerchief to her mouth as she passed by. Her eyes met Agnes's; never had Agnes seen such defeat, a look that dropped straight down into darkness, like a stone dropped into a well . . . a look too defeated even to signal an accusation . . . but Agnes accused herself . . . what kind of person are you . . . what kind of person are you. It was not a gift, to have a sensitive nose . . . she'd inherited it from her mother, who was the one who told her it was a curse . . . bad smells, she told her daughter, were much more disturbing than good smells were delightful. Agnes can't say to anyone, "I simply can't be near these people, my body revolts . . . I do not judge them, I do not, I understand, as Laurel says, how very easy it is to slip off the ladder. But my body will not allow me to be near them . . . the animal I am flees for its life."

As an act of reparation, she keeps in her bag a pair of rubber gloves, and each morning when she arrives, she walks around the property picking up the cigarette butts, the food wrappings, the dirty Kleenex whose provenance she doesn't want to think about, and puts them in a plastic bag, which she leaves in her trunk until she leaves, when she takes it to the town dump with a relief that she knows is disproportionate.

She admires Laurel Janssen; she trained as a librarian, but now her job is part social worker, part nurse. Which Miss Hilbury would never have dreamed of.

She is glad to be of use. It would be very possible for her to be of no use in the world at all.

She's glad that Leo is taking karate, although it was something she would never have thought of for a child of hers. But he is half black, and, as his father reminds her, he has to live with the knowledge that there are many people who, seeing him on the street, would prefer him dead. Leo is small of stature and by nature a conciliator; it assures her that if a bully approaches, Leo could, at least possibly, cause him physical harm.

What does that mean about her, that she approves of the possibility of her beloved gentle grandson doing physical harm? It is something she would never have imagined about herself. Since Maeve's birth she has known that it is impossible to be a truly moral person if you have a child, because you always wish the child's happiness, well-being, more than anything in the world, and you know that, if it came to it, you would sacrifice the lives of any number of strangers' children to protect your own. And that does away with any ideal of objective goodness; yet the opposite would be a monstrosity.

At least once a month, she drives to New York and spends two or three days. Frances, her mother's friend, has moved into a nursing home; her apartment is empty; she urges Agnes to make use of it; she assures her that when she dies it will be hers anyway.

Agnes knows that she is very lucky. She is close to those she most loves. She is of use to them, of use to the books in the library and the people who want to read them. She is over seventy, and it is of the greatest good fortune to be loved, to be of use. And to live in a lovely place.

And yet, the world has never seemed so terrible to her, so ugly and so cruel. Insult was the norm; crudity, the acceptable tone and diction. Last week, she parked her car in front of the library quickly, and it stuck out into the street. When she got into the car in the evening, there was a note under her windshield wipers: "Learn how to fucking park or stay home." She had been shocked; it made her feel dirty and vulnerable. Her less-than-ideal parking had hurt no one, had taken nothing from anyone. And yet someone had been angry enough to tear a sheet from a notebook, write a note, and place it underneath the wiper.

It is because of the president, everyone knows it is because of the president. He has poisoned the air; he has darkened the sky; the horizon seems threatening or unapproachable.

She is ashamed of her country, although she had never thought of herself as particularly patriotic; being American had never been an important part of her knowing who she was. Her earliest memories include the conviction that Europe was the superior place; her most cherished objects were what would be called "foreign": of course, Jasper's perfectly chosen presents: a ceramic doll with soft black hair, dressed in the costume of an Italian peasant; a wooden music box, with a yellow boat on a blue lake on its cover, which, when lifted, played "Santa Lucia." Souvenirs of Frances's many trips abroad: a wax model of London Bridge, a snow globe from the Alhambra, a pair of wooden shoes, handkerchiefs of crisp Irish linen bordered in real lace. Her father drove a Volkswagen; her mother's scent was called Ombre Rose. The books she loved most had illustrations in colors that she knew were European: mauves and teals and soft dove grays. What could America offer that would measure up? Pilgrim figures in joyless black and white, crepe-paper turkeys, punitive Uncle Sams, stories of prosperous, energetic kids—not *children*, no, always *kids*—in loud primary colors that made her want to turn the page. Briefly, when John F. Kennedy was president, she knew what it was to be glad about where you'd been born. But those days were so short, a thousand only, before the day on which almost everyone in her generation knew where they were (not the younger ones, of course): November 22, 1963. The end of brightness, the end of pride.

And she had come of age politically in the years of Vietnam, years in which it was impossible not to be ashamed of your country, the country that murdered its best, that basked in its own superiority like a fat, greased wrestler strutting the ring while his opponent bled beneath his foot. People, mainly Europeans, would insist that she glory in the achievements of American culture. Baseball, they would say, and jazz. Skyscrapers. Abstract expressionism. There were higher skyscrapers now; there was no canvas by Rothko, who moved her deeply, or Pollock or de Kooning, whom she grudgingly respected, that meant a tenth as much to her as the smallest corner of a Bellini, a Filippo Lippi, a Morandi. She had no interest in baseball and had to pretend to care for jazz. She had not been sorry to leave America; had been glad to call Italy her home. It was a relief to pretend to be a citizen of a country no one hated.

But even in the terrible time of Vietnam, it was not this bad. Johnson had seemed diabolical; Nixon a hideous avatar; there had been hatred and violence between those who believed in the war and those who believed it an abomination. And there had been the thousands upon thousands of dead: killed for nothing. Black men shot in their beds in the name of the government. But it was possible to believe that change was coming, inevitably for the better. That was what had changed since then: the belief in possible change.

She was afraid that she was of a people so cruel, or so stupid, or so unconcerned with the fate of the earth, that even her one small patriotism seemed in danger now. She had loved, even more than the great beauties of Rome, the trees of America, the trees she had grown up with. After her sister-in-law Giulietta came to visit, she wrote Agnes, "Thank you for the days of tall, strong trees." Pignut hickory, the largest, her favorite. The purple-red copper beech. The ash and elm, vulnerable to diseases, the stewartia with its silver bark. Her mother had wanted to die looking at these trees, and Agnes had made that happen. It is something she can feel, if not proud of, at least good about, something she can know she has done that is unequivocally good . . . never to weigh as much on the scale as the thing she had done to Heidi . . . that was unequivocally bad.

Her mother had died as she wished: in the sight of her own trees. Agnes hopes they will live after she herself is dead, but she is afraid they won't, because the fate of the earth seems so clearly in jeopardy. When people say, "We have been through dark times before and gotten through them," she thinks always, but nothing like this where the earth itself could turn against us, and it will have been our fault.

Will Leo have to use his karate skills to kill other children for drinkable water? Would it be better to kill someone for drinkable water or to die of thirst? Is this what we have done to our children . . . is this the kind of thought it is now reasonable to contemplate, the kind of choice?

She had come back three years ago, April 2015. She often wonders if she would have made the move . . . if her mother would have . . . if they had known what the outcome of the election of November 2016 would be.

She had come back not only because her mother wanted to, but because she knew that here, and only here, she could be of use. As a restorer, she was quickly becoming an anachronism. More and more friends were dying; she would not have wanted to be a young person in Italy now: its future seemed hopeless or trivial: a country whose major industry was tourism, with its inevitable falsities and corruptions.

And, in the end, she had come back because, for her, the personal weighed most. The people she most loved were here. She was grateful for the meagerness of her gifts; had she been greatly gifted—an artist, a scientist, a politician—she would have had to put people aside, would not have been able to put people first. It is right for someone who has a great gift to put the gift first. But she has always been aware that whatever gifts she had were decidedly minor. A negligible weight in the balance of the great weights of the world.

She knows that she is very lucky. And yet, she finds herself thinking, "It would be quite all right to die." These thoughts happen in the time between waking and getting dressed; usually they are gone by the time she has had her first cup of coffee, showered, taken herself to the couch with more coffee and the book she is reading so that when the dog jumps up on the couch beside her, the enveloping darkness has begun to lift.

Sometimes she is astonished about how much of this is due to the dog.

She would not say to anyone one of the things she—not believes, perhaps, but guesses at—that her dog suggests more strongly than anything else that there is a benevolent force somewhere, above, beyond . . . inaccessible, unconnected to thought or language, unknowable but present, nonetheless. The dog sleeps beside her, conforming her position to Agnes as she moves in the night. She would be mortified if anyone heard her talking to the dog: *I love you, I love you so much, you're the best dog in the world, I am so lucky to have you, you are the most beautiful, the most wonderful, the most intelligent dog in the world.* Nonsense words, a little language nearly devoid of meaning.

The dog arrived one day, in a snowstorm, a blizzard, really, shivering on top of a six-foot drift. She'd heard, in that pure silence that comes at the very end of a snowfall, something crying out, a whimpering, and she saw the dog: pathetic, unprepossessing, utterly in need. At the time, her mother was still alive. "There's a dog stranded out there." Agnes puts on boots, snow pants, parka, mittens, hat. She picks up the whimpering matted creature, takes him in, wraps him in blankets. "Whiskey," her mother says, "and broth." The dog laps the warm mixture. A female. Brown and white. Small. Smelly . . . but she must be warmed and fed before anyone can think of cleaning her.

After the snow is plowed, Agnes takes the dog to the vet—calling Jeanne Larkin, who always knows what to do, to find the name of the vet who cares for her horse. The vet says, "You can put up signs, put an ad in the paper, but she had no collar and she's hardly a candidate for the American Kennel Club. But she's healthy; I put her at about two years old, she'll have a good long life, I predict. I've never seen a more thoroughgoing mutt."

The vet is right. The parts not quite fitting together; one brown eye, one gray-blue, a tail much too long for the squat body, effulgent, luxurious, but in the middle an incongruous black stripe.

She and her mother do their part: they put up signs, they take an ad out in the paper, hoping, praying that no one will respond. No one does. After two weeks, they take the sign down. They get her licensed; they give her shots. She is theirs. They decided to call her Eccomi. *Here I am.* Ecco for short. People think it's Echo . . . but Agnes and her mother know.

Ecco spends her days at Agnes's mother's feet, except when it's time for a walk, in which she pretends to feign interest. She does sniff the ground, but no small wildlife arouses her attention. She is their dog; only Agnes and her mother interest Ecco . . . and it begins, this ridiculous love, this indefensible love. (A child in the developing world could be fed on what they spend on Ecco's food; a child could have a year's medical care on what it cost when the dog got into chocolate at Christmas and ran around like a demonic creature, nearly poisoned, force-fed charcoal, her stomach pumped, to keep her alive.) There was no defending it; there was no explaining it. How happy this dog made her. How good life seemed, after her morning's dread (making the dread seem false, self-indulgent, though it had not been), sitting on the couch with Ecco, with her coffee, her fruit, her toast, reading the Russians, reading George Eliot and Trollope and the Emily Dickinson and Shakespeare she had never gotten around to in all the years, art books whose text she had skipped. She relishes the large leisure, the open days, but not too open, because she is warmed, she is hedged, she is bounded by the love of her daughter, her son-in-law. Her purest passion: Leo, ten years old now, her delight.

She has no idea what will happen after death. She thinks it will be either nothing, something like sleep, or something quite wonderful that our brains are too small to comprehend, since we will not have our bodies, and so will not be what we think of as ourselves. She finds it a useless endeavor to speculate on what will happen. Only, she would like to die before she does something unforgivable. Or no, she has already done that. Something *else* unforgivable. Something even more unforgivable than what she did to Heidi.

The house is very quiet, entirely quiet except for the sounds that are so customary that they are no longer taken in: the settling of the house, the light wind in the branches. Her life is quiet, and she is grateful for that . . . but sometimes the house's quiet shifts its shape, is no longer a balm, a sheltering cloak, but an open pit that could swallow her up, an abyss into which she could disappear, a black sky into which she could be taken up and whirled, boundaryless, forever. She never felt this when her mother was here with her. It's nearly two years since her mother's death, her mother's dying. Her mother had been standing beneath the arbor where her father had planted Concord grapes. She reached up, just above her head, to pick a bunch. And then she fell down . . . and Agnes heard the crash and rushed out to see her mother on the ground, her hands purple from the grapes she'd crushed in her fall. A blank efficiency took Agnes over; she called 911; in a minute, two minutes, the ambulance arrived, but it was over. The EMTs lifted her mother, gently, reverently, and placed her, at Agnes's instructions, on her bed. Agnes called Maeve, and Maeve somehow stepped into the blur and made arrangements for her grandmother's last exit from her home.

In so many ways Agnes feels her mother's presence. When she opens the drawer of what had been her mother's dresser, what she uses now to store the linens only rarely used: cloth tablecloth, cloth napkins, the green cloth bag of silver napkin rings, the embroidered runners Pietro's sister Graziela made, linen hand towels, a clear plastic box of rose-scented sachets, her mother's scent. And the drawers lined with a pink quilted material were saturated with the scent of roses, she is determined that it will be there always: her mother's ghost, friendly, as her mother was, discernable, but finally apart.

She had loved her mother . . . there had never been a time (the commonplace for daughters) that she had not. But when she tried to grasp her mother, to say to herself, "My mother was like this," she disappeared, as if Agnes had tried to grasp a handful of smoke. Death and distance had made her mother no more comprehensible.

When she tried to make a single picture of her mother, she always failed. Her mother was vague, yet she was scientifically precise in her anatomical drawings; gentle, yet an aggressive driver, capable of shocking language if someone cut her off on a highway or took a parking space she had her eye on. Acutely sensitive. Reserved, famously reserved, yet capable of the occasional disturbing confidence whose effect on the listener she seemed entirely unaware of. "My greatest romance was not your father, but my time in college with Jasper and Frances"—not realizing that what she was saying to her daughter was, "There were people whose company was more pleasing to me than yours." The death of Agnes's childhood romance that her mother had always loved her best.

Her mother had always been hopeful, despite the world's evidence. "Things have gotten better, things have gotten better, don't forget that. When I was young, Maeve marrying Marcus would have been a scandal . . . at best, a great anxiety. Now, I'm not saying it's nothing now . . . but it's much, much easier than it was. And Christina and Jeanne . . . unthinkable even when you were young."

Agnes is very grateful that her mother died in June 2016, believing there would be a woman president.

Agnes misses Pietro in a completely different way, a way that is at once more and less physical. He spent very little time in the house, and so he left no scent, no fingerprint. But she had slept beside him for forty years, and sometimes she awakes in the night, cold, or aching, and reaches for him; then she feels the loss of him with an acuteness that robs her of sleep. And night after night for years they had made love. She dreams of sex with him, but waking, sex seems so remote that she thinks it might be something she only dreamed or imagined. She knows that she desired him passionately, but it is hard to call up the sensations those words suggested.

Because he was less reserved than her mother, it would seem that he was more knowable, but, as he had spoken very little about what might be called an inner life, he was, in some ways, even more difficult to comprehend. She misses him at breakfast or when she needs the stepladder to reach something she would have asked him for, or when Leo says something that would be their shared joy.

Thinking of her dead mother, her dead husband, she feels what she so often felt: the impossibility of understanding anyone. The futility of saying, "This person is this, this person is that, this person is not this, this person is not that." The wall that surrounded every life, so that it seemed impossible even to understand yourself, to acknowledge the creature that lurked in the mud, that raised its head in the moments between sleep and waking . . . that, too, was yourself. Was it that no one, even yourself, could ever be entirely known? And yet, you had to try, you had to try to understand, you had to try to determine what in your actions would do harm, what might, just possibly, be of some use. When Heidi Stolz had woken her from sleep, that was what she had failed to do: that faculty of discernment, however partial, had been stolen from her by her unawake brain. You had to try. So often you were wrong, but without the attempt, humans were only brutes, far worse than animals whose inflicted harm seemed to contain no other possibilities.

But even if you tried, there were moments when the vile or

careless beast broke through the covering of—what was it, she wondered . . . civilization, consciousness or conscience, with its ragged claws, its broken teeth?

The public terrors and the private ones. That the planet will destroy itself, that the world's hatreds will destroy it, and that if or when this happens she will be too old or ill to be a help to those she loves, but instead will be a burden to them, that she will learn that Heidi Stolz is someone whose life she has destroyed.

Sometimes it feels like another work: to remind herself each day of her good fortune, to enjoy the moments when the joy of the world brims over—with Leo, in the pond where she swims each day from late May to October with her friends, whom she is lucky enough to live beside. They often congratulate themselves on being able to still take pleasure in each other, although Christina notes that they drink more than they did when they were young. "Let's face it," she says. "Alcohol is the new sex."

Agnes wonders when the shape of that sentence came into vogue. Orange is the new black. Something is the new something. Suggesting a need for, or is it the possibility of, replacement or replaceability.

QUIN HAD FORGOTTEN how much she loathed New England. Their pride at their impossible climate: freezing in the winter, summer days soaked in humidity. Oh, the autumns, they would say, don't you miss having a real fall. Two weeks of color for fifty unlivable ones. Her contempt for fall-foliage week, when people drove for hours to look through their car windows at trees they had no interest in at any other time of the year, staying at bed-and-breakfasts that advertised a fireplace in every room, only most often it was a fireplace with a gas or electric log . . . the talked-over, coveted breakfasts, homemade muffins, homemade popovers—what were popovers, an eggy crust surrounding air. Then maybe a lunch of New England clam chowder—a bowl of white glue with pieces of tough, tasteless mollusk. The trees. The huge, oh-so-prized trees. Choking the clarity of whatever blue sky might occur. What she loved about the desert was its dryness: a landscape violent and broken and exposed, not perpetually sloping and sloppy. How much more preferable were the cactuses she cultivated: clean, sharp needles rather than leaves that grew null and bland and fell, and collected in damp piles year after year, each year's deposit covering the last, becoming what: mulch, mealybugs and worms crawling in and out. If you got through the top layer, damp dead leaves sticking to the bottom of your shoes in that disgusting way. But our trees, our trees, they swooned, in their L.L. Bean boots and L.L. Bean flap hats and L.L. Bean plaid jackets they walked through the woods, adoring the leaves in fall, tapping the maples in spring for inedible syrup.

Self-love hung in the air like a vapor, covered the windows and the railings like scum. Our Pilgrim fathers (she had loved reading about the Salem witch trials when she was a girl), now the PCers had discovered that all the wealth was built on the slave trade and boo hoo hoo, breast beating, oh, we're so sorry that our wealth was from the skin of our brown brothers, nevertheless, we will continue to enjoy it all . . . while saying it's been spoiled for us, but nothing had been spoiled, they'd do it again in a minute if they had the chance.

Everything too small, everything too cold or overheated. She thought of the Christmas parties in her upscale neighborhood.

Oh, they loved her mother . . . the blond athlete, the Northern goddess—the poster girl for what they secretly, ashamedly, adored, what they would have jumped on the bandwagon for in the '30s. Her mother would wait till she was sure she was the last to arrive, and as she stood at the door and looked at them, looked down on them, a hush came over the room, and the hostess would rush up to her and kiss her and the host would hand her a cup of eggnog—mostly rum, don't tell Reverend Sykes—oh, Liesel, how lovely, how lovely, your perfect blond hair, your perfect white skin, your perfect red lips, your perfect long legs (which so many of the hosts had seen in all their glory or at least had dreamed of seeing). Oh, Liesel, oh, Liesel, oh, tell us about Switzerland . . . tell us about the mountains, the wildflowers, the blue, blue skies. Eggnog and cookie parties from one end of the street to the other, and the wives vying with each other for the most absurd Christmas sweaters, perfectly matching their absurd names that would have been fine for a pug or a Pekingese but not these pigeon-breasted, thick-calved matrons . . . still calling themselves Muffy and Sissy and Pokey . . . their bursting pride in the presents they'd specially wrapped for each family: one year Pebble Prothero had gotten everyone a wind-up toy: tin mice at a piano playing "Silent Night." In every den of every man, a team photo of their glory days on the prep school football or lacrosse or tennis team: nothing would ever live up to the days of Andover, of St. Paul's, of Choate or Groton . . . and then Harvard, or for some of the more nativist: Brown. Maybe Princeton, which they said was, "let's face it, really a *southern* school."

The Lydia Farnsworth School had convinced itself that it was different, that it was open-minded, forward looking, unhidebound. But that was another lie. Everything was done to prepare "our girls" for one of the prized colleges . . . or, for the ones who didn't have the brains to write their name on an application, a genteel face-saving alternative: a year abroad, some college in Virginia or Pennsylvania, "which Buffy insisted upon because she could bring her horse."

She'd had contempt for it all as long as she could remember, but occasionally, breaking through, a sickish desperate desire to be part of it, to be given a place. That was what Agnes Vaughan had taken advantage of: the soft weak spot where she put her gently manicured hand—colorless nail polish, a modest engagement ring—the touch that broke through the precious scab that had kept Heidi Stolz safe from grieving over what she could not have, what she knew she was far too good for, but that the sickish spot yearned for, like the spot on a sore throat yearning for the soothing honey, that healed nothing, fed nothing, but provided a temporary palliation.

She hated being here; what made it all worthwhile, more than worthwhile, dressed the wound until it became one of those dueling scars her mother's uncles were said to have prized, was the idea that she, Heidi Stolz—no, she, Quin Archer—would ram through the brilliant glass carapace, lift up the polished stone, revealing what bred and seethed beneath, would shine light through the vapor, bright, painful light that would cause the tender hands of Agnes Vaughan to try to cover her eyes, to keep the punishing clear light from what she could not bear to see. What she didn't have the courage for, the courage to look straight on, to face up to what was there.

She imagines what Agnes Vaughan looks like. Like all those New England women who pride themselves on their plainness. She'll be wearing no makeup; her skin will be mottled with dark spots caused by sun damage: all those days on their precious beach. Her hair will be thin and a dull gray-brown, pulled back in a scrunchie or pinned up in a French twist . . . but wisps of straggly thin hair will always be coming out of the pins. She'll be wearing some loose-fitting shirt . . . some loose-fitting draw-string pants. Birkenstocks or clogs or some version of Mary Janes that Quin stopped wearing when she was eight. The famous shapely hands will be marked by thick blue veins; the nails will be ridged, unmanicured. Her glasses, which she will need for most things now, will be hanging around her neck on a maroon or gray or taupe or navy cord. Quin wonders whether her voice had changed. Too often for her comfort she had heard Agnes Vaughan's voice, first comforting, "You're really very gifted," then the words of complete abandonment, "How could you have let that happen?"

She gets out of the car and walks up the stone path to the Vaughans' front door. She hadn't counted on the strong response that lodges in her ribs, like a lit match held behind them. A burn-ing, but with none of the rush and energy of a real burn. This is where everything happened. Where everything was lost. The place, the actual locus of abandonment. Of betrayal. The betrayal worse than her actual violation. That had been a shock, but it was a shock delivered by a stranger; the knife had pierced the flesh, but then had been quickly withdrawn; no familiar hand twisted it, kept it lodged. Here, on the very stones she walked now, she had lost all faith in the possibility that she was, if not loved, then well regarded. Never again would she believe that she could count on anyone; all praise, each look that par-took even for a moment of approval or regard, any indication of fellow feeling or admiration must be held back, cut off; she was a fortress, one of those castles with only slits for windows, behind each one an armed soldier, his arrow ready for the next approach. She would not say that something had died there; she would not indulge in those high, heated words. Rather, some-one had been born there, a creature born armed and bristling, a new species whose success depended on believing in no one, and nothing.

Joe Mangan, her cameraman, follows ten steps behind her, the camera at his shoulders. She rings the doorbell; the tone is an insistent double ring. And she remembers now; the knocker in the shape of a dolphin. She uses the knocker; four sharp raps, redundant, perhaps because of the tone of the bell, but somehow satisfying.

The door opens. It is Agnes Vaughan.

What Quin had imagined: the style of her hair, the looseness of her clothes, her glasses on a string around her neck: all that was right. But for one thing she had not been prepared.

Agnes Vaughan is beautiful.

"Yes?" she says, her smile uncertain and yet not unwelcoming.

"Are you Agnes Vaughan?"

"Well, yes, I am, I suppose, or you could say I was. Now I'm Agnes di Martini."

"And I am Quin Archer. But you knew me as Heidi Stolz."

Agnes steps back from the doorway. She puts one hand to her throat. Her eyes close for a moment, and then open; she fixes them steadily on the two people at her door.

And she says, "So here you are."

~~~

WOULD SHE CALL what she was experiencing a fall; certainly there was a sense of downward movement, the shock, expected but not really, of a hard landing; it was as if, in the forty years since she had last seen Heidi Stolz, she had been sitting on a window ledge on the top floor of a very high building, waiting for what she knew would come sometime: the push off the dependable surface, then the free fall, taking no time, everything so fast that the pavement when it arrived seemed always to have been arriving, and, stunned, you lay motionless, waiting for someone to tell you whether you were alive or dead. She has to force herself not to keep her eyes closed. But even with eyes fully opened she can't see what is in front of her, can't see what she knows she should be seeing. Only available to her sight: a swarm, a stew, a background of a poisoned green, and spinning through it, whorls or circles: blood red, and lines or lightning shapes, purple and flashing. And through her mind go the words, "This is the hour of lead"—had it really been only this morning she had read that poem—because what she feels closing around her is a dense impenetrable casing . . . impeding movement, making each breath a risk, a near impossibility. And another kind of lead: the leaden sound of a struck gong, deep, and resonant and resonating out and out. She would like to close her eyes, put her hands over her ears, take herself to the couch and rock back and forth in desperation. But someone is at the door. Two people. Heidi and someone with a camera. They are at her door. They are here to see her. They will become her guests.

How ridiculous they sound in her mouth, the words that follow, the only possible words, required by convention, good manners, the slightest pressure not to appear uncivilized.

"Come in. Can I get you something? Coffee, tea. A glass of water, perhaps."

"Coffee would be great," Joe Mangan says, and Quin is irritated with him . . . she doesn't want him to be sympathetic to Agnes, to be seduced by her as Heidi had been seduced; she's learned that the cameraman's unconscious bias toward the subject influences the way the subject appears on the screen; if the cameraman is on the subject's side, she's more attractive; if not, her flaws show clear. Don't take anything from her, she wants to say. Quin has only minutes to do what she knows she is very good at: calibrating her persona. Preparing a face to meet the faces that she meets. It will be a challenge with Agnes, because Quin has based her career on rejecting the legitimacy of the posture of victimization . . . and yet the subject must be seen to have suffered, but in a way that hasn't leached them of energy, of the force that demands retribution. She has learned, though, that her audience doesn't like a subject on the attack, or someone who appears to be doing so much better than the person they're confronting that the confrontation seems not like justice but like persecution.

Agnes Vaughan . . . Miss Vaughan . . . is sitting on the couch, her feet flat on the floor, her knees closed, her hands folded on her lap, a perfect little girl, Quin thinks, a perfect lady. But the hands are clasped in tension, and Quin sees with pleasure that she has pricked the skin of the famous Agnes Vaughan composure, as you might prick the skin of a chicken you were roasting, to test for doneness. She will prick the skin again, more deeply this time.

"Before we begin happy hour, Agnes, I need to tell you why we're here."

She's learned that saying the subject's name with a particularly insinuating tone often knocks the subject off balance. But it frightens her a bit to say the name, Agnes . . . only the second time she's said it aloud in forty years, and the word in her mouth, then in the world, takes on a new reality, a new power, which she would prefer it not to have. "Yes, please," Agnes says. It takes all her courage to look directly at Heidi.

"I am the host of a TV show called *PAYBACK*. We're based in Brimston, Arizona, but we can be seen nationwide on YouTube. The premise of the show is that someone comes to us who is try- ing to redress the injustice of someone in his or her past having done them harm and gotten away with it: caused our subject suf- fering and did not suffer, maybe never even thought again of the person they harmed. My idea is that the only way to overcome the curse of victimization is to demand, and to receive, justice. Then, and only then, can the chapter be satisfactorily closed."

"I thought of you, Heidi, you must know that. You have never been far from my thoughts."

"It's Quin. Heidi is dead . . . I killed her when I moved west."

"I'm sorry, then . . . Quin . . . but I don't want you to think that I forgot you, forgot what I did to you . . . I never forgot. I've regretted that moment all my life, I know I did you harm; you trusted me, and I betrayed your trust. I am more sorry than I can ever say. And, of course, if there's anything I can do to make it up to you, you're perfectly right, that would only be just. And so if you want me to be on your show, of course I will agree to it. I'll agree to anything you want."

This isn't the response Quin was hoping for; it isn't the kind of response that makes good television. There's no arc, no move- ment, if the accused admits their guilt in the first minutes of the interview. Nowhere for Quin to go that doesn't seem like kicking a dead horse. She will have to find a point of resistance in Agnes; something she can prick and burst and watch the splash, the mess that is good television.

"Yes, well, there are some papers we'll need you to sign. Release forms. My colleague will be here shortly . . . I'll just phone him . . . you have good cell reception here?"

"Yes, I think so, I've never had any problems."

Quin reaches into her black patent leather clutch for her orange cell phone. Agnes is surprised that her long fingernails . . . orange to match her dress, her phone . . . don't impede her quick pressing of the buttons that will make her assistant appear.

"We're ready for you. It's a go," Quin says.

"I'll just get some shots of your house, then, if that's okay," Joe Mangan says.

"Yes, of course, anything," Agnes says. "I'll get you the coffee."

"A glass of cold water for me," Quin says. "No ice."

She's heard people call her the ice queen. She likes that. She sees herself, cold, sharp, discouraging the idea of touch.

"We don't have a lot of light here . . . we're going to have to bring some other equipment," Joe says.

"Yes, these old windows . . . they don't let in much light. It's an eighteenth-century house. They were reluctant to build houses with a lot of windows; glass was expensive and for a while there was a window tax: your property tax was based on the number of windows in your house."

"And better not to let the light in, better to keep reality out," Quin says.

Nothing in this room is bright; the walls are the color of sage; the carpets a faded rose and blue; the furniture a darker velvet sage; the lamps are small, the shades and ivory linen; there is,

she notices, no overhead lighting. On the wall—was it possible—
the portrait of an ancestor, a tousle-haired nineteenth-century
boy, everything in tones of brown except for the shocking white
of his shirt, the surprising redness of the full lips. Another small
painting on the wall: a stream, some woods, dusk . . . a rower
and a boat, again only the white shirt providing a place for lightness. On the shelves a white bowl of black stones; on the table
a blue and white bowl of potpourri; rust-colored pillows on the
couch, a russet-colored ottoman.

The cameraman follows Agnes into the kitchen, and she
resents the intrusion, feels the privilege, at least in relation to
him, of a small refusal.

"I'll just be a moment," she says, closing the kitchen door.

There is a pounding in her skull, so insistent, so relentless,
that she can't imagine it won't result in permanent damage. She
takes down the bottle of Advil from the cabinet to the right of
the stove; she takes three. Which she usually only allows herself
after dental work or with an ear infection.

The name pounds and presses. Heidi Stolz. Quin Archer.

Whom I have harmed.

Who has, at long last, come for her revenge.

Oh no, revenge is wrong. It's only justice.

The sharp bitter smell of the coffee seems like an intrusion
from another realm, the ordinary realm where, just this morning, she had been herself, letting the dog out, drinking coffee,
reading poetry. Now who is she? Now who will she be?

What she has been waiting to become. Completed. Punished.
Forgiven? Forgiveness is something she doesn't dare even to ask
for, is quite sure she won't be found to deserve.

She fills the kettle; puts it on the stove; measures the coffee into the glass cylinder and waits for the water to boil. She hopes it never will, because the sound of the whistling kettle will be her signal to go back into that other room, that other world. The world of punishment. The world where she, the criminal, will be judged and, she is sure, condemned.

How strange Heidi looks, she thinks, or no, Quin . . . what must she be thinking of to present herself that way, a way so insistent on harshness, on refusal, the demand for distance. The too-bright colors of her dress, her lips, her fingernails. The high heels . . . can they possibly be comfortable? Aren't they, certainly, a punishment she willingly inflicts on herself? The over-black, overlong eyelashes . . . as if the eyes themselves were not the point, were to be protected, concealed, kept from the possibility of any sort of revelation. The hair: a weapon; silver-white spikes, like small knives growing from a skull that insists that you remember it is bone . . . everything in Heidi-Quin refuses the suggestion of a caress, the giving or receiving of any tenderness at all. And Agnes understands that this is planned, and that this deliberate choice to make a weapon of herself, to keep herself invulnerable, inviolate, is her fault, because she had murdered the tender girl, the girl who showed her teacher glimpses of her yearning, of her vulnerable thirst for a connection. Which Agnes Vaughan had also killed.

I didn't mean to, I didn't mean to . . . she wants to cry out. But to whom? Certainly not to Heidi. To Quin. Who would say, quite rightly, looking at her with the strange curtained eyes, "That doesn't matter in the least."

The doorbell rings, and for a moment Agnes has trouble placing the sound, so far is she from anything she would have called familiar.

"Hey, sweetie pie," she hears a male voice say, answered by Quin's "Hey yourself."

Sweetie pie. How strange, the words connecting in any way to Quin. She is certain of one thing: the two words must be meant ironically.

It is required that she leave the kitchen, open the door, and walk into her own living room, which she feels is no longer hers but an occupied city now, its walls broken down, entirely invaded.

Joe Mangan is walking around the yard, looking at things, choosing what his camera will record. So the male voice must belong to this new man.

He is very good looking in a way that strikes Agnes as slightly unbelievable. The symmetries are perfect, too perfect perhaps; the high cheekbones in exactly the right relationship to the startling blue eyes, the blond hair—surely it can't be natural, and she tells herself that it is a fault of hers to be critical of a man bleaching his hair, why not if it's all right for women—with just the right proportion of gray, the light blue shirt harmonizing so perfectly with the startling blue eyes, the gray trousers picking up exactly the right tones of the shirt, the eyes, the proportional gray of the blond hair.

She has never seen such white teeth, and the whiteness seems another kind of invasion in the dim light of her familiar room. She wonders if he trimmed his moustache so that it became a frame, an emphasizing frame, for the white teeth. But he is, she sees, trying to be ingratiating, and there is no reason not to take the extended hand . . . the hairs on his forearms, she notices, are dark brown, nearly black.

"Rich MacParland," he says. "The prince consort. Mr. Quin Archer to his friends."

Agnes knows she is supposed to laugh, or at least smile conspiratorially, but numbness has overtaken her, and the best she can muster is a languid nod.

"I'm Agnes di Martini. You may know me as Agnes Vaughan. But of course, we've never met."

"No, but I risk the cliché, 'It's so good to meet you. I've heard so much about you.'"

"Agnes is making coffee. My husband is addicted . . . I've tried to get him to switch to green tea, one of the best antioxidants, but it's his funeral."

"My wife is kind enough to select my allowable vices."

Agnes understands that this kind of rough bantering is the tonality of their marriage, and there is no need for her to respond.

"I'll get the coffee, then," she says.

She stands in front of the cupboard where her mugs are kept. The task of choosing exactly the right mug seems daunting—everything will be noted, everything will be judged. She takes down the wooden tray her mother brought back from one of her Roman visits; on this tray, she'd carried cups (tea for her father, lemon, sweet, and for her mother, dark espresso, with the three teaspoons of sugar she preferred) to her parents, who had both been ill in this house, both died here. She would like to think of herself as a child, flinging herself on the beloved ghosts for protection. But there is no protection possible; it would be wrong to wish to be protected, to be spared, from what might plausibly be called her just deserts.

"Is it your first time in Rhode Island, Mr. MacParland?" she asks, hoping her voice does not betray the fear that has made her throat feel so constricted that each word must be squeezed out.

"Rich . . . nobody uses last names anymore unless they've just been arrested. Yes, it is . . . I'm a midwesterner, myself. Omaha, Nebraska, if you can believe your eyes and ears."

"How long have you been married, if you don't mind my asking . . . and once again, if you don't mind, Quin, I'm very eager to know how you've been . . . I mean, how you got where you are now . . . such an interesting place you seem to have arrived at."

"I'd like to chime in here," Rich says. "My wife is too modest to give herself the full credit for the remarkable success she's made of her life. Talk about the right place at the right time. We met in '82, just as Arizona was really taking off . . . we met because she opened a gym in Brimston . . . having the fantastic good sense to hire me as a manager. It was five more years before she'd let me carry her over the threshold."

Quin snorts. "You've never carried me anywhere."

"But to continue, she then got into real estate, at, again, just the right moment, did very well at it, as she does well at anything, and then became a feature on the local morning talk shows until the heads of the station offered her a place on one of them, until . . . this is the genius part . . . she came up with the idea for PAYBACK, this show you're going to be part of . . . Quin won't tell you this, but she's absolutely a local celebrity . . . everyone talks about her, people are glued to their sets, they build their days around PAYBACK, and they talk about it for weeks afterward."

Quin has taken an emery board out of her purse and is filing her nails. Is she really bored by this recounting of her triumph, Agnes wonders, or is this part of their act, the song-and-dance routine they have, Agnes sees, perfected over years?

"So yes, he's got it mostly right, and I'm glad we're getting this over with because this is the part of my life that won't be in the show we're doing with you because my audience knows it all . . .

what we're going to focus on is what happened to me after I ran away from you."

"What you've done with your life is quite admirable," Agnes says.

Quin won't let her stay in this cool spot; she wants her dancing on the burning coals she has prepared for her.

"It took discipline and courage to get where I am from where I came from. I won't give you the details, I'm saving them for the show, suffice to say that when I left here, I lived in absolute squalor for seven years."

Rich unzips a thin black leather envelope and lays some papers on the table. "These are release forms for you to sign, Agnes, if you will, and maybe we should firm up a schedule."

He hands Agnes a green enamel fountain pen. Usually, Agnes is fond of fountain pens, but this one seems too thick, its point too large and cumbersome. She briefly reads the words on the page. She agrees that she will not sue, she agrees that anything she says is true. Yes, she thinks, it is easy to say yes to both.

"We're staying in Newport," he says, "our crew hasn't been to this part of the world and we thought it would be kind of a hoot for them to see how the rich lived in their versions of McMansions."

She understands his response to Newport; it always seemed a hymn to wrong-minded excess; why build chateaux based on the domains of Renaissance French nobility whose domains were a long river when you were at the sea and lived in the place only for a few weeks in summer?

"I hope you enjoy it . . . I believe there are some first-rate restaurants . . . I haven't been in years, but I could ask my daughter. She and her husband try all the new restaurants."

"Your daughter, Maeve," Quin says.

It alarms Agnes to hear Quin say Maeve's name.

"Yes, Maeve, she is a doctor here in practice with Christina Datchett, you remember she taught science?"

"We don't have children," Quin says. "And I suppose I have you to thank for that. In my squalid years, I contracted PID, which rendered me infertile. And so, if I hadn't lived the way I lived after I left you, who knows?"

"I'm very sorry," Agnes says. She sees that Rich is a bit uneasy with this turn of the conversation; perhaps it's a raw subject, and he is not comfortable mentioning it publicly . . . but that would be strange, because it is, after all, their business, to make the private public.

"I'm going to want to shoot some footage at the school," Quin says, and Agnes sees she's someone used to giving orders and having her orders unquestioningly obeyed. "Who do you think we need to get in touch with about that?"

"Well, Jo Walsh is still the head . . . she's retiring in two years, but she's still in charge. I could certainly speak to her."

"Miss Walsh. MIZZ Walsh, the only one who insisted on that ridiculous syllable, which always sounded like some slave on a plantation . . . the Red Queen, we used to call her. Pretending she was interested in free speech but if you disagreed with her, she'd just beat you down with arguments until you gave up from exhaustion. So you still see your old friends."

"Yes, I'm lucky in that. And you remember Christina Datchett . . . as I said, my daughter's in practice with her. And you remember Jeanne Larkin. She and Christina were married last year."

Jeanne Larkin. The words hit a vulnerable spot, Jeanne Larkin, the only student she'd admired, Jeanne Larkin, who wouldn't give her the time of day, even the day they were both on the train, the day that led to everything.

"Well, isn't that all just cozy . . . was that going on while they were student and teacher?"

"No," Agnes says, more defensively than she wishes. "No, not at all, they met up again when Christina was in medical school and Jeanne was a graduate student."

Quin sniffs. "Whatever," she says.

"So, Agnes, let's say we'll speak on the phone tomorrow, and perhaps we can start the shoot the day after."

"Of course," Agnes says, "whatever you like."

"It's not about liking," Quin says. "It's about good TV."

She closes the door after them. She moves to the couch and calls the dog to sit beside her. She buries her head in the dog's neck.

She will have to call people now. Maeve, Jo, Christina . . . she'll have to gather them together and say—what? "The oddest thing has happened." And then what, say what to Maeve, who has never heard of Heidi Stolz, has no idea of that stain on her mother's past, or its power. Say what to Jo and to Christina, who had never sympathized with Heidi, had doubted, as had Letitia Barnes, that what Heidi had said happened to her had happened. Who'd thought that Agnes's frantic trips to New York trying to find Heidi were excessive, neurotic, a tribute to some stale, Puritan past. So she hadn't talked to her friends about Heidi after the first days, hadn't talked to anyone, had made a new life for herself in Italy, become a different person as Heidi had, moving to Arizona, becoming Quin. Agnes had kept things to herself, and keeping them to herself had seemed to her the only honor that attached to the whole catastrophe. And now, she would open it up, set it out; but what was it she was opening, setting out, and to whom? Not only to her friends, her daughter, but, at Heidi's—Quin's—insistence, the whole world.

"She's a very private person." That was the new phrase, spoken grudgingly, as if the person described were selfishly, deliberately, withholding something. It had been a relief to be in Italy, where, although there was no word for privacy, and life seemed famously to be lived in the open, people felt the compulsion to speak about what they had done, or what they felt about it. Was it the war? A whole shared past of shameful secrets. Or was it something to do with a taste for form, a kind of good taste or good manners, linked somehow to the way they set a table, wrapped a package, addressed an envelope. So you had your outdoor life, your street life, which anyone was welcome to, and then you had the life that was your own, invulnerable and valuable, unsusceptible to light and weather. A closed room, narrow, dim and shuttered, to which it was possible, to which it was desirable, to retreat. Not from shame but from a simple need, something like a need for sleep, ordinary, requiring neither excuse nor consent.

But now the room was forced, the shutters thrown open, the overhead light beamed toward the white bed at the center of the room, the room's whole purpose, where someone would be free to rest.

She felt now always in a glare. She realized that ever since Quin and the cameraman had appeared, she'd had the impulse to shield her eyes.

But was it a good thing, entirely, this withdrawal, this closing off? Would it have been good for her and Maeve as mother and daughter (so many years there'd been between them this slight but palpable unease) if Maeve had understood her history? Would it have been better for her marriage, would Pietro have been able to understand the coolness that had come upon her, which was never spoken of between them but which she sometimes, but not always, thought he had felt?

Yes, maybe it was a good thing, what she'd always interpreted as a contemporary mania for exposure, the unappeasable appetite to be seen and seen and seen, as if nothing could be looked at enough, nothing sufficiently revealed. It had offended her, instinctively she'd turned her imagination away. She'd refused Facebook and Instagram. She didn't send hundreds of photos to hundreds of people every time she went anywhere at all. She didn't even like taking photographs, it seemed to her a kind of abuse of visibility.

Privacy. The right to privacy . . . it had seemed to her endangered, like one of those species of birds suddenly extinct because of the thrust and press of contemporary life. Her love of privacy had made her seem to herself out of step, old and cut off, but she had no desire to live differently, as she'd had no desire to go topless on the beach in the years when every Italian woman seemed perfectly happy to do it.

And yet she was uncomfortable with those Middle Eastern women who were concealed, covered except for their eyes . . .

So perhaps they were right, the people who liked Quin Archer's show. *PAYBACK,* it was called, she'd said. But it didn't matter whether it was right or not. It was happening.

Agnes lifts the telephone. She tries to decide who to call first.

Jo or Christina. One thing she knows: her daughter will be last. Although it is difficult for her to determine which call will be the most difficult; Jo and Christina had never liked Heidi, had actively disliked her as long as they knew her.

Like, liking. Such a meager word, she thinks, such a minor concept. And yet, without it there was . . . what? Nullity, or worse, the opposite of liking: dislike. She had been interested in Heidi. She had even admired her; her relentless insistence on the unsentimental, her freedom from the usual teenage desire to be liked. Heidi Stolz. In the countless times she had tried to determine what it was she had felt for Heidi, she had never come to a satisfactory answer. Heidi had interested her; she felt a responsibility to Heidi Stolz. In that interest, in that responsibility, there was no doubt a large quotient of vanity. But did she like her or did she merely love herself for her unusual choice in not *disliking* her; she had to admit that the first sight of Heidi at the door of the classroom or making her way down the hall had caused in Agnes a drawing back, a slight flinching—Heidi had had only two postures, either she slunk, making her way through a doorway, around a corner, as if she wanted to be invisible; or she strutted with her head stuck out in front of her, like an animal not quite on the attack but ready for it should the need arise.

No one liked Heidi, so no one understood Agnes's distress; they thought of it—they didn't say it, but she knew—as neurotic, hysterical, excessive. The most people would grant was that Agnes had made an unfortunate mistake. Because people loved her and disliked Heidi, they focused on Agnes's side of the event, what Agnes had done, what Agnes was feeling, not what the effects of what she had done or not done had on Heidi.

She calls Jo first—she doesn't quite know why, except perhaps that both she and Jo are unmated, Jack Walsh having left Jo for an intern at his law firm, soon after the *Bush v. Gore* decision came down. He said he could no longer live beside someone who had "lost all political faith, all political hope."

"And perky breasts," Jo said one night to Agnes, when the two of them had gone to a movie. After all these years, it was still more comfortable to be one-on-one with either Christina or Jo; Christina had an impulse to needle Jo, and Jo seemed always to rise to the bait.

Only she and Jo had made conventional marriages, and only she and Jo were alone. A widow and a divorcée. She envied Jo the word that went with her condition; *divorcée* sounded slightly dangerous, slightly seductive; to be called a widow, Agnes thought, made you sound bereft and hollowed out, as if you'd been declared, based on your husband's deadness, half dead yourself.

Hearing Jo's panicked tone, she wonders if calling her first had been a mistake. She'd forgotten Jo's doomsday tendencies, and her first response did not promise well. "Have you been diagnosed with cancer. Are Maeve and Marcus moving back to Italy? To California. Has Leo been hit by a car?"

"Nothing like that. Nothing so dire. It's complicated."

"I hate it when people say that. What they mean by 'It's complicated' is 'It's a big stinking mess.' "

"Yes, well, Josie, that too."

Maeve and Christina were more difficult to schedule . . . but everyone was free by nine that evening.

Maeve would come with Marcus; Christina with Jeanne.

. . .

Maeve's car is the first to pull into the driveway.

Marcus kisses her cheek and heads for the kitchen.

"I've brought ice cream, and I need to put it in the freezer."

"What's up, Mom," Maeve says, stroking her mother's hair as if she were a feverish child.

"Let's just wait till the others get here."

Christina and Jeanne arrive on foot; Jo, as is her habit, is last.

"Let's sit around the dining room table."

"Are you going to read a new will?" asks Jo.

"Jo, can you bear waiting one more minute or will your head explode," says Christina.

"It's just. Well, it's worrying."

"I told you, it's nothing life threatening. It's just, well, strange. Maeve, this will all be very new to you . . . it's something I never talked to you about. It didn't seem to have anything to do with you, with my life after I married your father, after you were born."

"You're not going to tell me I have a sibling you gave up for adoption."

"Geez Louise," Christina says. "Can't any of you wait?"

Agnes laughs. "No, nothing like that, Maeve, I would never have done anything like that. No, it's, it happened when I was a teacher at the Lydia Farnsworth School."

"The three of us taught there, that's how we knew each other," Jo says to Maeve. "Only I seem to be a lifer. Your mother was a wonderful teacher. The students worshipped her."

"Not so wonderful, not so wonderful at all. That's the point. I was a disaster in one of my students' lives."

"Oh, Jesus," Christina says, "Heidi Stolz."

"I remember her," Jeanne says. "She was smart . . . you tried to connect us on a senior project, Agnes . . . we went down to New York on the train together . . . it was just before she disappeared. People kept asking me about her, but I didn't know her at all . . . we weren't friends . . . I didn't even like her. Well, I didn't like anybody then, but I disliked her particularly. She just gave off this weird vibe, like she was desperate for something, but she looked down on everything, too."

Jo shivers. "It's like a ghost walked over my grave."

"She's not a ghost, thank God," Agnes says. "All these years I've prayed that she wasn't dead, or horribly damaged."

"So, she's not a ghost," Christina says. "Why are we talking about her?"

"It's all so strange, it's all so strange . . ." Agnes takes her hair out of its clip and pins it up again.

"She arrived at the door this morning . . . with a cameraman. She has a reality-TV show. Somewhere in Arizona. It's called *PAYBACK*. She finds people who feel like someone in their life hurt them and got away with it, and she arranges for what will feel to the victim like a payback. She wants to do a show about the two of us."

"My sweet Lord," Marcus says.

"Well, you're not going to let her," Maeve says. "I mean, you have to agree to it, don't you?"

"I have agreed," Agnes says. "I've already agreed."

"I can't believe you did that, Mother. Why did you do it without asking anyone . . . without asking us."

"I didn't need anyone's advice, I didn't need anyone's permission," Agnes says in a cold severe tone that is so unfamiliar to the people around the table that they look at each other to be sure that they've heard.

"Well, that's the goddamn stupidest thing I ever heard," Christina says. "You made a mistake . . . you blurted something out . . . she woke you up . . . you were half asleep . . ."

"I'm lost," Maeve says.

"I felt sorry for her . . . I was interested in her . . . no one seemed to like her."

"Because she was completely unlikeable," Jo says. "She took pride in being the only pro-war girl in her whole class; every time anyone on the left made the slightest wrong move, she rubbed my face in it."

"She had her own ideas, and this is what I admired, although I wasn't comfortable with her ideas . . . I thought, well, this is someone who isn't afraid to say what she thinks, who puts her mind to things that no one else around her was . . . and yes, she was intelligent, and she could be witty."

"And she followed you around like a goddamn puppy," Christina says. "It was pathetic."

"I didn't handle it well. Yes, I knew she was attached to me, and the very fact that no one else liked her appealed to my vanity . . . I should have kept her more at a distance . . . I should have been much cooler with her. A good teacher knows how to keep the right distance."

"We were so young," Jo says. "And Letitia Barnes just threw us into the water with very little training, she just assumed that because we were intelligent and knew our subject, we would be good teachers."

"I was lousy," Christina says. "I was much too impatient."

"You were great for the bright kids," Jeanne says.

"You, for example."

"Me, for example. You were the only one I respected."

Agnes wonders if Jeanne realizes that she has just insulted her and Jo.

"Well, I was getting worried that she was becoming too attached to me . . . her parents seemed to be away a lot of the time."

"Her mother was a Nazi goddess . . . wasn't she a skier?"

"Yes," Agnes says. "Heidi felt her mother never cared for her . . . and I could see she felt she could never measure up. The father was a pathetic little man, though quite wealthy, I think . . . and he . . . well, talk about follow like a puppy . . . I remember, people smoked all the time, even in parent-teacher conferences, and she took out a cigarette and snapped her fingers and he lit it for her. She wasn't conventionally attractive, Heidi—by the way, she's changed her name now to Quin Archer—"

"I love it," Christina says, and Jo says, "Perfect, absolutely fucking perfect."

"She had these little eyes . . . like she was always waiting to find you doing something stupid," Jo says.

"I tried to encourage her interest in art, she did have talent— it was for a kind of art I found alienating—Warhol and Lichtenstein and Rauschenberg and all the pops—and I thought it would be nice if she and Jeanne could do something together—you were both so bright," she says, turning to Jeanne. "So I gave her a ticket to a lecture on *Guernica* at the Museum of Modern Art. It was on a Saturday, and I knew, Jeanne, that you took that special science course on Saturdays—I was hoping maybe the two of you could explore New York together or even if that didn't work I thought it would be good for her to explore New York— and that was where it happened."

"Please, Mom," Maeve says. "I need to know what's going on."

And Agnes thinks, Now I will say it, now I will make a story of it . . . of the moment of my life that changed everything . . . that made me know that I had in me something curled and dark and careless and capable, with that same carelessness, of great harm.

"And you haven't seen or heard from her since then?" Maeve says, when Agnes has finished.

Agnes shakes her head.

"You tried, Jesus knows, you tried," Christina says. "My God, you drove yourself crazy . . . she was covered with eczema, Maeve, she spent the summer in New York following up on what the private detective came up with . . . we were all so worried about her, and that was when your grandmother came up with the idea of Jasper and Italy . . . that was the thing about your mother, Agnes, she always seemed so vague, so in her own world, but she was always seeing everything and when everyone else was confused or paralyzed, she seemed to have a plan."

Maeve paces the length of the table.

"I never knew. Oh, Mom, I never knew . . . but you always, well, you always take so much responsibility for everyone . . . it drives me crazy sometimes because you always think everything's up to you, you don't let anything go . . . but oh, Mom . . . this has been such a burden for you and I never knew."

"Children aren't meant to carry their parents' burdens."

"But you wouldn't let us help," Jo says.

"I couldn't let you help because I knew you disliked her . . . you didn't even really believe her."

"We still don't know whether it's really true . . . I remember Letitia thought it wasn't true."

Agnes bangs her hand on the table, and says, "That was very,

very wrong . . . that was very, very wrong of all of you. You didn't like her and you didn't like thinking about what happened to her . . . because she wasn't appealing to you, you didn't believe her. You didn't want to. It was in the world, it was in the air we all breathed, not to believe girls, because we didn't want to believe in the reality of how unsafe we all were, that it could happen to any of us, at any moment, that there was really not much we could do to protect ourselves, and so it was better for everyone to say, 'Well, it was her fault,' that if she'd just been smarter, more careful . . . more modest or more chaste . . . if she'd done something that any of us could do to protect ourselves . . . then we would all be safer . . . and we wouldn't have to think things about men that we didn't want to think. And that, all that was in the air we breathed, all that was in our minds from the time we were girls . . . and so it was in my mind. Almost the first thing that came to my mind . . . to all our minds when we heard the word *rape,* so coming out of sleep . . . instead of sympathy I created blame. I believed her . . . I could see that she had been hurt, hurt badly, but what I couldn't bear to believe . . . you can call it my unconscious but it was still part of me, something that belonged to me, that was me—that there was something in the world that couldn't be prevented . . . by intelligence, or foresight, or self-protection or whatever else it is that we think keeps us safe."

Everyone is silent. Marcus comes behind Agnes and puts his arms around her and this touch releases Agnes's tears.

"All right, it's all right, we're with you. We're always with you. We'll do whatever you want."

"I want to do whatever she wants," Agnes says. "I owe it to her."

"You do not. You do not. You don't owe her anything," Maeve says.

"Oh, Maeve, I do . . . and whether you understand or not, we're going to do this."

"I don't think your mother's been so tough with you since you were in third grade and wanted to give up the violin," Christina says.

"Yeah, she made me keep it up for three more years although I hated it."

"It was so important to your father," Agnes says.

"Yeah, but he made you be the bad guy."

"Please, Maeve . . . it doesn't matter. Leo's got it, Leo's really a marvelous violinist," Agnes says.

"He's got my family's DNA for sticking to stuff," Marcus says.

"I don't think there's DNA for that," Jeanne says.

Everyone laughs, because Jeanne's literal-mindedness is an old joke for all of them, and something lifts, everyone is suddenly free to move forward.

Agnes turns to Jo. "She wants to do some shooting at the school."

"Shooting . . . I guess she means a camera, but somehow in connection to Heidi Stolz I think of guns," Christina says.

Jo says, "I will not, will not permit it. That the school should in any way be fodder for her hideous revenge binge . . . no, she won't be allowed through the gates of the Lydia Farnsworth School."

"Quite right," Christina says.

"And don't let her back in the house," Maeve says.

"No, Maeve, she can use the house as a backdrop . . . and Jo . . . please, don't be unpleasant."

"I do unpleasant. I'm a mother of two sons, I've taught for forty-five years. I'm good at unpleasant."

"And I'm the biggest one here so I'll stand at the gate with a pitchfork and keep her out," Christina says.

"And we're in a joint practice, Christina, so I'll stand beside you with a matching pitchfork."

When they have left, Agnes phones Quin. "I'm afraid Jo Walsh doesn't want you to shoot at the school."

"Well, that's just dandy, but no surprise. You all managed to make me feel like an outsider, that I wasn't welcome there . . . even though my father was paying through the nose."

"I'm sure we never meant—"

"No, that was the problem . . . you never meant."

"You're very free to use my house, though, if you like, or we can walk around the town."

"So you can show me your ancestors' graves."

"My ancestors aren't buried here, Quin," Agnes says. "We only moved here in the '50s when my father got the job in Providence."

"Fine, fine, whatever you say . . . shall we say tomorrow at ten . . . it'll be Sunday so I'm assuming everyone's free."

"I'll try to make it happen," Agnes says.

"Oh yes, Miss Vaughan, you're good at that."

~~~

"YOU'RE OFF your game, babe."

"What are you talking about?"

"I just asked you what spin class you wanted to take . . . I found a gym near the hotel that does day passes, and you were miles away. Also, I know you, Quin Archer, or whoever you are, and this lady's throwing you off. Remember, we play them, they're the drum and we set the beat. You're responding to her rather than making her respond to you."

"You stick to your part of the business . . . getting me a spin class. And I'll stick to mine. Take the earliest one . . . I like to be up."

She knows he's right. She was miles away, almost literally. Crossing the bridge to Newport she is back in the car with her father, visiting her brother. One visit only, but it pressed down, it set its seal, it made its mark on the wet soil of the life of the young Heidi Stolz. Hateful, everything about it. The shock of learning she had a damaged brother. His grotesque shambling entrance into the ugly room. His slobbering over the chocolates . . . the violent outburst, with chocolate-smeared mouth and hands. As if he's just been eating shit.

Her brother Jimmy. The rusting pole that sticks up out of the landscape, ruining its harmony, the element that Ayn Rand could never have incorporated . . . nothing could be done for him, except perhaps to kill him . . . and often she had thought of that, that it would be a mercy. But then she would be a criminal, at the mercy of the law. Lawrence had told her there was enough money to see to Jimmy's care; she didn't have to think about it. Well, she had thought about it, but decided it wasn't her problem. She didn't know if the money had run out . . . if it had, people would be looking for Heidi Stolz, not Quin Archer.

In justice, he shouldn't be fed, clothed, given a roof over his head. In justice, he should have been left out . . . perhaps in some fairy tale cared for by animals, but it was not a fairy-tale world, and in the world as it is he would not have been cared for by animals, he'd have been devoured. Which would have been right.

No one alive knows of Jimmy's existence. How easy it is, she thought, simply to erase someone from the pages of the living . . . easier to erase Jimmy Stolz than to erase Heidi Stolz . . . because someone alive still knew of her, still, it would seem, remembered her. Agnes Vaughan said she had thought of her constantly. She will not allow herself to take pleasure in that. It didn't mean anything . . . it led to nothing. Heidi Stolz had been killed. It would be better if Jimmy Stolz had been. More than anything, she hopes he is dead. She will not allow herself to think of him . . . it's the influence of this damn place . . . maybe it wasn't worth it, maybe this is a mistake. But it's not a mistake. Her ratings were way down. Nothing could be worse than the humiliation of being canceled. They won't dare cancel her now.

"I'm not sure you've thought this out all the way," Rich says.

"What do you mean?"

"She's no good for our kind of show. She won't fight back. But she's not pathetic—she's, what is it, I don't know, but I'm worried that the camera will like it, and the audience will like it. Quiet, reserve, that's no good for us. Think about it, babe; maybe it's time for us to cut our losses."

Anger flares, and she welcomes it, is drawn to it, as a traveler is drawn to a fire on a freezing night. Anger. Home and hearth. The good place. The safe place. Rich was right, she was off her game because she had stayed away from the flame . . . weakened by, what was it, sadness . . . a sense of having been abandoned, bereft. Those were the feelings that could suck you up, suck you in, so you were swimming up to your eyes in filthy mud. Anger was the flame that consumed the mud, dried it to a hard surface that you did not drown in, that you could walk on, in safety, in security, with the firm promise of support.

"Earth to Rich, earth to Rich . . . there's no cutting losses, we already went on the show with Valerie, if I back out now, I'm a total loser . . . to say nothing of what this was all about in the first place: booting up our audience, getting our ratings back. Or maybe you're interested in downsizing . . . selling the house, moving to a nice two-bedroom condo . . . using the town pool . . . and when it's time to visit Dr. Drew for the next touch-up, going to Walgreens instead to see what's on the discount-makeup rack."

Rich sinks into the seat. "You're right, of course you're right. But how do we put this back on track?"

"I've thought about it. Two things make our kind of show work: the audience's love of humiliation, and their endless appetite for displays of rage. Well, you're right, if we humiliate Agnes Vaughan the audience is going to be on her side, and she just doesn't do rage. But there's something else. I've said I wanted to shoot some footage at the school and her old friend Jo Walsh is the headmistress—oh, wait, they don't want to say that anymore, it sounds too sexy—she was always ready to blow a gasket about anything she perceived as unjust . . . so we'll rev her up to attack me . . . but that's not all, the other friend turns out to be a dyke who's married—oh, please, here come the brides—to one of her ex-students. So I just drop the hint that as students we all knew that the old dykes were diddling the young lovelies. That will get a reaction."

Rich takes her hand and puts it to his lips. "You are without a doubt, wife of mine, a genius. But by the way, why'd you plant that whopper about your being infertile because of an STD you got in the bad old days?"

"I was road-testing it."

He kisses her hand again.

"Three. Two. One. Action."

"Hello, I'm Quin Archer, and this is *PAYBACK*.

"You may be surprised to find me here, in the perfect New England town of New Canterbury, Rhode Island. But this is, you might say, my hometown, where I was born, where I lived till I ran away from it at age sixteen.

"This, my good friends, is finally my story. This is my PAYBACK.

"I'm standing at the gates of the Lydia Farnsworth School, where I was a student. As you can see, the gates are locked; the headmistress—she likes to call herself the 'head'—MIZZ Jo Walsh, has forbidden us access.

"Let me tell you what it was like at the Lydia Farnsworth School in 1972. My parents had sent me here because it was the place where the people—anyone who was anyone—sent their daughters. Well, let me tell you, they should have saved their money. What were they educating us for? To marry rich men . . . to be volunteers at the local museum . . . to be on the board of the local orchestra . . . to arrange flowers? Nothing I learned here was of the slightest use to me in my life . . . most of what I learned here I had to unlearn.

"We're starting here rather than in the house I was brought up in, because the house I was brought up in no longer exists. It was sold in the late '70s, to developers who turned it into condos. The development company that owns the condos has also denied us access—they say the condos don't want their privacy invaded. I've learned that what people mean by privacy is that

that they don't want their dirty dark secrets exposed to the light. Never mind, I don't need them. And this, my friends, is one of the reasons I've devoted myself to this show. To show other people who have had difficult experiences, people who might think of themselves as victims—well, to get out of that victim mentality, to take your own life in your own two hands, to feel your own power to undo the past—and how?—through justice. Through PAYBACK.

"But I didn't follow my own advice. For years, I've kept my own story hidden. And then, by chance . . . or maybe not by chance . . . what people call chance or luck is, in my opinion, just being awake, taking the hint and turning it into something you can use. Something you can use for yourself. Those of you who've known me for years in my home in Brimston, Arizona, know that I began here by running a program in the gym I owned called Selfishness Boot Camp. Selfishness has a bad name. But it's the fear of selfishness that keeps a victim a victim . . . or encourages people to think of themselves as a victim. And I've devoted myself to saying no, it's not the only way. Love yourself, think of yourself, take your past in both hands and make of it the future that you want.

"So you can say it was good luck that I discovered that the person who harmed me was back here in New Canterbury . . . but it was my good sense that continued to subscribe to the local newspaper here, and when I saw that the woman who had harmed me—my teacher in this very school, the prestigious Lydia Farnsworth School—when I saw that this woman had come back to New Canterbury after having lived in Italy for forty years—well, I knew it was time for my PAYBACK."

"Quin, walk toward me . . . walk away from the gates into the street. Great. Perfect."

"One way to describe what happened to me is to say that I was a victim of rape. But a better way to describe it is that I hadn't yet learned to rely on myself, that I relied on someone who said they were reliable, my teacher, I gave away my own power to her . . ."

"Quin, walk closer to the camera."

"Yes, this is my story. I was raped. You may be surprised that the person I'm confronting today is not the person who raped me. I didn't know his name . . . he was a stranger, someone who accosted me on the streets of New York, or a back alleyway of New York . . . no, I would never be able to get PAYBACK from him, because I don't even know his face—he wore a ski mask when he accosted me. No, the person who harmed me . . . and this will surprise you, but it is, my friends, the truth . . . was not the person who raped me, but the teacher I loved and trusted, who said that what happened to me was my fault.

"Okay . . . let's move to the house. Pack everything up. Do some footage of the neighborhood. Ooh la la, local color, the old houses, the beautiful old trees. They'll eat it up."

"I'm walking to the front door of the house of my old teacher, Miss Agnes Vaughan, now Agnes di Martini. This is the house she grew up in, the house where I tried to find comfort from her . . . the house I ran from as a desperate sixteen-year-old . . . I haven't been back in thirty-eight years . . . but, my friends, nothing has changed here . . . it looks exactly the same.

"This is the bell I rang, the brass knocker in the shape of a dolphin—that image always came back to me when I thought of that terrible night.

"And here is Agnes Vaughan, Agnes di Martini . . . and this is the story of a desperate girl who was betrayed by the person who had pledged to be someone who was always worthy of trust."

"Hello, Quin, you're very welcome."

"A bit late for that, Miss Vaughan . . . or Mrs. di Martini."

"We moved the furniture around, Quin . . . sit on the chairs we've put near the windows. The light is fabulous for you."

"Wait a minute, Joe, what's this? These people can't be here."

"They said you said they were going to be part of the show."

"Yes, but not yet. Not yet."

"Hello, Heidi," Christina says.

"It's Quin."

"Not to me."

Quin feels a cool sense of satisfaction, of mastery. The air crackles with energy, the energy of hostility . . . which is the energy she needs. She's done it again, what she's best at, sizing up a situation, calculating the pressure points: where to touch to elicit gushing tears and where to set alight a flame of anger. Alone with Agnes, Agnes's beauty, her mildness. Well, she hadn't thought of that. But now . . . the three women bristle with aggression, and aggression is something of use to her. The fuel that runs the engine that has made her name.

"Perhaps, Quin . . . if you have some sense when you'll be ready for them, they might come back later."

"We'll stay here," Maeve says. "We'll be in the kitchen or on the back porch."

"We haven't met. I'm Quin Archer."

"I know who you are," Maeve says, making no move to introduce herself.

"So, Miss Vaughan, Mrs. di Martini . . . it's still hard for me to call you Agnes."

"But please do."

"All right, then, Agnes, tell us about you as a teacher in the Lydia Farnsworth School in 1972."

"Well, I was very young, I was only twenty-five. I loved teaching. I loved my students. You made me feel so hopeful, and it was not a hopeful time . . . the Vietnam War was still going on."

"We're not here to talk about Vietnam. We're here to talk about you and me."

"Oh, yes, I'm sorry . . . but, well, it was a strange time, a difficult time."

"You taught art."

"Yes, studio art and art history."

"What was your background?"

"I had a degree in art history from Pembroke. That was the women's college attached to Brown. In retrospect, I think I probably wasn't qualified to teach. I had had no instruction in the methods of teaching."

"But your students loved you. I remember that."

"You may say that, Heidi . . . Quin . . . and if you say that you must add that in your case, certainly, I was unworthy of that love. I betrayed it."

"Betrayal. That's what we're here for, Agnes, isn't it, to talk about betrayal. So perhaps we should share with the audience what went on at the time we're talking about. April of 1972."

Quin stands, moves away from the chairs where she and Agnes are sitting, to a place in the room that has been emptied for her, so there is the sense of her taking center stage.

"It's 1972. I'm sixteen. A very unhappy sixteen, but most sixteen-year-olds are unhappy. There's this special teacher . . . she goes out of her way to make me feel appreciated, which none of the others did."

"I thought you were quite gifted. I hope you've gone on making art."

"This is my art, Agnes, and you're my subject. But let's move on. Let's talk about the boots."

"The boots?"

"The boots you gave me. The red boots. You gave me a pair of red suede boots. You said you'd bought them for yourself, but you didn't think they were right for you. But you said they were right for me because I had nice legs. Didn't it occur to you that that was crossing boundaries?"

"The boots," Agnes says. "I hadn't . . . oh, well, yes, the boots . . . I remember I bought them for myself and I thought, well, I wasn't the type, but I knew someone else would be. And I thought, well, you had such an original sense of fashion . . . I just thought . . ."

"You thought what? That those very sexy boots were too dangerous for you, were giving out the wrong signals, but they'd be fine for a shy sixteen-year-old girl."

"I hadn't thought about it . . . but you're right, of course you're right . . . I was very unwise."

"You see, I believe that the boots were the whole problem. Or part of the problem. The other part of the problem was your romantic ideas about New York City. That it was the great good place, that I needed to be there to . . . what did we say then . . . so I could find myself . . . but think about it, Agnes, New York in 1972 was a hellhole, and you encouraged a young girl who had no experience there to go down by herself . . . wearing your red boots."

"I thought it would be fine. You were going to a lecture at the Museum of Modern Art. It wasn't a bad neighborhood . . . it was the middle of the day."

"And I got off the train with the directions you gave me . . . I remember holding them in my hand . . . like you were with me, holding my hand. Only I got lost. And I guess I looked lost, because when this man asked me what I was looking for and I said the Museum of Modern Art, he said, Just follow me, and I did, and I didn't realize he was leading me into a deserted alley. Where it happened. Where I was raped.

"There are parts of it I just don't remember . . . I don't remember the man's face. I don't remember how I got myself back on the train . . . but I remember, oh, how well I remember, being on the train, cold, so cold . . . I was only wearing a miniskirt and a jacket I'd gotten at the thrift store and the train seemed freezing to me . . . I remember the blood, I had to go into a bathroom and line my underwear with toilet paper, and I remember how the bathroom in Penn Station stank . . . and on the train, the only scrap of comfort I could cling to was, 'I can go to Miss Vaughan, Miss Vaughan will understand.'

"I ran up the path—the same path that's still in front of your house. I rang the bell, and then I used the knocker. Your mother answered the door. She invited me in. She offered me tea. She said she would get you, that you were sleeping. You came down; you were wearing a pink chenille robe. Your hair was in braids . . . you looked startled, frightened to see me there. And then, when I told you what had happened, you said those words . . . do you remember, Agnes, do you remember the words you said?"

"Of course, Quin, of course, how could I ever forget?"

"Tell us, Agnes, tell us what you said."

"I said, 'How could you have let that happen?'"

"Move closer to the camera, Quin."

"'How could you have let that happen' . . . try to imagine me, terrified, overwhelmed, going to my beloved teacher, the teacher I truly loved, for comfort. And to be told . . . somehow it was my fault.

"That, ladies and gentlemen, that was the true violation. I ran like I was running away from the assaulter once again. I took what money I could from my parents' house. They weren't home . . . well, they traveled a lot . . . I took money from my father's drawer . . . I spent the last night in my childhood bed and then I left for good . . . went to the city . . . where else?

"And lived, for eight years, eight long years a life of squalor.

"New York, 1972 to 1980 . . . it disgusts me that some people think those times were glamorous . . . sexy . . . full of creative energy. And that's one of the reasons I do this show: to unmask that kind of lie. I lived in squalor; I squatted in empty apartments where there was no plumbing; I was filthy . . . the people around me were filthy . . . and we were in and out of each other's beds . . . or mattresses, or sleeping bags . . . passing diseases around . . . one morning I woke up and there were small mollusks on my private parts . . . a form of lice . . . and oh, we were always combing each other for lice, like monkeys . . . working at squalid jobs in squalid places . . . I'll never eat in a New York diner again . . . eight years and then . . . a kind of miracle, only I don't believe in miracles, I do believe that there was one part of me that stayed intact—call it my mother's athleticism, I don't know . . . somehow one night I made my way to a lecture on Ayn Rand. *The Virtue of Selfishness*. And I got my life back, because I knew it was my life, my life, and that it was all I had, all that was real, and everything else was a lie. So my life was stolen by one teacher, Agnes Vaughan, stolen and before that distorted by everything you encouraged me to believe was true . . . but it wasn't true, it was delusion . . . and a poisonous delusion that poisoned me . . . but I was saved by another teacher, another woman . . . and I have lived since then knowing that all I had was my life, that it was in my hands, and that there was nothing else to look to as the ground of reality. I left New York, thank God. Nothing would induce me to go there again . . . I moved to Arizona. And I made my life."

"I'm very glad your life has turned out well, Quin."

"Let's bring the others in, Joe," Quin says, standing up and smoothing the back of her dress.

"Jo Walsh and Christina Datchett were also teachers at the Lydia Farnsworth School; I was also their student. MIZZ Walsh taught history; Miss Datchett . . ."

"It's Doctor," Christina says. "Dr. Datchett."

"Dr. Datchett . . . so the connection to the school runs very deep and wide. I understand, Dr. Datchett, that you recently married one of your former students. When did same-sex marriage become legal in Rhode Island?"

"Jeanne was a student of mine . . . briefly . . . but we met up years later, at Brown; I was in med school; she was the TA in my anatomy class."

"What a funny turnaround . . . she graded your papers and before that you, when you were her teacher. Would you say she was special to you; would you say you were close? And MIZZ Walsh, would you explain to the audience here why you denied me access to the school today?"

"Because, Heidi," Jo says, through her teeth, "it has nothing to do with the school, and I saw no point in involving it in what was a private matter between Agnes and you . . . something that you've turned into . . . I don't know, some private little revenge drama . . . you need to know everyone around here loves Agnes—"

"Or is it that a private school with not a very good endow-

ment can't afford to have things investigated that might be better covered up. And there've been one too many scandals in tony
private schools, am I right, MIZZ Walsh?"

"Nothing's being covered up."

"Whatever you say. Dr. Datchett, I understand that Agnes's
daughter here is your partner . . . but by that I mean, only in the
business sense."

"I am Maeve di Martini, and Agnes is my mother, and I'm
very proud of her, and I'm proud of her friends who have loved
her and been beside her for all these years. I wonder if you can
say the same."

"Well, yes, Maeve . . . or Doctor . . . that's my point. I was
injured because of what's happened to me, I'm a survivor, and
survivors often have a hard time trusting again . . . and here you
are, all of you, so comfortable . . . and your mother with her Italian romance . . . and do you have children, Maeve?"

"I have one son."

"And you, MIZZ Walsh . . . as I recall, your husband was in
prison when I was your student."

"He had burned his draft card."

"And where is he now? Not still in prison, I assume."

"California."

"You're not together, then."

"No."

"But children. I believe you have two sons. One, I've learned,
still lives in town here. A carpenter, I think . . . or more of a
handyman. He still lives with you. And your other son is in New
York. What is his work?"

"He works on Wall Street."

"Well, that must be a challenge . . . I remember you saying

that Wall Street was the source of the infection that diseased the whole world. Do you see much of your New York son?"

"He's quite busy."

"Yes, stockbrokers work long hours. But I imagine, on Thanksgiving and Christmas . . ."

"We all get together on Thanksgiving and Christmas," Maeve says, "all three families."

"And you, Dr. di Martini, I understand you are the mother of a young son . . . and your husband is . . . a gardener."

"A landscape architect."

"African American, I believe."

"Yes, among other things."

"Joe . . . back in the living room. Back in the main spot."

"So you see, folks, I've come home. Or come back. I won't say I'm a victim, because I'm committed to the idea that that's only a hobble, an impediment, but I've had to work hard, work against things to get where I am. There are no warm extended-family Thanksgivings and Christmases for me. Rich and I are on our own. My greatest desire has always been to have a child, but because of the years I lived in squalor in New York, years of drug use and sexual promiscuity . . . I am incapable of having a child."

"There *is* a God." The cameraman swivels fast to pick up Christina's last word.

"Yes, Dr. Datchett, I suppose you think it's God . . . perhaps you even believe in him . . . but I say it's because of Agnes Vaughan and what she did . . . that I have had to make my way, inch by inch, on my own . . . relying on nothing, counting on no one."

"I thought you were married," Maeve says.

"Well . . . yes . . . of course . . . of course I meant except for Rich . . . we walk the road together . . . but it's a tough road, and we've made every inch of it ourselves."

"We'll do a wide pan now, Quin."

"So, I look at you, all of you here, in the place where you grew up, surrounded by such comfort, such love, and I think, well, perhaps I'll come back, perhaps my PAYBACK will be to find some of what I've lost, some of what was taken from me."

"You wouldn't think of coming back here."

"Yes, MIZZ Walsh, I might."

"You can't be serious."

"Oh, I am serious. I can see that Agnes knows I'm serious. Agnes understands me . . . or does she . . . wasn't that what she told me, that she understood?"

"I do understand, Quin, why you would want to come back to try to recover what you lost. I'm sorry for what you've lost, sorrier than I can say, for what's been taken from you."

"Well, thanks for your understanding . . . it would have meant everything forty years ago. But I can't come back here . . . I'd always be the outsider, as I always have been. Oh, yes, I can just imagine what you might do in the name of defending your mother, your friend, protecting her, getting back at me for exposing her. This is your place. Jo Walsh is the head of the town council . . . I can just imagine trying to get some sort of building permit and her holding it up for years . . . or calling a plumber and finding out that he's her son's best friend and he just can't get over to fix my toilet for a week. Your daughter and your best friend are the town doctors. If I had a heart attack, I'd have to worry that maybe they'd tell the ambulance not to rush—"

"My daughter would never do that . . . Christina would never do that . . . Jo would never do that. We're not like that."

"People always think they know what the people close to them would do . . . but people can surprise you. You surprised me, Agnes . . . I thought I knew who you were. And look what happened. No, I'm not going to stay. I'll be glad to get out of here. Back to my beautiful desert, to my people, who know to call me by my right name.

"Close-up, Joe.

"Quin Archer, saying goodnight for *PAYBACK*."

In an instant, the lights are taken down, the crew disappears through the door as if they'd never been there. Pushing past them, Jeanne Larkin walks into the living room.

Quin jumps as if she'd put her finger in an electric socket. Is it possible that Jeanne Larkin has not aged the slightest bit in forty years? Of course, the lights in the house are dim, the eyes play tricks after the harsh TV lights, but nothing seems to have changed: the tight gold curls, the long legs and boyish torso, the bowed horsewoman's walk.

"Hello, Jeanne," Quin says, "I often thought of you."

"I never thought of you," Jeanne says. "When they mentioned your name a few days ago, I didn't even remember who you were."

"Well, you'll remember me now," Quin says.

Christina puts her arm around Jeanne's shoulder. "Actually, knowing my wife, I'm not so sure."

Quin pulls Rich toward the door roughly, nearly unbalancing him.

"You're nothing but two pathetic old dykes," she says.

"Quin . . . ," Rich says. "You don't need to stoop to that."

"Oh, it's not stooping, or only partially, Rich," Christina says. "Because we are dykes, yes, we certainly are, and, in my case, probably old—but pathetic, no, that's where you're wrong . . . pathetic . . . never."

The door slams.

Maeve goes to the closet and takes out the wool shawl that belonged to her grandmother. She wraps it around her mother's shoulders.

"You're shivering, Mom," she says. "Chris, go into the kitchen and get brandy."

"No, no, it's all right, I'm all right. Thank you, thank you all, you were wonderful."

"Well, we weren't wonderful . . . we weren't wonderful at all. She held out the bait and we jumped for it . . . we jumped for it every single time . . . I seemed to be defensive about everything: the school, my sons . . . and she suggested . . . not accusing, mind you, no, never a real accusation, that my husband was an ex-con, that one son was a loser living at home, and the other a Wall Street tycoon I was estranged from . . . that Chris and Jeanne had been involved when she was a student . . . nothing direct, only these vile accusations, like being covered over in a spider's web you can't get off your skin even though you thought you'd passed right through it."

"You know," Maeve says, "I never believed in evil . . . but I think I just met a truly evil person."

"She wasn't like that . . . she wasn't always like that . . . it wasn't her fault . . . it was because of what happened to her . . . what I let happen."

"Oh, Agnes, for God's sake . . . you're swallowing her story whole . . . think critically . . . come on, you're smarter than that, we're older than that. First, she was always like that; she only seemed happy when she was shining light on someone's faults or weakness. Well, congratulations to her, she's made a career of it. But it's not you . . . it's the world . . . the kind of world that watches shows like that . . . and glorifies it with the word *reality.* But it's not reality, and it certainly has nothing to do with the truth."

Agnes feels as if she's been wandering aimlessly, half asleep, or through a fog, and suddenly she's walked bang into a pole or pillar, struck her forehead on rough stone. Her forehead throbs, and when she puts her fingers to it, she's surprised that it is cool, and that there seems to be no swelling, no abrasion.

The truth. What Quin had said was not the truth.

He said, Just follow me, and I did, and I didn't realize he was leading me into a deserted alley. Where it happened. Where I was raped.

Agnes knows that she remembers exactly what Heidi said all those years ago . . . she's played it over in her mind thousands of times . . . she knows the words . . . it wasn't possible for her not to have remembered them exactly. Quin just said she was raped in an alley. But Agnes remembers that, when the words came rushing out of Heidi's mouth that terrible night, the words were not that she'd been led into an alley by a stranger. "I was raped. I went to the lecture in New York and I met this man and he invited me to his apartment for lunch and then he raped me."

Those were the words, Agnes knows it, she knows it absolutely, that had elicited that terrible response, "You knew better than that. How could you have let that happen?"

It takes all her discipline to remain silent, not to say what she knows the others don't: that Heidi—or was it Quin—had lied about what happened to her.

She is lying to the camera, to the hundreds—or is it thousands—of people who will believe whatever she says. Unless Agnes Vaughan, whom she has painted as her betrayer, betrays her once again, by saying, "No, Heidi, that's not it. What you say is not what happened at all."

But she will not do it. Nothing has ever caused Agnes to doubt that Heidi was actually raped; the image of the desperate girl, the terrified girl, the wounded girl has appeared before her eyes thousands of times over these forty years.

Something dreadful had happened to her . . . and perhaps it was her right to use what had happened in any way that would be of use, that would help her to make a life.

To make it into a story that could be told to her advantage, a story where she could only be pitied, because she was pure victim. But whatever happened to her, she *was* a victim, and the man—what had happened to the man? Here she was, here Heidi was . . . the focus was all on the two of them. But the man . . . he'd not even been mentioned. The world had swallowed him up, had absorbed him as if he had never been. It was she, Agnes, from whom Heidi was demanding payback. Nothing, it seemed, was required of the man. Was it because to call up that face would be unbearable to Heidi . . . less unbearable to relive the moment when her teacher had failed her . . . less unbearable to make up a story that could form a backdrop to a larger story: that the world was easily divisible: that it was possible to locate the darkness, to corral it with a series of phrases, of images: New York, the '60s. In its way, it was enviable: to have that kind of story, with a beginning, a dark middle that everything in the beginning led to, and to which everything, every dark thing that followed, could be traced. Heidi, or Quin, had made up a story to save her life. She had to survive, and she has, Agnes sees, mastered the survivor's cunning . . . a skill that would not be necessary had Agnes not failed her when she did. And so, to say, "No, Heidi, no Quin, that's not what happened. What you're saying happened to you is not what happened at all," would be to destroy what Heidi—or Quin—had created to be able to survive.

She forces herself to come back into the room, to the present, to the presence of other, real, living people.

"We live in terrible times," Jo says.

"Oh, Jo, don't universalize it . . . it's just one little woman, one little show, in one little town in Arizona . . . no one we know will ever see it . . . we can let it go . . . it's over . . . it's all over now," Christina says.

"I don't think so," Agnes says. "I don't think it's over. I'm not sure it ever will be."

PART VI

Newport, Rhode Island

April 2018

L end me your jacket," Quin says to Rich, "I'm fucking freez-ing. Who would live in this part of the world?"

He knows better than to say anything to her. That there's a problem with the show; that there'll have to be a massive amount of editing . . . less time spent on Agnes, more on her daughter and the other women . . . maybe even reshooting some of Quin and pasting it in. Because she was really off her game.

She'd never aimed for being likable, not in any ordinary way. It worked as long as you felt she was righting wrongs . . . that she rose like an Amazon, protecting the weak, the Owed, who had to be likable, from the Ower, who had to be seen to, at least in the past, have been unworthy of regard. But Agnes Vaughan threw the whole formula off, and threw Quin off: she didn't seem avenging, she seemed vengeful. She became the kind of Owed that Quin would never have signed on: a bully, a hec-torer. If it were going to work, Quin would have to have been playing two parts: Quin Archer, the avenger, and Quin Archer, the wronged justice seeker. But the mask had slipped. She had become only one person. She had become herself. Like the most gullible members of her audience, she had confused reality with reality TV.

~~

SHE KNOWS that what Jeanne Larkin said about not thinking about her is a lie. It has to be a lie. Everyone in the school, everyone in the town, must have been talking about her; it must have been the subject of conversation for months. But she remembers that everyone made fun of Jeanne Larkin because she seemed to have absolutely no imagination and no humor. In the school plays, she did the lighting because her delivery of lines so lacked any sense of drama. Most often she didn't get a joke. She got herself and other people in trouble refusing to be in on trying to convince the teacher that she hadn't told them there was a test; she was known to be inflexible in not bending the rules. Yet people didn't dislike her. Heidi never understood why people liked Jeanne and didn't like her.

The show wasn't good. If she could, she'd pull it. But it was too late . . . she'd made the big splash on Valerie Singleton's show. She'd work on the edits . . . somehow, she'd make it look the way she wanted. The way it was supposed to be. What she had to do now—what she was waiting to figure out—was what the payback would be. It annoyed her that it hadn't come to her already. She knew what the problem was, she just didn't know how to fix it. She'd made a point of suggesting that she'd gotten everything she wanted in life on her own, through her own efforts. That she needed nothing. But a payback was only satisfying if the Owed seemed to need something. If it was more about justice for the Owed than punishment of the Ower.

She taps her fingernails impatiently on her armrest, opens the cubby that holds bottles of spring water. She knows it will come to her, but it's not coming yet, and she wants it now. She's tired. She'll take a quick shower and get into bed. Her sleeping's been off. Maybe it's jet lag. She'll take an Ambien; in the morning, she'll be back on her game.

∿

THERE IS a knock on the door. "Get that, will you?" Quin says, and Rick slips on the hotel's terry robe and answers the knock. It is room service; she's ordered for herself: green tea, a poached egg, a fruit plate, ice water. He is annoyed, but not surprised, that she hadn't thought of ordering for him.

He has no idea what she's up to, but he's glad something's absorbing her so he doesn't have to talk about the disaster of yesterday's taping. She snaps her fingers at him, pantomimes signing, points to the desk where she is sitting.

The server lays the tray in front of her. She signs the check. Rich gives the server an extra five dollars. He'd been a server himself and always augments Quin's notoriously meager tips.

"Listen," she says, "why don't you go into Newport and wallow in the lifestyle of the late rich and famous . . . it's your thing, knock yourself out. I'm tied up all day."

He's glad to be out of the room. Glad to have a day of sightseeing, which he very much enjoys but almost never gets to do: Quin has no patience for it. And he knows it's his job—his livelihood depends on it—to be always at her beck and call.

He's pleased with himself that the outfit he's chosen is exactly right for where he is, what he's doing . . . khaki pants, oxford shirt, blue blazer. Tan loafers. No socks. He fantasizes about living here in the high season: sailing, hobnobbing with old blue-bloods, accompanying widows on shopping trips for sunglasses or antiques. Quin spears a piece of melon onto her fork.

The great houses please him: the extravagance of building some version of a French chateau to live in for a month or six weeks a year, the high rooms, the chandeliers, sparkling in the light from the long windows, the view of the ocean almost an afterthought, everything about these houses for display of extraordinary wealth. For lunch, he allows himself a lobster and luxuriates in dipping the rosy flesh into all the melted butter generously provided; Quin would never have allowed it, and there is the double pleasure of consumption and transgression: his favorite combination, the more precious for being infrequently indulged.

When he gets back, she's sitting in a white terry bathrobe. She's treated herself to a massage, a manicure, a pedicure, a facial. Something has gone her way; he feels the shimmer that surrounds her.

"So, what have you got . . . I can tell you've got something."

"Oh, I've got it all right. Couldn't be better. We'll nail her. We'll nail them all."

PART VII

New Canterbury, Rhode Island

July 2018

A harsh, threatening noise wakens Agnes from an unrefreshing sleep. She looks at her watch. Ten thirty. She has slept badly since Quin Archer arrived three months before. Her eczema has returned. Half asleep, she scratches her dry flesh, wakes to find that she has left tracks of blood; her skin is a torment and none of the remedies she's bought at the drug store are of the slightest help. She hasn't asked Maeve or Christina for a prescription; their worry for her would make things worse.

She puts the pillow over her head, but it isn't possible to block the noise. The dog jumps off the bed and barks insistently. Ecco has accommodated to Agnes's late rising, but once awake, her needs are imperative, and she won't stop barking till she's let out.

Agnes throws her bathrobe on and runs down the stairs. She opens the front door. The invasive, violent sound comes from across the street, at the Dolan house. A chain saw. The noise agitates the dog, and she paces back and forth in a desperate aimless circle. Agnes leashes the dog, opens the screen door, and walks down the three stone steps.

Pressing close against the Dolan house, there have been, for as long as Agnes can remember, two enormous cypresses. Now three men stand in front of one, which is already half cut down. She lifts the dog into her arms and walks to the edge of her front lawn.

And then she sees her: standing at the edge of the Dolans' front lawn: Heidi Stolz/Quin Archer.

She can't comprehend what she's seeing. For a moment, she thinks she might be still asleep, dreaming one of those dreams that includes in itself your own voice saying, "What you're seeing is all wrong."

"Hello, Agnes," Quin says. "Sorry about the noise. But like they say, you've got to break eggs to make an omelet, and you've got to make noise to cut down trees."

"But why are you cutting them down? They're perfectly healthy trees. They've been there forever."

"Oh, I guess you didn't know. I've bought the property. The Dolan house. Or what was the Dolan house. It's mine now. I'm cutting down the trees because I just bought the house as what we call a teardown. By the end of the day, every one of them will be gone."

Agnes puts her hand to her mouth. She is afraid to speak, afraid of what happened the last time words came out of her mouth and fell on Heidi.

"It's my latest investment. I've been doing some research, and this town is just as ripe as it could be for development. I mean, you're sitting on a gold mine. The beach just minutes away . . . and property more than affordable. I'm thinking it could be the next Hamptons. But if that's going to happen, you've got to anticipate your market. I mean, if it's going to be the New Hamptons, nobody wants pokey little dark houses the size of something in Munchkin Land. So this is going to be a teardown. And to follow . . . well, I hate that term *McMansion* . . . it's just something the naysayers and sour-grapers came up with because they can't get it for themselves. What people want to pay for is space and light. And statement . . . something that says to everybody, right away: See, this is what I could afford.

"But the Dolans have had this house forever. The children . . . or the grandchildren . . . they've always come here in the summers."

"Let's say I made them an offer they couldn't refuse. Let's say cash is king."

"You're going to tear the house down? When?"

"Not right now . . . not fiscally wise for me at the moment . . . not that it's any of your concern. But after I move a few things around . . . I'm not quite sure . . . maybe the end of the calendar year, maybe next spring. It's all under consideration."

Agnes forces herself to meet Quin's gaze. To look at her without flinching, without looking away. Everything about her is dry and sharp and tight; the skin stretched across the cheekbones, the hair like spikes . . . the nails painted the color of danger . . . the shoes . . . as high as stilts and pointed as a dagger. Her eyes: small, lightless, outlined in thick black kohl: eyes like darts or dares: I dare you to look, I dare you to look away. A starved look,

MARY GORDON

darting, with the cunning of the starveling. Agnes remembers how she would slink around corners—who had said it, Christina, maybe—that she was like one of those street dogs that slunk around begging for handouts but then would bite your fingers off if it didn't feel you'd given it enough.

"All these are going to be gone by the end of the day," Quin says, making a sweeping motion with her arm.

Agnes hears in her mind the names of the trees that the sweep of Quin's arm has taken in: sugar maple, pignut hickory, copper beech.

"But why, why, if you don't know when you're tearing the house down?"

"I like the feeling of knowing that things are on the move . . . that I've made a definite first step. I am simply constitutionally unable to bear anything vague or wishy-washy. This makes a clear statement: It's going to happen; it's already happening."

Agnes shivers and wraps her arms around herself.

"Don't stand here shivering, Agnes . . . you probably don't want to be in the middle of the street in your bathrobe."

She had run out of the house forgetting that she was still in her bathrobe. Quin, coiffed, buffed, perfectly made up, expensively shod, looks Agnes up and down, her gaze an even mix of contempt and satisfaction.

"Well, Agnes, as far too many people in my part of the country say, *Hasta la vista*."

And Agnes remembers the literal translation: Until we see each other again.

So she must live her life ready for the sight of Heidi Stolz. Quin Archer. At any moment. And always at Heidi's pleasure. At her will.

"Thank you for letting me know your plans," Agnes says, knowing even as she says them the foolishness, the falseness, of her words.

"My pleasure," says Quin.

And Agnes sees that it *is* her pleasure. The greatest, perhaps the only, pleasure Heidi Stolz, Quin Archer, will ever know.

There is nothing to do now but turn away from Quin and go back into the house. The dog trembles; the noise of the chainsaw is still a torment to her. Agnes carries the dog to the couch . . . buries her head in the rough fur, and sits, immobile.

And then she feels the urgency to flee. From the noise, and everything that the noise represents. She considers the possibility that she will have to leave her house forever, that perhaps this impulse to flee will never go away.

She showers quickly, pulls on cotton pants, a striped T-shirt, her old rose-colored sandals, bought in her favorite shoe store on the Via del Barbuina near the Piazza del Popolo. She carries the dog to the car and backs out of the driveway, trying not to look across the street at the Dolan house. The Archer house? Quin's? Heidi's?

The Dolan house. She wonders how many times she's been inside it . . . she is sure it must be fewer than ten. The Dolans were neighbors, but they moved in after Agnes had left for Italy; her mother said they were "very nice, but dear God, you don't want to get into a conversation with her. Septic tanks, problems with wiring, problems with storm windows or screen doors, or joints or rotator cuffs . . . and I don't think I've heard him utter more than ten words."

Children Agnes hadn't known had been young there, then grown, then gone. The Dolans had lived there for forty years . . . who had it been before that? The Andersons, unmarried sisters whom you could never imagine as anything but old . . . she remembered that her father would tip his hat to them, and they would invite Agnes and her parents for a glass of sherry and cake on New Year's Day. But Agnes could not remember one detail of the inside of the house. It had simply been there: a brown-shingled Cape Cod with shutters that were green or white. Now it would be torn down. Why should she feel that as so great a blow, so great a loss, this house she had rarely been in, whose furnishings, the proportions of whose rooms, she wouldn't be able to describe if her life depended on it?

The house had been there, but its meaning was simply as a marker, solid, unassuming, with the modest clear righteous (self-righteous) proportions of the best of New England architecture. She had never thought much about the house itself, but she had loved the trees, the beautiful sugar maple, blazing orange and yellow in autumn, lush and opulent in high summer; the hickory, whose branches dipped and swayed; and the copper beech, with its solemn, reserved, wine-colored leaves.

She wished she had the courage to throw herself in front of the trees and say, You may not, you must take me first. But it was not something she would do, give her life, her one life, for a tree. She had a child; she had a grandchild. Perhaps it would be a worthwhile gesture, but she would not make it. No, she would drive down the road, gunning the engine like a runaway or a thief, barely able to see the road because her tears made her driving, she knew, a danger.

She had to be away before they were taken down. The

cypresses were bad enough, but the loss of the others would be unbearable.

During a long red light, she pulls down the visor to look at herself in the mirror. She had run out of the house without combing her hair, and she sees that she looks wild, half mad, her hair tangled, her cheeks red and wet from weeping. She feels a shock go through her body, as if a torch had been held to the base of her spine.

Hate, she thinks. I am hated. She is destroying these trees because she hates me.

It frightens her to have to say it: I am hated.

Without thought—it is a drive she has made for as long as she could drive—she heads toward Ralston Beach, where she and her family and everyone else she knew went to swim or walk or look at the ocean. She wants to walk and walk where there seems to be nothing but horizon, suggesting nothing or everything, the indistinct far-off that could be the end of the world.

Only now does it occur to her that there is a dark side to this place that had been, for as long as she could remember, the place that represented nothing but good. It was a private beach; you had to be a member; membership was not expensive, but you had to have been a New Canterbury resident for a long time. She knew that membership was limited—it was a parking issue, the board informed the members in the letter that came with the request for membership renewal—but never before did it occur to her to wonder what the criteria were for inclusion, which, of course, implied exclusion. People who came for a few weeks in the summer were excluded—except for the ones whose families had been coming for a few weeks in the summer for more years than anyone could count. She is thinking of what Quin said: it could be the next Hamptons. But Ralston Beach, at least, would not be vulnerable; it abutted wetlands that the local Nature Conservancy had bought so they would be carefully preserved. Heidi's plans had nothing to do with Ralston Beach.

Agnes swerves wildly, pulling into a sandy driveway to turn the car in the direction of the public beach. She drives down streets she hasn't driven down since she left for Rome forty-six years ago. Because she never thought of going to the public beach. Had Heidi known that? How had she known?

Turning down South Beach Road, she sees that the houses are well off the road, invisible or only just behind high hedges and large old trees. But as she drives closer to the beach, the look of the place changes so drastically that at first she imagines some blight had struck, and was responsible for the sudden nude expanses, the wide, out-of-place lawns leading up to houses whose unsheltered and insistent self-presentation, in relation to the road, the other houses, feels like an aggression, an assault.

Every house she sees is an example of some kind of wrongness. Out of scale: three times larger than the older houses, too close to the road, fronted by garish aprons of grass, kelly green—the green, she thinks, of golfer's pants, a purposely false green to announce itself as a purchased import, rather than a native species. Each house is, most importantly, not a house, but a declaration: of its newness, its refusal to conform to what was expected, what had been, for generations, done. In this part of the world, where architecture is famous for its modesty. Each of these new houses is pretending to be, not a house on the shore of New England, but something else, a barn, a chalet, a docked yacht, Tara.

Anger rises up, beginning in the backs of her knees, traveling upward, settling for a moment in her pelvic floor, then moving with a toxic effervescence to her mouth and throat; the urge to vomit, which she knows has no physical cause, is impossible not to take notice of. Anger is something she's felt rarely; it took its place alongside other unusual sensations—like sexual arousal at the image of something she considered perverse—something she knew must be hers but that she barely recognized.

Two words flash against the inside of her skull, which has become a kind of screen. Hatred and ugliness, hatred and ugliness. She had been spared them her whole life. Now, because of Heidi (or was it Quin?), they would be her daily bread.

She hears, as if it were on this street, not miles away, the noise of the chainsaw, and she sees the sight of the fallen trees. She doesn't even get out of the car; she has no impulse to walk on the beach now.

She must go home. She cannot simply run away. If the trees are to be taken down, taken away, she must be there—to what? To witness, to accompany? At least not to spare herself the most brutal evidence of what hatred had done.

She drives up the road to her house. In the driveway of the Dolan house—Heidi's house, the Stolz house, or was it Quin's house, the Archer house—a truck is being filled with amputated branches, their playful leaves bristling, unconscious of their doom, like children singing on their way to the guillotine.

What has been left behind: stumps, each the size of a round dinner table, planed raw in the afternoon sun. The sign of brutality, of brutalization. Impossible to believe they were ever connected to something lovely, something desirable.

Now her home will never be the same. She will perhaps give

up using the front door entirely; the door her mother had always insisted be painted a shining red, the dolphin knocker her father had found—for a song, he said—in a junk store in Providence.

Her home has been stolen. She will never be at ease again; no step, no gesture will ever again be quite natural.

She sits at the dining room table and beats her fists on the polished wood. "Hatred and ugliness. Hatred and ugliness," the two words circle her mind like a rabbit circling a racecourse.

Hatred and ugliness. Hatred and ugliness. And there is nothing I can do.

Heidi knew how ugliness would torment Agnes; she had listened as Agnes had spoken to her students about beauty, the importance of beauty, its protection from the ugliness of the world, which was a form of death.

And hatred, Heidi hated her . . . and did the hater know the hated as the lover knew the beloved? For the beloved and the lover, she thinks, there is no more precious sentence than "Knowing, I am known." But for the hater and the hated—the sentence is indeed a sentence . . . a life sentence . . . the punishment capital and never done.

Being hated. It was a shock, as if an electric current ran through her body. And then she understood: Heidi hated her because she had loved her. When she went over the words of the interview, she had to realize how many times Heidi had used the word *love* . . . "my beloved teacher," "everyone loved you." And she realized that by "everyone," Heidi had meant herself.

Heidi had loved her. But she had not loved Heidi. Heidi had interested her; she even respected her for being unconcerned—so unusual in a teenager—with what people thought of her. But she hadn't loved her. Was that an accident . . . if she had not stood too

close when she spoke to people . . . if she hadn't raised her hand
before everyone else in the class and waved frantically if one of
her classmates gave an inadequate answer . . . if her laugh had
some other tone than that of mockery . . . if her eyes were larger,
if the palms of her hands weren't always damp . . . would she
have been more lovable? Was there any world in which Agnes
Vaughan could have loved Heidi Stolz . . . in which Agnes di
Martini could have loved Quin Archer?

And she knows the answer.

Never.

No.

~~~

IT IS nearly dark when she hears a car pull into the driveway.
There is no one she wants to see; there is no one who can be of
help to her. But now, she must try to understand how to live a
new life; to answer the door, to open her house, which is not her
house—to pretend that it is a normal thing to be living here.

"Jesus Christ, what happened over there?"

The sight of Marcus, his plain young strength, the depth of
his voice—loosens what had been clenched, and she allows herself to weep.

"She bought the Dolan house. She cut down the trees. She
cut down the trees so I would have to look at what she knew I
couldn't bear to look at."

"Who, Agnes, who did that? Who cut down those beautiful
trees?"

"Heidi," she says.

"Heidi?"

"Quin Archer."

He reaches into his pocket and takes out his phone. "I'm calling Maeve."

"Don't call her . . . don't bother her. It's not her problem."

"Of course it is. It's all our problem. She'd be furious with me if I didn't call her right away when I saw you were in distress. But it's not really a problem. It's an assault. Everyone in the neighborhood, everyone who drives by, has to look at those hideous stumps where there were beautiful trees."

"I don't know, Marcus . . . I don't know . . . do you think anyone cares that much?"

"I don't know. And neither do you. But I'm getting everyone together. You're not alone, you know. Order pizzas. I'll bring beer. We'll meet here tonight. We'll fight this. You'll see. We won't let her win."

"What would winning be, Marcus . . . hasn't she already won?"

"We have to do something, not just nothing. Remember, Agnes, it's not just for you. Do it to protest about what was done to those wonderful trees."

She feels herself able to stand straight for the first time. It's not just about her. It's not just about Quin hating her and punishing her. It's about the trees.

"I'll order pizzas," she says.

"She doesn't know who she tangled with. She won't get away with it."

"Probably, Marcus, she already has."

~~~

ANGER FILLS the room, righteous anger: lit and hot like a summer storm.

"I'll help you put the food out," Marcus says.

It comforts her to see him moving so slowly, so deliberately, making piles of forks and knives and napkins, putting them out on the wooden tray she'd used to bring tea and meals to her mother in her last, weak days.

"I keep thinking of something I heard in Sunday school," he says. " 'The children of the darkness are wiser than the children of the light.' "

"The worst thing about it, Marcus, is to know that someone hates me so much."

"You've never had anything like this in your life?"

"No, I guess not."

He turns away from her and closes the silverware drawer with his hip.

"Black folks know it from the first minute we walk into the big world. It would never surprise us."

She feels deeply ashamed; she feels her face grow hot and red.

"One good thing about being black is you don't blush, so no one has to know you're embarrassed. I embarrassed you, didn't I. I didn't mean to. I just . . . well, it just struck me hard, the difference."

She doesn't know if she's glad he said what he said. Because she has to feel it once again, that pain in the front of her forehead, as once again, she bangs her head straight against the pillar of her own limitations. She wants to ask, "Does Leo know it? Does he know it already?" But she's afraid of what the answer will be.

Marcus puts the tray on the dining room table. Maeve sets out place mats, lays pizzas on them, opens the boxes, and prepares to serve.

"Okay, everyone gather around. As my grandmother would say, let's put on our thinking caps."

Hearing her mother's words, Agnes eyes are pricked by tears. It is obvious that Maeve and Marcus are in charge of the evening. How beautiful they are. "She has your eyes," people always said, but they were not just hers but her mother's, gray in some lights and, depending on what she wore, sometimes blue, sometimes green. "Thank God she has your fortunate nose," Pietro had said, but she was glad Maeve had his springy hair, his high domed forehead, definite chin, the full lips, the large strong white teeth. How beautiful they are, she thinks, and will they make less of a mess of it—their lives, the world—she wonders. Of course, she thinks. How could they not.

"Mom," Maeve says, handing her mother a plate with pizza on it. "Don't get that deer-caught-in-the-headlights look. You remember what Papa used to call it, *Il viso della Protestanta congelata*."

"The face of the frozen Protestant," Jeanne says. "I've been studying Italian on an app on my phone. That's a pretty funny thing to say about your wife. Very funny."

Agnes had noticed before that Jeanne was one of those people who said, "That's funny" as an alternative to laughing.

"All right," Maeve says. "So this is the deal. Quin's bought the house. She says she's going to tear it down and build what she says she doesn't like to call a 'McMansion.' She says she sees that our town is all ready to become the next Hamptons."

"Well, yeah, that's where she's wrong. Not this part of the town, anyway," Jo says. "Remember, it's been designated a historic zone. And if the Dolan house was built before 1850, she won't be able to tear it down. As you know, I'm on the planning board. There are more rules here than in Leviticus. Why do you think it took us seven years to get affordable housing approved? Height, for instance. No house can be more than fifty feet high. So that's not on the table. Quin just said that to upset you. And she must have known that—Heidi, Quin, whoever she is. No realtor would have let her buy without knowing it. She was just yanking your chain."

Yanking your chain. Another expression that had come to America while she was away. A good one . . . entirely apt for what Heidi did to her . . . she feels herself a chained animal, trapped behind bars, and Heidi—what, the zookeeper?—just pulling the chain around Agnes's neck for the pleasure of it. Just because she could. She thinks Jo must be right that Heidi knew that she couldn't carry out the plans she mentioned to Agnes, that everything she said was possible was not possible. Was a lie. She had lied during the taping of the TV show about the circumstances of her rape. Letitia Barnes had called Heidi a "fabulator." Fabulator. Liar. The effects were the same. Heidi had probably lied, or fabulated, from pathetic motives. But what were Quin's motives? Did she know the difference between a lie and the truth? Did she have any moral consciousness at all? Was there anything Quin Archer wouldn't do, if she could get away with it? Agnes knows the answer to this: there is nothing she wouldn't do, and the chilling knowledge of this diminishes the comfort of what Jo has just said.

"Those McMansions near the beach are outside the historic zone. But the frozen Protestants did some good things. There's no way this part of New Canterbury is going to be McMansioned."

"I don't think you can use *McMansion* as a verb," Jeanne says.

"Your English teacher would be proud of you," Jo says. "Poor Florence Gould."

"She liked my limericks," Jeanne says.

"Your limericks were wonderful," Christina says, kissing the top of her wife's head.

"Even if she can't do any more than she's done, she's still cut down the trees and left those horrible stumps," Marcus says.

"That's probably why she did it so quickly," Christina says. "Just to get her licks in as early as possible in case she can't do any more."

"I've been doing research," Marcus says. "There are things we can do. Quick, remarkably quick growths. I'll plant a row of larches . . . you won't believe how quickly they grow . . . so people curse them, call them invasive . . . I hate it when people call plants 'invasive,' but in three months you won't be able to see the house from your windows, you won't be able to see it at all."

"Blackout curtains," Christina says. "Then thick winter drapes."

"Pack yourself up, spend a month in the city in Frances's apartment," Jo says. "We'll come and visit."

"We'll send Leo down for a week, at least. He's dying to be in New York," says Maeve.

So this is it, Agnes thinks, the only solution. To run from it, until the gate finally closes entirely, shielding from sight what must be kept from sight. We'll call it landscaping. We'll call it decoration. We will not use its proper name: concealment. Hiding. Denying. Blocking out.

"It'll be all right, Mom, please don't look like that. It will be all right."

"Of course it will. I know that," she says, because she must say that, to thank them for their love, their goodness, their intelligence, and their imagination.

But she knows it will never be.

Not all right.

Not all.

Not ever.

PART VIII

New York
New Canterbury, Rhode Island

October 2018

It was much harder, having a dog in the city. She was looking forward to not having to get dressed to take the dog out, simply opening the door, making her coffee while Ecco went outside, letting herself in and jumping up on the couch beside her; the pleasure of taking up a book and reading as she drank her coffee, ate her toast. But the room would be different now. Living in the house where she was born would never be the same. There were new curtains; there were new trees bordering the road. Only the back of the house would be light filled; she was thinking of adding a back porch, glassed in for winter.

She was glad to be going home; she was less at ease in New York than she imagined she would be. It wasn't that it was a city; she'd lived in Rome for forty years. But it was a Rome that contained her neighborhood. There was no neighborhood on Fifty-Fifth Street between Third and Lexington. She didn't even know who her neighbors were; they might be pleasant to the dog in the

elevator, but they always seemed rushed, and the idea of inviting them in for a coffee was out of the question. She had made
a connection with the people she met on Tuesdays and Fridays
when she had to move the car to obey the alternate side of the
street parking regulations. The exchanges had been pleasant in
that light neutral way that marked the talk of citizens engaged
in a common, slightly onerous task: having to sit in your car,
ready to move it at the last second when the cops arrived—like
the driver of a getaway car for a bank robbery. It wasn't possible
to have a conversation with the others; everyone was in her or
his car or standing next to it on a cell phone. People waved, nodded, shared their annoyance on the days when the cops didn't
show up, feeling the waste of their time as a personal assault
by a hostile government. She had told one woman—about her
age, about her level of dress and makeup—that she wouldn't be
around anymore, and the woman wished her well. She didn't tell
her where she was going; that seemed provincial, and appearing
provincial was something she'd worked hard to avoid.

Walking the dog was a task, but she'd miss it, miss the
exchanges with other dog walkers, or the dog deprived, who
swooned and mourned and talked about the dogs they'd left
behind . . . the impossibility of having a dog, working as they
did, living as they did. And she would greatly miss walking the
dog in Central Park.

She knew she'd be back frequently; she felt newly bound
to visit Frances in her nursing home, although she sometimes
thought it was a fool's errand—Frances, lost in dementia's fog,
never even recognized her. But she knew that the nurses were
aware of what patients were regularly checked up on, and which
were abandoned, with no one to report malfeasance or neglect.

She wished Frances didn't have to be there; she considered taking her back to Rhode Island. The nursing home was drab; the smell of old age was an assault when you walked through the door; the walls were a sickly green; if she brought flowers, the next time she came they were dead in their vase on top of Frances's plywood dresser. Occasionally, someone cried out; down the hall a woman regularly shouted, "Margaret, Margaret!" The food was clearly meant only to keep the old people alive; no care was made for its preparation, and Frances lived mainly on Ensure, a liquid supplement that INSURED the necessary nourishment. She sat all day, her head in her hands, rocking back and forth, sometimes moaning. She was incontinent; she couldn't walk . . . occasionally she became violent when an attendant tried to dress her. No, it would not be possible for Agnes to take her home. But she mourned her clever, elegant friend, reduced to this remnant of what it meant to be human. Somehow, though, the animal that was Frances refused to give up; and Agnes vowed that as long as Frances wished to go on living, she would visit her regularly.

She wished Frances would die. She prayed for it, in the only way that she could pray, not to God . . . she wasn't sure what that meant, God . . . if such a one existed, he was the God of countless universes and could not be expected to favor this insignificant bumbling species that happened, through some accident, to have a faculty called consciousness, which meant that it knew it would die. She couldn't pray to that kind of God for the same reason that she didn't like looking at the stars with her father, because the size of the universe made her feel unhinged, physically sick.

She prayed to her beloved dead. To her mother and Jasper,

who had been young and happy together, to call their friend
Frances to join them . . . out of this misery, out of this pathetic
body to which she seemed, against all odds, to cling. She prayed
to Pietro when she could see no prospect but darkness; to her
father when the world seemed to have lost its reason.

Her beloved dead. For so many years, no one she was close to
had died. That was because she had been young, and although
she didn't think of herself yet as old—though some, she thought,
probably did—she knew she was no longer young. Now her husband was among the dead, and both her parents. She had been
present at their deaths, and at Jasper's. What had struck her was
the enormous difference between the living and the dead; the
body of the dead was there, but it was not the same; something
had departed . . . and so it must be spirit, and it must, having
loved and been loved, she believed, still be somewhere.

Her last meetings with Quin Archer had troubled her belief
in the endurance of the ties of love. Because if love went somewhere after death, where, then, was hate? She had understood,
in Heidi's case, that it was the other side of the coin of love. Even
after death would Heidi's hatred follow her, spoiling eternity, the
cracked note in the harmony, the dark spot in the radiance? Since
Heidi had come back into her life, Agnes had, for the first time,
been truly afraid to die. She had to make herself believe that the
love of those who loved her would surround her always, like the
cloak of the Madonna on the first statue she had restored, keeping
her from the hatred and ugliness that Heidi had shown her. She
had to believe it; otherwise . . . the otherwise was too unbearable
even to name. The otherwise was a wall of briars, like the briars
that the hero and heroine in fairy tales were challenged to hack
through, blinding, occluding, light, and beauty, and the possibil-

ity of joy. Some days it was impossible to believe that there was any getting through. That must be fought, that must with every strength be refused, resisted. You hacked a small hole through the briars; you got glimpses only, inches only, of clear light.

And today the light was *very* clear. October light: the clearest of the year. The sky seemed rinsed and drenched with color. Last night's wind—at times exciting, but you were glad to be indoors, not subject to it—had scoured the air, and every atom that might block light had been stanched, absorbed. Today it will be a joy— the kind of joy that must be clasped and held, tight—to walk in Central Park.

She's proud of Ecco. Although she pees in the street just outside their building, she holds her bowels till she gets to the park, considering grass the minimum necessity. It takes some discipline on Ecco's part, because the walk to the park is three long cross-town blocks. Agnes regrets that Frances's apartment is in one of Manhattan's least appealing districts, and not conducive to the noncommercial aspects of human habitation. There are no food stores; if she wants a quart of milk, she has to go to the Duane Reade drug store on Madison; there are shoe stores, high-end restaurants for the people working in the high-end offices, a storefront offering Chinese massage. Only two buildings are worthy of her notice: a synagogue with peacock-green Moorish turrets and Stars of David carved into its brick façade; and a building on Madison and Fifty-Fifth that is said to be a post-modern masterpiece but to her is only depressing, a ghost house abandoned by its tenants, a landmark, the signs say, welcoming all to relax in what is called an *atrium,* but the space is anything but welcoming: too large, too metallic . . . the shops that once tried to make a go of it have given up, leaving behind them the trail of their failure. The pride indicated by the plaque describing the atrium seems only pathetic: "This space contains the following: 8 planters with trees, 104 tables and seats. Green restrooms." But everyone there seems as if they'd rather be somewhere else, they just happened to stop there, too tired or too rushed to look for some place really pleasing. Even disliking it, she always walks past it because to walk to Fifth, the entrance to the park, to pass by Trump Tower, with its phalanx of armed guards.

Walking in Central Park, she misses Rome, misses the Villa Borghese with its pavilions and formal statues; most of all she misses Pietro. Sometimes when she hears someone speaking Italian, she wants to join in their conversations, but she doesn't, and he would have, and most likely something pleasant would have happened. She would have liked to tell him how odd it was that Europeans and Asians took picture after picture of gray squirrels, whom Americans considered at best ordinary, at worst a pest. How amused he would have been by the couple today . . . twenties, early thirties . . . arm in arm . . . "Is it source of irreducible meaning or irreducible source of meaning?" she asks him, but the dog stops to sniff something and Agnes doesn't hear the answer.

She has time to walk the twenty blocks so she can wave goodbye to the Metropolitan Museum of Art, which, she congratulates herself, she has visited several times a week during her time in New York. She concentrated on African art; because of Leo she had a stake in learning about it, and she felt shame that she had never made her way to the parts of the museum that housed art whose sources were not European. That knowledge had been daunting; there was African art, which she could know only superficially, and there was the Chinese, the Indian, the South American . . . and located next to the African, the art of Oceania . . . a name, a designation she had never, before this, heard of. She felt overwhelmed, as she had felt overwhelmed looking at the stars, at the things that would be marvelous to know that she would never know . . . looked at another way, things it was her responsibility to know if she were to have any kind of genuine understanding of the world . . . and it was impossible. Even what she knew of the Italian art of the Renaissance was superficial. She understood this because she knew the pleasure of knowing something, one thing thoroughly, as she knew the elbow or the fingernail of the statue she was restoring. The problem was: if you were going to know one thing thoroughly, there was no time even to know the names of what you would never know.

She had determined that it would be a good use of her time to learn at least something about African art. She was most drawn to a wooden statue from Ghana: a mourner bent over, his back scarified, his head buried in his hands . . . she wondered what went into its restoration, and, for the first time, she missed her work with a dull, spreading loss. She created a routine: walk the dog, drink coffee, have breakfast, read one of the books on African art she had invested in. Leo came for a week, and his company was the sheerest pleasure: she took him not only to the Metropolitan but also to the Museum of Natural History, and to the precious, semisecret Frick. They went to Shakespeare in the Park and Mostly Mozart at Lincoln Center. They ate ice cream at tables set out on the sidewalk. Then he was gone, and she realized, after a few days, that she was genuinely lonely. She found eating by herself depressing; her dinners were meager—cut-up vegetables, hard-boiled eggs, tuna salad—quickly consumed, something merely to be gotten through. She was too old to make new friends; she had no work, so there would be no natural way of meeting people. And, despite the satisfaction of

learning something new, she needed people . . . she needed the
nourishment—or was it the protection—of the ones she loved.
She knew she was not a person for whom the mind is dominant,
or even the eye. Was it too crude to say the heart?

She was glad when she had visitors; she cooked elaborately
for them, asked them to stay the night. Christina came with a
book of samples; they needed to choose the fabric for the new
blackout drapes.

She was astonished at Christina's excitement; Christina,
usually so ironical, so suspicious of strong feeling, of strongly
expressed emotion—Jo's extravagant diction always annoyed
her. But, stroking the fabric, page after page, Christina herself
grew extravagant, showed a delight in the world of the senses
that Agnes had never seen. So, Agnes felt, it is more important to
me than to her, I will let her choose.

It was obvious she had already chosen. "Just feel this, just feel
this," she said, taking Agnes's hand and placing it on a rectangle of purple velvet. "And we'll line it with this"—she flipped
the pages of the sample book—"just feel this creaminess . . . it's
expensive, but every day you'll feel like you've just popped a perfectly ripe fig into your mouth or eaten blackberries and cream."

Agnes knows how important it is to Christina that she share
her excitement, so she pretends to be excited. What she wants to
say is, You don't understand. Nothing can make up to me for the
reality that these drapes are needed . . . nothing will take away
what has been done.

"Well, what's money, anyway . . . the planet will probably be
uninhabitable in twenty years. I might as well have nice drapes."

"That's my cockeyed optimist," Christina says.

Marcus and Maeve come . . . Marcus shows picture after picture on his phone . . . as excited as Christina at the quick-growing

trees. "When you come back, at the end of October . . . they'll be six feet high . . . and next year . . . we'll have to be pruning them like mad."

And because Agnes knows that his pleasure in the new trees is engraved with the mourning of the great old trees destroyed, her gratitude is twofold: he wants to help; he understands the loss.

She and Jo go to undemanding movies; the one they like best is about women stealing a jewel from her beloved Metropolitan Museum. But it's the part of the museum she doesn't like . . . the Fashion Institute. The part rich women feel most drawn to . . . the part that pays all the bills.

There is no part of her that considers moving full-time to New York. Nothing makes up for it; the love of those she loves that shelters and nourishes. Shelters and shields. But today, her last day, she will not fail to enjoy the light, wafers of light falling through branches. The yellow leaves . . . aspen, elm, maple, beech . . . taking in light, presenting light, transforming it into tangible lightness.

She tells the doorman she will be coming down soon with heavy suitcases. Ramon, the doorman, whom she loves in an easy way that carries with it not the smallest obligation—a tip, perhaps lavish, some might say . . . but if he were sad or ill or impoverished, it would not be to Agnes that he would bring his troubles. Ramon, elegant and yet lighthearted . . . Nicaraguan . . . what had he seen of horrors . . . had he been on the side of the tyrants or the rebels, who, it seems, had turned into tyrants. There was, she was grateful to believe, no need to ask, no need to know.

"I hope we'll be seeing you soon. Tell Leo this year the Knicks will make a comeback, and I want him to be here to see it."

"Oh, we'll be back. We'll be back."

He scratches the dog's head; the dog sniffs a cuff, lifts her head to give him what Agnes thinks of as Ecco's famous farewell smile.

~

CROSSING THE HUDSON is a sign, as if, once you're over the bridge, you show your passport to another country. The country of Not New York. She was going home.

But what home was she going to? Its shape, its texture, its nature had changed. Quin Archer had changed it; it was possible to say that she could not destroy it, but it was not possible to say that it had not been changed.

How did the dog know, a quarter of a mile before their exit, that they were nearing home? Ecco stood up; she sniffed at the window so that Agnes knew she wanted it open. As they approached their own street, she started whimpering, but it was a whimper not of distress but of pure joy. She had missed it all, Agnes thought . . . she's happy to be home. There is no mixture in Ecco's feelings; what does it matter to her that there are ugly stumps where there had been grand trees, that there are velvet drapes where there were muslin curtains . . . new plantings where there had been a view of the road.

Turning into the driveway, Agnes forces herself not to look across the street.

The dog jumps out of the car, runs to the backyard, sniffs the ground as if she'd been starved for something all these weeks.

Agnes goes in the back door, the kitchen door . . . the one she will now use exclusively.

Leo runs to her. "Nonna," he cries, "I'm so glad to see you."

She can no longer lift him up. He loves measuring himself against her. "I'm up to your chin now. I'll be taller than you when I'm twelve."

"We keep telling him not to grow, but he seems to do it in his sleep," Maeve says, taking her mother's bags. "I'll put them in your room. I know you, you probably want to unpack right now; I honestly think you believe clothes rot in a suitcase if you don't expose them to the air within ten minutes of arrival."

"We're only doing finger food," Jo says. "Everything you like best. Everything everyone likes best, if they're honest. Pigs in blankets. Meatballs. Grape leaves. Taramasalata . . . and for dessert . . . miniature cream puffs."

"And most important," Christina says, waving a wooden spoon over her head, "using the last of the season's mint . . . my very own mojitos."

She wishes she didn't have to go into the living room. The room that Heidi Stolz has spoiled.

It is only four o'clock in the afternoon, but the new drapes— the fig-colored drapes, or is it blackberry?—are closed for the day. Marcus—she assumes it's Marcus—has lit a fire, so the tonality of the room is far from grim; she remembers how vain her father was about his ability to light a fire quickly and efficiently; she never lit a fire when she was on her own. Now, she resolves, she'll do it regularly.

Christina hands her a drink. Leo passes pigs in blankets. Maeve and Marcus pass other trays.

"Did you see the trees?" he says proudly.

"No," Agnes says; even just a sip of the mojito makes her feel free in her speech. "I was afraid to look at anything."

"Don't be a wimp, Mom," Maeve says. "Marcus has done a wonderful job."

My daughter is happy, she thinks. My daughter loves her husband.

She follows Marcus out the front door. Abutting the road there is a feathery screen, the trees are thin, the leaves sparse, but they have been planted close together so that nothing in front of them is visible.

The young trees are lovely and hopeful. She can't see the stumps. There is nothing she need be afraid of looking at. The ugliness has been taken away. By people who did it for love . . . or to bleach out the trace of hate.

It is not possible to thank them sufficiently. They love her; they are intelligent and gifted. They had summoned loveliness, and it had taken root.

Christina is telling a story about the man who runs the fruit and vegetable stand whom they all call Eeyore . . . because his predictions are always dire. "There will be no strawberries this year," he said, before Agnes left, "because of something called a wet drought . . . the plants were ruined, ruined." It had, in fact, been a bumper crop. "There'll be no beans at all to speak of. No melons, no peaches worth a damn." Jeanne Larkin is, for some reason, his confidante in the area of romance. He has never married.

"His dog died while you were away," Jeanne says.

"And so," Christina says, "he told Jeanne the story of the latest woman throwing herself at him. 'She sent me a condolence card when the dog died. But I wasn't falling for that one. I've been around the block a few too many times for that.'"

"There's one woman who seems to have taken his fancy," Christina says. "What did he tell you about her, Jeanne?"

"He said, 'At my age, it's about going on drives and finding a good place for dinner.'"

They're working hard to amuse her, and she pretends to be amused. She goes into the kitchen to feed the dog and give her water. She is pleased by the sight of her bowls, her pitchers, her platters, chaste and orderly on the white-painted shelves. Opening a drawer, she lifts the salad servers, a gift from her mother-in-law, enjoying their silver heft, the ice cream scoop that was her father's, the napkin rings with their painted blue, red, and purple flowers. She stoops to put the dog's food on the floor, and, rising up, feels a lightness in her head: she wonders if it's the mojitos.

The windows over the sink show that the sun is setting fast. What an unsettled and unsettling month October is, she thinks, this morning the sun shot all the colors through with the greatest possible brilliance, but now, in the time it took her to spoon the dog's food into her dish, put it down, and rise again to standing, the sky has turned indigo, the last light disappearing, swallowed whole, as if some shade or curtain had been roughly, angrily, pulled down.

Her sense of well-being is entirely gone now, the disappearing light has snatched it clean away. She tells herself there is no reason for what she's feeling, nothing has changed; everyone is as they were, my daughter, my son-in-law, my grandson, my friends, my dog, my bowls, my pitchers, my silver, my napkin rings. My and my and my and my. She has always known her range was very small. But is there nothing larger, nothing so capacious that there is no place for it following the word *my*? It frightens her to keep saying *my*: to say *my* is to call up a web of lucky accident, of a good fortune so capricious that it could be taken away in a moment, as if it had never been.

Maeve comes into the kitchen. "Don't stay out here brooding.

Come into the living room, come on, Mama," she says. "Let's enjoy what's there to enjoy."

Her daughter has seen the shade pulled down, the curtain drawn. She takes Agnes's hand and then pushes her, almost roughly, into the living room, then takes her hand again, walking her to the couch, pulling her mother down, sitting beside her.

"Leo," Maeve says. "Now you must play us something wonderful."

"Sure," Leo says, picking up his violin case.

A jet of love for him rushes up, like the water in her beloved Roman fountains, arching and then returning to its base or basin, endlessly replenishing, endlessly refreshed. "Sure," he says, but, she wonders, what is there to be sure of? Nothing. He doesn't know that yet; she doesn't know if she wants to be on earth when the time comes that he does know . . . she will be able to do nothing to help him . . . she will only be an encumbrance. We are not safe, she thinks . . . no one is ever safe. From what she saw when Quin cut down the trees. Hatred and ugliness. Hatred and ugliness. Perhaps nothing can keep them back. Even here, in this small house, on this small street, in this small town, what they have done will be only partially effective. Whatever they do, they cannot keep Quin away. She will come back whenever she wants; she will do whatever she needs to do.

"This is the Schubert Sonatina in A Minor," Leo says. He begins to play.

Agnes stops thinking about Heidi, about the fate of the earth, even about her love for Leo, and allows the music to wash over her, to penetrate her, to allow her, for a moment, a sense of something beyond destruction, some place where these notes are housed and preserved, a shelter that will, despite everything, and in some way she can't fathom or name, endure. But even if there is, even if it does endure, she thinks, it cannot keep us safe. The distance is too great, no one could span it, it is much too far, remote, and inaccessible.

It is what it is. Not keeping us safe, but keeping something. Something. Somewhere. Those words, she thinks, vague and imprecise, are what we have.

Leo puts down his violin. The music ends. Her love for him flares; a gold light rims the room.

"Please, play some more," his mother says.

Once again, he picks up his violin, puts the handkerchief on his shoulder, places his violin on top of it, rests his chin against the instrument's dark wood. He raises his bow.

And, once again, there is music.

PART IX

Brimston, Arizona

February 2019

The women meet for lunch, after hot yoga, at Brimston's newest restaurant. SloCoLoSo, named for its principles: Slow Cooked, Locally Sourced. They feel fortunate to have gotten a table, knowing that they needed to reserve a week in advance.

The menu provides two choices, each accompanied by a narrative.

"Cauliflower nest. Poached egg (from our own hens, living behind the restaurant . . . The gift of Polly and Molly, our star layers)."

"In a nest of cauliflower grown down the road at one of our dear providers: Willow Moonstone, organic farmer extraordinaire and star of Valerie Singleton's *Morning Circle*."

"Our vegan option: Celeriac soup, lovingly slow cooked by our own Traci Windsor, grown a quarter mile down the road by our treasured Mike and Cissy Lloyd. Rumor has it that the avocados they are growing in their greenhouse will be available within a month or two."

The women do not balk at the price of each entrée: twenty-four dollars. They call this "splurge day," and they know that they deserve it: they have been good wives, good mothers, and they fear the day (later, they hope, rather than sooner) when their husbands retire; they have been warned: "Might be some belt tightening." But there will be no belt tightening, rather belt loosening, if they have to cut down their classes at the gym . . . and can no longer lunch at places like SloCoLoSo, which tend to be pricy.

"It's great to see that Willow's farm is working out," one of the women says. "And that she and Valerie and Alison are still with us. I still can't believe that PAYBACK's been canceled."

"You could see it coming. She was losing her edge . . . it seemed to be the same thing all the time, money and sex, money and sex, and then she really blew it with the show about herself and her teacher. I mean, come on, the teacher seemed like a nice lady, she was sorry, she really was, you could tell, and Quin had made such a point of not being a victim, buying the house across the street from the teacher, well, it just seemed over the top, just a spoiled brat acting out. And she really had to stop wearing those sleeveless sheaths: I mean, maybe you can't be too thin or too rich, but those arms were really looking ropy."

"I wonder what they're going to replace her with."

"There was some talk of The Real Housewives of Phoenix, but I don't think it went anywhere."

"Yeah, well, whatever it is, it damn well better be entertaining."

Acknowledgments

My deep thanks to Professor Michele Marincola of New York University, who generously gave me the benefit of her expertise on the restoration of wooden polychrome sculpture. And to Irene MacDonald, honorary goddaughter and lawyer to the stars, for her advice about the ins and outs of reality TV. And master proofreaders Jonah and Max Mirer.

A NOTE ABOUT THE AUTHOR

Mary Gordon is the author of seven novels, including *Final Payments, Pearl,* and *The Love of My Youth;* six works of nonfiction, including the memoirs *The Shadow Man* and *Circling My Mother;* and three collections of short fiction, including *The Stories of Mary Gordon,* which was awarded the Story Prize. She has received many other honors, including a Lila Wallace-Reader's Digest Writers' Award, a Guggenheim Fellowship, and an Academy Award for Literature from the American Academy of Arts and Letters. She lives in New York City.

A NOTE ON THE TYPE

This book was set in Monotype Dante, a typeface designed by
Giovanni Mardersteig (1892–1977). Conceived as a private type
for the Officina Bodoni in Verona, Italy, Dante was originally
cut for hand composition by Charles Malin, the famous Pari-
sian punch cutter, between 1946 and 1952. Its first use was in an
edition of Boccaccio's *Trattatello in laude di Dante* that appeared
in 1954. The Monotype Corporation's version of Dante followed in 1957. Although modeled on the Aldine type used for
Pietro Cardinal Bembo's treatise De Aetna in 1495, Dante is a
thoroughly modern interpretation of the venerable face.

Typeset by Scribe,
Philadelphia, Pennsylvania

Printed and bound by Berryville Graphics,
Berryville, Virginia

Designed by Cassandra J. Pappas